JEFFREY WOOLF

Apples of Arcadia

BLACK UMBRELLA BOOKS

This is a work of fiction. All characters and events portrayed in this book are either fictitious or used fictitiously.

Copyright © 2008 by Jeffrey Woolf

All rights reserved. Printed in the United States of America.

No part of this book may be reproduced, stored in a retrieval system, or transmitted in any form, by any means, including mechanical, electronic, photocopying, recording, or otherwise, without prior written permission of the author.

To contact the author, please send correspondence to:

Black Umbrella Books
P.O. Box 241
Duluth, MN 55801-0241
www.blackumbrellabooks.com
admin@blackumbrellabooks.com

Excerpts from *Rimbaud: Complete Works, Selected Letters* by Wallace Fowlie reprinted with permission by The University of Chicago Press, copyright © 1966 by The University of Chicago Press. Excerpt from "to kiss the worms goodnight" from *Burning in Water, Drowning in Flame: Selected Poems 1955-1973* by Charles Bukowski reprinted by permission of HarperCollins Publishers, copyright © 1963, 1964, 1965, 1966, 1967, 1968, 1974 by Charles Bukowski.

ISBN-13: 978-0-9797-614-1-6
ISBN-10: 0-9797-614-1-7

10 9 8 7 6 5 4 3 2 1

Apples of Arcadia

3.30.12

To Emily —
Here's to the start
of a
remarkable friendship.

— Jeffrey

To The Unnameable

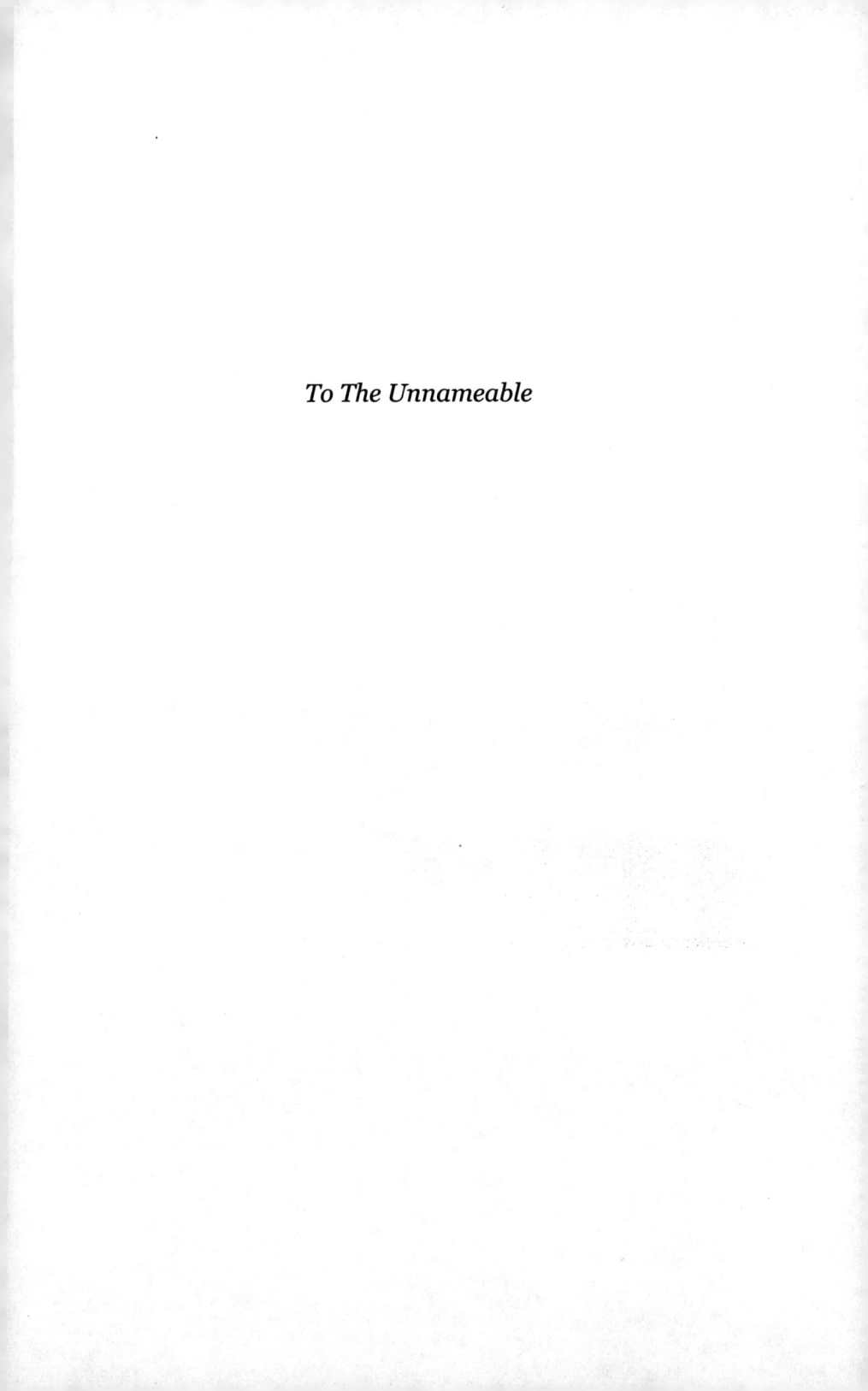

Book One
Latrinalia

F ive o'clock.
I walk through the door into a swarming bar. Joe's the first to greet me, a look on his face like a bloated fish. "For Christ's sake!" he shouts as I corner. "Find me some fucking vodka!" It looks as though Shelby quit early again.

My coat isn't even on the rack and already I'm dodging orders from some pup who's demanding a drink, of whom in turn I demand ID. "Just get the goddamn kid a drink!" shouts a gruff voice from a boorish face. The paternal semblance is hard to deny. No more questions. Sonny Boy gets his drink.

While pouring I'm muzzled by shouts from all sides – mostly beer, thank Christ, with the occasional whiskey thrown in by the foreman. He's the one in the corner with the pepper-toothed grin, the walrus surrounded by his trained arctic seals, the driving force behind our (which is to say Superior, WI's) main operation: mass resource deportation. We stock 'em, you dock 'em, yessiree. And with an operation like that, rocked between the rocky coasts of the Great Lakes Waterway, it's no wonder our boys get the wages they do. There's much to be made mixing water with grain...of this I have no doubt.

Down the bar, not far from my station, sits Shelby. Her husband's a grainer, works mostly the night shift, and while he sleeps it off and waits for the moon she sits on her stool as faithful as a cucumber and sips her vodka. So faithful, in fact, she doesn't even think about sex while Doc, professor of philosophy at the University, slides a few saffron fingers up the coarse of her thigh; she just imagines the callused fingers of her man. I find time to fill Doc's glass and as I do Shelby hands me a sleepy-eyed wink which I hide safe in my pocket. Doc turns pickle green.

A crack-jawed barrage begins on all fronts, the ramparts surrendered to the slings of limp soldiers who spit and fart, curse and ulcerate and hurl forth orders like crazed croaking frogs. No longer, it seems, are they pleased with their swamp; they need more juicy insects, choked and fermented, and softer pads for their pimpled asses. Red as radishes, their cheeks flap like deflated balloons as they cry out for spirits to silence the echoes. And if, at seven bells, those hellish echoes persist, then there's no potion potent enough for relief. All one can do then is just stumble on home and hope for a stroke – husbands and sons dunked up to the eardrums dripping in through doorways and belching off a barcarolle, a "Honey I'm Home!" worthy of withering mothers and teary-eyed housewives. Soon they'll find time for a plate of steamed grain (again...with thanks for the foreman), all pray, then fall upon cone-shaped piles, the coarsest seeds spat to a fat, panting mutt. Then after, bellies bursting with wheat germ and churning, it's off to the couch for a doze and a snooze to the drone of a voice from an electric void and as they sleep and snore and fondle themselves firm to the cadence of wind and rhythm of waves the mothers and housewives get down on their knees and scrape the filth off their gray, flaking feet....

Off they trot to fulfill this scenario and as they do Joe and I enjoy a brevity of silence, a mother-of-pearl moment when the pennies of the past two hours are peeled off our hides and tossed with a clink into an oversized jar. And it's now, when the room has finally been drained of its dusty grainers, the Brothers Draught begin to make their appearance. Already present is Doc, the predatory type who has evolved from the tiresome chasing of prey, opting instead to sit silent and still, patient as a squid enticing an attack – then, when one finally

Apples of Arcadia 11

does decide to pounce, he slides quickly aside and watches with savor as his hapless victim falls flat on its face. And as it lies there, blinded by pain, Doc leisurely proceeds to pluck out its eyeballs and swallows them down with a rich oyster sauce and a butter biscuit.

Now comes Cardigan Paul, an apothecary at a local pharmacy. He earned this name from his red cardigan sweater, his self-appointed smock which he wears every day of the year without fail. Also, this sobriquet serves to distinguish this Paul from the other, dubbed *Football Paul* on account of his passion for sports and subsequent betting habit. The latter soon strolls in and takes his seat alongside the former, then slaps down his dollar and salivates at the thought of the first cool, crisp sip.

The next is Cole, a pseudo-intellectual whose solipsistic technique has left his orbs dangled by Doc many times. Pride, however, is epoxy for punishment and he always looks first for the open stool nearest the professor and his swallowings. They exchange sour-blooded glances before Cole turns toward me to call out his order...as if it were necessary. Of the three years I've stood behind this slab nothing with this man has ever changed. Always the same mug of beer and the same pack of smokes always settled with a twenty-dollar bill and always he keeps every fucking cent for himself. The only time Joe and I ever see a coin from that pod is during the gift-giving season, and never anything more than a Canadian quarter.

Now here, lumbering in like a mute elephant, is Sexton, a quiet, common creature near middle age who has worked the same grid at the strip-mall appliance store the past fifteen years...that is, until the damn place shut down four months ago. Since then the lucky sod has been sifting his account while also enjoying a nice monthly stipend compliments of the Assistance Office. All this good fortune, however, hasn't raised his spirits any as he still finds it a pain to crack a laugh before half in the bag, at which point he suddenly becomes jolly as a juniper berry. Hell, at least he's not one of those mad, cathartic tosspots who spit blood the instant their ulcers are under.

And last, stepping now to center stage, is Jude, a sullen Jew fresh from the synagogue, and Lawrence, a third-rate politician who somehow managed to secure a stale office in the municipality. Together is the only way these two can be seen for the simple reason these two alone none other can tolerate. With Jude it's his mother, that sandy bag of brine, whose ill health has caused a spread among all who have to hear of it, not to mention his incessant whines concerning the money woes now that Pop has passed on. And Lawrence, since being anointed, has taken a fancy to crying out "Foul!" at the first sign of decline in this city's streets, proudly taking the role of "civil servant" to the obscene. Together they sit and sip their beers, every so often taking the time to wipe the tears away off their salty, seaworthy cheeks.

Ladies and gentlemen, the players....

ACT ONE

[*The Lounge, early evening.* THREE GRAINERS, *obviously intoxicated, sit hunchbacked in a booth alongside an L-shaped bar, at the end of which sits* SEXTON, *sipping silently from his glass. At the opposite end sit* COLE *and* DOC *and between them* SHELBY, *whose defiant posture betrays her stray glances. Seated next toward the center are* FOOTBALL PAUL *and* CARDIGAN PAUL, *seemingly, inaudibly in the midst of an argument. At the angle of the L, adjacent each other, sit* JUDE *and* LAWRENCE, *both gesticulating wildly during an expository discourse.*]

JUDE [*twirling a pale finger*]: I say, a good beef stew should go further than a fortnight.

LAWRENCE [*nodding vehemently*]: Too true! Too true!

[*Tweaking a nostril.*] But how, then, friend, do you atone for your cheesecake?

JUDE [*proudly*]: Quite simply, dear zealot, I scrape off the zwieback and feed it to Mother.

LAWRENCE [*delighted*]: Ah, by bearing! How very wise!

JUDE [*suddenly sullen*]: O, if only her bowels could be as congenial.

LAWRENCE [*seemingly distraught*]: Aye, an elder's innards are a sewer of sadness.

JUDE [*sighs*]: Perhaps. [*Thumbing his navel.*] Dear me, a son's wounds go straight to the source.

LAWRENCE: Aha! [*Points upward as if enlightened.*] A city in source is a seed in soil!

JUDE [*offended*]: And you, strange sir, are a sodden soul! Know you not of your mother's milk?

LAWRENCE [*chuckling*]: Aye! [*Cups his breast.*] And a mother's milk must never spoil the meal, eh? He, he....

JUDE [*startled*]: Eh? What's that?

LAWRENCE [*sensing something*]: Err...a mother's name is a father's shame. [*Rather meekly.*] He, he....

JUDE [*enraged*]: Oh, ho! Now you speak of my father's shame?! And what of my mother, man?!

LAWRENCE [*aflutter*]: Err...umm...he, he...well, uh, I will say this.... [*Pauses, spits and curtsies.*] Heavenly peace is a prudent mother's promise!

JUDE [*exalted*]: Ah! Ecclesiasticus! I know it well! Here, try this one on.... [*Clears his throat and checks his resonance.*] Honoreth thy mother, layeth long in God's favor!

LAWRENCE [*relieved*]: Sir, you speak divinely! Have you another?

JUDE: To be sure. [*Stands straight and stiffens his whiskers.*] Angereth thy mother, endangereth thy father's finance!

LAWRENCE [*laughing*]: By law, that's a promise! [*Suddenly serious.*] But have you a motto by my design?

JUDE: If you so demand it. [*Clicks his heals and salutes like a soldier.*] A curse on thy mother is a national iniquity!

LAWRENCE [*excitedly*]: What governing goodness! Sir, grace us again!

JUDE: Without wait. [*Licks his teeth and clacks his tongue.*] A mother in scorn...wait.... [*Pauses.*] A mother in scorn...hmm....

LAWRENCE [*befuddled*]: What's this? A stumbler?

JUDE: Some room! [*Unfastens his waistcoat.*] A mother in scorn seeks...sought....

LAWRENCE [*mockingly*]: Seeks! Sought! Well, which is it, man? Give us a clue!

JUDE [*unbuckling his belt*]: Seeks...sought....

Apples of Arcadia 15

LAWRENCE [*annoyed*]: Come on, then, you groaner! [*Punches him in the midriff.*] Out with it already!

JUDE [*doubled over*]: A mother.... [*Coughs.*] Scorn.... [*Coughs.*]

LAWRENCE: Oh? [*Brandishing his fist.*] Need you another?

JUDE [*raises his hand, pauses, recuperates, and continues*]: A mother in scorn seeks...sought.... [*Tries to contain a cough but cannot.*]

LAWRENCE: Right. [*Makes as if to strike.*]

SEXTON [*monotone*]: A mother in scorn sought coition in porn.

[LAWRENCE *halts before striking* JUDE *and both peer toward* SEXTON *who stares straight ahead and sips off his glass.*]

LAWRENCE [*putting his arm around* JUDE]: What, you dare sling such words at a wounded fool?

SEXTON [*dispassionately*]: Aye, and not just the fool but his king, too.

LAWRENCE: Aha! The sword of sedition! [*To* JUDE.] Beware the double-edged dagger. [*To* SEXTON.] Vile villain! A thousand tugs on your tussock, you dreg!

JUDE [*still hunched*]: Aye! [*Coughs.*] And a ream of... [*Coughs.*] ...rank eggs... [*Coughs.*] ...on... [*Coughs.*] ... your... [*Coughs*] ...prepuce... [*Coughs.*] ...you... [*Coughs.*] ...python! [*Coughs.*]

LAWRENCE [*to* JUDE, *impressed*]: Ream of rank eggs? By my ears, man! How does one find such a pregnant stench?

JUDE: Well, you see, friend... [*Coughs.*] ...I've quite the mind for... [*Coughs.*] ...the maternal 'n' stink.

[*Both* LAWRENCE *and* JUDE *begin laughing obnoxiously as* SEXTON *goes back to the solitude of his beer. At this time the argument between* FOOTBALL PAUL *and* CARDIGAN PAUL *escalates violently to the foreground.*]

FOOTBALL PAUL [*loudly striking the bar*]: Horseshit!

CARDIGAN PAUL [*protecting his glass*]: Tell it to Williams!

F.P. [*querulously*]: Yeah, and who is this Williams, anyway? Some dune bunny, I'd bet!

C.P.: You'd lose.

F.P.: Huh?

C.P.: He's a biochemist.

F.P.: Oh. [*Thinking.*] Well, one botch ain't so bad.

C.P.: How about two?

F.P. [*confusedly*]: What?

C.P.: Not what. Who.

F.P.: Huh?

C.P.: Dr. U.D. Register.

F.P.: Register?

C.P.: Right. From Loma Linda.

F.P.: Linda?

C.P.: Loma.

F.P.: Who the hell is Linda Loma?

C.P.: Loma Linda.

F.P.: Who?

C.P.: Not who. Where.

F.P.: What?

C.P.: *Where* the hell is Loma Linda.

F.P. [*frustrated*]: How the hell should I know?

C.P. [*calmly*]: I'm not asking you...I'm telling you.

F. P. [*anxiously*]: So tell me, then, before I explode!

C.P.: California.

F.P. [*shocked*]: What?! You mean right here in the States?!

C.P.: You know of another?

F.P. [*confusedly*]: Then how in the.... [*Pauses.*] What, is she some kind of anarchist?

C.P.: Not she. He.

F.P.: What?

C.P.: Not what. Who.

F.P.: Huh?

C.P. [*annoyed*]: Look...*he* is Register who, like Williams, related the relation between alcohol and the typical American diet, only Register used rats.

F.P.: Rats?

C.P.: Right. He fed them sausage and sweet rolls, spaghetti and soda, then set out a choice between water and whiskey. In no time all those rats were lapping up a gallon of the good stuff per week.

F.P. [*laughs*]: Stupid rats! [*Takes a gulp of beer.*]

C.P.: Not really. They didn't have a choice.

F.P. [*confusedly*]: Huh?

C.P. [*slowly*]: See here...Register's rats were avitaminotic. Their intake consisted of minimal nutrients. This type of diet ultimately leads to confusion, irritability and a physiological craving for a neuroanesthetic. He had his rats so bloody imbalanced they were begging for the bottle!

F.P.: Whatever. [*Takes another gulp from his glass. Thinks.*] Hey, were these rats really American? [*Pauses.*] I mean, what if it turns out they were from, say, Nova Scotia or someplace? Wouldn't that blow his whole theory to hell?

C.P. [*after a short reflective pause*]: You're missing the point. And besides, any body from Nova Scotia is biologically the same as that same species from the States, right? [*Waits for confirmation. Then, with concern.*] Right?

F.P.: So, you're saying a running back from Lakeland is the same as a linebacker from Rainy River?

C.P.: Biologically...yes.

F.P. [*laughing repulsively*]: Ha! Man, are you medical types dumb! Imagine...a mud duck the same as a muskie! [*Laughs.*] And you call yourself educated!

C.P. [*reserving patience*]: And what, then, friend, do you pretend to call yourself?

F.P. [*suddenly serious*]: Why, American, of course!

C.P. [*amused*]: I see. And let's say we send you east and set you straight on the Axle. What'll you be calling yourself then, I wonder?

F.P. [*pauses, thinks, then extends his hand*]: Hello, there, sand nigger. Call me Abdul.

[*Both laugh heartily. By this time* JUDE *and* LAWRENCE *have regained composure enough to attempt conversation with the* THREE GRAINERS, *who appear thoroughly annoyed though politely allow the presence of their intruders. Suddenly, a horrible, high-pitched shriek turns attention toward* SHELBY, DOC *and* COLE.]

DOC [*half-serious*]: Don't bruise her, now, you brute.

COLE [*to* SHELBY, *excitedly*]: Come on, then, missy.

[*Tries to tickle her.*] Stop your squirming!

SHELBY [*laughing mad*]: I will once you stop poking me!

COLE [*laughing*]: You hear that, Doc? She thinks she's being poked, eh, he, he....

DOC [*with a smirk*]: Perhaps that's all she thinks you're capable of... [*Points up his pinky.*] ...a little poke, eh?

[*Both* DOC *and* SHELBY *let loose a laugh.*]

COLE [*to* SHELBY, *feigning good humor*]: Oh, is that so, now, Miss Pissy Britches? Well, if you think that's all I'm capable of.... [*Tickles her relentlessly until he tires.*]

SHELBY [*catching her breath*]: Well... [*Pants.*] ...judging by my... [*Pants.*] ...blood clots... [*Pants.*] ...I'd say you're quite capable of... [*Pants.*] ...making your mark.

COLE [*rather priggishly*]: In truth, dear girl, there's only one mark I ever intend making, he, he....

DOC [*aside to* SHELBY, *mockingly*]: And with such a small marker it's a wonder it's ever made, he, he....

COLE [*prickingly*]: Eh? What's this? Shielding pigeons from the carbineer? [*Tries to tickle* SHELBY *but she clouts him in the mouth.*]

SHELBY [*snappishly*]: Enough, b'Jesus! My sides are beginning to swell!

DOC [*to* SHELBY, *with an air of concern*]: Careful, my coquette. Such actions to a sadist may only spawn more of that unwanted swelling.

SHELBY [*gently massaging her side*]: I seriously doubt there could be any more.

DOC [*chuckling to himself*]: Or less. [*Laughs aloud.*] Most certainly not less.

COLE [*to* DOC, *annoyed*]: Alright, now, you potted sage... profess! Why this fascination with my wick, eh, what?

DOC [*haughtily*]: Purely philanthropic, my dear underling.

COLE [*intrigued*]: Oh? And how's that?

DOC: Well, you see, the way I figure, it's best to make light of one's problem by, say, simply softening up the issue.

COLE: I see. [*Mocking* DOC's *professional tone.*] And what problem, pray tell, are you alluding to, good sir?

DOC [*with an air of sympathy*]: Why, quite simply, the softness of your issue, of course.

[*Both* DOC *and* SHELBY *begin laughing aloud while* COLE *broods over his beer. After a moment he realizes he has but one sip left and, unwilling to part with another dollar, begins squirming in his stool. Shortly after,* DOC *empties his own glass and calls over the* BARTENDER.]

[*Enter* BARTENDER.]

DOC [*to* BARTENDER, *indicating* SHELBY *and himself*]: Set us up with another, young sir.

[*Exit* BARTENDER.]

COLE [*insulted*]: Hey, there, Doc, why not come round complete?

DOC [*gazing up* SHELBY]: Some comelier time, perhaps.

COLE: No comelier time than the present, I say.

DOC [*angrily*]: Aye, you and every other feeble-minded banality! [*Calms down.*] Alright, since we're in the habit for sharing shopworn remarks, here's another for the rounds.... [*Smoothes his brow.*] My mind-eye's fortune lies present while your present is past.

COLE [*confused*]: Meaning what?

DOC: Meaning this, you simpleton...my money has grown myopic. [*Puts his arm around* SHELBY.] Beauty beyond the second stool simply does not exist.

SHELBY [*to* DOC, *sincerely*]: Ah, my dear old philanthroper.

[*She then takes a quick sip of her drink and begins choking violently.* DOC *eagerly offers his handkerchief.*]

COLE [*to* DOC]: Am I to believe, then, benevolence a boon to be granted only for the beautiful?

DOC [*axiomatically*]: Better to be beautiful than beholden.

COLE: How's that?

DOC: It's like Socrates says in the *Symposium*.... [*Impersonating Plato.*] He desires that which at present is impalpable.

COLE [*peeved*]: And the lesson?

DOC: Just this.... [*With a sneer.*] Be patient! [*Then, with a chuckle.*] The future may find you a proportionate man.

[COLE *retreats to his near-empty glass. At this time a disturbance breaks out between* JUDE *and* LAWRENCE *and the* THREE GRAINERS, *the latter moving fluidly around the former who stand huddled backs-together so as to keep a constant eye on their enraged aggressors.*]

THIRD GRAINER: Say, brothers, dost thou smell a swine?

SECOND GRAINER: Aye, a swine and a sailor's wife!

JUDE and LAWRENCE: Come, now, fair gentlemen. Let us have peace!

FIRST GRAINER: Peace?! We hate the word! And if we be fair instead of foul then thyme shall sprout from my scabby stump!

ALL: Thyme! Thyme! Scabby stump! Peace be gone! Time to jump!

[*The* THREE GRAINERS *attempt a blow but are dodged.*]

LAWRENCE [*to* JUDE]: Holy Christ! These cats are quick!

JUDE [*to* LAWRENCE]: Tooth your tongue, you sinuous ass! Your wicked words already hung us thrice and now you make me swallow Christ?! Sin upon sin! Silence, before you find yourself aflame!

LAWRENCE [*to* JUDE]: A searing tongue shall never tame a flame! And besides, it was not mine but *thine* own words which fanned our devils' fury! Therefore, bite yourself and do it hard, you whimpering son of a wayworn widow!

JUDE: O, Yahweh, the blade hath been brandished! My dear old mother has been laid upon the table!

LAWRENCE: Aye, the table...and the chair...and on the velvet divan...and in between the sheets of thy father's mossy bed....

JUDE: Enough! By God, the day of this affliction shall not be forgotten! [*Raises his fists.*] Prepare thyself for Hell!

[*Sets himself upon* LAWRENCE. *Together they spin in a whirl of violence before the* THREE GRAINERS *who look on in amazement.*]

THIRD GRAINER: By all quarters, this most certainly is a curious display!

SECOND GRAINER: Aye! My penthouse lids are bent up like bats' wings!

FIRST GRAINER: Then turn, my brothers, and forget these two, for my belly and the brew have conspired a spell of the testicle tingles. Come.... [*Starts toward the door.*] Let us make haste toward the nearest hole!

SECOND GRAINER: I'll give thee wind! [*Farts.*]

THIRD GRAINER: Aye, and I as well! [*Also farts.*]

[*Exit the* THREE GRAINERS.]

CARDIGAN PAUL [*nudging* FOOTBALL PAUL *and pointing toward* JUDE *and* LAWRENCE]: Look there! It appears the war out East has made its way inland!

FOOTBALL PAUL [*peering toward* JUDE *and* LAWRENCE]: So it has. [*Pauses.*] Care to make a wager?

C.P.: [*thinking*]: Hmm...I'll place two on the Jew.

F.P.: Ha! Only a fool would bet on the Jew! I'll match your two and take the other!

[*Both shake hands, after which* FOOTBALL PAUL *drinks down the last of his glass.*]

F.P. [*to* C.P., *indicating his empty glass*]: Look here, chemist, how's 'bout an advance?

C.P.: Advance? On what?

F.P.: Why, on my winnings, of course!

C.P.: Control your tremors! Each side has yet to find its aim!

F.P.: My tremors, eh? And I suppose for those you'd even have a pill?

C.P.: Most certainly! [*Extends an empty palm.*] A lovely dose of cattle liver, coated and all!

F.P. [*disgustedly*]: Hell, mine best be coated in butter and onions if I'm to take it.

C.P. [*laughs*]: Right! Butter, onions, and a nice spicy chipotle sauce.

F.P. [*confusedly*]: Chipotle? Shit! Sounds like a taste for

Doc's perverted tongue.

    C.P.: True, but only if poured atop the tender tips of Shelby, eh, what? He, he....

[*Both laugh.*]

    COLE [*to* DOC, *overhearing the two* PAULs' *remarks*]: Hey now, Aristotle! Mind the course hecklers! [*Points toward the two* PAULs.] Them there aim to make merry of your name!

    DOC [*extracting his tongue from* SHELBY's *sockets.*]: Eh, what's this? Still pining for a pour?

    COLE [*indignantly*]: How poor is your sight! A friend shines his light and you dim his wits! Is that how it's to be, then? A curtain between us?

    DOC: Better a curtain than a cup. By Christ, can't you tell when you've been yanked?

    COLE [*to* SHELBY]: Is this true? Am I a loose tooth?

    SHELBY: A little too loose for my taste, perhaps.

    COLE [*laughs*]: Ha! Too loose for you is like infinity times two...utterly incomprehensible! [*To* DOC.] Come on, man! It's only a buck!

    DOC [*absolutely annoyed*]: Alright, then, if only for the sake of your insipid persistence...and only if you promise to take yourself away!

    COLE [*crossing his stomach*]: I swear it on my soul!

    DOC: Here, then. [*Hands him a dollar.*] Take it and be

gone!

COLE [*waiving the bill*]: Aha! A victory! [*Calls the BARTENDER. Enter BARTENDER.*] Look here, boy! I have an even trade!

BARTENDER: I see...if only your take wouldn't have taken so long.

COLE [*confusedly*]: How's that?

BARTENDER: Our time is up. The taps have all been shut. [*To* ALL.] Down the gullet! The second bell has rung!

FOOTBALL PAUL [*to* CARDIGAN PAUL]: Aha! My man's on top! That's two for me! Pay up, you pusher!

CARDIGAN PAUL: You're confused. You took the other, as you'll well remember, and whichever is winning the other is well losing.

F.P. [*angrily*]: A common sort of trickery! Come, you dog! Hand over my kitty!

C.P.: Tell you what.... [*Stands.*] We'll discuss this sometime over underdone eggs...my treat.

F.P. [*standing*]: Well...okay...so long as some sausages find their way onto my plate.

[*Exit both.*]

SHELBY [*to* BARTENDER]: But what about my man?

DOC [*to* SHELBY, *standing*]: I assure you, my dear, a man of much worth shall no doubt come anon.

SHELBY: Really? Where?

DOC: Wherever you wish, my young seminal sponge.

SHELBY: Really?

DOC [*leading her from her stool*]: Really.

[*They exit.*]

COLE [*to* BARTENDER]: Look here, friend, this bill is yours if you see fit to fill my glass.

BARTENDER: Alright, then. Here it is.... [*Points toward* JUDE *and* LAWRENCE.] Send those brawlers out the door and I'll pour your fill for three days hence.

COLE [*excitedly*]: A dandy of a deal! [*Hurries over to* JUDE *and* LAWRENCE.] Well, poor souls, it seems my belly has gotten the better of you both! [*Grabs their ankles and exits, dragging both behind him.*]

[*The* BARTENDER *walks to the tap and fills two glasses, then toward* SEXTON *at the end of the bar.*]

BARTENDER [*to* SEXTON, *handing him a glass*]: To the rousing night.

[*They clink glasses and drink.*]

When drinking, the strange and curious never escape my senses. Must just be something in the act itself...a dampening of the ordinary, so to speak. Take, for example, that libertine doll sitting alone in the center of the room, her thin, libidinous wings flapping like semaphores each time a musky scent meets her pale, powdered nose. Strange, wouldn't you say? Or how about that stiff shirt three stools down tugging his necktie and thumbing his cock to the surge and sway of the stock market news? Curious, indeed! Then again, both these (and countless others like them) have happened all too often and, because of their frequency, have been dubiously colored the same dull, synthetic tone as seedless fruit. Without effort I could devise an exhaustive list of such occurrences and at the top, etched in bile, would be that lackluster moment a person of your past appears suddenly as if born by the thick, embryonic air around you. What does one do in such a case? Two choices: 1) either tend to it, nurture it, or 2) blow by it like a banshee and pray to Christ it doesn't start wailing for your nipple. What I'm leading up to is last Saturday night when, while having a drink in some dump after work, who should appear but she who gave birth to a thousand such bewailing babes: Sara.

As it were, this was one rare moment that defied choice. To tuck tail and turn and blow by her surreptitiously (at such a choiceless hour) could kill the clement of this gracious gift of Fate. No, such gifts must be recognized, and in the name of the Norns I resolved to be seen...and allow her to come to me. This is the key move in the game. If I were to spot her, and be spotted spotting her, then the burden of approach is all on me, at which time I lose all advantage. If she sees me and does not come, well, then this gift of Fate was nothing but a bitter pill. But if, upon spotting me, she *does* come, then the stars will shoot confetti and the moon will spew champagne in honor of my renewed faith in fortitude. So, drink in hand, my head in my book – trying like the devil to look lonely and forlorn – I sat patient and awaited that singsong voice and a soft, pleasing tap on my folded shoulder.

Two drinks later, and still no tap, and my faith in Fate was slithering fast into the gutter. Just minutes till closing and already I was beginning to imagine that long, dark walk back to the apartment; just me, the moon and the green plastic garbage cans singing our lament, the pitch of which tuned true by electric light beams and the painful screams of sirens; the stumbling, bumbling, meandering, mopish, picayune Panpiper playing his solo and playing it well on his purple, palpitating parasol prick, his long limber lumber slung over his shoulder and under his button hole, belladonna lily bulbs blooming from his umbilicus, omphalos, anopheles, anomalous bed bites and achromous appetites, apostrophe pointing at safe and sound people whose carpenter's cross is a good Christian's crutch (sempiternal hellfire my temporal ass!), anodyne ointments and diuretic teas meant to stave off our ailments and cataclysmic inclinations, agenbite of inwit, silk of the kine, crepuscular functions and nocturnal unctions, a lecherous laugh is a priestly scream with a crackajack slingback of pedigree bees sip your sluices of brandy with peaches and pee and sing "Bing-bang-tallywag, Bloody Bloody Douche Bag" on hollyhock harps strung with Silvertone strings, Paris green pianos and verdigris keys, nicotine, tamarind, capsicum cream, St. Ursula's vitriolic, vaginal bleedings all over America's dear, dour, sour, syphilitic sheets...

"Jeff?"

Jesus Christ! I nearly fell off my stool! Blinded by surprise and scarcely with a wit, I barely managed to squeak out a weak "Hello." Then: "How long have you been here?" to see if she guessed my scheme.

"Oh, quite some time now," she chirped. "I noticed you earlier, though you seemed so upset, your head down and staring at your book, I thought I'd just let you alone."

Okay, so my plan could use some revising. At least the frame could still support the façade...I hoped. I noticed her hands were empty and offered to buy her a drink.

"You can't," she said. "That's why I came over here. The bartender gave last call ages ago. He's throwing everyone out." She then stared at me some before asking if I was OK. Just dandy, I told her. A little tired from work, is all. Hey, I know! Perhaps some coffee might do some good. I asked if she cared to join me.

"Not tonight," she said. "I'm here with some friends from home." Then: "This is their first time in the Twin Ports, don't you know, and listen to this...they've never before seen the Lake, not even pictures! Can you believe it?! It's impossible to describe. I had to bring them here myself and show them all this amazing beauty!"

Yes, yes, dazzling, to be sure. A dizzying display of Nature meets Nadir. *Tickets, folks! Tickets! Get yer tickets at the gate! Only a dream or two for a dream of a view!* Ah, well, the only crime is in not even trying. Without looking too dejected (just a dash of pity to freshen the palate) I stood off my stool and reached for her hand. "It was good seeing you, Sara," said I with a soft, gentle squeeze. "Be sure to give your friends an aquatic eyeful." And with that I turned my back and made for the door.

"Wait!" she shouted...just as I expected. A little indifference goes a long, long way. "Give me a moment," she smiled before trotting off toward the rear of the room. I always was good at reading her this way. In truth, it was partially this which split us in the end; it all got to be so goddamned boring. So dull it was I soon resorted to tearing out a few chinks in my own armor just to even the odds – that is, until it all began to seem like masturbation.

I stood in the entrance as she gossiped with her friends,

gave one final giggle, then sauntered back with that feline sway, tossing all about those luscious honeydew hips of hers. Good Christ, those hips! There's much to be said for a woman who knows how to bounce around her hips with such vitality and verve as if she were attempting to seduce the Messiah Himself. Even if it's all meant as a tease, it's still one hell of a knee-bending sight. One lovely thing about Sara, however, is she hasn't a Salome bone in her body. With her, this dance is natural. She means every ounce.

I took her to an all-night café just up the street. We made way through the moonlight sediment and found a small, quiet spot in the corner. We sat opposite each other. She ordered a blueberry muffin (somewhat typical, I thought) and I was contented with my coffee...for now.

"You know," she began as her muffin arrived, "it's been almost a year since we've seen each other last."

"Really?" I asked. "Have I changed at all?" (Silly, I know, though I thought it best to keep the pot bubbling.)

"Jeff," she began in her motherly way, spreading margarine atop her mushroom-shaped muffin, "you'll never change. You'll always be the same self-centered, stubborn, obstinate little boy."

"Obstinate and stubborn are the same thing," I snorted.

"See?!" she snapped. "See what I mean? You always gotta have the last word...just like a little boy. You even dress like a little boy!" She laughed aloud at this as if she were really enjoying herself. But what matter if she had her fun? She deserved at least this much for the times I broke her down. I decided just to sit there quiet with my coffee and listen, perhaps even amused a bit.

She went on to list all my faults, the likes of which were nothing more than simple variations sung by every girl who ever got to know me: selfish, mulish, narcissistic, insensitive, incapable of affection, incapable of love, deplorable, delusional, an inactive dreamer, yippidy-do and dippidy-dee. No harm in it, really. The coffee was good and her chiming voice, which I always enjoyed, somehow made her chidings sound pretty, charming.

Finally, after an emphatic chomp off her scrumptious muffin, it all came to an end. Quite impressive, really, these performances. I wouldn't dream of interrupting a ceremonious moment. For some reason, likely because I've become so accustomed, I've grown to enjoy listening to them all with great attention, trying to notice the slightest nuance as one might do when attempting to detect the subtle differences between a keyed-up symphony and its myriad conductors.

After the snakes have all been drained of their venom the rest of the conversation seemed safe on all sides. So safe, in fact, I even got to slide in a few references to a romp...all subdued, of course. Then, suddenly, the talk turned toward this town.

"Any plans yet?" she asked.

"Plans?"

"Yeah, plans...to leave," she explained. "You always said you hoped to escape one day. I'm just wondering if you've made any plans to do so."

I pondered this over a slow, slurping sip. It's true, and to call it an "escape" would not be melodramatic. Nobody ever leaves this town, at least not for long; the allure of nostalgia seems too magnetic. I've often wondered if all hometowns are this way. Are all domestic fields across America's Great Plain nothing more than vast, hovering vacuums which suck the souls of their weary inhabitants and spin them there eternally? Surely not, it can't be, though what must it take to tear oneself away from so crippling a gravity? Everyone I know who has left this hole has returned, and each more disillusioned than the last. None excluded. The closest example of this is my older brother. With him it was a woman. After only a year of marriage and a short stint in Kansas his new wife got homesick. *Homesick!* Homesick for what?! Hangovers and old boyfriends?!

"Who knows," I sighed. "Perhaps I'll never leave this town.

Perhaps this is the perfect place for a stubborn, starving, self-centered artist, what with all the ennui..."

"Christ," she scoffed, "don't give me any more of your *ennui*! You know as well as I do there's no perfect place for you. You're restless, dissatisfied, always craving more of your blessed *ennui*. You prefer your precious suffering to even the smallest pursuit of pleasure. A starving artist, you say? *Pshaw!* You'll never be starving, at least not in this town, and you'll never be an artist...you're not sensitive enough. An artist creates in order to admire, to bring out life's beauty. Do you honestly believe you can create something beautiful? Do you even know the meaning of the word? I doubt it! All you seem to know about is the base, the obscene, the vulgar, the ugly, the ugliness in everything...."

I turned a hollow ear. In all my years of bartending the most important thing I've learned is it's never wise to pay mind to the hiss of a pissed missy. Besides, I've heard all this before; her lines are so rehearsed, so brittle with wear they turn to dust the instant they touch oxygen. In fact, given the moment's temperament, I thought it best the whole thing were abandoned. I started from my seat and reached for my coat.

"Where are you going?" she asked as if surprised.

"Look," I sighed. "All I wanted was a cup of coffee and a little conversation but it seems as though you can't handle even that." I tossed some coins on the table. "So long, Sara." Then I turned and made for the door, trying like hell to conceal my smirk.

Outside and starting up the walk I wondered how long it would take before...

Before the thought even left my mind she came bursting through the café door swearing up and down how sorry she was, that she didn't mean any of it, all she wanted was for me to feel the same way she felt those two years together, the frustration, the fights, the hurt feelings, the...whatever. The moment was primed. I reached for her waist and pulled her close, pressing our lips tight together. And somewhat to my surprise she resisted very little; just a bit of a stiff leg at first, though after a moment of that hard human warmth her hand was heading straight for my fly.

"Wait!" I laughed. "We're in the middle of the street!"

She hesitated, allowing her fingers to linger over my buttons, then she giggled and said, "By chance do you remember where I parked my car?"

Right this way! The entire time I kept pinching her ass, not just as a means of rekindling the flame, but also as a reminder of my true intentions. I was not about to amuse any hope for a full-on reunion, and it might seem arrogant to speak thus, though not if you knew Sara. She's the sort of girl who would proudly swim through a city of sewers in search of a lover, and it's this which attracted me to her, though the problem arises the instant she finally does find her man: at first whiff of love's sweet aroma she sets in like a leech and with her tireless tongue begins draining all the life from her unsuspecting host. What causes this in a woman, this need to latch on, this parasitic desire to seep herself deep into a man's very soul once the skin has been broken? I realize some men might want this (some even *need* this) and lust for the teeth of an impatient nymph, though the rest of us react to such a sentiment as an aborigine to the bite of an infested flea, our vital signs diminished, our skin cold and clammy, our bowels dyspeptic with undigested affection.

Anyway, the furthest thing from my mind at this point was dyspepsia. To be honest, I found myself salivating at the thought of a juicy slice of overbearing ass, and Sara's got a dandy...a meaty, succulent sirloin cut! I can't keep my hands off it as we approach her car, the thought of escaping out of public view whirling like a maelstrom in my brain, making me behave all hands-down-the-pants. And wouldn't you know, it's now she decides to play coy with me, squirming like an eel out from under my advances. All this manages to accomplish, however, is a bubbling over of that effervescent emotion, an inner explosion of pure spermatozoa. By the time she finally gets the car door open my cock has sprung loose and is sniffing about like a blind, hungry polecat. She has her tiny fingers wrapped tight around it and in her other hand her keys, dangling and chiming like an Egyptian charm. "You drive," she said. "I've had too much to drink." Without a word I hop straight for the driver's seat, my dong bouncing in the night air like a bald, frightened bunny.

The instant I'm inside she has her hand back on my prick and is stroking it soundly. All this cock squeezing has blurred my vision and I find it a hassle just to get the right key in the ignition. Nevertheless, I must press on. I'm up for a night of it and I know if I let myself go now before we've even left the parking lot she'd feel so damned ashamed of herself I wouldn't even get a wet kiss goodnight. With all my might I try to keep my mind on the task at hand, which is to get her someplace indoors as quick as possible and into the mind-numbing warmth of a comfortable bed. As it is, it's all too much just to manage the strength to roll down a window and to make matters worse no longer is she satisfied with letting her hand have all the fun and down she darts and starts tonguing my prick as if it were made of molasses and honey. Must press on, I repeat to myself.

We're speeding down the side streets now and I'm beginning to get nervous. Already I've knocked over three garbage cans, a park bench and a "Do Not Enter" sign and if this keeps up, I think to myself, we'll both be spending the rest of the night trying to find a hole between each other's holding cell. Suddenly it occurred to me I hadn't the slightest clue as to where I was driving. She must be staying with some friends in town, but whom? I've never known her to keep any friends in Superior. "Hey, there," I said, softly patting her head. "Where to?"

She let up with a smacking sound and, in a groggy voice, asked, "Where are we?" The East End, I told her. "You're way off," she laughed. "It's on Baxter...by the Bridge," before settling back into my candy-coated lap.

Finally we found the place and slithered out the car and scurried indoors. It was dark, though just enough light shone in through the windows where I could make out a figure lying motionless on the couch. "Who's that?" I asked.

"That's Rebecca," said Sara. "This is her apartment."

Oops! I hurriedly tried to hide my cock from plain view. Sara let out a wry giggle at my awkwardness, then laughed, "My, aren't we shy all of a sudden?" After watching me suffer awhile, she leaned over and whispered, "It's alright...she's asleep." Then she held my hand and led me past the couch, pants open and all, down the hall toward the rear of the flat. Nearing the bedroom I asked why, if this was her place, was Rebecca on the couch and not in her bed. "Because," said Sara, "I asked for her bed tonight as a favor...just in case."

Ah, finally inside the comfort zone! So relieved am I, so relaxed and peaceful it's now I realize my bladder is about to explode. I excused myself and made way toward the bathroom, beaming at the thought of eventual relief.

Upon leaving the toilet, after the last exquisite drop had been drained, I had a strange desire to get an eyeful of this Rebecca. It struck me odd she should surrender her bed on a Saturday night...or any night, for that matter. Any unsightly distortions? I wondered. I tiptoed quietly to the couch and peered down.

Though dark I could clearly make out her features: long strawberry-blonde hair woven over alabaster skin; soft eyes; a bit of an aquiline nose, though her full, parted lips drew the eye away from this, forcing attention instead toward the continuousness of her demure chin and the curves of her naked neck and shoulders. She must have been warm, for one leg rested bare atop her blanket, revealing a long, slender stem of silvery flesh. I noticed nothing wrong with her. Quite attractive, really. So much so, in fact, my erection again grew to obscene proportions. It was high time I made way back toward the bedroom.

When I walked through the door I was disappointed to

find Sara still fully dressed and, what's more, a book in her lap. "Remember this one?" she asked while fingering a page, then read:

> There was a little girl, she had a little curl
>   Right in the middle of her forehead;
> And when she was good, she was very, very
>   Good,
> And when she was bad she was horrid.

After which she laughed and said, "Or how about this?"

> He drew a circle that shut me out –
> Heretic, rebel, something to flout.
> But Love and I had the wit to win:
> We drew a circle that drew him in!

Yes, yes, very clever, Calliope. Christ, there's nothing worse than a tipsy bitch clutching a book of common poetry in her paws. Always sounds like the breaking of bones. All right, then, Miss Bradstreet, since you're in the mood for tripe....

> The shining fat buttocks
>   Of the big baby
> Who on his knee sticks
>   His white snout into the cups

And then, my sweet....

> Rubbed by a muzzle that growls
>   With a gentle tone,
> And licks the round face
>   Of the little dear...

Or, if you found those lines a bit too abstruse....

Apples of Arcadia 39

One evening you consecrated me poet,
Blond ugly one:
Come down here, that I may whip you
On my lap...

I walked toward her, took the book from her hands, then pulled her to the bed. Slow, I popped open each button on her blouse, letting loose her warm, heaving breasts. I always did adore her tits; supple and full, the mounds of a woman. We fell upon the bed, her atop me, and immediately she sets in working upon my fly. She's got me so excited, her rose petal lips poised just above the buckle, when she undoes the buttons and pulls down my pants my pecker smacks her straight in the chin, which she's quick to play off with a coy, girlish giggle. My pants now off and tossed to the floor, I flip her beneath me and feel up her skirt. I'm shocked to find she's not wearing any panties (hardly her style), though perhaps she chose to do away with such restraints as a personal favor to herself...just in case, don't you know. Moving forward, I pull down her skirt and begin kissing her stomach and just as I'm approaching the *abricot-fendu* she starts bursting juice like an overripe peach. At first I just tickle the outer folds with my tongue, every so often sliding it in to steal a sip of the glistening dew. She shivers at this, holding on tight to the back of my head, and soon after I start lapping her bean like some mad, thirsty pit bull she pulls me up by the ears and plunges her tongue deep down my throat. Then she grabs my cock and places it into position and with her hands on my ass thrusts it in to the hilt. The first few strokes are so deep, so surrounding, I feel my balls start to bubble and swell though somehow I manage to maintain, the pleasure fast reaching that fine point of torture. Her legs held high as if suspended with stirrups, I work my way into her trembling womb and then further still, though for some reason it seems I can't reach her itch. She wants my blood, of this I'm certain, and as I work faster, then faster and faster, as fast as a piston on axle grease plasma with gasoline corpuscles bursting in my veins a cramp starts to swell in the base of my back and quickly stiffens and worsens in pain and I wonder how much more of this I can take. I don't dare stop now (she'd tear me to shreds!) and a change in position is out of the question; she now has her legs wrapped round my ass like a boa. My only hope is in making her blow, thereby turning her limbs into dandelion stems. At first I nibble her neck. Nothing. Then a little tongue-play on the nipples. Still nothing. Frustrated, I stoke my brain to try and remember the teachings of Kama Sutra science but my mind's so heavy with pleasure and pain I can't concentrate on anything but the sting. Aimless with despair and needing wings like a lemming, I thrust my hands under her ass and begin squeezing like a maniac...and at this, thank Christ, she responds! Excited, I squeeze on, listening with glee as she squeals even louder with each fierce pinch, my fingers still searching like frantic explorers for that one special spot that will make her explode. The cramp has now spread from my back to my legs and I'm on the verge of tears as I give one last desperate poke at her puckering hole, her moaning now like the whine of a puppy. Convinced this is it, I dive straight in and relentlessly massage round the rim and within. She's got her body glued to mine and gyrating wildly like a suffocating fish when finally she lets loose a high-pitched squeal and a series of thrusts, abrupt and acute, and then BLAMMO! off she shoots into space like a missile and spins round the earth with the grace of a satellite before falling to the surface and crashing at sea, exhausted, surrounded by soft, smooth, rapid, rolling, oscillating ripples. I soon follow with a gusher, then quickly slide off to stretch my back, the groan from which is even greater than the orgasm. And after the pants and sighs of pure satisfaction we both fell back and closed our eyes, soon to drift off into a deep, smiling sleep....

After what must have been a few hours I awoke to the feel of female skin, her smooth, naked ass pressed up against my prick. My back now much more rested, I wasted no time in caressing her leg while offering a few firm thrusts to see if she'd respond. After some time of this and nothing I slid my fingers between her slippery thighs and began tickling her tingtoddy and at this she started to stir, though only to push my hand away. At first I thought it just a reaction to the spiders of sleep...a brushing off of the cobwebs, so to speak. Again I slid my hand between her legs and again she pushed it away. A bit miffed, I went straight for the source and this time got a slap on the arm. "Behave!" she said before turning her ass and legs toward the wall, inaccessible.

What the fuck?! I wondered. Could the immodesty of alcohol have worn off so quickly? Did her dreams reveal to her the sinful visions of some cheap, brazen hussy? Whatever the reason, that one word was enough to dampen all desire and all I longed for then was to make my exit without having to speak to her another word. After a while of lying still and listening to her breathing I finally heard it get hard and heavy. Easy, I got out of bed and began to dress.

Making way through the apartment I passed the couch and turned a thought of having a go at Rebecca, though she looked so peaceful, so angelic in her sleep I thought it best if I just made my leave.

Outside the sun was rising. After a few blocks I began to get a headache from all the squinting. This aside, the only thought that occupied my mind was how wonderful would taste a strong, steaming cup of coffee.

Ah, springtime in Superior, when the air is heavy with the smell of muddy exhaust and defrosting dogshit! Literally hundreds of lawns smothered in the stuff, leaving little room for even the narrowest path. And on the first of the marginally sunny days, the weather soft and soothing for even the skinniest pup, one can view these quadrupeds, quivering with excitement, lined up for blocks around the corners and alleyways, their owners chained and dragging headlong behind them through the mess and muck of a winter's worth of waste. Quite honestly, I don't know how those mutts can manage. It's impossible to imagine anything pushing its way through all those layers.

Also in spring is when the Bridge crew continues its on-going task of masking the rust with a thick metallic coat of Columbia blue, the municipal tint of this freshwater town. I've often wondered, since this massive passage connects the two, who is it who must foot the bill once this lofty venture comes to completion...Superior or Duluth? Then again, the answer is obvious. One must merely compare the two and follow his nose to the sweeter scent. Due to the view of that majestic Lake the magic word is *tourism*, and it would seem extremely hard to attract a dollar with broken-down buildings and sewage pools when rose gardens and lakeside cafés await abroad. Superior is an orphan, the daughter Mother America never wanted, the offspring of some sloppy affair with a man named Pierre and sent away the instant the cord had been severed. The result is a novelty, a mockery of childhood. Forced to listen to the cheers of other children who slide down silver chutes and swing from golden branches, pathetic little parks and salty streets were all she had to play upon, that and piles upon piles of all types of filth. Now well into adulthood, all she has to look forward to is the bending and tending to the tainted demands of scabby patrons in dilapidated bars, returning at night to rest her sight inside a dimly-lit slum, all the while her sister on the hill sitting high upon her throne, blue and gold oriflammes flowing from her crown, drowning out the soil from the sun's essential warmth....But still she persists, somehow finding nutrients in the putrescence like some saprophytic parasite, leaving behind as her mark on her hosts a spider's web of varicose veins. And because of her years spent steeped in debris and disease and decay she cannot be killed. She has been inoculated. She will outlast them all....

The Lounge is the first bar off the Bridge and as such it attracts all those dizzy, dehydrated brush pushers who swarm in like locusts to drink the place dry, and Joe and I do our best to oblige – for one very good reason. Whoever it is who pays these people obviously has a dizzying well from which to dip. These guys are loaded, dollar bills bouncing off their backs like lice. Not once do Joe and I forget to cast a smile when seeing our boys in blue blow in from the windy heights off that monument to free trade, tongues wagging, wallets waving, willing to drink the spilt booze from our bar rags if need be. This sort is always the easiest to please. Simply plop a bucket someplace near their faces, allow plenty of room for the first fierce splash, then sit back and watch as they drink themselves stinking. In a few hours they'll begin to think us saints sent from above, worthy of the most esteemed obscene gibberish and, more important, a fistful of the world's most circulated bank notes. Needless to say, they get first service. This causes quite a stir among the grainers and the Brothers Draught who view their being snubbed a gross indecency to their loyalty...as if there was such a thing.

The leader of the Bridge crew is a tall, oily Greek called Kosta who drinks nothing but Ouzo and who always pays with a fifty-dollar bill, even if his pockets be stuffed tight with twenties (which they most likely are). His second is a round, bulging man with wiry whiskers and an insociable thirst for Canadian whisky. Together they sit in the covetous corner booth, the others bouncing around them like bees, the hive constantly worked over to find the most delectable honey. And if none can be found (which is usually the case) then they'd gladly settle for a plate of scorched meat and a potato found in the restaurant upstairs. An incredible piece of entrepreneurship, this place. Long ago the owners of the Lounge (referred to as "The Family") discovered the first thing a drunk reaches for toward the tail end of a bender is a hot, greasy something-or-other served by someone else. Shortly after this enterprising observation the upstairs (formerly low-income housing) was snatched up and turned over into the hands of economic vision. The Family was even thoughtful enough to leave one of the units intact and properly furnished so that Grandma Greenback could sit quietly, comfortably inside her own safe surroundings the rest of her life losing her mind and decaying of cancer. Since then the menu has progressed with the venture's success and now the joint is considered the area's premier spot where a guy can get a little steak to go with his sauce. The house specialty is prime rib (Black Angus, no less) and our blue-blooded boys would gleefully sit back and gobble it all if only their bellies would allow it.

Most of these guys are nothing more than the sordid sort who prefer little else than a good time, an icy cold brew and, when both those have gone flat, some juicy tail whereby to occupy the mind. The only notable member of the entire bunch is a gangly Negro from the Dominican Republic named Henry. Oh, Henry likes his liquor and his laughs, to be sure, though there is one hairy detail which separates him from his single-minded cohorts. "Come 'ere, Joffree," he says in his thick Domingo accent. "Me wish to speak to you. You listen, Joffree? You listen to Enree? Ah, good. Now, tell me, Joffree...you got woman? Ah, is good, Joffree! Is very good!

Apples of Arcadia 45

You know how much man need woman. Man no good if eem no got woman to keep eem happy, ain't that right, Joffree? But still, even if man got woman is no sure thing. Woman like to run if eem no make her stay, is not true? Is true, Joffree. You listen to Enree. Now, you look there...you see Kosta? Eem very rich man, Joffree...very rich. Eem take home any woman in town. Why you laugh, Joffree? Is true! Now, you look 'ere at Enree. Enree have his money, is true, but Enree's money no truly his. Listen to Enree...eem explain. Kosta, his hair always slick back, always make sure eem smell good...Kosta get his woman, is true, but Enree notice something. Sooner or later woman always want to run. Why you think this is, Joffree? You listen...Enree explain. Is because Kosta no treat woman like woman...eem treat her like dollar bill. Eem put her in his pocket and eem try and possess her. Now, you look 'ere at Enree, Joffree. Enree is man. Enree see woman and eem want her, but eem no take her. Why eem no take her? Is because eem no in need. Enree got eemself one good woman and two good children back home who Enree send money and when Enree see them again...." He wipes a tear off his dusty cheek, then downs a mouthful of booze and continues. "Kosta, eem always be in need...never enough money, ain't that right, Joffree? Enree? Eem see woman as woman...as wonder to walk with...as love, Joffree. Ahhh, love...." This with a lusty sway of his bony hips. "Now, you listen to Enree, Joffree. Is very important. You listen, Joffree? You listen to Enree? Ah, good. Now listen, Joffree....Man never possess love. Never in all his life. It possess eem. You listen, Joffree? You listen to Enree?" The others are pushing him upstairs to eat and as he disappears through the ceiling I hear him say, "You listen to Enree, Joffree! You listen to Enree and you be happy just like eem!"

As they all stagger upstairs Joe and I are left to rake the bills they've left behind, our eyes glistening as we stuff them tight in our jar. I soon learn, however, there's another reason for Joe's beaming orbs. It looks as though Monica, his latest lay-on-the-side, just strutted into the bar, her brother Ned not far behind. Ned is never far behind. For some reason he's got it into his crackpot crop he and I are destined to be pals, co-patriots of the first infantry commanded by the Big Chief himself to take on with extreme prejudice the *taedium vitae* of this entire town...all because I once beat him in a game of foosball. See, Ned is of the sporty type who both admires and abhors all those of equal or greater skill than himself in anything. As it so happens (which is usually the case with this sort) he is an utter failure in everything he assumes, including the maintenance of a healthy marriage. Long ago he realized he wed himself a woman of even lesser value than himself and ever since then he's not been able to muster the courage it takes to cut the cord. Instead, his distorted head has twisted it all into an opportunity to prove to another human being his blatant supremacy, this by treating his wife as sludge and slighting her every chance he gets. Thus, Ned has taken to the bar scene at full steam, bagging the first broad who tosses him a soggy glance. At least with Joe his infidelities are not so narcissistic; Joe just likes women, and a variety at that. After about an hour of nibbling Monica's lower lip he steps into my station and with an obsequious grin asks, "Say, isn't Lizzie spending the week at her stepfather's farm?"

"Yeah...so?"

"So...how's about a little after-hours action at your place tonight?" A moment of silence, then: "What, you don't expect me to bring her home to meet the wife and kid, do you?" Actually, I thought you'd just throw down a few dirty blankets in the back of your pickup, or would that be too much of an expense? This isn't the first time Joe has asked this of me, and I've learned from before it's pointless to argue with the guy. Even after you give him the final no he still shows up at your door at three in the morning with a girl on his arm complaining of nowhere else to go, that the wife just dumped all his shit on the front lawn and would you be so kind as to lend a guy a bed? And how's about a little something to eat?

Better make it enough for two – Miss Nameless Screw hasn't eaten in over a week, don't you know. Spent her last dime on the telephone bill, or the laundry tab, or on a much-needed new pair of silk stockings hand-stitched by Burmese monks. After a while of pretending to think it over Joe takes my silence as a confirmation, then slaps me on the back and says, "Thanks, bud! You're the best!" Righto, that's me. Always merry and bright.

I spend the next hour floating around the bar like a specter trying to avoid Ned and the feeble ramblings of his bloated ego. I'm damn near scaling the fixtures and heading for the air ducts when finally he ropes me in and paralyzes me with his poisonous tongue. "Hey there, partner," he starts. "Y'up fer a little foosball action later? Kick yer ass!" Then do it, you sap, and let me sink back into the blissful void enjoyed by your other mindless victories...but no. This guy likes to toy with his prey before delivering the deathblow. "Guess what, partner," he goes on. "Played this asshole the other night... man, what a wet nurse! After kickin' this guy's ass ten times straight he starts wimperin' like a wounded puppy, talkin' 'bout how he hadn't so much as seen a bar in over a month, tryin' to blame it on the booze and all. Can you believe that shit? Hell, I s'pose he had to blame it on somethin' cuz this guy sucked so bad I wouldn't let him blow my dog, know what I mean? I mean, shit, this poor bastard couldn't find the hole in a fifty-cent whore. I even told the sonbitch, I says, 'Look here, asshole. Even if you had been belly-to-the-bar the past year solid you still couldn't get the ball by me, you limp prick!' Know what he says then, partner? Guess what this sonbitch says then...."

I couldn't care less for the rest of Ned's jack-off scenario.... I've just spotted pure sex waltzing in through the front door. Busty and blonde, the perfect image of the modern-day floozy in tight, black, flower-cuffed polymer, no room for panties; glowing, glittered nymphean skin oozing out from under her loose-fitting, low-cut pink satin top which has a mind to melt off her ivory shoulders by the bounce of her hips and three-inch heels. Peach juice poured atop oleander rose petals. Caviar cunt, to say the least! Every guy has his eyes glued to this girl, even Ned, who has managed to pocket his tongue long enough to lick the spermatic film off his useless sack. Heads spin as she glides past the bar toward the corner booth and as she does I think to myself, Shit, if those horny bridge bastards spot this sprightly faun she's done for! They'll tear the poor girl to shreds! Her only hope is this guy she walked in with, some middling beau whose T-shirt and jeans routine has me wondering if maybe he's her brother. Well, whoever he is, at least he'll be able to buy her some time should the lions stray their cages.

Just as I'm about to step out from behind the bar and introduce myself I find Joe has beat me to it. Christ, how much ass does one man need?! And with Monica still panting like a poodle on her stool! This guy's balls must run on petrol. When he comes back I cut him off to find what he knows.

"Hey there, Humbert," I start. "Who's the nymphet?" He just stares at me, confused. "The girlie," I say with a nod to the corner. "Friend of yours or what?"

"Oh, her," he says with a sigh. "That's just my cousin, Nora."

A bit muddled myself, I glance toward the corner to see the resemblance only to find she's no longer there. I turn toward the door just in time to see her walking out, the beau ideal of boredom close behind. I look again at Joe for an explanation.

"She's visiting the Northland from down south," he begins, "hoping to break free from those rural doldrum blues, as you'd say. Where else would she visit but Superior, eh?" he laughs. "And besides, at least here she has family."

"Who?" I ask. "I mean, besides you."

"Are you kidding?" he coughs with a crooked brow. "Just look around you, pal."

I do...then it hits me. Joe's relatives make up more than

three-quarters of the bar, and it doesn't take long for me to figure out why. Joe is of that special breed of bartender who has long ago learned the nature of the beast, who has taken as granted that with such an important role in society – a society whose genetic seed has maintained itself steadily throughout dozens of decades – those who stand to benefit most from his position are the members upon members of his immediate family. Cousins, aunts, uncles, nephews, nieces, neighbors of half-brothers, etc., et al. All line up to claim their stake in the name of nepotism, and Joe, being of the clever sort, decided it best just to drift with the flow. Why fight the stream when so many fish are willing to flop into your boat? With a service on the sly comes a bundle of bills – no one understands this more than a bartender in a room full of familiar faces. And at the Lounge, where the *modus operandi* has barely surpassed that of the Neolithic Revolution, such dealings go undetected, perhaps even encouraged. The more booze that's poured underhanded the more patrons return to collect their share, creating the illusion of a booming business. Joe gets a pat on the back by the boss while at the same time filling his pockets to their wide, tattered brims. Everybody wins, or at least until inventory season, at which time Joe is always quick to offer a hand to make sure a few extra hash marks find their way into the ledger. As for myself, though with considerably less than Joe's local fanfare, I've been able to cast my net as well by way of playing along as if Joe's family were my very own. And they're such the receiving bunch, so kind and courteous as to welcome me into the fold with open arms...that is, so long as the drinks keep coming gratis.

But what about the girl?

"She's the daughter of my uncle Jesop," starts Joe. I've already heard the story of Jesop, who's not Joe's true uncle but the husband of Julie, Joe's aunt. Before the two had even met Jesop had had a previous marriage, the wife of which gave birth to the nymph Nora. The former soon kicked off due to some ridiculous disease and thus developed the sinewy bond between a wifeless father and a motherless child. They were inseparable – that is, until Julie arrived. "She didn't feel like sharing her man," explains Joe. "She'd cry and wail and carry on with a fit if Jesop didn't devote all his time to her demands, which were really nothing more than a deep desire to rid her home of the no-good, beautiful Nora. I suppose she might not have been such a bitch if it weren't for that ugly mole on the tip of her nose. I swear, it's that mole that drives her crazy, makes her cringe at the sight of Nora's beauty. It must have gnawed on her like battery acid having to sit and watch her husband dump all his affection silly on his sweet, adorable daughter. Shit, even after they finally had a kid of their own she still wasn't satisfied. She wanted Nora gone, simple as that. Of course, it didn't help matters any when the kid came out retarded." He goes on to tell how Jesop, after Julie's unrelenting torrents of rage, finally gave in and shipped his daughter off to his sister's home in the southern part of the state. And Julie was never so nice than during Nora's absence; so nice, in fact, she saw fit to shit out a son in her husband's honor. Then one day who should appear upon the front doorstep but the object of Julie's hatred...and not alone. In her arms was a month-old baby boy. "She was too damned ashamed to say anything before," says Joe. "And Jesop, still eager to play the doting Pa, took her *and* the kid indoors without so much as a word. Julie, however, had a mouthful for the both of them. She spat out every indecency from half-wit to whore and then back again for letting herself get knocked up and, worse yet, for not having the sense to keep her mitts on the guy who'd done it. Back they fell into the same old scene till one day Jesop comes home to find Julie gone and Nora on the floor bleeding, the kid upstairs screaming bloody murder in its crib. Later that night Julie came home drunk, telling Jesop how his precious daughter hadn't the sense to take care of her own screaming brat and how she, to knock some sense into her, knocked her straight on her ass. Jesop bought the bullshit story and once again sent Nora off, this time with a fat check meant to help her find an apartment and a job or, failing that, a man and after a hug and a kiss and a promise to write again she was gone and he and Julie could go back to pulling the curtains down over their black, bloody windows." That was over four years ago and now it seems Nora's back, as Joe puts it, "to scrape the scabby mole off Julie's pig nose." Knowing all this it isn't hard to see why Nora left when she did: there was no point in staying. Tonight is Jesop and Julie's bowling night. They won't be back till next week.

And the guy?

"He's nobody," says Joe. "The boyfriend of some girl she's staying with in town. She only brought him along 'cause he has a car."

Hmmm....

After a short while and further attempts at turning a deaf ear in Ned's direction I notice a steady trickle flowing from the restaurant upstairs. Must be near closing time. I prepare myself for a new breed of customer.

The first to fly down are those post-dinner buzzards who crave a little something to settle the stomach, *viz.* strong, acidic concoctions and facetious conversation served with a splash of sarcasm and just enough honesty to allow them all to feel ashamed of themselves a short while, then off they trot to their leather-clad cars to lick the wounds and redress the bandages.

Once gone, down come the others. Skin leprous, conscience crippled, they limp toward the bar for a chance to fold their hands upon my mock-marble altar. Unlike the others, these souls come to me for absolution, a quick and painless cleansing, a spiritual catharsis of all that is impure in their unholy lives. My Eucharist consisting of tobacco and neck oil, I offer these sad few a promise of forgetfulness, a warm, soothing ointment for the stings of tomorrow, a staving off of the carrion crows. They crave only that which is soaked in false passion, cloaked in the might and mystery of foreign discontent, concealed within the gifts offered them by my steady hands inspected and approved by the Clerk of Courts herself to serve this town's downtrodden, an incomprehensible underworld of spavined pachyderms, the blood of a billion fatlings as proof poured thick over a thousand cigarette-stained, polyurethane slabs.

And just as every priest has his congregation, so must I administer my flock, the most faithful of which are Steve and Sadie Sunderson, a cute, affable couple born and bred in the Evergreen State who've so carefully plotted a homestead some safe, pleasant place nearby lakeside property nearby a reputable school within a quiet community far off from the vice of a sinful metropolis. So flush and proper they've prepared their family's upraising, taking into account every possible danger from busy streets to power lines, that once the unexpected happens, that one unforeseeable something they never could (nor would) imagine, the glass palace which had sheltered their dreams came shattering down, scattering everywhere into innumerable, irreparable pieces. This something is the death of their son, a handsome lad judging by the pictures they've shown, who managed to get himself drowned just months before emergence from adolescence. Since then they've reacted in typical fashion for people who've denied the possibility of such a cataclysm: complete withdrawal. Their son's untimely death has caused Steve to dissolve his sorrows inside a bottomless bottle, his wife Sadie (as always) right beside him, ready to offer her matrimonial support in the form of purblind acceptance. Thus, they maintain oxygen intake by safeguarding their pain inside an airtight reservoir, submitting themselves to the mindless minutiae manifested primarily as dry silences over medium-done steaks and easy smiles from the wait staff above, then down below to bask in the comfort of hollow aggressions and surfaced conversation. Everything subdued, submerged, secured tight inside the mind's alembic. Not once would they ever consider straying from this script drawn out for them by some mad playwright nestled high above the land in his secluded loft and gazing out the window through crippled eyes and half-cracked lenses. And even if they somehow found the courage to stray the only sure promise is a loss of perception. No, better if left to what's been published on paper. And I'm such the good cleric, so cunning in my counsel, so intuitive of their subtle, histrionic undertones not once do I return the sentiment behind Sadie's sleepy-eyes, nor do I jostle Steve's hibernating senses. Like any decent man of a drowning faith I'm obliged to remain oblivious to the tumultuous undercurrents whirling beneath the glossy, waxed-over surface.

"Say, Jeff," says Steve, "did you happen to notice the forecast for the following week? Looks like falling mercury."

"Yes, Jeff," says Sadie. "Perhaps it's best if the scarf and mittens were left on the rack...for fast reaching and all."

"To be sure," says Steve. "Preparation is the rooftop when the weather's on the wane."

"Most definitely," says Sadie. "And precaution is the pillar of a well-guarded acropolis."

"Quite," says Steve.

"Indeed," says Sadie.

And on and on it goes, my head nodding along with a distant grin till finally they're satisfied with my silent affirmations and again it's all right to retreat once more to their insulated town and steel-sided barricade whose wooden frame is infested with a million insatiable, imperishable termites.

It's near midnight now and the restaurant upstairs is shelving its trays and down pour those left snoring in the gazebo, mostly consisting of a few bloated bridgemen whose stomachsful of beef have given them all a taste for their own saliva. Like caged beasts who've just slaughtered the keymaster they've chased and devoured all resources in sight, their swiping claws laying to waste all within reach until no flora nor fauna remain and what's left is to set out in search of more copious forests. And because the Lounge is so far off from the abundant pastures of Tower Avenue, thus begins the long, dark quest for the cornucopia as they hanker out the door, their bloodstained teeth glistening behind bestial grins.

Them gone, the only ones left are Joe, myself, and a few hangers-on, namely Monica, Ned and Jenna, a waitress upstairs who just happens to be the eldest daughter of the Family itself. As of recently, most likely due to her age (fast approaching the legal dousing age, she is), she's taken a sudden interest in the inner workings of the Lounge. At first Joe and I were a bit leery of taking her in, fearing an eventual leak in our operation, though once assured she was just some curious bird we found ourselves amused at the thought of leading this green, bathybic creature through the belly of the whale...and the daughter of Poseidon himself! Soon we were feeding her all we knew with the enthusiasm of two lonely tombsmen who suddenly found themselves escorting a princess through the dark, moldy catacombs beneath the castle.

With just us five and no chance for a surge, Joe thinks to lock the doors early and pours us all a libation, a primer for the thick, acidic coat sure to come. Monica, fresh in becoming a bartender herself, takes to this type of drinking scene with great gusto, her arms flailing wildly like a wing-clipped albatross, pointing to the next bottle she'd like to see emptied. So wrapped up is she in this newfound science no longer is it enough just to know what each tastes like but smells like, pours like, mixes like, burns like, pisses like, pukes like, which ones turn color when poured over ice, which ones bring flies when left out overnight, which induce the worst hangovers, which seduce the best illusions, which are most likely to send her muliebral membranes into a blackened oblivion quickly regained with a swift dose of oxygen. It isn't long before her calls become shouts and we all hope like hell she'd just order a beer, especially Joe, who's the sort of drinkslinger who has no faith in his multifarious arsenal. "For Christ's sake, mix your own fucking drinks!" he shouts before snatching a beer from the cooler and wandering off to sulk. Since my first day here I've noticed this in Joe. He has a keen, uncanny ability to communicate with all types of customer from the base to the nebular, though one thing he never could fathom were the chromatic demands of the female clientele. A severe scowl would curl his lips whenever he'd have to pour anything but wine for these women. "Such colors weren't meant for human consumption," he'd snort while scraping his feet across the floor to find the bottle. "Only a poison would be given such a tint...as a warning, don't you know. Now, orange I can understand. After all, it's been given to us by Nature...an honest, juicy color fit for a dusty taste bud. But who in their right mind would drink something blue? Or green? Or even pink, for that matter? Shit, the only time I find myself drooling over such colors is when they're smothered cream-like round the hole of a Swissified cake...or a young girl's panties...."

Speaking of young girls, I'm suddenly curious to see how Jenna is managing. Before now she's only been able to stomach a tall highball, and never anything stronger than a Chablis spritzer. Now, however, during Monica's deluge, she suddenly finds herself at the mercy of someone who could drown the eyeballs of a Highland trawler. I look at her face, at the eyes in particular to see if that bronze strain has furled the brow, though I notice nothing that leaves me wondering. She's even donning a smile – a broad, beaming grin as if it just occurred to her that one day all this will be hers once the king has kicked on. I drop all concern for this monarch-in-wait. In fact, I make it my duty to pour a stiff one in her Highness' honor. She thanks me kindly, then throws it down like a true tavern heiress.

After about an hour Monica's mood turns obnoxious, no doubt due to her incandescent insides. She wants to ditch this dump and hit the Avenue, and Joe and Ned are quick to agree. I stay silent in hope of somehow worming my way out after noticing that strongman-gleam begin to form in Ned's eye. The thought of being dragged to the tables by this dupe has me flipping through my index of excuses and ready to choose before it occurs to me I'm not the only one who's turned inward – it seems Jenna doesn't think it a good idea either on account of her age.

"No problem," says Monica. "We'll just go someplace where one of us knows the bartender is all."

Jenna is unimpressed. She's convinced every bartender in town knows her father and, consequently, her. Monica, however, is adamant and with Joe and Ned on her side she manages to fold Jenna's objections like a cheese omelet. Soon we're all headed toward the wilderness of downtown.

The first place we hit is a broken-down refuge on the fringe of the strip where supposedly Joe has a friend behind the bar. Jenna is outwardly apprehensive though she's right behind us as we file through the door and find a table near the rear. Joe walks off to get us all a drink and as he does I take the time to glance at the décor. The theme is typical of any joint on an outskirt: a glorification of a bygone era with low ceilings and soft, quiet lighting meant to aid the mind on its retrospective journey, and it's only fitting that the nostalgia of choice for this watertown tavern should be set on the nautical. Frayed fishing nets, archaic weather instruments, captains' caps, pea coats, pages upon pages upon shelves upon shelves of shipping boat logbooks, glass-encased portraits of young, eager crewmen whose hapless fate was laid flat by the raging waves, their graves now hollow, picked clean by mollusks. How perfect this motif suits the people of Superior, what with their urbane appreciation for the distant Then as their own infant Now is ignored and abandoned, dumped along the wayside like the contents of an ashtray. This love of the past is most evident in death, in the passing of a period of intense ambition when the people of this town could be proud of their lot, jubilant in failure as well as success, anticipating joy with each new stake. Somewhere in time, though, this joy mill slipped its cogs and since then all anyone could get out of the goddamned machine was a noxious fog which swept over the land like an avalanche, razing to ruins the color and pride of these weatherworn people, their faces now waxen and

Apples of Arcadia 57

atavistic. Once this happens all there is left to do is sell off the rites of the whole bloody mess to Posterity and advertise the demise as if it were all planned and organized, thought through with keen foresight and innocence, every minute detail drawn out *en masse* inside the imprisoned minds of our *non compos* precursors. And as a result of their audacity, their desperation borne out of emptiness and ennui, all we have now to gaze our eyes upon are the stale, foreign relics of that glorious season, redeemed and restored, preserved in pewter and polished to shine no matter how bleak and shopworn and pitiful the image. Then suddenly, in the midst of my mind's transgression, the strangest thing happens. Once I've resigned myself completely to this sentiment, this Superior sadness which has evolved into a passion, I find myself comfortably submerged, sentient as a fetus, allowing it all to seep in through my skin like a calming balm. I look up again at the photos on the wall, at the faces of those who've slipped beneath the surface, and it occurs to me that perhaps there is no manner more American than to decorate calamity, to idealize death, to be content at having the countenances of our pedigree suspended like certificates upon the walls of taverns and tourist attractions, a little more faded with each passing year by the glances of day trippers who bend and curtsy and bow and salute the Statues of the Fallen because, quite honestly, at such an awkward moment, if they did anything other than lay themselves prostrate before these canonized idols they'd be carted away as emotional mongoloids, sentimental lepers, as severe enemies of the State and sentenced to the most heinous, most degrading death this outstanding, noble, just nation would allow...then honored as martyrs for the progeny of their country.

I remain like this, sedated, until Joe shows up with the drinks. Seeing him wobble with an armful of alcohol jolts my senses like a shot in the ass and I spring from my seat to assist him, passing around each bottle and glass with such obnoxious glee you'd think I was the one who sprung for the lot. My sudden burst of energy draws attention in the form of seditious sneers from the surrounding tables. Fuck 'em! I feel cheery, cajoling, all chim-chim-cheree from the base of my bowels to the tips of my incisors. So infected am I by my newfound mirth, so drunk with delirium, so insanely awake as if injected with nitrate I'm on the verge of spilling my tips upon the counter and demanding a drink for those traitorous tables, the whole seditious bar, for the entire treacherous town before being brought to my senses by Monica's objections. It seems this place isn't quite what she had in mind ("The people here are too goddamn peaceful!") and Ned agrees, though for a different reason: the walls here are too shallow to allow any kind of entertainment other than conversation. He practically leaps at the proposal, his tongue wagging and slobbering all over Monica's sour puss. Joe couldn't care less one way or the other, so long as he gets what he wants in the end (among other places). Now that my mind's in the right place I realize that Monica, being the one who initialized the idea, has adopted the burden of the first round and only a fool would forego a free drink. Jenna hasn't anything to say about any of it and soon we all follow Monica out the door into the street.

    She leads us toward a more modern joint up the strip, an enormous, cavernous hall draped with life-size portraits of local sports heroes in purple and yellow, green and gold; meaningless bar league trophies; cigarette-marred buddy bars; slick linoleum floors meant for swift, easy sweeping and immediately I cringe as I notice an endless row of bar games lined along the walls and down the corridor. It should only be a matter of time before I find myself face-to-face with Ned's inanity. Ah, well, in any case I was right about the booze as we can barely keep up with Monica who races toward the counter in the center of the room. At this time Joe informs me this is where Monica was hired just four weeks ago and we both think of Jenna and wonder how much influence a month can buy.

    The instant we're all in plain view the girl behind the bar asks Jenna her age. The latter hesitates, listens and waits for

Monica, who is obviously among common company, to come through with what she said upon leaving the Lounge. Monica senses this and realizes she must say something, though only a feeble protest escapes her lips which is quickly shot down by the bitch in charge. She then looks at Jenna, gives a shrug as if to say, "Oh, well, I tried," then giggles and turns away. Joe and Ned follow suit, both eager to cash in on Monica's new friend. Jenna, glossy-eyed, quiet and stiff, slowly unseats herself and begins walking toward the door. Watching her as she goes – head down, feet shuffling, shoulders drawn as if she had been scolded – I'm suddenly embarrassed as hell to have been a part of this whole bloody scene. It's high time I parted ways with this group. Besides, while Jenna was leaving I managed to get a good look at her violoncello figure and her synchronous, symphonic ass cheeks as they metered out their sad lament. An ass like that can always use a friend and I quickly change my order from a beer to a scotch (top shelf, of course) and toss it down, then turn my back on Monica, Joe and especially Ned, who can find some other sap to spew his childish taunts upon, and chase after Jenna.

I find her just outside the door, peering about as if she had lost something. She doesn't notice me so I just watch a while, waiting for her movements to show me the angle of approach. Strange, but she doesn't look at all upset. I now detect a faint glimmer in her eyes, the same silky countenance as that of someone who, upon awakening, has just opened the shutters to a bright, sunny day. Perhaps it's all an act – her way of pulling down the veil before the gaze of strangers. Whatever the case, at last she chooses a direction and starts walking away and it's now I decide to make my move. "Wait," I shout while trotting toward her, catching a smile as she turns around.

In these situations it's always best to begin with a brief, apparently sincere apology.

"Oh, that," she laughs. "It's no problem. Didn't I warn you it would happen?" She goes on to tell how she recognized the bartender as the daughter of a friend of her father's and still she went along with it, explaining, "It was the only way I could get away from those assholes you call friends without being called a bitch behind my back." I have to laugh at this. Soon my laugh turns into a full-blown guffaw and she joins in before asking why I run with such a crowd, that I seem like such an intelligent, nice person and surely someone as nice and intelligent as me can find other nice, intelligent people with whom to spend my time. After listening to this I nearly turn on my heels. This girl needs consoling like the Congo needs disease and I'm about to give her a heartfelt farewell before she asks if I'd like to go for a ride with her in her new car. The scotch I tossed down in haste just now found its way to the top of my head and I'm beginning to think perhaps some cool, whirling air might not be such a bad thing. Anyway, what other prospects do I have? I accept with a smile.

Walking up the street toward her car she again brings up the subject of my friends, Joe in particular. "There's something about him that frightens me," she begins. "I'm not exactly sure what it is. Perhaps it has something to do with the fact he's stood behind that bar over five years now and never have I ever heard him speak a wish for anything different. I can't understand that. I mean, it's impossible for me to imagine anyone wanting to stand behind that stupid bar and serve all those smellies. He never used to be like that. I remember when he first started working there...how he made me laugh with his goofy impressions of all the drunks....How I adored him for that...like an older brother, I mean. Now...I don't know...something's changed. Now he seems more serious, more...*not goofy*. He never pokes fun at the drunks anymore. In fact, he seems perfectly happy just to be with them, as if it was his destiny or whatever to stand behind that bar and.... That's it! That's why he scares me! It's because he's somehow come to terms with that stupid bar and all those drunks and smellies. He's somehow become one of them...."

Finally we come to her car, an intoxicating, sparkling sapphire blue gem with diadem rims and sleek, tinted windows. She says it's a gift from her father, the king, in honor of the princess' upcoming birthday...and how fitting a chariot for a future queen! "Only," she says with a sigh, "what I really wanted was a year's worth of rent like when I turned eighteen." Ah, well, with each new age comes a fresh affliction. She disarms the alarm and unlocks the doors, all with one push of a button on her twinkling key chain, then pushes another for a world-wide weather report and a down-to-the-decimal-point gold standard quote before finally settling her perfumed ass upon the plush leather seats. Once in and situated she starts the car and asks, "Where to?"

Where else? "The Point," I say and off we go.

Once on the road she continues where she left off. "Don't get me wrong," she says with a bent neck. "I mean, I know what's being said about me behind my back, about my being the king's daughter and all, and I'm sure there are plenty other things I don't know about, too. What's not being said, though, is I never once asked to be born into the Family. I mean, why can't they all understand I'm just a person like them...all of us simply spinning about in life and playing out our own separate roles....That sounds clever, huh? I got it from this course I'm taking at the University...the plays and poems of the Elizabethans or something. Holy cats, were those people depressed! Nothing but kings and queens killing each other over kingdoms and castles...always some princess running off to meet her prince beneath some sycamore beside a river, then tossing herself head-first into the water once he winds up dead. Jayzus, the silliness of some people!" After this a chuckle, then: "Ah...all I want is to be able to bend my back and lace my boot in the manner of the commoner....Another good one, eh? That's why I came to you and Joe...to prove to you both I could just as well be some average, ordinary person like you, don't you see? And now that whole thing about Joe changing on me like that...and that bitch Monica! What's with that witch's grin and cackle act, anyway? Who does she think she's fooling? And Ned...well, I don't know what to say about Ned. Anywho, I don't know how you do it. After hanging around those three for only an hour I began to feel a rash coming on. With you, though, it's different. You're not like them. You seem quiet, artistic...I knew you'd be the one who could see me for *my* sake and not my father's. You know, I only agreed to wait tables in that dump 'cause he said it was my duty as a Family member and all....Well, fine for now, but if he thinks I'll still be serving smellies after graduation he'll be sorry! That's the only reason I'm even going to college...to flee that stinking hole. I'm gonna write my own ticket on the back of a degree, yessiree!...Only, I wish I knew how to write... I mean, what kind of degree I want. Father says I should go into business, thinking I'll help out with the Family biz, and he thinks he has a right to tell me since he's paying for it all.... Well, to hell with that! I'm gonna pursue what *I* want...what interests *me*! Only, I wish I knew what that was. I think I might have a natural artistic eye 'cause once I drew an ad for the restaurant and everybody said it was great. They even showed me around the mailroom the day it was printed and let me push the red button that straps up all the bundles. That was fun, only I don't think I could ever get used to a job like that...they say it takes a week to wash off all that ink. Then the other day one of my girlfriends suggested something in sales but her father sells insurance and he's the most boring, most unartistic man I've ever met and there's no way I'd ever surround myself with such duds. Imagine the husband I'd end up with! Hey, I'm not boring you, am I? You're such a good listener. I knew I did the right thing asking you on this ride with me. I mean, so far we've only talked a little but already I feel we understand each other, both of us being so artistic and all. You even went to the University, didn't you? What did you study? Like, people or something? What kind of job can you get with that, I wonder? It doesn't matter.... What I really wanted to ask you is your advice on this whole school thing. You being so smart and artistic and having already been through the University and all and having just listened to me talk about me...what is it you think I should do? Come on, now, don't laugh! I'm serious! I've been meaning to talk to someone smart about this. My friends? *Pshaw!* All they care about is how cute their toes look in discount sandals. Don't you see? You're my only hope so stop laughing and tell me already....What is it I should do?"

Set it all on fire and flush it down the shitter!

Luckily, before she has an opportunity to put any real pressure on me, we pull into the sandy parking lot of the Point and I jump from my seat as if yanked by a rope and follow the sound of waves and hop the nearest platform leading out to one of the thousand lighthouses spotting the Lake's shoreline. These various plateaus are nearly a mile long and chopped to bits by years of corrosion and vicious storms. One false step and you just may find yourself unconscious with a cracked skull or, worse, submerged within the icy waters and pulled beneath the surface by a merciless undertow. Either way, a bitch of a predicament. And it doesn't make matters easier with the sky black as pitch and the wind a restless wench, though I have an advantage: I've been making this voyage ever since I could drive and have gotten to know the rocky terrain like my own pale skin, memorizing from repetition the pattern of these jagged plains stretching out to meet the illuminate Palladium. I've run this stretch so many times it's gotten to be I can almost go full speed over these slants and angles leading toward a rise just slightly off-center and bent toward the left, then down again and right and damn near vertical before coming to a precipice where one must jump with arms like wings lest he lose his balance and find himself impaled as if upon a palisade. I keep running like this, my eyes fixed upon the movement of my feet, until I come upon a stretch of stone attached to the lighthouse itself. Once still and standing on level ground I snap out of my trance and suddenly Jenna comes to mind. I turn to see her silhouette halfway back crawling clumsily over the rocks. Figure I have at least a twenty-minute wait. I light up a smoke and stare out into the Lake.

A local writer once likened the Lake to God, stating one night when his mood was in a demonic funk that "vast, holy freshwater sea" with its "great, glinting orchid-gold" delivered him from his despondency and offered his intelligence a new religion: the religion of Nature. Not once have I felt this way. Even all those times I came crawling down that broken, jagged aisle like some crippled parishioner chasing the proverbial promise of prayer; even then, as I laid myself bare upon this cold, stony altar and offered up my sins with outstretched arms, my face swollen and wet with tears and sweat, my mind open and willing to swallow any consoling morsel this great god Nature would bestow upon my brow; even then, with the lights of the shoreline spangled like stars atop the water's surface, saturating the horizon with a rich violet hue; even as I begged and pleaded for just one word, just one syllable to be uttered into the ears of this sad young man and receiving...nothing. Silence. Those same lights of *glinting gold* seemed to mock my boyish naiveté and with shoulders folded I slid away, my wounds now gaping, carpeting the rocky aisle in a shroud of blood. The last of these draining pilgrimages was made five years ago and I've not returned since...until tonight. Once again I find myself face-to-face with this black, heartless Being and still I'm unable to muster even the slightest sense of veneration for such an emotionless mass that to me now seems to resemble a slab of volcanic glass. No longer is this scene able to spin its illusory magic on a young, sensile mind. God, you say, you perfidious wordspinner? Why call this great venomous void God? Why not reserve your idolatries for more compassionate things in Nature such as, say, a freshly trimmed hedge or a row of sown chickweed? For if I am to believe this aquatic graveyard is God then He is without a doubt as invalid as an aborted fetus when it comes to mending the spirit of His most loyal lamb; as inadequate as a cassock to imbue His greatness, His wisdom, His serenity within the souls of His spleen who are drifting aimlessly through Hell's circles. Well, then, for the sake of our own metaphoric lickspit, let's just suppose this black mass of bile is God. What wouldst thou speakest whilst in the shadow of such divinity?

"Alright, you bastard," I'd begin. "Here I am once again, a child, blind and stumbling, though no longer the faithful candle-holder you once mistook me for. Your silence all these years has made a martyr of that spindling servant boy and now before you, his tear ducts dry and wasted, stands a bitter man...bitter, yes, though not yet in the grave. I wonder....How will you receive him? You have another chance to dress the wounds of that whimpering boy, his heart peeled at your heels like a bruised apple, his sins doused in alcohol and set aflame, ready to be used as a torch to guide him straight toward your kingdom. How will you receive him? Will you finally decide to speak? A small reward, perhaps, for all his youth spent kneeling at your throne. Or will you once more brush him off without so much as a whisper? If you have anything to say then say it now. Your people down here are starving for just one gasp from your black, cavernous throat, hungry for any voice other than the gurgles we get from those sad angels you've sent – so hungry, in fact, we've resorted to flesh and bone like barbarous cannibals, desperate to regain just the slightest sense of nourishment even if it means taking the knife to our neighbor, only the meat we take is rancid, the bones brittle, infested with rot. We are all left gnawing on the rotted flesh of cadavers and we won't stop until you let loose a sound, just one decipherable note from that *orchid-gold* esophagus, one acidic belch from that bellyful of souls you so greedily gobbled up and have it resonate throughout the hearts and ears of all us scavengers so there'll be no mistaking the significance of its meaning. Only speak, damn you! SPEAK!!!" Then I'd wait....

...For nothing. Silence. *Aujourd'hui comme hier.* I draw the final drag from my smoke, then let the butt fall into the black, whirling water.

I'm still exhaling the toxic plume when Jenna finally reaches the plateau and wastes no time in cursing me a scoundrel for leaving her behind in the dark all alone. She's spitting so furiously now, frothing at the mouth like a rabid beast, I'm actually beginning to get a bit frightened and before she has a chance to take a swing I pull her close and squeeze and try to smother her scoldings with the warmth of my mouth. And whaddya know...it works! Soon her wild fury has dwindled to smoldering ash and I pull away, holding her still at a safe distance in my arms. She's so bewildered by this sudden burst of lust all she manages is a blank stare. I suppose I should say something.

"There's a bit of a chill tonight, wouldn't you say?" She nods. Then: "How's about getting out of this night air into someplace warm?" Again she nods. I give a wolfish grin, then pull away and immediately begin the leap back toward shore. Before I get too far I hear her yell, "Wait! Don't you at least want to look at the Lake?"

We get to my building and climb the stairs and immediately I notice a crack of light between the door and the frame. I can't remember if I left it there myself or if Lizzie returned early from the farm. Either way, I think it best if Jenna wait on the porch while I investigate. She's not at all attracted to the idea, though after I assure her it's most likely nothing and in no time at all we'll be listening to soft music and sipping chilled cherry wine she smiles and slithers down the stairs like a salamander. Once she's out of sight I turn toward the door and peer inside.

Sitting cross-legged on the floor is a woman I've never seen before. She's so damn drunk she can barely keep balance, weaving back and forth like a top that hasn't been spun properly. After a full minute she finally realizes someone is watching her and blinks stupidly and says, "Oh, my dear Neddie...you came back!" Just as I'm about to ask who the hell she is I hear a noise from the kitchen and soon after out trots

Ned, a fresh beer in one hand, an enormous sandwich in the other. Upon seeing me he lets loose a nervous grunt and mutters something obscene through a mouthful of meat, nearly choking himself to death before swallowing and saying, "Well, hell, if it isn't my hero! Tell me, Superman, where's the damsel in distress, eh? I thought for sure both of you would be back here by now *disdressing* each other...ha, ha! Get it, partner? *Dissssss*dressing? Ha!" after which he chomps his sandwich and snorts a piggish laugh, letting half-chewed pieces of ham and cheese fall from his mouth, and as he snorts and chews the drunk chick chimes in and the two of them together are causing such a ruckus the door to the middle bedroom swings open and out comes Joe, half-naked with a bottle of vodka dangling from his mitt. Upon seeing me his first reaction is to look ashamed, though it isn't long before he realizes just who it is he's dealing with and a sheepish grin stretches his lips as he hands me the bottle. "You know, bud," he begins, coy-like, "you really oughtta keep your doors locked at night. There's all sorts of strays out there just waiting till you leave to eat all your food and drink your juice." After which he chuckles, then suddenly gets serious and says, "Speaking of strays...where's Jenna?"

Before I even have a chance to answer in storms Jenna through the front door, pissed as hell for being left alone in the dark...again. This time, though, she really lays it on and as she does Monica peeps out from the darkness of the middle bedroom, whereupon Jenna spins on her heels and makes as if to leave but before she gets far Monica starts hissing, "What, can we really be so lucky as to once more see her royal ass heading straight out the door?" This stops Jenna dead in her step and the two glare at each other like leopards about to pounce though before either can strike Joe steps in and with a slap on the ass sends Monica spinning back into the bedroom. He soon follows, though not before snatching back the bottle of vodka.

The Monica problem now modified, Jenna calms down

and we both take a seat next to Ned on the couch. Suddenly, as if possessed, Ned leaps off the couch and snatches my guitar and, still spitting soggy bread and cheese, in an apoplectic fit of drunken inspiration begins crooning like an alley cat to the achromatic key of some sappy overplayed radio melody. It's obvious he's playing for the puddle on the rug, and at first she manages a painful smile, though after only about a minute of this mangled act of romance she thrusts her hands over her mouth and darts like an arrow toward the toilet. Ned follows, guitar still in hand and laughing like an idiot. Once gone I nod to Jenna as if to say, "Quick, before they come back!" and together we race off toward the master bedroom for the final lesson of life in the cellar....

Daybreak.
My tongue like perfect tinder, I stumble out of bed and crawl toward the kitchen. On the way I peek through the middle bedroom door. The bed is in shambles and empty. The entire apartment is empty save myself and Jenna still asleep in my bed. I slake my thirst with a glass of cold water and cringe as the hunger hits, then frown as I stare into a foodless cupboard...then the cooler. Nothing, not even a crumb. It's all in Ned's stomach churning a massive turd, the thought of which sends me straight into hysterics. I'm nearly on the floor when Jenna finds me, wondering what the hell could be so funny. I tell her and she laughs too, then frowns and confesses she's also hungry. I check my pockets and find a few crumpled bills, enough for rolls and coffee. Before we leave I think to wash the sheets before Lizzie returns from her stepfather's farm.

Book Two

Bottle-Assed in Love

"Lizzie" - charcoal on paper. Sketched by the author.

Henry Miller once wrote, "A beautiful woman will never starve." If this is true it is only because she is forever feeding off the will of a weak man.

Lizzie and I first came together toward the tail end of my abortive episode as a slapdash writer in a hotel in Canal Park. Our lives just seemed to collide when both were searching for something new: she a new man and me a new life miles away from the loneliness and despair of that sordid hole stacked to the roof with derelicts and drunkards. I was fast approaching my end with this joint. Not one room had a toilet to itself – just a mucky bowl in the center of a spider-draped room which we all shared. What's more, each trip down the hall would strike a spark of inspiration for conversation in one of the demented minds of the other occupants. I'm thinking now of Felix, an overblown, broken-down walrus of a man who hadn't shaved in over a month and whose stink made my eyes sting. By him I would find myself detained indefinitely. What's worse, the only thing this man could ever think to talk about was his younger brother whose high status in some public office someplace helped rake poor Felix from the coals of an arson charge a few years back. Always the same story. Never the slightest deviation from the most maladroit detail. Finally, during a fit of inspiration myself, I got wise with old Felix. Whenever he came calling while on my way to the crapper I'd raise my hand like a politician and say, "Sorry, old chap, can't talk now. There's a butt on the bed I gotta get back to." At this he'd shoot a twisted look of concern, his eyes darting wildly out the door and down the hall before finally diving back into his dark, forsaken room. Problem solved. Next issue.

Other times, during one of my half-hearted attempts at tackling the machine, I'd hear a tap on the door and, like a wounded gorilla, in would walk Cedric. Cedric was a drunk and a darkie who (fittingly enough) fancied himself a poet and who also (as luck would have it) was damn near seven feet tall and built like a brick house. Needless to say, though neighborly hospitality has never been my best suit, I never found it difficult to summon a smile whenever good Cedric came knocking. I did, however, try countless times explaining to the man that I wasn't a poet (I somehow thought better than to admit I despise the stuff). All the same, he considered us kindred spirits, destined to share with one another the fruits of our creative labors. Looking back, it all seems more amusing than anything to see this looming, shadowy figure of a man, the stink of cheap gin following after as he made way through the room toward a chair before finally taking rest and unfolding a torn, beer-stained sheet of paper, then proceeding to spit and stutter through a few lines of perfunctory verse which choked the atmosphere nearly as much as the booze. His muse was his daughter whom he hadn't seen in years and whenever he'd reach the third line or so he'd invariably break into a series of sobs. A line or two later the sobs would turn spastic until finally, under the pretense of fetching a tissue, yon Cedric would unsettle himself and slither off toward his room for a mouthful of medicinal relief. I wouldn't see him for days after.

The others in the house weren't quite as intrusive, save an inquisitive peek every now and again through a crack in a doorframe, and if it weren't for that I'd had never suspected their existence. Toward the tail end of the month, however, a noxious odor would always and mysteriously seep through the hall, at which time the proprietor would be forced to make an appearance and sort out the problem via quick and painless evictions.

There are only a few joints like this in Duluth (none in Superior) and I would be lying if I said my main intention in choosing this dive was to live out the typical romantic notion most dilettantes have of the forlorn artist living on the outskirts of an artless society. In truth, all I wanted was my chance at the treasure, at forging my own tools and digging for gold, and as chance permitted my mother's aunt – whose mind had already long diminished past the point of dementia – passed on, leaving behind in her wake a sizeable, though disappointing sum. (She had once been wealthy, though since being diagnosed ill someone saw fit to see that she settled for nothing less than pure luxury in her final days, never mind the fact she couldn't even process her own name let alone the posh amenities of a five-star rest home.) That which she did leave, however, was just enough to fatten my courage and within a week after receiving the check I quit my job and left Sara to hide in the least financially demanding hole I could find, allowing myself as much time as possible to practice my alchemy. Thinking the only sustenance needed was that which nourished the mind, I set aside the bare minimum for bread, cheese and coffee as well as just enough for cigarettes and, to help keep the corpuscles coursing, a few cheap bottles of *vin ordinaire*. Surrounding myself with an armament of man's best books and enough blank paper to rewrite them all, I set myself down with fierce resolution to excavate the English language of all its gems and exploit the constantly raging river of thought which flowed like lava through my brain's terrain. Six months later, broke and burnt to a crisp, I found Lizzie.

Strange now to think, after first being drawn toward her beauty like a funeral pyre, just one year prior I had looked upon her radiance and immediately wrote it off as nothing more than a dream. Still, the memory of this dream caused a doubling-over in the solar plexus, a searing pain throughout the viscera as graphic and mysterious as stigmata, the result of which set forth the foundation for a new faith, a new religion, the resurrection of a citadel where decadent citizens of ancient civilizations performed the rites of Dionysus and Apollo without insight or peril, privation or need; a long, cavernous hall where the portraits of the past were diminished to cone-shaped piles of rubble and ash. All this from one chance encounter completely beyond my control.

She and her man walked into the Lounge one fall night about midway through my first year behind the slab. Everything about this girl stalled the gaze of every guy with the mind to comprehend the rarity of true Proserpine beauty. My memory vivid as an autumn constellation, I can still see her every step, every facial expression, every glowing detail, however trivial or surreal: her scent floating freely through the thick, smoky air, infusing the very essence of feminine vitality; golden-spun sunshine twirling atop her crown and down around two pools of lapis lazuli; the chorus of a thousand seraphim piercing straight through the slumber of all us drunken dreamers. And as she walked, her skin glowing like phosphorescent snow, those silver-blue eyes never once betrayed her station by feigning to entertain the smiles strewn before her like rose petals. She was obviously above such mundane gestures of adoration; she couldn't possibly have settled for anything less than a man's soul. As it were, not one of us had a soul to speak of – all any of us truly had to offer were a few thin feathers and a tarnished halo. We held before us a beauty so stellar, so unmatched by any of the perfumed floozies we'd become accustomed to it left us trembling like atheists who suddenly found themselves standing before the gates of Saint Peter. So startling an image left us chasing false passions, our filthy hands fumbling to try and recapture the purest vision of paradise.

Such visions of beauty always impress me thus: as indecipherable equations whose symbolic properties have grown so absurd, so abstract and unreal their significance has transcended all human comprehension. They leave me cold, lonely, scornful, an inhuman taste like lead in my mouth. All too often it seems we are eager to digest the popular ideals of the day – ideals such as Sex, Peace, God, Love, Money, Race, Country, Etc. It's as if our human evolution has reached a state of advancement so far above the ignoble demands of preparing our own meals we've become accustomed to having them force-fed down our throats by thieves, by those who've stolen the key to the cupboard. Imminent with this arrangement, however, is before too long those same ideals lose all sapidity – soon, instead of steak, we find ourselves gnawing the flesh of *corpora delicti*, tongues swollen, gums bleeding, teeth rotten through, though still we gnaw on having long lost the faculty to recognize the difference. And Beauty, that most palpable of all human ideals, held close to the bosom of mankind since the birth of thought, Beauty has finally lost its ability to inspire life. In fact, it has become the very opposite of life, existing now only within the realm of the imagination. No longer are we able to perceive it as attainable, as something worth the energy of a waking conviction. This degradation, this destruction of an ideal's essence has been a constant merry hell in the history of mankind, the most notable instance being the veneration of Christ. To be sure, we were supposed to adorn His image, the image of human perfection, though the true meaning behind His perfection, His purpose, His message is the *realization* that such an image, such a life as He realized (I speak now of Jesus the Man, not Jesus the Christ) is an ideal attainable, nay, *existent* within us all. He meant to direct us in the direction of His will, which was and forever will be a wholly *human* will. What we have done with the image of Jesus after His departure from this world is one of the most inexcusable acts of treachery ever executed by this diabolical race. Those who recognized the true power of His image, His true human beauty were no doubt so goddamned ashamed of themselves, so overwhelmed by His message and their own human weakness that, once gone, they assigned for Him the only explanation for His supremacy their pitiful minds could muster: they deified Him. They turned Him into a god. No, the *Son* of God. No, the *only* Son of God, eternally begotten of the ugliness and vileness of our own wicked sins, which, since the image of Christ is now suddenly as lofty as the right hand of the Father, have now become tolerable, enjoyable even. Ever since this moment, the moment man abandoned the Man among men, we've twisted and contorted His (which is to say Man's) image into such a state as to mock man's divinity...*every* man's divinity. And Beauty, belonging to every man just as flesh, blood and bone, Beauty has also been distorted, contorted, alienated from our own inner radiance, our own inner passion. Like Money, it has gone beyond the ken of its creator. It breathes and heaves, building prowess and strength with each new dream it digests, taking refuge in men's minds and shitting out its essence through the assholes of those it has chosen to entertain us with plastic skin and prosthetic tits. It has become an ideal, an abstraction, maintained within a mold so airy and ethereal even Heaven couldn't contain it.

Lester! That was the name of the deadheaded dolt who sauntered in behind our Aphrodite as if he were the Almighty in Headdress incarnate. And for the fact that she allowed the company of such sludge not one of us blamed her. Like weeds, white-tipped dandelions one and all, these putrefactions plague America's soil, spreading their rancid undergrowth throughout the land until all that's left is an arabesque web of anhydrous roots, the earth around it lifeless and barren. Their number has become so dense, so massive and firm even the strongest must bend beneath its venomous girth. They've become a reality, which is to say they simply won't disappear once she closes her eyes. And what about our mistress with the silver-blue eyes and deplorable brow? What has she to comfort herself if not the sunbeams of dreams? Why, she has only the privilege of drawing the curtains down upon her strangled pride, then weeping while repeating: "At least I'm not alone." She has reached the point where pleasure is nothing more than a gravel yard, the groundskeeper of which a perfect facsimile of inanition who, after spilling his seed, puffs his pipe and waits for the moths to reclaim the flame; a simian dolled up in logo-tagged lapels proclaiming to all he is magically immune to the jeers and taunts of us transparent types whose longing eyes just happened to fall upon his captive treasure, a declaration that it is with *him* where she belongs and *you*, you social misfit, you human anomaly, all you may do is gaze imploringly upon this gleaming stone as a penniless bum through a department store window. What this sort always fails to realize, however, is that though at present he be palming a truly dazzling gem we poor, lowly types, us paupers of fortitude have developed through lack of resource innumerable methods of thievery and deceit. Like warriors armed only with pebbles and twine we've taught ourselves to sling a rock with deadly accuracy. Being neck-high in filth for so long we've evolved into a species of superior sensory perception, our olfactory glands surpassing even that of the shark. One might even argue it is only we who are truly capable of detecting the aroma of ambrosia. What's more, we can even detect the odor of impending death. And as they both made way through the bar toward my station it was I who began salivating at the scent of gaping wounds.

    I awaited them both with a cocksure grin. I decided it best just to get the idiot's order out of the way so as to allow the lady my full attention. He ordered a beer (the most tasteless, to be sure) and after a shallow gesture I flipped him the bottle and forgot about him entirely. My ears now pricked and quivering for the first inflorescent word to fall from her passionflower mouth, I asked what she wished. I could tell from her smile she would try and test me. No brown bottle for this miss, no siree! The words "vodka martini, straight up with a twist" dripped off her lips like opalescent pine drops and with one swift step I roped the bluest bottle on the shelf before righting myself in preparation for my one act pomp, a rory-cum-tory harlequinade needing equal nimbleness both in arrogance and legerdemain, the latter damn near that of a prestidigitator, the former essential to season with zest and zeal an otherwise pallid and tasteless display. Strange, but her being with her man (and him being an utter sap) equipped my nerves with unspeakable cheek as I whooped and wheeled through the entire routine with the castle-building confidence of an ostentatious flunky suddenly called to the scaffold. A constant smirk beset my lips as I swirled the steel strainer and poured out a long, silvery stream into a frosted glass chalice, my movements as fluid as the vodka itself. A twist of rind curled round the rim like an asp consummated the concoction and with a sleepy-eyed grin behind my steel rimmed spectacles I handed over the golden apple...and she smiled! (Later, once together over a homemade martini, we spoke of this first encounter of ours, how my princely knave and bombastic bartender routine reminded her of some sappy actor from the silent film era.

"Which would that be?" I asked her once, a bit tipsy and somewhat suspicious. "Valentino or Keaton?"

She looked at me with an expression of disappointment. "Chaplin," she said, as if I should have known.)

After that first facetious episode neither she nor her man ever set foot inside the Lounge again. She later explained this was because Lester, presumably keen on my overstated antics as well as her reaction to them, thought it best just to distance us as much as possible, the light of which actually lifted him a few notches in my mind; it comforted me some to think he was at least clever enough to take action once the diamond had threatened to slip his grip. In any case, after she left my life as airily as she came, I quickly moved on. A good many others (though not nearly as stunning) were willing to wisp my thoughts away from so distant a luxury, the most notable being Sara. Unfortunately for the latter, however, that one chance encounter with a tangible ideal had etched upon my mind an impression as indelible as a semeiotic scar. These "chance" encounters, seemingly as coarse and savorless as found in most fiction, are, in truth, not nearly as stale as their label implies. Initially as fruitless as an octogenarian's womb, they secretly take root and blossom and flourish. Unlike earthly ornaments, however, they fail to whither and curl once the Old Man turns a cold streak. They prove themselves immune to the frosts of Time, their scent fragrant and potent as ever through thick glacial layers of snow and ice, their fruit still as enticing as the apples of Arcadia. Every minute detail – the magnetism of her eyes; her scent like sunlight through the nocturnal fog; her limbs like the locks of a Gorgon's mane – each seed burrows itself deep within the mind's fertile soil and infiltrates one's dreams, especially during waking hours. It had gotten so I would see her haunting beauty even when Sara and I were making love, which, to be honest, at that point not so much resembled the mystical experience of love making as it did the tilling of untamed lands. Those eyes, those lips, that paralyzing smile actually aided in prolonging mine and Sara's relationship. Through her nebulous existence I learned to transcend myself into another sphere where Happiness and Sex weren't just illusions used to sell magazines and movie tickets. I actually began to believe in the true power of beauty. Still, her empyreal existence wasn't enough to maintain the corporeal demands of real life and the bitter demise of Sara and myself as *Us* soon became manifest. Once again I was on my own, though this time I resolved to make something of my solitude. I would attempt to produce a testament so stunning and unique as to justify the years spent sifting through all those web-filled tomes in a pitiful attempt to escape my fate. Out of my own despair I unearthed a determination as thrilling and frightening as a gushing oil geyser. All I needed to do (or so I thought) was plop my undernourished ass in front of the machine and punch out the masterpiece I felt germinating within me. What matter experience when faced with such fury? Wasn't my drive, my inexhaustible desire enough to guide me straight toward my goal? Wasn't it this, this white-hot force generating immense energy and acumen, wasn't it *that* which I had learned about while thumbing through the lives of such literary lions as Whitman and Joyce, Balzac and Proust? Wasn't it Balzac who never left his garret other than to fetch a bag of coffee or to flee the financial gadflies constantly nipping at his heels? And as for Proust...an invalid at times unable to leave his own bed! Yet there he was, there they all were, taunting me to try and etch out my name in the massive, Babylonian edifice of Art. *Alright, then, you bastards!* I said to myself. *I'll show you!* All I need is a little time and a warm, steady breeze to blow my way and I'll catch the breaker that brings to shore the most passionate, most astonishing display of pen and ink human eyes have ever seen! I'll tear the leaves from your autumnal trees and build a fire so high and bright it guides me straight toward your celestial sphere where the glories of men's minds blaze the night sky like stars. I'll scratch and bite and claw and tear till the blood flows like treacle through the thousands of pages I've prepared for you all like some black, coagulated tomb! Do you hear me?! Do you, you dust hounds?! If not now then soon, for I've already saddled Pegasus and am yanking his reigns like some crazed, sadistic cowpuncher. Onward, Pegasus! Onward, you tamed eternal relic! Onward toward Truth and Beauty and man's Immortality! Onward toward the timelessness of God's greatest gift! Onward, you son of a bitch! Onward! Onward! Higher! Higher! *Henceforth, excelsior!!!*

Six months later and busted and all I had to show for my money and arrogance were a few useless pages and a slew of fettered nerves. In my resolution to set myself down and write in earnest I had actually become more lost, more alienated from myself than I had ever been before. Mindless hours, days, months spent sitting before that torment of a machine and not one phrase, not one word worth the sweat on my brow. In the midst of my own white-capped sea of blank, crumpled pages I realized I was drowning, suffocating from the worst type of asphyxiation: asphyxiation of the Self. I needed air. Dejected, depressed, but most of all suffering from a loneliness the likes of which I had never known, I stood from my chair and stepped away from my desk, then out the door and down the hall, down the stairs and out the exit till finally I found myself standing on the sidewalk like a somnambulist.

The first thing I noticed, aside from a drizzle, was I felt completely detached as though I were floating high above the city and peering down upon the streets through the purplish glow of a moonlit fog, my mind an element of infinitesimal influence, my body as strange and unknowable as fairy dust. I stood like this for some time, separate, indifferent, my legs as marble pillars fixed by steel bolts to the sidewalk, my head hovering over the icy waters of the Lake and shooting like lightning between the islands and inlets and bridges and canals until violently thrown back by the obnoxious bellow of drunken tourists, their shouts like the acrimonious cries of hyenas, and instinctively I walked away from the ignominious waters of the Lake and Canal Park.

Crossing the viaduct over the railroad tracks which once were alive (now inanimate as fossil) I noticed behind me the distant sound of footsteps and instantly I thought of the tourists and how, their luck between the legs being nil, they'd now gladly settle for a satisfying game of chase-the-sickly-antelope though when I looked back I saw not the tourists at all but an elderly couple seemingly out for a midnight stroll. How very strange, I said to myself, then walked on toward the orange-yellow lamplight glow of downtown Superior Street.

Before entering I have to fight my way through the nettle of nostalgia which drapes like Dacron from the billboards and buildings. Once inside, the scene escapes and disappoints the imagination as something so false, so obviously contrived; every edifice painted deftly and polished with strict instructions as props to a play; electric lampposts assuming the likeness of archaic gas-lit lamps casting their pyretic glimmer across coeval cobblestone; shops and eateries lined along the street like carnival booths, their bright, obtrusive canopies as disturbing to the eye as dancing corpses; poorly reproduced icons of Mother Europe who bore them out of necessity, out of honesty and beauty now shamelessly stolen and recklessly assembled as the backdrop to a town of ceramic trinkets and cheap keepsakes, the shopkeepers of which trading secrets with the gentry as often as possible, each garbled, hematose note scribbled down as gospel to be recited in praise and honor and glory to their common god: Monsieur Almighty Commerce. Countless times in my youth I've walked down this very street and found myself in awe of its beauty in simplicity, an immaculate image of some peaceful, far-off hamlet the likes of which I had only seen in books and magazines. I used to fall into a daydream while watching the people in black and blue suits scurrying this way and that with mindless tenacity, the others in earth tones more relaxed, composed, probably content upon procuring their daily bread; the scents of cider, cheese and sausage, incense and candle wax; the lights of cars and shop signs gleaming like diamonds off the rain-soaked streets and endless walls of glass. The entire city seemed magical, a brief but abundant glimpse into another land, a land of milk and honey and windmills and giants and dragons and knights and brightly colored banners flying high above a tower where a princess looks down upon the land below and dreams. How crestfallen I became the day I discovered this fantastic world existed only in my imagination. That which was revealed to me upon repeated visits to the various shops and eateries, made substantial by the utter impersonality of the people I encountered who, like myself, were really nothing more than hopeless dreamers – the total lack of anything resembling the reality I had invented in my mind – all came crashing down around me in a cloud of dust, the remains of the great brownstone façade forming two huge heaps of antiquated rubbish. Fortunately, though, out of every destruction comes some form of restoration and for me this restoration took on the manifestation of grayish-green slabs bound together by twine and stacked askant like sarcophagi, the entire scene encircled by raptorial birds and barbed wire.

About this time I again noticed the sound of footsteps, more familiar than before, and when I looked back I saw the same old man, though this time he was alone, the old woman no longer by his side. He seemed closer now and I could barely make out his features: chrysolite cap; sallow complexion; sharp, bony shoulders which gave a pitiful shape to his frazzled jacket; long, sweeping legs which moved steadily toward me. The presence of this ghostly figure made me ill at ease and, forgetting all about my earlier despondency, I thought I'd try and evade him by turning right at the Phoenix Building and hiking up the hill, thinking in his old age he'd never attempt such a climb. After a few blocks up I turned back to realize I was right – he was nowhere to be seen. A bit weary myself, I turned off on Fourth Street to straighten my legs.

If the Lake is the heart of this harbor town and Superior Street its prime aorta, then Fourth Street is the portal vein which threatens to explode and flood the entire organism in its own rejectamenta. Crab grass, gravel lots, overgrown foliage, pawnshops, thrift stores, soup kitchens, secretions, neglected pets, pellagra, subsidized housing projects, the sidings of which permanently stained from the smoke and smog of the industry below, their windows and doors, once new and promising, now lifeless and hollow as sunken eye sockets. These houses, erected for the sake of poor families whose descendents some time ago found themselves stranded on this frozen land of evergreens and steel-and-ice airs, these shacks are now barely able to stand upright on their own, some needing the help of pine beams and planks nailed haphazardly to the porches and unpainted windowpanes. Many times I've found myself wandering down this desolate street not knowing for sure what drew me there (the only concrete street in a cardboard town) though there I was, feeling sad and elated all at once as I tossed a passing glance through the cracked glass of some sad home built with bones and rusted dreams, so familiar a scene I can almost see myself sitting comfortably inside.

In fact, I nearly did find myself living inside one of these shitholes, just after Sara and I began dating serious. Up until then she had been living with a co-worker of hers, a *male* co-worker of whom I wasn't too concerned about seeing as he was thoroughly homosexual, a truly sad and queer fellow who, as Sara once related, would fall fatuously in love with a fellow queer and wouldn't find the courage to do anything about it until three sheets and stinking from drinking gimlets all night, after which he'd then proceed to unwittingly spew forth his cockled heart's affection upon the unsuspecting beau, the latter invariably proving himself a sadistic prick who enjoys nothing more than toying with a man's emotions as a cat to a dying mouse. All in all, though, he seemed a decent bloke and sometimes I'd even take to flirting with the guy to try and inject him with a little confidence. In the end, though, it was Sara who decided he should go. "He's simply too much of a slob," said she and with that she was alone and in need of a roommate.

One night after dinner, myself desperate as hell to alter my situation (in truth, all I wanted was out from Superior, even if it be just across the Bridge), I pitched her the idea of pooling together our resources and finding a place together. At first she was against the idea, saying it was too soon in the relationship and I didn't make enough money and what would her father say? I didn't dare suggest she forsake her father (a remark like that to a Norwegian wench would mean the same as sacrilege), though I did manage to dissuade the issue by placing more importance on the others, such as arguing in favor of the relationship, that I had never before felt as comfortable with anyone as I had with her, that together we could surely manage to make ends meet, that I would take up a second job if need be and aren't you at all the least bit curious? As it turned out, none of the above was the deciding factor, though money did play its part. After all the talk about raging fathers and relationships her one real concern was the rent. Already it was approaching the end of the month and she hadn't a single response to the flyers she had posted in the cafés and bookshops and bars about town. Fearing embarrassment should she have to borrow money from the landlady (or, worse yet, her father), she accepted my offer, however hesitant, and before the month was over we were living together, swimming in pseudomarital bliss, drenched in the joyous sweat of stolen hymeneal sex.

This lasted a few months before it started showing signs of a declining glory. As it turned out, her words concerning my earning powers were prophetic. During this time the idea of becoming a writer grabbed hold of my brain and wouldn't let go, causing all sorts of distorted ideas. At first she was excited, the thought of having a writer for a lover acting as a sort of aphrodisiac, though soon after I sold my car and expressed a desire to quit my job she began to worry. She protested against such rash acts, to be sure, though anything other than wholehearted enthusiasm for what I was doing fell entirely on deaf ears. In any case, not long after selling my car (for which I got very little) I persuaded Sara to seriously consider moving closer downtown and the more frequent bus schedule. This wasn't at all difficult since by then we both had had enough of our landlady (an obesely overweight woman who lived directly above us and who suffered from insomnia, her constant night pacings causing the ceiling to seem as though it would collapse) and it wasn't long before we were sifting through the classifieds to see what we could afford, the findings of which eventually leading us toward the trenches of Fourth Street. Day after day we would trudge through the hillside in search of something, anything other than the dumps we were shown. If the previous lot had cracked ceilings and plaster flaking off the mucus-yellow walls then the next was sure to have both those as well as no kitchen sink and a family of vermin living off in a corner. Some were in such a state as to actually induce between the two of us an hysterical fit of laughter, one of those rare moments of shared joy which sprang up every so often like bladderworts in our boggy affair. It was just after such a moment when she surprised me with what proved to be the most genuine, most completely pure and unexpected gesture I had ever experienced in any relationship.

After an entire day of disappointments and hysterics we decided to sooth our throats in one of the neighborhood bars. Once seated and sipping on something cool, our spirits high, our wallets low, she leaned toward me and almost in a whisper said, "You know, Jeff, I really enjoyed being with you today."

"Yeah, I know what you mean," I laughed. "I can't believe they actually advertise those dumps."

"No, that's not what I mean," she said, a strange smile on her lips which to me seemed foreign, maniacal almost. "I'm not talking about the apartments," she continued. "I mean *you*. I enjoyed *you*...just *being* with you."

This little pleasantry, delivered without the least bit of sarcasm, still impressed me as bittersweet. To tell someone you enjoyed being with them, then imply as if it were unexpected, that what you had prepared yourself for was, in fact, the exact opposite isn't quite the ideal compliment one hopes to receive, even if that someone didn't deserve as much. Ah, well, what matter life's trivia! The weather was fine with the sun in the sky and we still had a few bucks tucked away tight in our jeans and it all made me so pleased to be alive, to be breathing and drinking, even if it be inside a dive such as this, I smiled in response to her bittersweet observation and reached for a butt. Seeing me go for my pack, she asked for one as well which took me by surprise since never before had I seen her smoke, not even after a good tongue-tingling fuck. Amused at the thought of what she must look like with a cigarette dangling off her dovelike lips, I handed her a smoke and chuckled and, still chuckling, reached for the matches in the ashtray on the table. Just in mid-reach, however, I was stopped to a halt by an unmistakable sound and when I looked up I saw in her hand the most peculiar, most beautifully exotic lighter I had ever seen. Silver and cylindrical with blue and green engravings as trim around the base and lid which, when pressed, would light the flame and, when released, would self-extinguish and protect the wick, its presence before me seemed awesome and baffling as a priceless stone the likes of which I could never imagine existing within America's run-of-the-mill, throw-away culture. (And I was right. It was made in Austria.) After lighting her cigarette she reached toward me with her dollish hand and lit mine and said, "Here...this is for you."

All I could do was stare at it, stunned. The thought of asking where she got the money for such a gift never entered my mind, the only thought blooming in the brain at the time stemming directly from the nature of what was being presented to me and why. She must have guessed by my reluctance to reach for it that I was struggling for an explanation as to the meaning of it all because it wasn't long before she shrugged her shoulders and said, "Look, I just thought every writer should have his own lighter is all."

I remember wondering if she realized the significance of what she had said, given the way she said it, for even if she'd suddenly changed her mind and decided to keep the gift for herself the importance of that lighter, of that gesture in general transcended all meaning she could have possibly conceived. The instant she likened me with that sacred group of mortals, a group hitherto held so high above my head, a height at once incomprehensible and unreachable, what she really was saying was that she could see me standing among such glorious company, that not only would I one day become the writer I so desperately wished to be, but that, in fact, *I already was that writer*, even if at that point I had written nothing but piffle... piffle and epitaphs. All the same, the confidence which was suddenly injected into my veins, and by someone whom I had already written off as a nonbeliever, was so powerful, so potent a fix of narcotic conviction it circulated its course for the remainder of the relationship and well into the period of voluntary seclusion. Though suddenly, while walking through the very neighborhood where it all took place, the emotions of that day and that wonderful lighter came gushing back, extinguishing my faith with the force of a fire hose. Instead of intoxicating elation the only thing now I felt coursing my veins was the raw panic of a junky in limbo. My head in the gutter, the lighter an icy reminder of failure in my pocket, I folded my shoulders and quickened my step as if to escape the tyranny of my own despotic memories.

It was then when the drizzle suddenly turned into a cloudburst and I rushed like hell from the middle of the street toward the nearest row of shoe stores and cafés and bars where I crawled beneath the awnings till finally stumbling upon the neon likeness of a steaming cup of coffee. The invitation was irresistible. I opened the door and stumbled inside.

The light was blinding in contrast to the street and for a while I just stood there, blinking, till finally my eyes focused upon an empty stool at the counter. I shook the rain off my shoulders and walked toward it whereupon a waitress (mid-forties, vacant smile) flew down off the rafters and asked my order. "Coffee," of course, which she brought back at once and just as I was swirling in the cream with my spoon my attention was stolen by a violent eruption somewhere near the wall. My vision now clear, I turned toward the burst to see a threadbare man in rags bent over the table of a comely young couple, the beau of which obviously perturbed by this blatant breach of privacy and, failing to free himself by civil indifference, by the force of frustration suddenly leapt up like a Pharisee and made as if to strike. This sent the ragged man back on his heels, forcing him to reconsider the option of partition. He stood still a moment in the center of the room, regaining composure, all the while searching for a kind, generous face. Somehow our eyes met and I tried to turn away but it was too late. I lit a smoke and prepared myself for the inevitable.

Without a word I heard him take an empty stool beside me. The waitress, less sedulous than before, drifted down like a leaf and asked the man, "Well?" He stalled to think a moment, then reeled off in freeform a comprehensive list of most items on the menu beginning with banana-nut tea and on into everything from sourdough toast to baked Alaskan halibut before at last concluding with a double Swiss mocha topped with whipped cream and barbital. After the barrage the waitress turned to me as if to confirm, whereupon I (on the sly) slipped a few fingers into my pocket to feel for a bill, then, when successful, shot her a woolgathering grin. She smiled sardonically, then ruffled her feathers and flittered off once more toward the nighthawk nest. Once gone, the dingy one turned to me and slurred, "Helluva night, innit?" I gave a distant nod and slurped my coffee.

To this day I've never uncovered the twisted force which invariably attracts me to the most desolate soul in any setting, day or night. As far as I remember I've always possessed this gift (assuming something so unsettling can rightly be called a "gift"). I could be walking through a park some warm, sunny day, the pavement soft as hollandaise sauce, my nostrils filled with a flowery philter, in my ears the joyous sound of psalms and after deciding to soak it all in and stretch my legs on some sun-warmed bench by a river near a tree who should I suddenly find sitting alongside me but Beelzebub himself donning a blood-soaked grin and cupped in his hands a steaming pile of poo. This "gift", as I called it, likened only to the transonic magnetism of suicidal atoms, has countless times left me stranded with some sad fool who's in need of consolation and suddenly, without warning, I'm roped in for a sucker and hog-tied and gagged while the *fatigue fatal* sucks the life from my aura, then licks his chops and saunters off afresh while I'm left lying there like Hilda the whore: ravished and phlegmatic. Such emotional transfusions have become so common, such a part of my own *Comédie Humaine* they've come to take on the properties of oxygen...that is, invisible and everywhere. They blend in perfectly with the elements of Everyday, never once failing in their veering oxidation which leaves my resolve tarnished by a bluish-green film of pity and apathy: pity for myself; apathy for whole of human suffering. So draining are these vacuolations all I'm ever able to do when playing host to these parasites is sip my coffee and nod politely and smile and wait for the needle to finally be drawn from my drained, wasted vein.

After a few minutes spent in silence our mistress in misery brought forth the man's coffee which immediately he threw down in a single gulp and, wiping his sleeve across his salt-and-pepper chin, kindly requested another. The trench wench scoffed, then slid the entire pot down the counter like a curling stone. The man mouthed, "Thank you," before filling both our cups and with an up-turned digit took a slow, dainty sip, then smiled and slouched across the counter like a wounded soldier, sighing, "Yessir, helluva night. Hellenic, I'd say. In fact, if my memory serves, it was on such a night as this I first learned to sing songs of Grecian love triumphant. May I?" he asked while pointing at my pack. I nodded absentmindedly, still trying to ingest all he had just said. He lit the cigarette and with a deep grunt drew in a healthy drag, then exhaled and, staring at his cigarette, said, "Ah, just us two for the turpitude, what?" At this I laughed a little which must have encouraged him, for suddenly he began flapping his arms like the wings of a wild goose, the stench from which nearly knocking me off my stool. He was still flapping wildly when the waitress returned with a plate of pickled smelt and sneered, "Alright, now, you peddler. Listen here! Steal this boy's peace and smoke, if he lets you, but not for one instant believe your luck demands we must all sit and watch your wits reduce to rubble, right!"

"My dear auburn woman," began the man, "these wits you so tenderly referred to as rubble are, in truth, no less than the early-autumn plumule of God's own chrysanthemums hidden deftly in the hollow of my mind's meadow labyrinth."

The wench simply baffled her brow, then with a buzzard-gray glare let fall the plate of smelt and scoffed off toward the kitchen. After, the man leaned to me and whispered, "In any case, I've yet to see the day I'd forsake my wits, autumnal though they be, for her dried-up, sour, mummified sacs, eh, what? Ha, ha, ha!" Once he realized I wasn't responding he leaned in closer and, even softer, whispered, "You know, boy, I've heard music in every form imaginable."

At this I looked up. He was wearing a pedantic grin and nodding his head as if he had just proven an irrefutable claim. His hair was the color of harvest hay which contrasted sadly with his apple-blossom complexion, setting to life the Bacchic impression of knowledge coupled with youth.

"It's true," he continued, "and what's more their visions and stale, acrostic styles have left my heart cystic as a bloated gin blossom, a dense and troubling nausea which sinks below the belly of a black, spasmodic sea. I've seen the sun spotted with Hell's mystic horrors as drunken corks dance upon summer's green waves, their songs sung in false cadence and melting in the moonglow, a stagnant larghetto floating along the twilight and fitting my skin with fantastic disguises, a thousand starry sufferings composing my accouterment: cantankerous twaddle. An impotent dream. A vain hope, fame. Forgery! And now that same sun approaches autumn. Autumn! Autumn already! The season of dead leaves, wet smoke and drunkenness!"

He was cut short suddenly by the arrival of the waitress delivering the second course. He smiled politely, she not at all, and the moment she was gone he turned to me and continued:

"But in truth, boy, I have wept too much. Every sun is bitter, every moon atrocious. Autumn's drunken rays are like the felling of trees...mournful, but necessary. The day this dawned on me the streets no longer seemed as blood, their pale stone entranced as sun-bronzed skin shot through with beryllium – their shallow puddles now as luminous currency. No longer do I swim beneath the fearful eyes of prison ships."

At this the aroma of his food grew too great and, forsaking all utensils, he plunged forth his fingers into each plate in order from nearest to farthest and then into his mouth. After he had licked clean his thumbs and fingers he looked up and, with a childish grin, said, "It's all as simple as a musical phrase. Take, for example, this fools' café. In this dense haze my eyes were searching for maintenance while you, like an Emperor near the end of his decline, you were looking to die a little, no? And here we are!" Again he plunged forth his fingers into his food and again he sucked them mercilessly until: "Men as us must always remain modern. After all, an artist's thumb is no better than a plumber's. The bone-worn products of an ancient age give young men pleurisy and cause a mighty chaos to whirl within his brain. All is eaten. All is drunk. There is nothing more to say. What's to happen when you leave this world? Nothing. Those senses of yours to which you hold so dear will one day serve as fodder for the urges of another. I say, go forth and satisfy your dark heart's desires! Dance upon that haughty breast and sleep a dreamless slumber, your fierce, monstrous pride now as somber as a house cat. It's there, I tell you, where true treasures lie, where hordes of young men much stronger than yourself have already been tended on by many a naked, perfumed slave. An intoxicating death! A hero's grave, what! Oh, in my mind's eye my memory serves well. Mind your memories, boy! Mind your memories like lice! Why, just the other day...or was it yesterday? Yes, yesterday, while dancing through the Armory, my mind was burst asunder by the rise of man's fall and his futile, mirthless remedies for...."

He stopped suddenly, groaned and grimaced, then, with both arms wrapped around his stomach like two snakes, said, "Oh! Aye, me! It seems my memory has made way for dysentery!" Then he pushed aside his food and stood off his stool and, still holding his stomach, began stumbling down the counter, shouting, "Remember, boy! Remember! Remember your memories like...*oh, my licentious stomach!*" before finally disappearing through a hallway door.

Once gone I turned toward the window behind me and noticed the rain had ceased entirely. Determined to make the most of it, I fished a bill from my coat pocket and, not even

Apples of Arcadia 95

noticing the denomination, left it half-hidden beneath one of the empty plates and made for the door.

The instant I was outside and in the open air I sighed for relief from the bum and his conundrums. Mirthless remedies? Memories like lice? What manner of talk was this? The half-cracked drivel of a drunk, that's what. Why ponder it further? The recent downpour mingled with the late summer night air causing a lithic fog to settle between the pavement and level of street lamps. Lost in this fog, and not concerned about direction at this point, I followed the gurgle of a gutter rivulet flowing away from Lake Avenue toward the end of the block and down around Second Street where it flowed so fast I could barely keep up before going underground beneath an iron drain. My inspiration now flowing somewhere below the city, I lifted my head in search of its replacement.

There before me stood the lugubrious gothic arches of Duluth's First Presbyterian. This towering structure with its pinnacles and parapets, gargoyles and buttress, is exemplary of the charade which has engulfed this town like a tomb. The presumptuous cravings of these necrophilic people, their need to surround themselves with the landscape of the past has tainted the horizon with timeworn monuments, the silhouettes of headstones. Small wonder, then, while staring up at this cold residuum resembling so much an unearthed casket, I suddenly found myself awash amidst the icy currents of some midland stream, the likes of which held dear by such names as Dante, Dostoevski, Rabelais, Rimbaud – all the tortured souls and masters of sorrow who've invariably sprung up along the banks of still waters. While swimming through the words and minds of these men I've vicariously, yet vividly experienced the awe and mystery of a land which has fostered both flood and fire, bacterium, delirium, psychosis, psychoanalysis, pointillism, cubism, pasteurization, anthrax, the Albigensian Crusades, the King James Version, revolutions, reformations, evolutions of civilizations, a vast and whirling wind of life and destruction, death and rebirth, all of it orchestrated beautifully beneath an ultramarine blue, salmon-pink sky. Strange, then, on this night, when standing before their shrine, instead of a glorious landscape gilded with wonder, instead of the promise of salmon-pink skies I saw a sky darkened by blood, its horrific red light like a suffocating shroud across the rooftops and street lamps, the entire city now resembling a raging river of blood, the blood of the past and present and future, of progress ad nauseam, tormenta infinitus, dark and vulgar catacombs reeking of doom, doom of starvation and eternal sleep, of dignity ashen and airy as dust only to be revived by the moisture of tears, of man's sharp martyrdom, the dreamer of dreams, the Builder and Seer whose fruits were as manna now sour as headcheese, the sacristy of life's ornaments reduced to rubble and rebuilt as formless and false as Hell's windmills, the river Styx gurgling like a sewer below, a cataract as putrid and malignant as the Plague, its fiery waters stinging my face, neck and eyes, forcing me to turn away and then back upon the church, an image so mundane, yet so strange and perverse as any within the murals of Hieronymus Bosch. Crass, vainglorious pedagogues impaled through the pelvis and dangling from the gables; purple-faced prophets leaning out the eyelets and preaching the New Word with esoteric tongues, their voices as slop between apoplectic fits of vomitous wailing; vicious beasts feasting on the charred flesh of Prometheus; men and women joined at the genitals and masturbating like monkeys – a man, mid-thirties, barely visible behind his shadow, a ridiculously long mustache protruding from his lip, an eerie blank stare like dementia in his eyes; behind him a woman dressed in faded black canvas, in her hand a leather strap which she whips him with repeatedly, that blank, empty stare never once leaving his eyes – a thousand million faces made pallid and cold where once were tears now ice locks the eyelids and now I have the feeling I'm no longer alone. I look behind me and there stands the old man, his countenance cold and lifeless as stone. Too terrified to move, my legs as hollow shells, I tremble and stare as if in a trance until I feel his icy fingers press hard upon my shoulder and the other rising up from the periphery and pointing toward the tortuous scene. Instantly and without effort, almost as if we're floating, we start toward the carnage, his frail hand guiding me steadily onward and onward, closer and closer, closer and in my ears the sound of screams and mangled cries of torment entwined like the harmony of some hellish symphony and we're so close now I feel on my forehead what can only be the random rainsplatter of blood and I turn toward the old man but he's no longer there it's just me now shivering beneath this terror and above me the blood-red rain stinging my eyes and in my ears the echoes of anguish and pain and the next thing I know I'm running like mad away from it all, away, just anywhere away, away to wash this blood off my face and neck and eyes, away out of earshot of echoes like sirens, away from the suffocating shroud of the night and dark city streets and searing isolation, just anywhere away, away, away, away....

I didn't stop running till once again I was surrounded by the lampposts of Superior Street, though this time their light seemed less offensive, less lacerating than before. Two long rows of purple-pinkish light (the color of shaded naked flesh) extended several blocks down each side of the street. So many there were, like two enormous tiers of luminescent stars, their glow as inviting as a drunken sleep, they seemed to swallow me whole as I wandered through their midst like a cosmic thief, the sensuous warmth of semidiaphanous rays caressing my skin and suspending my legs and arms, lifting me up and on toward Andromeda's solarium, the sun-star alveola, her rose-colored crustacean bearing silver-bluish streams of secretory pearls, the wellspring of reason, the reason for reason, isolation incarnate, the spectrum-spangled clamshell dancing nude in the moon like soft, concupiscent seaweed waving between two long, smooth, celestial, gravitational constellations. I looked up: a beacon burning in the likeness of a Broadway marquee; to my right a man and woman engulfed in an embrace as though they were attempting to devour one another. Dispassionate, I strode past them and in through the antiquated entrance.

Scarlet carpet covered the corridor floor and seemed to breathe and heave between two enormous walls of slate mirror paneling sending off the illusion of an endless sea of blood and immediately I was reminded of the First Presbyterian though instead of screams I heard the muffled sound of music seeping in through the ceiling. Looking up I noticed what appeared to be a balcony, a black iron staircase coiling toward it.

Upstairs a small crowd had gathered and was nodding its head rhythmically to the melody made by four men at the front of the room. The music they made seemed soothing enough and after finding an empty stool at the bar I ordered a beer, lit up a smoke and sat facing the scene.

The entire crowd seemed solemn, sedated, engulfed by the collective consciousness that defines the crowd. Aside from a subtle hand-to-mouth movement or an accidentally upturned ashtray there was nothing, not one particle of meaning in their common plasticity, not the slightest gesture to suggest a single sulfuric thought. Even the music seemed metallic, automatic, devoid of flesh and bone and sanguineous emotion, of genuine elation or heartache or grief or a sudden combustion of dystopian membranes; nothing but an undulating, entangling mesh of electronic inertia incubated in the world's tepidarium womb and embraced by the crowd as its very own seedling. Still, though they bowed and curtsied and applauded the four men for having so pleasingly championed their mediocre offspring, one couldn't help but have the feeling that, should the lights suddenly and mysteriously shine on, they'd all scatter and flitter up the walls like frightened cockroaches shitting all over themselves while frantically searching for any dark crevice in the framework of the bughouse. We are all scared shitless and witless that one day the light will be shown through our skulls and into our thoughts, that one day there'll be no wall, no dark crevice, no hole in which to hide. What then? Well, then perhaps the crowd seems a perfectly acceptable place wherein to sip a pensive potion and drown one's conscience. Perhaps it's best if we all got used to the idea of a collective voice, a collective language, a collective custom, race and ancestry and currency and tax levy and tobacco company and tampon factory and tooth decay and bone disease and cancer and cirrhosis and neurosis and *morbus gallicus*. Perhaps we've already fashioned ourselves for a life inside the bughouse. Perhaps we're all well practiced in diving headlong into the lockbox. Perhaps those buggers in the Big White Wooden Kimono are onto something. Perhaps they have it all sussed out. Perhaps their high position demands they be well versed in the human disposition toward self-destruction and deem themselves delegated to hasten the outcome – a political and global *coup de grâce*. Perhaps none of this means anything at all. Perhaps one day we'll all awake as cinder, in which case perhaps it's best if we assemble ourselves in one mass collective huddle for quick and easy sweeping once the angels take control. But still, when the fear of assembly and loss of privacy fill the atmosphere, what does one do when that same fear is coupled with an even stronger, more infectious type of fear. What then when the Self instills just as much suspicion as a room full of shitting cockroaches?

  The music stopped. Cheers abound. I swallowed what was left of my beer and snuffed out my smoke and made for the door when from nowhere the words "Leaving so soon?" wafted over my shoulder like smoldering ash.

  Had I an ounce of courage I'd have run for the door.

  Instead, I spun around. A cascading rainfall of fire and ice floe like diamond glissandos through clouds in Beulah. I stood frozen, immobile, my limbs as unyielding as fortified lodestone – silent and petrified, a gaolbird on the gallows... but what was I guilty of? Silence, to say the least. I felt I should say something, anything, if only a gasp to let her know I was alive, but my lips wouldn't budge from their flintlike lock, my tongue a lifeless slab of chromite in my mouth. After a few pathetic attempts at speech which produced nothing, not even a gurgle, she smiled and, seeming to free me from my torturous silence, asked, "You were leaving, weren't you?"

...But to no avail. I managed only an idiotic nod.

"Oh, that's too bad," she sighed. "I was hoping you'd stay. You see, I saw you walk in and I've been meaning to come talk to you, only I got stuck talking with someone else about something important and, oh, I wish you weren't leaving, not just yet."

Leaving? Who's leaving? Nobody's leaving. Not even if the devil himself sets fire to the ceiling and fills the air with a phosphorous fume. We'll all just stay right here and breathe in the poison till our pores bleed, if that suits you.

"Oh good!" she exclaimed, her voice like cathedral bells. "You wait here. I'll be right back."

Whatever you wish.

Christ, what the hell just happened?! Was the sky raining stars as the Aztecs predicted? Was this some fantastic effect of the recent alignment of Venus and Mars? Whatever it was I felt wholly unprepared, a mere apparition who'd just stumbled upon a treasure amid the mishmash of the poorhouse... spiritually inadequate in every sense. I had a moment's thought of making a run for it, in retreating to try and nurture what little dignity I had left, but damned if her scent didn't linger like valerian, restricting my movement like nebulous bilboes. I was done for. And besides, I hadn't a single crumb of dignity to sit on. Any dignity I had at all was engraved in the matrix and had turned to lentigo when plucked from the uterus. All the same, that didn't stop me from trying like hell to compose a confident air when I noticed her gliding across the floor toward me.

In her absence I instinctively guarded two stools for us to sit. She took one, then smiled and reached for a cigarette. I reached for my lighter. As I held it to her, the soft light licking her luminescent skin, I noticed in her eyes a strange glimmer, almost covetous, as if they'd just caught sight of what they dreamt but never seen. Once the cigarette was lit she withdrew the plume, then said, "I don't suppose you remember me, do you?"

Remember her? How could I forget? How could I let go the memory of the woman with whom I've traveled the world over into every capitol of every country, down every dirt road of every countryside leading off into the garden of some far-off, forbidden courtyard where we'd steal the lush tomatoes and radishes and strawberries and tuck them in our shirts and run off together somewhere beneath a sycamore beside a river where we'd eat and make love and watch the sun fall asleep and give the stars names and where I'd wait to watch her golden skin breathe life into each new day. Remember her? I remember everything about her...everything but her name.

"I'm Elizabeth," she said extending her hand.

Elizabeth.

"Lizzie, actually."

Lizzie. A new constellation. *Rara Avis*. The star with downy plumage....

"Well, I remember *you*," she said. "You're that bartender from the Lounge...the one who made that magnificent martini."

I smiled. So that night left an impression on *her* as well. And up till then I'd figured it all but a waltz in a dream.

"You know," she went on, "yours is the only bar martini I've enjoyed. It's so rare to find someone with this simple skill, don't you think? Especially in Superior. You'd think it'd be the opposite...a town full of bartenders and wasters...you'd think *they'd* be the ones to perfect the drowning art...but no. They'd all much rather just pinch their pennies and reach for the cheap stuff...the more for the money and all that, I suppose. Nothing but a bunch of penny-pinching groaners, if you ask me." Of a sudden her eyes got round and wide as if with fright. "Oh, I hope I didn't offend you!" she gasped. I gave a confused look as if to imply such a thing were impossible.

She tried to explain: "I mean, I know you're from there and all and...."

"Wait," I interrupted. "What makes you think I'm from Superior?"

"Well, you *do* tend bar at the Lounge, don't you?"

"Not anymore," I replied. Now it was her turn to look confused.

I wondered how I should handle this. I didn't dare say anything about sequestering myself in some seedy hotel to punch out my masterpiece. Such a comment would mean the same as revealing the knotted flesh of an amputated stump. Nausea, plain and simple. And Sara? Perhaps this might be a go, but still the subject required an expert hand whereby to sketch the scene with both pathos and passion. I decided I hadn't this hand, not after tonight. With all my pride freshly slain on the chopping block I was now operating under a protective intelligence. No great leaps with the imagination, I told myself. Not just yet. I shrugged my shoulders and said, simply, "We just parted ways is all."

Luckily, she accepted this explanation, however sparse. "All the same," she said, "I didn't mean anything by it. I mean, I could never say anything *too* nasty about Superior. You see, I live there myself." *Was that a shiver up my spine?* "Not that I was born there or anything. God, could you imagine! Could there be anything worse?!" *Perhaps not....Just a draft.* "No, I've only been living there a year or so now...shacked up, don't you know." *Yes, most definitely a shiver.*

She went on to tell the story of how she and dull Lester, both of Duluth, hooked up two years earlier while working in the restaurant (she the hostess, he the cook) of the Gilded City's most reserved hotel, so noted for its revolving roof which gives the diner a panoramic view of the entire Twin Ports in precisely the time it takes to choke down a dry, overpriced steak and side of creamed asparagus. Their income not so steady, however, and heartily advised by her sister who had already weathered three winters and a husband on Superior soil, they decided to pool together and take advantage of her slums (*"Surely there must be one with a window facing the sun, doncha think, there, hun?"*) and off they sped across the bridge to build their nest with lush, youthful illusions. (Actually, she disclosed he wasn't so youthful after all; fast approaching thirty he was with all the accompanying signs including a swollen belly, balding head and halitosis.) After a short while of barely making ends meet (even in the slums) yon Lester thought it best if he went back to school to better his lot and after a quick thumb-flick through a local trade school catalogue he decided swabbing toilets was the way for him and soon he was enrolled in a two-year course on the art of castellanship and severed completely from the culinary for good. This sudden change in Lester (which, most likely, was for the better) was quite disheartening for Lizzie who'd developed her own crystalline vision of how she and her man would coexist among the rolling clouds of Coupledom, and this fantasy involved nothing so obscene as the reality which was now manifesting itself. The belly, the baldness, the bad breath, the castrating desire to become (of all things) a custodian, all this was simply too much (or too little) for young Elizabeth to accept as her given lot in life...and who could blame her? All any man had to do was just glance in her direction and immediately he was struck dumb by the presence of the Divine.

While all this was unfolding from her splendid, supple lips I couldn't help but wonder, *Why?* Why had she chosen to reveal this most personal side of herself to *me*, a guy of whom she knew nothing other than his ability to mix a proper martini? There I was, unable to relate to her even the simplest detail (good God, have I even told her my name?) and already I could compile an exhausting symposium revolving round that which she confided in me in the course of an hour. To be sure, it wasn't anything anyone wouldn't have been able to untangle after a short conversation with the girl. The sadness would have pervaded the tiniest pause and seeped its way into every sentence, eventually flooding out every emotion other than an intense desire for something else...anything else. We all have this desire somewhere inside us, especially those who seem the most content, and it's these especially one must keep a constant eye on, for God only knows how much they've suppressed below the surface and for how long. One minute they might be tittering like a teenager over some amusing bit of minutiae and the next they've got the axe in hand and are swinging mad with murderous accuracy. A typical story, is it not? And still we have the audacity to wonder how in the hell Bob could have done such a thing to his darling family when most likely poor Bob was just defending himself. Perhaps within a month's time his dear adorable wife or two wonderful children would have done the same to him. Who's to say? To deny the fact that we recognize this murderous potential in the eyes of our neighbor is to deny his very existence, and to deny the fact that we recognize loneliness in the eyes of the beautiful is to deny God. In fact, it is their beauty which makes it all the more evident, all the more painful and unbearable to endure, as if God Himself were weeping for the misery of mankind.

Sadly, all too soon the night came to a close. The band was packing and the cockroaches scurrying and the time had come to say goodbye. We finished our drinks in silence, a "deafening silence" as they say, then walked toward the door at the rear of the balcony. Both seemed to want the night to go on. There was something in the air, a heavy something like lead around our legs and ankles which made it impossible to take a single step, to speak a single word, to make a single sound other than a burdensome grunt. There was much more to be said, at least on my part...far too much to try and reel off before the night split us apart. The night spelled doom for her and me and we knew it. The night would forever spell doom for us both...this we did *not* know. We stood at the door, the words gurgling in our throats like acetate, the moon drifting over like sodium bicarbonate, the previous hour's raindrops dripping down the drainpipes like burning magnesium when finally one of us decided to speak.

It was she.

"I enjoyed talking with you tonight."

These otherwise ordinary words when let from her lips suddenly took on new meaning, like "faith" or "joy" after a life-threatening experience.

"When do you think I might see you again?" she asked. She was looking me in the eyes. I wondered how she managed such strength. All I could do was flitter about from her hands to her mouth to her waist to her feet to the pavement they stood upon.

"Whenever you'd like," I garbled.

"Next Tuesday?"

I smiled.

"Like tonight?"

I smiled brilliantly.

"Good. It's settled then," she said. "I'll see you here next Tuesday night." And with that she disappeared into an ocean of shadows.

Jubilant, inundated with elation, yet curiously sad, I ran back through the balcony and down the stairs through the bloody corridor and out the antiquated entrance past the two lovers who'd devoured each other whole, back into the black, suffocating shroud of night though now it all seemed exotic, enveloping, yet distant, like a black rose found dead center in the middle of the Sahara. Even the buildings, those fallen structures with their windows like eye sockets, even these failed to inspire contempt, for were the buildings not life? Or *of* life? Or at the very least *in* life? And as such, like the trees and rivers and lampposts and automobiles and bridges and viaducts and even the railroad ties, did they not also possess the ability to cast a shadow? And was not she, the black rose, the sun-star alveola with rose-tinted aura, was she not at this very moment resting in the delicate embrace of shadows? So I say unto you all, Fall down, ye dark shadows! Fall down upon the brow of the holy black rose! Fall down upon her precious, silken petals and nourish them with your vespertine, sable-vested light! You must not falter, for you have been chosen! You have been chosen to blight out the sun for the sake of her corona, her inflorescent halo! Don't you see? The sun would steal her luminosity...you must steal it back! So, then, you ghosts, I shout unto you all, Blight out the sun! Blight it out with all your might! Build more buildings and bridges and billboards and more shadowy monuments to man's mediocrity! Yes, if anything, more mediocrity! Nothing destroys the sun like these phallic obelisks! Build more bridges and buildings and billboards and automobiles and airplanes and highways and byways and parkways and driveways and pornographic websites and pharmaceutic sunbeams and bottle shops and tea bags and dried fruit and dildoes and new editions of dictionaries and cosmos-scented candle wax and handjobs and holograms and cellular receivers and slow revolving restaurants and space ships and astronauts crashing to the surface like meteors and nuclear missiles and manhunts and botched treaties and bungled opportunities and paranoia and disease and starvation and death and more! More! More! *Basta! Basta!*

 When I got back to the room I was so wound up, so electrically charged I could have shot lightning through my fingertips and follicles. I tried to sleep it off, though even as I lay stretched on the bed I could still feel my muscles twitch and my temples pulsate. I got up. I tried to read but my eyes wouldn't move fast enough to satisfy my brain. I desperately wanted a drink and would have downed a whole bottle of pure firewater if only one were handy...but no, nothing, not even a drop. I drank it all during previous bouts with failure and despair. I checked my pockets. A few dirty bills. Good. Just enough. I looked at the clock. One thirty. Shit! The stores were all closed. Cedric? Screw that! I'm not that desperate. Back to the bed. No go. Back to the book. Might as well be Chinese. *Christ! What to do?!* By chance the corner of my eye caught the battered keys of the machine. *Fuck it!* I said, then leapt at it like a lunatic.

The following hours are a blur. I remember only the imprints – the machine's incessant tapping; the flurry of my fingers as they moved across the keys like ants devouring an elephant; the weightlessness; the automatic maneuvers like reverse telekinesis; the sheets upon sheets of paper falling and rising and flirting and flushing and osculating and copulating and teeming and birthing; the blood on the walls; the phantom made flesh. And when it was over, when the last drop of protoplasm had been drained and bottled, I reached for a cigarette and the silver-blue-green lighter and fell back into a puddle of hollow bone and membrane.

*   *   *

I tripped through the ensuing week in blissful delirium. Nothing too substantial – a few visits to the library (for no real reason), a few stops by the food shelter, a few long walks up and down the Lakefront, a few letters written but never sent (all to anonymous nonentities). It seemed I was surviving for one purpose only: to reenact the scene of one week prior. Like the novelist in the process of penning his *magnum opus* I was contented to live out the rest of my days in the landscapes and castles of my own imagination.

Finally next Tuesday night. I thought I might purchase some flowers, perhaps some violets or belladonna lilies, but the money I managed to save throughout the week wasn't nearly enough for such an expense. I had enough for a few drinks, that was all. I sifted through the shambles. Nothing but torn paper and apple cores. I was frantic. Only an hour till we met and the thought of appearing before her empty-handed had me terrified. I was just about ready to put the knife to an earlobe when my eyes caught the shimmer of the Austrian lighter. Would this work? Hadn't she looked upon it the other night with dazzling eyes? Those deep, suffocating, azurite eyes. It would work. It had to. I snatched up the lighter and shined it on my shirt, then found an old candle box and some stuffing from my pillow and placed it gently inside before trotting off once more toward the warm glow of Superior Street.

I had to do some retracing before I found the right place. In my previous haze I failed to notice the club's name. Still, the marquee was unmistakable. The Mezzanine, it was called. So be it. I braced myself and stepped in.

I sighed for relief when I noticed she wasn't in the lobby. Strange, but a sense of dread mingled with the anticipation, causing a slight tingle in the back of my throat. I wanted her, desperately, though even still I feared her company. If only she were like these mirrors, I remember thinking. Obvious. Obedient. Impossible thoughts.

Upstairs the scene was the same. Four same men, same smoky atmosphere, same empty stool, sameness in solemnity, somnambulism at its best, soporific soap suds seeping in from the ceiling and down upon the throng....

There she was, among the crowd. She hadn't yet spotted me. *What should I do? Should I pretend I don't see her? Should I order a drink? No, wait for her. Should I light a cigarette? With what? Perhaps there are some matches on the bar. Should I find out? Perhaps there aren't. I'd look like a fool! Perhaps I should forget this whole damn thing...*

No, wait. She's spotted me. Yes...she's waving. Should I wave back? No, just nod. Yes, that's it. Don't forget to smile. Mustn't look too disinterested. Does she look disinterested? God, she's gorgeous! What the hell am I doing here? I must be out of my mind. Yes, you're completely insane. You still have time, you know. You can run for the door and never look back. You'll never have to meet or talk with her again. You'll only have to live with the memory of her beauty. But, oh, what a memory! Still time. Why won't your legs move? Run, you idiot! Run! Save yourself! Flee!

Too late. She stood before me, a glass of wine in her porcelain-white hand. A haunting portrait. *Blonde Judith with*

Wine Chalice.

She spoke.

"I'm so glad you could make it."

As if I had a choice. She was wearing a black Kashmir sweater with a long white skirt draped just above the ankles. She looked fucking sanctimonious.

I noticed her looking at the package in my hand. I raised it to her. "This is for you."

"For me?" She smiled and opened it. She recognized the lighter immediately, her mouth agape in awe.

"I noticed you looking at it the other night," I said. "I thought you might like it."

"It's beautiful."

"It's Austrian," I told her. It sounded pompous. I kicked myself in the teeth.

"It's wonderful. Thank you."

A smile. An awkward silence. She placed the lighter in her skirt pocket.

I needed a drink. I noticed her glass was near empty and offered to refill it.

"Yes, thank you."

I ordered her a wine and myself a stout. *It's beautiful, it's wonderful,* kept running through my head like a refrain. *It's beautiful, it's wonderful...it's Austrian! Ugh!!*

The drinks arrived. I had just enough for both and a little change besides, which I left on the bar. The bartender glared. "My apologies, friend," I said silently. "That's all there is. That's the last of it." Just then a panic swept over me. All the same, I remembered the matches.

I handed her the fresh glass. Another awkward silence. Then, apropos of nothing: "Those are the same guys from last week, right?" meaning the musicians.

"You remembered!" she chimed. She seemed genuinely pleased. "Yup, that's them," she went on. "They're here every Tuesday night. I guess you could say they're kind of like the soundtrack for Poetry Pavilion."

Poetry Pavilion?

"Yeah. That's what Ian calls it."

Ian?

"Uh huh. Ian and Irene."

Irene?

Just then her face dropped in shock. "Oh, my God!" she cried. "You haven't met them yet! Well, then...come on!"

She grabbed hold of my hand (the first time we touched!) and led me through the crowd toward a table near the rear where sat two people in what appeared to be an incestuous embrace. The man, a frail, troll-like figure with a rust-colored tuft atop his pale, freckled head, was leaning over and tongue-tickling the ear of a much, much younger and much more attractive girl. Upon approaching the table the latter leapt up and danced toward Lizzie like a nixie and showered her with an onslaught of kisses and hugs. I stood off to the side, trying not to look embarrassed.

Once it was over the spritely one turned to me and smiled and said, "Hi. You must be Jeff. I'm Irene."

We shook hands. Soft. Feathery. Fairy-like.

"And I'm Ian," said a dry, salty voice rising up from the table. Short. Guarded. Like a leprechaun.

We all sat down, Lizzie beside me, Ian and Irene as before and it wasn't long until Ian's tongue again began tickling the tender edges of Irene's tympanic membrane and she wiggling and giggling with girlish delight and me instinctively turning away as if witnessing something illegal and Lizzie at last revealing the lighter and she and Irene crooning over it like a couple of religious devotees and Ian leaning back in his chair, distraught. After a short while of their unsociable coos he figured he'd had enough and decided to examine the lighter himself. Averse, Lizzie handed it over whereupon he set to work lighting it and extinguishing it and tossing it up and down with his callous, freckled paw (weighing it, I suppose) and sniffing it and tasting it and testing the blue and green filigree with his yellow, elfish fingernail till finally, after the sniffing and testing and weighing and tasting, he gave it his dignified nod of approval and turned to me and asked, "Where on Earth did you dig such a find?"

"It's Austrian," answered Lizzie in a haughty voice. I was singing.

"Well, that explains everything," laughed Ian. "If it were mine, though," he continued, "I'd have a tough time letting go of it, I'm not ashamed to admit."

"Well, it's not yours so give it back!" cried Lizzie. She seemed on the verge of tears. Ian laughed heartily. Had I a pistol I'd have thrust it in his groin.

Finally he handed it back and she cradled it gentle as an infant in her arms, smiling weakly up at me as if to say, "I promise I'll never let anyone touch it again, not ever!" I was bellowing the aria to *Tristan Und Isolde*.

"So tell me, Jeff..." (it was Irene speaking) "...what is it you do with yourself?"

"Yes, Jeff," chimed Ian. "We're all curious as devils to hear how you busy your day, especially Li'l Miss Pixie over here," he slurred, smiling seductively at Lizzie. I slung daggers at his skull.

I had the odd feeling a trap was being set. Something in their tone struck me as suspicious. Even Lizzie was looking intently toward me, waiting for me to give some piece of the puzzle. After all, hadn't she already revealed so much about herself? Wasn't it only fair that I now come clean on at least this much? Just the name of a building or an honest trade? But I hadn't a building or an honest trade. Christ, I hadn't even a penny to my name! And there I was, sipping stout and handing over seemingly expensive gifts and sitting alongside the most beautiful woman who had undoubtedly ever set foot inside this sleepwalker's wet dream. Better say something, even if it only be an out-and-out lie. Otherwise they'd all gasp and point fingers and cart me away as an imposter, a criminal. Yes, go ahead and lie, if need be. Nothing too outlandish. Something earthy. Something ordinary. Something clouded over with common terminology. Something easily disguised beneath a mist of perfumed airs. In other words, a modest, supple swirl of flower-scented horseshit.

"I write for the paper," I told them with as straight a face as I could muster.

Lizzie smiled. This was something, was it not? Irene was also smiling, smiling and nodding. Ian, of course, wasn't satisfied. Not in the least.

"Which paper would that be?" he wanted to know.

I panicked. Perhaps he had a crony on the payroll...but for which paper? A slip here would mean exposure. In haste, I scoped the more political way out.

"Pick one," I grinned, hoping to muddle the issue with a modicum of wit.

"Ah, freelance!" he exclaimed. "I've done a bit of that myself...for the *Tribune*, of course. Perhaps your column and mine have rubbed elbows, what!"

"Perhaps."

"What's yours called again?"

I stalled a moment as if inspecting the air. "*Thoughts on Pennies*," I said finally.

"Hmm," he grunted, scratching his forehead. "No, sir. Don't think I've read that one. Where'd you say they run it? The editorials?"

I shook my head. "The appendix."

He winced, his freckled head bent toward the table, flustered. Dead issue. Next question?

Of a sudden, the music stopped. Ian leapt from his chair like a man possessed, a childlike glow of excitement in his face. I looked searchingly at Lizzie who, unfortunately, now had full concentration on Irene who looked positively terrified. The one had her arms slung round the shoulders of the other and appeared to be whispering something in her ear. Why did Ian suddenly tear off like that? And where to? And why was Irene now white as a sheet? And what was Lizzie's role in all this? I felt as though I were a spectator to a play...a

Apples of Arcadia 113

play *in promptu*. Entirely out of my hands. All I could do was sit back and watch and applaud, if deserved. I hoped it would get bloody...Ian's blood, I mean.

Within a moment I heard Ian's voice echo off the walls and ceiling and instinctively I turned toward the front of the room to find him standing in the center of a makeshift stage, microphone in hand. It was then the words "Poetry Pavilion" came flooding to memory. *Bloody hell!* I yelled inside as I sat there, stupefied, while Ian ran through his routine like a weary old magician. He was telling jokes and pulling poems out of his ass – long poems, short poems, fierce poems, fluffy poems, poems with little pink noses like jelly beans, poems that bounced on your knee, poems that pissed in your shoe, poems that took one look around the room before diving headfirst into an unflushed biffy. And then, after his bucolic colon had been properly excavated, he invited Irene to join him on the sump pit. She was shaking nervous as a newborn calf but still she went to him and took the microphone and unfolded some paper and began choking through a few poems of her own. She seemed to have the rhythm down all right (in truth, all she was doing was mimicking Ian's) and after a few minutes of listening out of politeness I fastened my gaze on Lizzie. She was staring intently at Irene, smiling, her hands folded lovingly beneath her flawless chin. It was then I realized her role in this charade: she was the nutriment, the nurturer, the mother hen, the one Irene entrusted to keep her confidence warm under eiderdown wings...and she played it to perfection. She could not be discouraged, nor could she be distracted once the curtain had been raised. By now Ian had returned to the table and was cheering obnoxiously, exaggerating even the slightest reaction Irene's lines demanded, robbing the performance of any genuine impression...but Lizzie just sat there, smiling, her eyes fixed in a constant, trance-like beam of adoration. Nothing contrived, just properly executed. Watching her, my heart began to swell and flood and float off in every direction, first inward, then out around the room under the chairs and stools and tables, over the scent of sweat and patchouli, eventually finding its way onto the makeshift stage and trying like mad to contain Lizzie's gaze but it could not, her eyes stared straight through it, searing as it did a hole which spewed black blood and charcoal bone and tissue and self-cauterized and again my heart tried to steal her attention and again a fiery hole and still the stench of sweat and patchouli and Ian's impish laughter like a drunken punchinello courting humdrum musicians pouring soap suds through the ceiling and down upon the throng and in the drinks and on the matches in the overflowing ashtrays and in the bartender's pockets the last of my pennies and in my ears the rhythmic flutter of Irene's tympanic poetry and on my skin the lucency of Lizzie's icy-blue eyes and their impenetrable stare and her hot hand holding mine and squeezing and squeezing and leading me straight into a whirling pool of fire....

Once again the night was closing and again the musicians packing and patting each others' backs and Lizzie looking radiant walking beside me toward the door when suddenly she stopped and turned to me and said, "You know, it doesn't have to end like this."

I looked at her with searching eyes. Of course it didn't, but how?

"I have the mornings to myself...mostly...and...." I tried to listen without seeming too assuming. Still, I couldn't help but smile when she continued and said, "...and I was wondering if maybe you'd like to join me at Ian's and Irene's house tonight and maybe...I mean, that is if you want to, of course...maybe... spend the night?"

Was this really a question? Still, I tried my best to answer nonchalantly, "Sure...why not...that is, if they don't mind." In truth, I couldn't have cared less what thought Ian and Irene. The sun-star willed it so. Nothing else mattered.

Lizzie had a car and I rode with her. On the way she made full use of the opportunity to explain a few things about Ian and Irene. "You must understand," she began, "I adore Irene more than anyone, anyone in the world. Sometimes it's as if we're sisters, you know...that's it, it's like we're sisters, and like sisters, I suppose, we don't always agree." She seemed hesitant to continue. I sat patient, coaxing her along with my silence. "It's like this," she went on. "Remember before she went up on stage, how scared she was? Well, it's obvious that wasn't her idea, right? Don't get me wrong, she really does write some beautiful poetry, some truly wonderful poems, if my opinion means anything...I mean, poems I couldn't even dream about writing, see? And at times it seems she's reciting all those beautiful, wonderful poems...at times it seems she's reciting them to me, understand? It's only...God, how I hate him!" I had a feeling I knew where this was going. Still, ever patient. "As I said," she continued, "it wasn't her idea to go on stage like that and recite her poems, all those wonderful words and images meant for me and only me. Ian thought it would be good for her, to express herself on stage like that, like some damn dancing ninny! And she listened to him! All those beautiful, wonderful poems meant *for me* and every drunken asshole in the joint tittering over how awkward she looks and how goofy her voice sounds. Christ, it makes me sick! I wish he'd go to hell!" She might have cried if the anger hadn't blocked the tears. "I know why she does it, though...why she listens to him, I mean. It's because she feels obligated to him, to his every whim, so to speak, and all because he supports her and her daughter. That's the only reason she married the guy. Yeah! Didn't you see the ring? She got knocked up a couple years back by some jerk who split and Ian was the only one who'd mop up the mess. Why am I telling you this? You don't mind, do you? Good. Anyway, she and Ian dated back in the day. Why, I don't know. I suppose it was 'cause he was always around, always on her heels like, and then one day she just gave in. It didn't last long, though. Turns out she couldn't stand the guy. Easy to see, right? So, along came the stud and soon she was in the family way with no way of making a family. Her folks? Oh, she could have gone to them,

I suppose, if they weren't both such lunatics. Her mother's an activist, does mostly volunteer work for stricter penalties for drunk drivers or whatever and her father's a minister, a real Lulu. Anywho, once they found out about the condition she was in they decided that, since it was Irene who had been so irresponsible, the sole responsibility of it all should be hers and hers alone. Nice, huh? Enter Ian, and ever since it's been nothing but black days all around." We were pulling into the driveway when: "Oh, I remember now why I told you all that. It's because Irene's daughter is...well, you'll see. I only wanted to prepare you is all."

We exited the car and strolled toward the house, which really was a duplex seated square in one of those peacefully pleasant, horrifyingly mundane neighborhoods where each house is identical and each only meets his neighbor when the sirens begin blaring to warn the town of a toxic spill or some other catastrophe – one of those communities which seem to exist solely for the sake of the damned who wish nothing more than to own a home and a tiny lot a land, none of them ever realizing such a thing impossible. Only those who advertise the sale of such ghosts are those who own homes and to stoke our hope in the everlasting struggle they give us the illusory title "investment". In the end, however, we on the outside are nothing more than prisoners left groveling in our sleep with permission to dream...that is, so long as the payments are delivered on time.

Inside the kitchen sat Irene and Ian and between them, gumming soggy graham crackers, the tike and secretly I thanked Lizzie for the flea in the ear, for after one look at their supposed darling offspring I'd nearly let loose a boisterous, disastrous laugh, for atop the child's head swirled a thick black mop, which wouldn't have seemed strange if either Ian or Irene had a single hair darker than an Englishman's toenail. Ian shot me a sarcastic smirk as if to say, "That's right, buddy. Now you know the lot," though Irene seemed content just to leave it alone, busying herself with the final demands of the day, never once looking up from the dishes and dolls until all was accomplished and, under the pretense of a sleepy bairn, all trotted upstairs and left the house in mine and Lizzie's hands.

We took a seat at the table. I couldn't help shake the feeling all had been arranged, that I was nothing more than a subject for experiment. How else to explain the way things were turning out? This night, the past week had already been driven entirely on speculation, on the thought that at any moment I might awake naked in a wheat field somewhere, the syringe still prodding my purple, swollen vein. What's more, as I sat there wondering when the dream would finally burst into a horrid bloody mess, there sat Lizzie, sending off angelic, effervescent beams as though Heaven itself couldn't be more of a certainty. Everything seemed dramatic, rehearsed, choreographed to perfection and practiced a thousand times over, and perhaps it was this which fascinated me most: she could compose herself and her role within the airy mold of Time. She was Time itself, it seemed – neither real nor imagined, either accepted or neglected...but never denied.

"We should have something to drink," she suggested and I agreed. She reached into a cupboard and extracted a bottle and poured out the liquid and handed me a glass. I didn't bother asking what it was. It could have been strychnine; I still would have tossed it down with a Benedictine grin.

For a long while we sat in silence just sipping and smiling, waiting for the other to speak...but in vain. And besides, what matter words when the moment is all, when your tongue is already aflame with ineffable fire (or was it the booze?) and to speak a word would only mean a blister on the lips. As it were, however, she didn't share the sentiment and soon she was searching for any subject she could think of – art, music, movies, our interests in each – until finally her attention strayed out the window and, noticing a soft nocturnal breeze, decided she'd like to take a walk.

Outside and treading through the sleepy, weblike streets

she still had trouble breaking through the sticky film of talk. It seemed all too much if I asked her anything other than what she'd already volunteered. She was determined to leave it all bobbing on the surface, the bait hook invisible but able to be envisioned. Her family? What of them? she wondered. Did I happen to notice the drawing on the refrigerator door? Irene's daughter drew that for her and wasn't it just delightful? And the music at the Mezzanine...what did I think of it? It was all very good, she answered herself, though sometimes they have a habit of getting too experimental, too "out there", don't you know, and on and on like that until I thought I might explode. What did I care about those monkeys at the Mezzanine or the bastard baby's drawings? Couldn't she tell by my steel-metal stare all I was interested in was *her*? That the whole world could spew sewage and swallow us whole and still all I'd care about was if her feet were keeping dry? Even still, all I could do was nod and listen patiently, playing that little game where one tries to uncover the truth behind the trivia, the purpose that lies at the base of every diversion. What was she trying to hide? Or, in fact, was she hiding anything at all? Was she telling me in her own cryptographic way all she intended to say? That to proceed further would force her to feel (most heinous of all crimes!) vulnerable? It was an adroit skating maneuver I never before bothered performing. Up till then I simply decided what it was I wanted and went after it, that was all, and damn the consequences. Though now, the consequence of losing her at the hands of such folly meant devastation, nothing less. I wanted her, madly, and if that meant standing outside the silent cocoon waiting for the silken threads to unravel then so be it. Could there be a more splendid way of wasting one's time?

All the same, as with any great tactic thought through in theory, nothing's so contradictory as that which happens on the stage of operations.

We had just finished circling the neighborhood when a chill began rising off the Lake's icy surface, forcing us to start back toward the dull warmth of the duplex. Standing on the steps, our hands buried in our pockets, laughing aloud as we cursed Duluth's weather, we experienced for the first time that delicious moment when the eyes fix in a deadlock stare and smiles turn to slightly parted, upturned lips of lust and promise to enfold the ancient Then with the distant Now and not even Jupiter Optimus Maximus himself could have stopped me from trying to kiss this girl and as I leaned forward to steal a taste of passionflower dew she pulled away, smiling as if anticipating my every move.

I looked up. The moon laughed in my face.

She spoke.

"Remember last week?"

Of course. I remembered everything.

"And what we talked about?"

I turned from the moon toward her in horror. I hoped like hell she wasn't about to say what I thought.

"About Lester?"

Damn it all.

"It's like this," she explained. "We're still together and..."

I'd heard enough. In those first few words of her untimely explanation I was able to gather the gist of its entirety. The only reason to continue attention would be in satisfying any curiosity I had as to the originality of her awkward words. With fishnet ears, I gave a listen...

"...A diamond, maybe. I don't know. Only, I want to be absolutely sure before I throw him away just like that..."

Christ, did she just call him a *diamond*?! And I thought *I* was the ridiculously romantic one. At least I can tell a diamond from a dung heap. What else?

"...Even though he smells. And the sports! Good God! That's what I like about you. You don't seem to be hung up on that whole thing. Did I tell you about the time..."

Good God indeed! What was supposed to be a speech on the virtue of abstinence instead turned into a synopsis on why Lester was the wrong man. Did she not see the irony in all this? Finally...

"...And even though things aren't exactly bliss between Lester and me...haven't been for a long time...still, I wouldn't feel right if I were the one who betrayed the relationship. You understand, I'm sure."

I most certainly did not! I wondered what the absent, inept Lester would say to her courting another man on the sly and feeding him drinks and smiles and hope for more. Would he not view this as a sort of betrayal? Would he still give her the benefit of two years' attestation? And where the hell was he now? Did he not see her straying? Did he not do nothing to try and prevent his oily grip from slipping? She had already been betrayed, plain as day, so why should she concern herself with such ill-deflected guilt? I say, Uncork the rare vintage! Let loose the love fountains! Tonight the streets will overflow with everything abundant!

That's how I saw it, though such visions to a woman waxing virtue on the brain would have been flatly refused or, worse still, accepted. No matter how many times in a night you make the Madonna see God, she'd still only see Satan lying next to her in the morning. After that, she and I as *Us* would be nothing more than a Mephistophelean nightmare. And though I had a hard time placing her in such sacramental company, I had to bow before her wishes. After all, this *coup de main* of hers was really quite cunning. It was obvious she was taking great care not to replace the dolt with an absolute dud. By rejecting me she was, in fact, placing herself wholly in my hands (however figuratively) as well as securing our then currently illusive future history...or at least that's how I rationalized the moment's insanity.

"You're still more than welcome to stay," she went on. "After all..." (with a giggle) "...I brought you all the way up here, didn't I?" *The Queen of Heaven is alive and well and letting cells in Sing Sing.* "Only..." (now serious) "...only I must have your word you won't try anything funny. Promise? Promise you won't try anything funny?"

Cross my cock and hope for herpes.

We stepped indoors and had one final drink (rather awkwardly, I'll add) before preparing ourselves for sleep. There was a bathroom on the lower level and when she was through I shut the door and pulled out my cock. "Now listen here," I started, bathing it in cold water. "You're not gonna screw this up for us, hear? We have to work together on this one. She's not like the others, understand?" It smiled sickly up at me which I mistook for confirmation. "Right," said I, tucking it tight between my legs. "No honey muffin à la mode on the menu tonight, there, John Henry." Then I looked in the mirror and repeated the same to myself.

Exiting the bathroom I found her setting a makeshift mattress of blankets, quilts and pillows on the living room floor. Obviously, she expected we sleep under the same covers all warm and cozy as a couple of cousins. What's more, in my absence she had stripped down to nothing but a tee and panties, her black lace bra draped over the back of a recliner like an ammunition belt. This left no doubt: this girl is a sadist.

"Now remember," she said with a mischievous grin, "no funny stuff, right?" before slipping between the blankets like a Northland dominatrix.

I felt like diving through the front bay window. There's no way I can do this, I thought as I unbuckled my belt and pulled off my pants and shirt and folded them neatly to buy some time. She watched the while, thoroughly enjoying the havoc she created, giving a sadistic (though still thoroughly enticing) giggle as I lifted my side of the blankets and slithered in.

"Just pretend she's got the syph," I said to myself as I closed my eyes and prayed for a quick slip into the protective folds of sleep...but no go. Her warm, near-naked body kept heaving beneath the covers beside me and immediately my glands began brewing a wicked froth. It took every ounce of strength (which had diminished considerably after the stout and strychnine) just to keep the covers from forming as a fingerstall. To make matters worse I could hear her tittering on her pillow, the sound of which brought to mind visions of Kokoschka's canvases and their whirling cathexis on Alma and neurosis. So, then, I thought, is this to be my *Bride of the Wind*? My *fata morgana*? Am I destined to carry under my arm forever this tittering portrait of the *femme fatale*? Well, then, never fear, Oskar, for even in your bitter swirls of blues and greens and yellows you are not alone. I am right beside you to help carry out the task, to darken the day and illuminate the night with each quivering stroke of my pulsating stick. What's that you say? Stab her swift and fierce with the blunt end of my saber? No, no, one cannot cheat Destiny. One can only carry out the task and set fire to the night and illuminate the darkness and nourish the heart, for is that not All? To set fire to the heart and beat it bloodless with lust and desire and deliriously vivid swirls of greens and blues and yellows, the glorious hues of saturated agony? Is that not what God intended by making animate the flesh of Man? As fodder for the heart to consume whole or piecemeal or whichever way it wants to maintain its flow? And if so, is that not *her* heart beating its hot blood beside me, alongside my swollen flesh and laughing with delight as it consumes me whole or piecemeal or whichever and digests my soul into a cesspool of desire, a swirling flame of fire and lust licking my wounds and melting my flesh into a muddled mass of teeth and meat and bone and nail and all used as pigment on the canvas of Mankind...but I am no martyr! No, I am not even a man! I am only fodder for her strong heart's desire, her blood burning fire, feathery, four-chambered heart and laughing lips and golden body like raw ember beside me....

The next morning I awoke to the smell of freshly brewed coffee and bacon burning. I also awoke alone, Lizzie nowhere to be seen. So, then, this *rara avis* has flown, was my initial thought just before I heard voices drifting in from the kitchen, hers among them. I recalled the moments just before sleep to see if I'd done anything to jeopardize the prize. I vaguely remembered my knee brushing up against her naked thigh, perhaps even a wandering hand roaming up the back of her warm tee, though nothing which had pierced her supposititious hymen. I smiled and stirred to claim my reward and when I did I noticed the pony had strayed from the stable. What's more, a thin film of dried saliva had formed about the jowls. Nothing but a little dribble after being roped so close to the oats, thought I, and left it at that. I jumped up off the floor and began to dress.

All three and the babe were sitting at the table munching jellied toast and eggs and I could tell by their chatter they had been up for some time; more than one cup of joe was bubbling round in their bellies. Irene was the first to see me standing in the doorway and greeted me with a warm Hallo! and a steaming cup of coffee with just enough cream I nearly fell on my knees and proposed then and there though just before I did my glance fell on Ian who was wearing a weird, twisted smirk on his pale, speckled mug. Wanted to know what it was like sleeping on the floor, he did. Fine, I told him. Quite refreshing, in fact. I suggested he try it sometime. He agreed, then turned attention back toward the brat, chuckling to himself like a Shetland cur. I ignored him as a matter of course.

My hat duly doffed in both hosts' direction, I then turned to Lizzie expecting a congratulatory grin on her glistening lips and receiving...nothing. She didn't even bother looking up from her bacon, toast and eggs, the latter of which she poked repeatedly with the spear-end of her fork.

"Good morning, Lizzie," I said as if it were a question. No answer, just a nod, her fork stabbing mercilessly the bloody eggs. Ian chuckled.

Irene invited me to the table. She had a plate all set up and for the moment I allowed myself to forget about Lizzie. If something were truly bothering her I would find out eventually, no? In any case, best not prod. Probably nothing but a stiff back from the bedding, eh? Aye. I dove into the food like a backsliding glutton.

"Ho, now, Jeff!" jeered Ian, an air of worry. "Watch out you don't choke yourself, hear? Irene's food can sometimes turn out tough." I steadied myself and swallowed down an enormous chomp with a mouthful of coffee. Then: "Hymie, who'd have thought you'd be so hungry after all those delicious dreams you had last night, eh? He, he..."

I looked up at him questioningly. Stifled laughter had twisted his face into a contorted mass of spotted flesh. I then looked at Lizzie; her face had reddened considerably. Irene didn't dare turn away from the dishes and dolls. It was obvious I was missing something, but what? Who cared? The food was good and the coffee was getting cold.

After the table had been cleared away and everyone had had their fill of coffee and folderol it seemed they all suddenly had something pressing to do. Turned out Ian was a cabby (rather fitting, I thought) and the time had come for him to begin his daily rounds and once gone Irene related it was high time she dropped the bundle at the babysitter's and scooted off to class. What was it she studied? I wanted to know. Speech pathology, said she. Fitting as well. The pathological poet. Judicious, even.

Lizzie drove me home. She still hadn't said a word to me all morning, barely even acknowledging my presence save a spiteful glance every now and again. I was beginning to wonder if maybe she'd caught me in eye-lock with Irene, though this happened only once and only after that first seductive sip of coffee. Still, I thought it a bit early in the game for upbraiding and about halfway to the hole I decided she had out with it.

"Enough!" I shouted, surprising even myself. "Tell me, already! What the hell did I do?"

Stunned, she looked straight at me, a strain of disgust on her brow. "You mean to say you don't know?"

At this I wasn't sure if she was disgusted at what I did or

the fact that I didn't know. In any case, the fact I had caused this disgust in her *at all* disgusted me. Still, I maintained my innocence. I honestly couldn't think of anything I did wrong. "That's exactly what I'm saying," I said, a bit gentler.

She stared straight ahead, her eyes peering through the windshield in a distant haze as if trying to decide something. At last, she spoke.

"You...you...."

What? What? What could she be struggling at? What could I have done that was so unspeakable?

"You...you...."

Good Christ, the agony! All these accusatory *you*'s and knowing they meant *me*. Finally, she let out with it.

"You...you...jizzed on me."

My mind must have replayed this sentence a thousand times in the span of a few seconds. Perhaps I heard her wrong. Perhaps the pronunciation of her words got jumbled with a passing siren or a crashing spaceship or something less likely.

"Did you say...I...*jizzed* on you?"

At first she didn't speak, just stared straight ahead. For a moment, thinking she hadn't heard me, I thought I'd have to repeat the question. She must have read this for, in an attempt to close the subject for good, she said definitely: "Yes. You jizzed on me...on my back."

"On your back?"

She nodded. That was all.

My mind raced back through the past few hours. It all made sense: Ian's chuckles, Irene's discomfort, the crusty cock, the poking pony. Perhaps that wasn't my hand roaming up her warm tee after all, the thought of which nearly sent me into hysterics which would have been disastrous had it not been subdued in time by a heavy dose of guilt...but for what? For shooting a wad while in the Land of Lipothemia? Shit, might as well hang a man for burning holes through his wife with a Martian ray. And did she have to use the word *jizzed*?

This alone nearly set me twitching. Why not say *sprayed* or *spunked* or *blew spew* or *fish egged* or *yolk soaked* or *shot hot jelly* or anything other than *jizzed*? That last one to me always sounded like the dialect of a delinquent. It's a man's act and should be described as such. Still, even if my guilt was imaginary, her anger most certainly was not, and I was prepared to treat it thus. To her I had committed a vicious crime: I had violated the sanctuary of sleep. I was made to feel criminal.

We were pulling up to the front of the hotel and I'm sure if I were able to read her thoughts I would have cringed at the violence in vengeance and dismemberment. How to remedy this? I wondered. Perhaps it was past remediation. Perhaps not. Perhaps an apology, at the very least.

"Look," I began, "I'm sorry if I embarrassed you, but you honestly can't hold it against me, can you? I mean, it's obvious I have no memory of it, right?"

Silence.

"And anyway," I continued, "shouldn't *I* be the one who's embarrassed here? After all, it wasn't *your* fault. *You* were only at the wrong end of the gun, so to speak?"

A horrible blunder. Humor only seems to turn these already nitric situations into a veritable barrel of TNT. Finally, after a few seconds of silence, she broke from her stare and said, simply, "Get out."

That was that. I fell from the car onto the sidewalk and watched her drive away, praying to Christ her car would suddenly run out of gas or drop an axle or anything...but no. She was gone. And not a word about next Tuesday night.

I crept up the stairs into my room and wept inwardly. I say "inwardly" because deep inside I still considered myself innocent. I was no more a criminal than a dog on the street, and I definitely was not no dog, no sir! I was a man, by God! (The actions of the previous night proved this much alone.) Nevertheless, in *her* mind I was a dog. In desperation I resolved to show her that, in fact, I was a man and, what's more, a man worthy enough to hold her hand as she walked down the street...but how? Which weapons were at my disposal? I had no money, no job, no car, no clean clothes, no confidence. Perhaps I might swipe some colored chalk from the corner shop and scrawl her name in blues and greens and yellows on her sidewalk as she slept...but no! Again the sleep offender! *Ugh!* And besides, I had no idea where she lived. She was careful enough to keep that bit of information from me, the minx. I nearly fell on my knees and admitted defeat though just before I did it hit me: *the pages!* I would sift through the saturnalia and sculpt and mold and polish those pages till they resembled the mended remains of my terebrated heart. Then, next Tuesday night (blast it all if she didn't invite me!) I'd present to her the spectacle wrapped in ribbons and dripping with everything I meant to say but couldn't. Then she'd accept me. She'd have to! What woman can refuse a man who spills himself freely at her perfumed feet?...so long he doesn't miss and douse her splendid back.

The next week straight I added and omitted, reduced, embellished, borrowed freely, stole shamelessly, invented, created, destroyed, razed, ruined, demolished and resurrected right up until the very hour it had to be delivered and even then I wasn't satisfied. No such luxuries, however. I couldn't allow my insecurities to get the better of me. I hadn't another Tuesday to waste. Weary, I rolled up the pages and bound them with a ribbon ripped from the satin edges of my blanket and slung them under my arm and made for the Mezzanine.

Once again I stood amid the smoke and soapy music and once more I was the hollow spirit that had wandered in off the street, though this time I was prepared. This time I had a weapon.

The plan was to find her sitting at the table in the rear with Ian and Irene and maintain a safe distance till I'd had enough time to assess the situation and plan my approach...or at least until my courage recovered. At once I saw the table and Ian and Irene, but no Lizzie. Perhaps she scampered off to the powder room, thought I, then made way toward the entrance thinking I'd catch her off-guard to my advantage and as I waited, lingering about the door like a pervert, I felt on my shoulder a soft, feathery tap.

My backbone shattered like a crystal stalactite.

I turned to see Irene, a timid smile stretching her sylphidine lips.

"Lizzie's not here," she said airily.

I waited in silence to see if she'd explain. Sensing this, she added, "She's not feeling well, is all."

Would she return next Tuesday?

"Tough to say. She sounded pretty sick on the telephone, though. Could be bronchitis."

Right....Or cardio-acidosis. However, message received. I gave a nod to let her know I understood, then, feeling the pages in my palm, I held up the scroll and (not knowing what else to do with it) said, "This is for Lizzie. Could you see that she gets it?"

She said she would and accepted the scroll, then watched me sulk away.

So that was it. I'd fucked up good and proper, or, rather, my *prick* had fucked up good and proper and there was nothing I could do about it. She had even gotten Goody Flower Sprite to lie for her. T'would be a black day in Fairyland, that's for sure. Exit the sun-star. Enter eternal night.

After the Mezzanine I roamed the hillside like an insect, my antennae bent, my body a crumpled mass of broken limbs and lamellicorn. I must have limped through the entire city, even wandering down Fourth Street and beyond hoping some poor, desperate soul would do away with my misery with one swift stab...but no. The dregs of the street seem to strike only at the scent of fear. As it were, I floated through the streets in a stupor, the usual companions Fear and Caution left snoring in the subconscious. All I could think of were the past few months of my millipodic life, the body of which once hopeful and bright, now spliced into a million bloody segments of failure and rejection.

By sunrise I'd made way back to Canal Park. Exhausted, I flopped on a park bench someplace and witnessed the brilliant sun seemingly being born from the cervical canal of a blushing Lake, my tired brain processing it all as the paralytic birth of another stillborn day. Crestfallen, I crawled toward my bed, determined to spend the bulk of it asleep.

It was dusk when I awoke, the warm orange-red rays of an ephemeral sun casting hellish shadows along the walls and ceiling and for a while I just stared and allowed my drowsy mind to toy with the images. I had an incredible hard on, one of those pulsating, near painful erections which threaten to burst from the casing and pulverize everything in sight and this was probably why most of the images took on long, lance-like projections with heads and limbs dangling from the arrowhead – dark and dreary images, insanely sacrificial, with genitals and organs left draping from the lamp shade and coat rack and door handle in a bloody carnal mess of slaughterhouse carnage and still too groggy to feel shock or disgust I just rolled my eyes, making mental lists of all I saw when suddenly my eyes fixed upon my protruding cock. A shameless apparatus, what! Even after its mutinous act the previous week it still stood stiff, puffed up as a beefeater smiling at me as if to say, "So, then, what's on the menu for this evening, there, guv'nor?" I remember wondering what it might be like if I suddenly went mad and gave it the axe. Would my mind be recompensed any? Would I become more composed, more studious, my musings like those of a young seminarian? Would I become sage-like, wise as a Carthusian monk? Or would I be constantly awoken in the middle of the night, a burning itch like fire between my legs – the ghostly sensation of a severed appendage driving me to madness? What strange cud the mind tongues over when fresh from the comforting folds of sleep – the last few frames of a cinematic mind flipping frenetically just before the blindfold of everyday life is promptly tied into place. Nothing the mind sees in this mediatory realm is too fantastic, too bizarre for the brain to comprehend. We understand the story instinctively and accept the morals as faithful as children. It's only when these morals are filtered through the meshwork of the waking mind do we question their sincerity, their veracity and meaning. What we label "strange" or "bizarre" in "real" life are really nothing more than the pressures of conformity strangling the mind and restraining the natural impulse to manifest itself creatively, to bring to life the majesty and depth of our being. In "real" life we scurry along the ocean floor like crustaceans fleeing from a common enemy which is ourselves. In "reality" we are nothing more than fear-stricken, castrated crabs.

And so, like Cancer the crab, I crawled out of bed no longer able to enjoy the blissful lunacy of Dreamland; "reality" was already forcing its way through the sand. Famished, I walked to the icebox to find what was left: the butt-end of a bread loaf and a knife's worth of butter. And it was then, munching absent-mindedly on this tasteless morsel, a warm, calming thought crashed over me like a tsunami: this was to be my final meal in solitary. The end of the month had finally arrived and I hadn't a penny to put toward the rent. My sentence was over. By tomorrow I would be a free man, free in the truest sense of the word, which is to say beholden to nothing, no one, not country nor creed, each road before me leading nowhere but the future. I might choose West or East or South...but not North. No, my bones are already brittle with the cold. I could see Spain or France or Egypt or Greece or Guatemala. I could make a pilgrimage to the Western border of China to see man's greatest monument to his manic xenophobia or I could sail the Red Sea and trek through Abyssinia in search of forbidden cities between Somaliland and Harar. All I needed was a passport and a little travel money. I might find work as a deckhand on some Russian freight vessel christened the *Pavlov Pavlovich* or *Ivan Ivanovanov* or some crazy name and float like a cork on the Fresh Water Sea carrying timber or coal or peat moss or peanuts or coffee or Q-tips or orange pekoe tea. That's the best thing about failure: no matter how devastating the downfall, how complete the disappointment there is always an abundance of options awaiting you once you're through kicking yourself in the ass. Excited, I choked down the bread and butter with a thimbleful of creamer and threw on my pants and crept quietly through the hall for a quick piss and a spritz bath, then down the stairwell toward the door to greet whatever were to blow my way and just as I was about to close that door for what might have been the last time I looked down and there on the bottom stoop, head hung, back hunched, bewitchingly sad and wondrously sullen, sat Elizabeth.

Upon hearing the door she sprung up like a fawn and spun around. Her hair was tied back, no doubt to allow the light to taunt and tease two prismatic diamond earrings and the apricot complexion of her columnar neck. She was wearing a long-sleeved lavender blouse (seductively unbuttoned), a khaki skirt (with pockets) and cream-colored stockings. A ruby pendant danced between her half-exposed breast. She looked as though she had just come from a wedding.

A wild, startled look filled her eyes, her bag clutched tight to her belly. She looked terrified. For the first time in my life I felt what some might call pity.

For a while we just stared at one another, neither of us seeming to believe our eyes. I didn't say a word. I didn't feel I had to. And besides, I was too busy letting my eyes ride the curves of her pear-shaped hips and professional dress. Quite a difference from the mutilated body parts still strewn about my room. For reasons unknown, even to myself, I've always harbored a bizarre fantasy for professional women – that is, women in professional dress. Perhaps it has something to do with the awesome task, in successfully stirring up that which everyone takes for granted as null and void. Or maybe it's simply the sight of the female form suggestively obscured behind a velvety veil. Nothing quite excites the mind as that which eludes the eye, no? My penetrating gaze must have been transparent.

"I just came from work," she said by way of explaining her dress. Then: "Well, not *just*...that is, I started to work but couldn't. Actually, I've been sitting on your doorstep all afternoon. I would have rang but I didn't know your number."

I didn't tell her I didn't have a phone. She seemed nervous, fidgety, almost frightened as she stood there shifting her weight from one leg to the other and toeing the pavement. An onlooker might have gotten the impression I was scolding her by sheer mind power, though in truth it couldn't have been more the opposite. I was overjoyed at the sight of her standing at my door. What's more, she had come without my calling her. She had come at the call of her own free will...or had she?

It was obvious she wished to tell me something and she tried several times though just before she began she stopped and looked around as if she'd committed a crime. I thought maybe the overzealous eyes of Canal Park's pedestrians were holding her back. I invited her inside. She accepted.

Upstairs in my room the fear in her face took on chameleonic changes, first to alarm and confusion, then disgust and contempt, then embarrassment for her innate, involuntary *faux pas* before finally recovering with bold, sympathetic eyes aimed directly at my ego. I deflected her offering and offered her a chair, which she took rather anxiously as though a snake might suddenly spring from the matting. I then offered her a drink which she declined (thankfully, since the place was dry) before taking rest in a chair by the desk.

Then I waited.

Of a sudden a strain of nuisance bent her brow. "I never asked for any of this," she began, just like that. "I mean, it wasn't any part of some scheme of mine to invite you up to Ian and Irene's last week. It was all was their idea...well, Irene's, mostly...and it's no secret now that it was all a mistake...a big, awful mistake."

My heart spat bromine. Is this why she came? To twist the stake still lodged in my chest? I was about to say something before she quickly continued: "And as for us meeting at the Mezzanine that night...a coincidence, nothing more. Don't you see? There was no star, no cosmic power of the moon or fog or streets or lampposts or anything. I've never believed in fate or destiny or any of that crap, not ever...well, maybe once, a long time ago, when I was just a little girl. But I'm not a little girl...not anymore. I'm a woman now...a grown, mature, intelligent woman who is completely in control of her life, got me?!" She nearly shook her fists before righting herself and saying as if awaking, "Look, I'm sorry about all that. I shouldn't have gotten so upset...not like that. I only wanted to make that perfectly clear before...."

She stopped herself short, then reached into her bag and pulled out the scroll and asked, "Did you write this?"

She was looking straight through me. I felt as though I had committed a crime...again. I tried to remember what it was I had written, if it was anything vulgar or indecent or obscene, but I couldn't summon a single line. In my haste to complete the pages on time I was throwing around words and images like a gravedigger throws dirt. It must be obscene, I thought. Why else would she be glaring at me like I'm some drunken hick who tried to pinch her ass in passing? All the same, it was an easy enough question. I answered it in silence.

"Why?" she wanted to know. "Why did you write me this... this....Oh, I don't even know what to call it!"

Why?! How the hell should I answer that? Then again, *why* the hell should I? She didn't have to come all this way just to throw it back in my face, did she? In fact, she didn't have to do a goddamn thing, not if it upset her so. How dare she come to *your* hole and treat you as some filthy, flea-ridden mongrel! You're no mongrel! You're a man, remember? (*Woof!*) So, then, stand up to her like a man, you mutt, and take back your bone! (*Grrr...Woof! Woof!*)

I straightened my shoulders and stood from my chair, then, extending my hand toward her, said, "Never mind. Just give me back the pages and let's forget the whole thing."

"*Never mind?!*" she exclaimed, protecting the scroll from my grasp. "Is that all you have to say? Never mind?! Forget it?!"

What manner was this?! Only a moment ago she treated me as Chinese fondue; now she refused to allow the finger down her throat. I hadn't a clue what to do next. The only defense for my offensive behavior were the pages themselves, and since I couldn't recall so much as a comma I was lost, stuck, sinking, standing on quicksand. I sunk back in my chair, smothered in frustration.

Another silence. Then:

"Jesus, this room!" she sighed, eyeing up the walls and ceiling like Alice in the rabbit hole. "How can you stand it? I'm not claustrophobic or anything, but...ugh! It feels like the walls are staring down at me!" Then, looking at my desk: "Is that where you wrote this? Well, that explains everything! How anybody can write anything but death and disease while sitting in this dungeon is beyond me." Finally: "I can't stand it any longer. I gotta get outta here. Come on...let's go for a walk."

As you wish, Esméralda.

Back outside and on the street I began walking toward the Maritime Observatory when I heard a voice behind me ask, "Where are you going?"

"I thought you wanted to go for a walk," I answered.

"Well, that was then," she said with imperial airs. "I've changed my mind. I'd rather go for a ride instead." She pointed toward a parking lot. "Come on...my car's over there."

For a brief, magnetic moment I thought I'd keep walking. Something in her voice resounded of disaster. (Later, usually at night, my mind would replay this moment over and over again in increments, like the looping of spliced film.)

"Well?" she whined. "Are you coming or aren't you?"

(*woof...woof...*)

Sitting comfortably inside her car I had the feeling I had finally pierced through her epithelium shell. The effect of this event, though, wasn't quite as I'd imagined; there were no grand explosions, no cellular infusions. Instead it was more like uncorking a bottle of expensive champagne you'd been saving for years only to find someone beat you to it and had polished off the bulk. I felt bottle-assed, plain and simple. So, then, why didn't I flee? Just open the door and roll out into the street? Easy. Never before had I a more *délicat* bottle-ass in all my life.

About midway to wherever she decided to speak.

"I hope you don't mind what I said back there in that room." (Strange, but just now it struck me she never called it *my* room...just *this* room or *that* room or *the* room.) "Only, it took me by surprise is all...what you wrote me, I mean. I never would have thought you so...descriptive...so brutal, yet at the same time so...poetic. I'm not used to reading such things, you understand. At first it made me sick..." (*Christ, what the hell were in those pages?!*) "...though after reading it over a few times I began to realize something...you're not like the others, are you? I mean, I know that sounds corny, like a line out of some movie or something, but...oh, I don't know...somehow it seems to fit you because you're so...so...*different.* I can't put my finger on it. You sit there so quiet, so easy, so willing for anything, but deep down I can't help the feeling you're hiding a pistol or maybe a machete. Sounds crazy, doesn't it? All this didn't occur to me till after the pages, mind you, but now, now when I look at you I still see someone who's helpless and weak, but at the same time dangerous. Does that make any sense? God, it all sounds so silly."

Not at all, dearie! Quite impressive, this compendium. And with what pluck, what faith in her inner eye did she reel it off so readily, so unreservedly. (More on this "inner eye" of hers later. For now...) I began to think perhaps I'd been a bit hasty in my earlier urge to flee. Perhaps she's so imperial, so commanding in her expression because her beauty, her belief in her supremacy demands it. She truly is a woman, inasmuch as I understand what little I know about such creatures: she is strong, cunning, sensitive, sensuous to the point of bursting; she likes to play the pet, the captive tigress and all that, though the moment the game starts to get too real she instinctively claws you to shreds, just to let you know she could never be subdued...not *truly*. This last bit revealed itself full bloom back at the hotel. I listened further for what other morsel she'd let fall from her calico tongue.

"It's like this," she continued, "I really *do* like you...I like you a lot, despite what happened the other night..." (I cringed.) "...and I can tell from what you wrote that you really like me too...a lot."

"Okay, forget all that 'supremacy' bullshit," I said to myself. "If she says *like* one more time I'm jumping."

Luckily, the car came to a halt. I looked out the window (I'd been staring at her legs the while) into a landscape I recognized all too well: Superior.

We parked in front of a drab, two-story house next-door to a mission which had towering from its chapel a blood-red neon cross which cast its ominous light across the adjoining lots and rooftops. It was night.

Before we left the car she turned to me and said, "Listen, I hope I didn't sound too upset...about what you wrote for me, I mean. I mean, I suppose there *could* have been something curious between us that night...that first night, that is...and I suppose the thought of it has me worried. It's just not something I'm ready to admit yet is all," after which she smiled, then leapt out the car.

Did I mention the female tendency for duplicity?

I followed her through her door and up the stairs to her apartment. The first thing I noticed was the smell of patchouli mixed with stale cat piss. (She has three, I soon discovered, one of which is overweight and shaggy and can't help but get the dingleberries. He's also got a mean streak three miles wide

Apples of Arcadia 137

but is far too fat and lazy to do anything about it, which makes for fun taunting. The other two – one a skittish neurotic, the next a mental simpleton, even for a cat – make for absolute hell in litter box maintenance. That, however, is one chore I flat-out refuse.) It was also incredibly dark, the only light being that of the neon cross which shrouded the hardwood floor and panel walls in a cerement of blood-soaked beams, setting to light the gory scene of Judas' Aceldama. Instantly, the cats all came rushing to our feet like starving Spanish brats. I stepped on the fat one's tail...on accident, of course.

After tossing her keys and bag on the buffet she then religiously strode round the room lighting one candle after another, then the incense, then an oil lamp in the kitchen till finally no trace of that bloody cross remained. This put me more at ease. Even more so when she said, "Make yourself at home. I'm gonna go change out of these grammie clothes."

Righto!

First thing first. I went straight to the kitchen to find the delectables this bird likes to keep stocked and, of course, get a good bellyful before she came to her senses and kicked me to the curb. I didn't know how much longer her hospitable mood would last.

At first I saw nothing but an unsightly display of pastel plasticware and a sickly-looking milk carton. I didn't dare open either since God only knows what I'd find inside and I wasn't in the mood for a spoiled appetite. After further digging I uncovered some pickled herring and a few bottles of imported beer. In the cupboard were some crackers. I fixed myself a plate and trotted off toward the living room.

It was obvious she had style, a certain decorous *savoir-faire*. An enormous tapestry modeled loosely after Sixteenth-Century Indo-European style lay dead center in the middle of the floor, commanding the room. The furniture – consisting of one folded-up futon, one old easy chair clawed to shreds by caterwauling cats and the aforementioned buffet – all stood attentively along the walls like sentinels awaiting further instructions from their Commander in Chief. Off in a corner were a bookcase and stereo.

Most of the books were nothing more than the usual clamjamfry of mystery and suspense and romance novels as well as the obligatory and exhausting Stephen King collection. In other words, pure gobbledygook. Fitting material for a sanctimonious mind, thought I, before wandering on toward the music.

If it's true what's said about only truly knowing a person once you know their taste in music then this girl is undoubtedly a precocious schizophrenic. Never before had I seen such an eclectic collection in all my life! It's as if she walked into a record store one day and said, "Alright, now, listen up. I'll take one of each including all you got on that Rastafarian flugelhornist from the Malay Archipelago or Chicago or wherever and Big Johnny Jacknife's B-sides, '56 to '70. Oh, and don't forget that rare edition of Teutonic sensation Siegfried So-and-so who plucks out allegros on the lyre with his toes." This girl had everything from Carrie Newcomer to Blur to bloody Crystal Method. All Folk and Pop and Futurama. No Blues, though. Or Wilco. Whatever. I chose one at random and put it in the player.

It was then, when sifting through the *musica insania*, I heard a voice like a siren beckoning me from the bedroom.

I found her standing at the foot of the bed wearing nothing but a smile, a sea blue gown and slippers, the latter of which I pretended to ignore. She had her knees folded like Venus on the half-shell, her hands clasped loose behind her back as if to offer me her touting breasts. "*Tout à vous*," she seemed to say. "*Tout à vous le monde!*" A motley array of candlelight and incense smoke filled the room; the incense smelled of opium, the candle wax of ether. Through the chloroformic haze the corner of my eye caught the queen-size bed adorned with celestial sheets and parish lantern pillows, all of it seeming to float and heave on waves of smoke. The whole room had the feel of a sacrificial lair.

Without a word and still smiling she came to me, took the beer and pickled herring and crackers from my hands and set them on the vanity, then took hold of my wrists and drew me toward the bed.

"What about Lester?" I asked like a fool.

"Shhh," was all she said. She must have traded him in for those earrings she wore earlier.

We were standing at the threshold, my hand beneath her gown and gliding steadily toward the goal when suddenly she pulled away and said, "You don't like living in that awful room, do you?" I shook my head. "You never did. Tell me you never once liked living in that awful room." Again I shook my head. At this she let her body fall limp into my arms and sighed and said, "Good. Because you won't have to...not anymore...not ever," before smothering my lips with her warm, wet mouth.

We fell upon the bed, first on our sides, then upright on our knees going at it like mad, me in a wild frenzy to get my belt unbuckled, she doing all she could to help. My hands wet with sweat and trembling like wartime stucco, I fumbled a moment before leaving it all to her, instead throwing my attention toward what she had concealed beneath her silk and satin gown. Already the straps had fallen off her shoulders and it was only a small matter of letting her arms fall down along her sides (which she did instinctively) before revealing what till then I had only seen in dreams. Her boobs were more oblong, more papaya-like in person and I was amazed at their elasticity as my thumbs and forefingers caressed and tugged her taut nipples. I was just about to go down around her belly when finally she succeeded in unfastening my belt and freed my stiff cock and fell upon it instantly, her lips and tongue massaging with such precision, such passionate fury my hands convulsed and twitched as if she were electrocuting me with that passionflower mouth of hers. After only a few moments of this and realizing much more would result in disaster I gently pushed her away and eased her pouting lips with my mouth before lowering her to the bed on her back to resume exploration of her glorious torso. I soon discovered her navel was pierced with a dumbbell pin and she squealed with delight as I flipped and tossed the gem with my tongue, all the while my fingers mimicking the motion down below. Before long she had worked up such a lather she couldn't stand it any longer and with both hands on my shoulders pushing downward I dipped my serpentine tongue into the nectar reservoir of Corpus Christi and by God in Heaven I honestly believed I was sipping His Divinity, the Sweet and Holy Spirit consecrated and secreted and flowing like a river through the Isthmus Uterinae down the Rugae Vaginales before pooling in the pink shoals of the Labia Minora where I bent my neck and praised His name and then suddenly, without warning, she swung her legs round my shoulders and grabbed hold of my neck and flung me to the bed and tore off my pants and underwear and threw them to the floor and straddled my groin and began grinding her hips like a bitch in heat, all the while her hot mouth on my neck and sucking and sucking as if she were expecting a mouthful of manna. All I could do was lie docile and lissome as a lump of clay – that is, a lump of clay with a jet pump sticking out of it. And as she dipped and slipped her dipsy-doodle duckhole down around and over and strangled every breath from my fibrous being I couldn't help but have the feeling I had suddenly become detached from the writhing pleasure and consciousness of my cock, the mindless seminal vesicle...but no, it's just the hypnotic power of her neoprene tongue tickling and teasing the purple veiny prong with metronymic accuracy and undulating potency and though possessed I still manage to break free from the velvet chains long enough to steal a peek of the primordial paramour who now looks strangely hideous as flames and shadows dance about her face and naked flesh, distorting the angelic into the alien demonic, an insular exotic semblance of pure spermatic membrane which twists and turns with each new thrust and I tell myself I'm not frightened, just excited as I see the orgasmic grimace begin to creep into her countenance and swallow my resistance and it's no use now my limbs are as latex, my joints as raw rubber and I stop fighting entirely and allow my body to be consumed whole or piecemeal or however by her vibrating hips, a whirling undertow of high fructose and clumps of clay and jet pumps and papaya and plumbago and her glorious golden torso like flames of supravaginal fire licking twin-leaf sheets and ligaments and now it's me spitting up poetry from the bowels of my being like cystic mucilage, bulbocavernous or otherwise or could that be Rachmaninoff I hear pounding away in the background his *Rhapsody on Paganini* or *Concerto No. 2* or *3* or no or yes it is but I thought I played Brahms or Bach or Liszt or Beethoven or *DeStijl* or *The Bends* or what the hell difference does it make it's no use now I'm about to blow sperm oil like a seismographic whale from the base of my spine to the second sacral vessel and visceral and Holy Ghost homunculus and crus and Christ and BLAMMO! off I shot like a rocket-powered dyad through the azimuthal bellyband into the soft folds of a powder-blue aureole till finally taking rest among celestial sheets and moon clouds and mollycoddled safe and warm and snoring inside the paramortal womb.

*   *   *

The months following the placental fall were quite soothing, quite soothing indeed compared with the *rigor mortis* days of the Shithouse Hotel, the lot of which has since passed on to the realm of Rhadamanthus. For a long while I did nothing, absolutely nothing which exerted any energy save bathing and eating and every so often allowing Lizzie to lick clean my thin, catechetic skin. I was born again, and like every newborn, every fragile infant, I was obliged to give myself fully, without the slightest mistrust into the bosom of the woman who bore me. Anything resembling any other life before her was to be thrown to the fire and forgotten (never mind the roughage of her Lester days still strewn about the walls and dresser tops like trophies). Not so much as a faint, nostalgic sigh was to escape my lips, not even when asleep. And lay to waste any notion for objection or question as to her wisdom in the matter. Body, mind and soul were hers and hers alone for the mending and reforming into whatever shape she wished.

The first to go was my wardrobe. Far too impractical (in the slovenly sense), thought she, for this new life which had been laid out before me. I was to watch and study with keen acumen the airs and fashions of the famous, for whom else to pore over when learning the clowning art but those whose bodies have become public property and whom the world over has selected as its dress-up dolls? Made perfect sense to me. Magazines, videos, television shows, movies – together we sat and watched and relearned the method for proper image management and I must admit I was a bit awash when it came time to choose between baggy-pant or boot-cut, button-down or flat-front; such matters the mind ignores when wondering how and when the next meal will be served or if the butter's gone rancid. Now, since such quandaries are quagmires of the past, with what agility can I whip and wheel through the mindless ads and columns of her endless stacks of magazines. Ah, what swell luxuries have the well-fed and sedated!

Other facets of my upraising included relearning how to walk and stumble, sleep and snore and keep my stomach small, how to hold a spoon, how to toss a meal, how to test my plate before adding salt or pepper, how to win at war games, how to lose at gin, how to gaze suitably upon her naked flesh (which is to say, how to turn my eyes before she felt the burn), knowing when and why or how loud or soft to play her favorite songs and when the same had turned to sludge, how to ignore and/or protect her insecurities (of which the beautiful are undoubtedly the most bountiful), inventing new and amusing ways by which to keep her entertained while pretending I'm the same, learning and aptly using the esoteric language of her snooty friends and family, themselves as much a mystery to the modern mind as Sanskrit (they're Scandinavian, doncha know), neglecting all my prior "impotent" pursuits so I might better be prepared upon her arrival home with towel and salve in hand to soothe her aching feet and if, upon inspection, I had performed my duties well she'd swab my brow and shower me with gifts such as cigarettes or beer or wine or marijuana or a fleeting, salivary glimpse into the maiden Amalthea, perhaps even later, just to nourish my faith, she'd allow the tongue a taste of the sacramental element which always leaves my resolution blissfully intoxicated for hours on end, my dizzy head dancing with dreams of the New Jerusalem and Happy Valley apples and oranges and bananas and plums and pears and papayas and waking the next morning willing to begin it all again.

As I've said, she showered me with gifts (which became more and more abundant and altogether exuberant since her recent promotion from part-time hostess to full-time cocktail waitress) all as a token of her maiden appreciation, sure, but also as a means of keeping us in cahoots when in view of her friends and family whose eyes were hawkish and ever-present. Already they questioned her decision-making in discarding Lester, longtime friend and (if they had their way) eventual family member. And who was this popinjay, anyway, who presumed to take his place? From whence did *his* family hail? England? Hmm. Ireland?! *Pshaw!* A drunkard, no doubt! Or a drug addict! Or, worse yet, *a Democrat*! I was ostracized outright...though not outwardly. No, the airs of their ancestry (which in the Northland is equivalent to the holy royal papacy) would not permit them to lose the least bit face by unseemly ungentility (a farce later revealed to me in spades). In short, I was dealt with coolly, if at all. And Lizzie, reacting to their reaction to me as though her grandeur had been damaged, took it upon herself to prove to them all that she, Elizabeth Marie John Paul XXIV, could not be disproved. Thus, everything needed for my introduction and elevation and sustentation in the eyes of onlookers was seen to with great care and mercurial attention. I was indeed a dress-up doll done up in the form of her Highness' desires, a product of her own papistical pride. It was this same pride, however, which inevitably betrayed her and, consequently, me.

It seems her family thought it odd I did nothing all day but read books and magazines and rub her aching bunion despite her protests as to my inherent worth, *viz.* my degree, my employment history, my aspirations in learning (which are nil), my aspirations in art (which are less than nil), my ability to wash dishes, my ability to lick boots, my ability to soothe the throbbing man-in-the-boat, etc., et al. In the end, though, the poison of her family's pointed arrows soaked through the skin and up into the eyeballs, causing her to view with distorted suspicion my apparent sloth. They succeeded in making her believe I was somehow taking advantage of her advantageous situation (the restaurant, remember). She was forced to reconsider my role in the ranks: now that I had been well fed and preserved and had procured enough equipage for a speedy Roman conquest I was forced out of the barracks and on toward the battlefield. In other words, it was high time I got a job, thought she, and I heartily agreed. After all, how long must one endure the laws of isolate relationships? I was bored to the orbs with sedentary seclusion. I needed new scenery. As it were, however, the thought of pounding the proverbial pavement for so narrow a reason as employment had drained my ambition straight after its resurgence. After only a week of pretending to scan the classifieds and collect blanks and send out résumés I sacrificed adventure for the sure thing: the Lounge.

To do so seemed obvious. Her apartment is just blocks off the Bridge and, subsequently, the Lounge, which makes for safe stumbling after a drowning night of work. Also, for some odd reason unbeknownst to me at the time, I left on good terms – my place behind the slab (should I ever want it back) was guaranteed. I was even given a raise, which struck me as ironic since previously I had taken that place for quite a penny. All the same, there it was and I took it, of course, and upon first resurfacing from my Bassalian subterfuge I was greeted highly and congratulatory as a gilded war hero, the patrons all patting me square on the back and singing songs and stuffing crisp bills into my pockets and welcoming me home with warm, tearful salutations. I fell back into the fold. I had set out on my quest like a brave young lad and had returned to them a success (that is, I hadn't committed suicide) and now it was time I tightened my belt and accepted my lot. *Now, repeat after me, yon Icarian son: I am now and forever will be a bartender in Wisconsin, Thirtieth state born tippybob and toppling and bound to by blood this great and gloriously hamstrung and soul-sick American Empire. Good. Now pour me a drink.*

So it went. Once again the days blended together in fog-filled oblivion sustained indefinitely by black coffee and bacon and underdone eggs, the usual nocturnal company falling sluggishly into file like so many drunken, chilblain-ridden infantrymen. Our mission: to protect and serve with judicial indifference the tosspot tendencies of a Northern population. By night we display unbreakable bravery and swiftness in operation as highly trained cannon fodder treading through enemy trenches; by day we dry our clothes and siphon out the poison and nourish our morale with black coffee and bacon and eggs and toast and tea and honeymuffin cornmeal cakes and movies and martinis and clumsy, sticky fumblings under gossamery sheets. Always the same story, each day a dry facsimile, each night a new lesson in the vulnerability of humanity with only ourselves to share our misanthropic knowledge. There comes, though, with this knowledge a power in its secrecy, albeit a wholly destructive power...destructive of its owner. Like lithium it may calm and soothe the demons of within, though once ingested it renders the spirit as listless as vermiculite, forcing one to wallow in a warm, hypnotic haze seemingly innocuous as a needle squirting saltwater, yet pestilent as a vial housing *Variola vera*. Only through each other's company are we able to maintain our posture – this by keeping the other in constant ignorance of his misdeeds, our deaf-and-dumb obedience to the civic reciprocity via drip-drop injections of a local anesthetic. Night after night we all partake in the vice of our own administration, every so often dragging along those few who've (thus far) proved themselves impervious to our mythomanic fashion, all of us laughing and joking and dancing and singing and carrying on as drunken cloud hoppers, though beneath the laughing and joking and drunken dance of false joy we, the chosen ones, are reveling at the thought of their bibulous demise as we lead them from the field toward the coffin-varnish coverture.

And for a while, in the spirit of celebration for my recent restoration, *my* place was chosen as the opiatic den, no doubt due to its location more than any sentimental reason. At first Lizzie treated the intrusion with a sympathetic mind. She agreed to suspend her suspicions as to the character of such people and give heed to my apparent social needs, viewing it all as healthy...that is, healthy in the sense I was settling back into the world, a few comforting shoulders upon which to fall. For a while she even allowed herself to enjoy in the fruits of such company, indulging in the constant flow of bodies, booze and drugs which invariably follows the after-hours crowd, though after only a few weeks her hospitality started to wane. Again, her faith in her infallible inner eye forced her to reconsider her previous open-mindedness. It seems there's something wrong with my taking confidence in the very people with whom I spend the whole night working and, what's more, those others whom I help get all hopped up and poppy-eyed. How could I stand to run with such dregs of human wreckage? she'd like to know. Doesn't the very sight of them make me want to vomit? Aren't I at all the least bit worried they'd suddenly get the mind to reach into their pockets and pull out a knife or a pistol or a septic hypodermic? It was impossible for her to imagine that never in their puff would they ever consider harming a single hair on my frail head; that even she, being so closely connected to me, as close as flesh and blood, even she was safe from any wrath they may reap due to the fierce hostility they harbored against humanity...that is, so long as she were willing to accept them all as equals, as members of a coexisting, substratal social order. As it were, her infernal inner eye could not be ignored. The eye told her the lot of them was nothing more than scum and not to be permitted in her home's sacred halls. At first she tried voicing her variance mildly, opting instead to say nothing at all, just making herself scarce whenever they came around, sequestering herself inside the bathroom or bedroom or wherever, every so often coming out of seclusion to toss about the crowd a condescending eye to let them all know it was time they retreated back into the holes from whence they came...a potentially fatal blunder. Her unearthly beauty already having them suspicious, once her true mind of their character was known they retaliated in true vandalic fashion, first through indignation and inflammation of her ego, then, once realizing her ego is non-flammable, through the only form of retribution their harrowed lives have taught them: they stole. First food from the fridge, then simple, silly trinkets and sentimental keepsakes, then on into the expensive stuff like silverware and party bowls and pewter candelabras. All harmless acts of treachery, to be sure, and since they never stole anything of mine I soon found myself amused at how much they'd take before Lizzie caught on to their scheme. It was curious indeed, these missing items of hers, and the randomness of their disappearance made for all the more intrigue (in her mind, anyway). At first she accused her sister who has her own key and who always stops by unannounced, even while we're away. An eruption soon ensued between the two despite the sister's violent protests of her innocence. I, of course, never said a word. Strange she never accused me...not *openly*, anyway. Just a few scant-eye slits every now and again to feel me out. Fishing for chimera, as it were. She was dumbfounded, frustrated, coming up only with fistfuls of hair till finally, as it happened, the culprits got cocky, a bit too sloppy in their series of successes. No longer, it seemed, were they satisfied with the lifting of crockery and candlesticks and other household gimcrackery. They decided instead to go straight for the source, the *sanctum sanctorum*, and defile the walls and halls of that which she held the highest and most holy: her beauty. They ransacked her wardrobe and jewelry and vanity and cold cream and lipstick and nail polish and imported Parisian toiletries and everything else which reeked of pretentious finery until finally, after her sister had been given the clear (her key was retracted temporarily), by process of deduction she caught on to the game and laid a trap. On a night I was to work, bound to lead the devotees toward the chapel antechamber, she excused herself for the night, explaining she had to watch her sister's newborn brat and wouldn't be back till morning. The outcome is obvious, and to say I saw it coming wouldn't be entirely untrue. I suppose in my mind I decided it all had to come to a vile end somehow; best if it be at someone else's bidding. After all, I'd still have to greet these people everyday with a smile, would I not? What's more, to lose their confidence might just as well mean a prolonged loss in underhanded income. Why piss in my own flowerpot? And besides, imagine what I would have missed...

As expected, we all sauntered back to my place after hours and on this evening in particular, no doubt due to Lizzie's absence, they allowed themselves to act especially despicable, spraying expensive perfume on the cats and in the litter box, playing handball with her powder puff, using black lace bras as slingshots and catapulting cosmetics and contraceptives and catshit and all the while the lot of them done up in war paint like some militant troupe of Times Square transvestites dancing about the room as lewd as can be envisioned, their faces drawn on in clown-like fashion and miming the gestures of a princess on the parapet waving down upon a crowd and wearing as a crown a satin panty coronet and me in the corner wearing eyes of perfect satisfaction making damn sure I

Apples of Arcadia 149

took no part in any of it whatsoever. And when she walked in, catching them all in the midst of their mayhem, I raised my glass to her in salutation and promptly aided in ushering out the traitorous riffraff and collected all her personables and filed them neatly in order from Ankle Band to Zephiran and congratulated her on a plan well wrought. As to be expected, it took some persistence on my part to assure her all was understood, that, indeed, I was on to my cohorts' petty thievery, the scamps, yet knew of no way by which to bring them all to justice since accusing them outright would no doubt result in my disfellowship at work and, possibly, disemployment. Then, like a gentle stroke of genius, her clandestine scheme smoothed my thwarted brow and surely I would have stepped in before anything of value fell through their filthy fingertips and *Bravo, beautiful! Bravo!* As it turned out, my appeal to her intellect as well as her beauty was a stroke of brilliance in its own right and she bought the bullshit story, though not without the customary cold shoulder for having so foolishly allowed admittance of such lowlifes in the first place. All the same, I escaped the ordeal unscathed, saving face both with Lizzie as well as my friends, perhaps even gaining a notch in the eyes of the latter; they could only imagine the wrath I received after their hasty departure. Needless to say, never again are any of them allowed within the royal temple walls... at least not while Her Holiness is prowling about.

To continue on with this inner eye...

I don't mean to belittle it. After all, she had my friends pegged from the start; it was her snobbish pretenses which prompted their rebellion. The eye was dead-on – *she*, on the other hand, was the faulty one. If only she'd learn to curb her conjectures, shelve them high in the mind's mental library brought down only for future reference rather than hasten their veracity. Still, countless times I've stood in awe, absolute awe of her ability to gather from just one encounter the gist of a person's character, whether they're trustworthy or not – "shady" she'd say – then watched while her assumptions proved true as God's law, usually at the expense of some sap whom she'd condemn as a dupe, an utter ignoramus who deserved to be deceived. Countless times, I say.

There was once, however, this inner eye of hers failed, and miserably.

Just last week, in fact, while raking up crab grass cuttings beneath a warm red zinc ore sun and drifting off into a daydream (Since her recent promotion Lizzie aligned for us a new arrangement: she pays the rent while I tend like a slave to the household needs, everything from dusting to dandelion slaying. It seems her generosity knows no bounds.) I was lifted from my reverie by a soft, zephyrean voice blowing in from behind. I turned to see a man dressed in rags, filthy and torn as one might imagine on a wartime refugee or a hungover football hooligan. He was obviously neither, though the patched canvas bag slung over his shoulder might have suggested the former if he weren't wearing such a broad, beaming grin.

"How do you do?" he asked, extending his hand. Rough and sweaty, yet steady and sincere.

"Fine, thank you," I said, greeting him in turn. "And you?"

"Not bad...not bad at all. Wonderful day, wouldn't you say?"

At this I noticed he also wore soiled deerskin mukluks with thick wool trousers and a battered blue-green parka tied loose around his waist. Normally this wouldn't strike me odd, such clothing quite easily kept on the rack well into May and maybe even June, though this was July. Even in the Northland we have our few days of sun and for the past few weeks it's never been below seventy.

"Wonderful enough for yard work, anyway," I replied.

"So I see," he said, chuckling. "Mind if I help?"

"Not in the least," said I, handing him the rake.

After the grass had all been bagged and the sidewalk swept and the dandelions slain I thanked him for his help and stirred up some lemonade and invited him to join me for a cool, well-won glass. He accepted, of course, and after a tall eager gulp on both our parts we settled ourselves on the front steps to catch our breath and wipe our brow and it was then he decided to tell his story.

His name was Jim. He'd been on the road for nearly six months now...on foot. From North Carolina originally, said he, though to listen to him he might just as well have said New Hampshire or California or Nepal; in either case I'd have been hard-pressed to prove otherwise since he had no trace of accent or sense of nationality. An ex-lawyer educated at Columbia, he explained he just woke up one day and decided the life he was living was not the life for him. Since then he's traveled across the country with the trade winds, so to speak, just trying to keep ahead of the snow-and-ice season. "Sometimes, though, it's not so easy," he confessed. "What with all the unforeseen setbacks, the weather and otherwise." Thus, the mukluks and parka and thick wool pants which he swore he took up for a song at the Salvation Army in Bismarck four months back. Good thing too, he proclaimed, for his shoes were stolen while asleep in some boxcar and his "spring trousers," as he called them, wore clean through the seat just last week. "Lucky I had anything at all," he laughed. He's seen Texas, New Mexico, Montana, California, Florida, Idaho, West Virginia, Washington, Iowa, Wyoming, Oklahoma, Arkansas, Ohio, Hawai'i. ("First time in Wisconsin, though," with a humble, hangdog grin.) He's scaled the Adirondack in search of witch hazel ("In vain"), scoured the Aleutian Islands for a wife ("Also in vain"), took shelter from a tornado in a Carlsbad cavern, braved the waters of Campeche Bay "on a bet", soaked his bones in the sulfur baths of Big Sur ("Bliss!"), swam with the Stream off the coast of Cuba ("Never again!") and now he planned to plot his way through Michigan's Upper Peninsula and down toward Lansing where supposedly there's some family with whom he'll lay up a while and regain his resources and then, "Who knows? Maybe Nova Scotia or New

Guinea or the Narragansett inlet, only..." (his enthusiasm suddenly dropping dramatically) "...only it's been so long since I've slept in a bed or even had a bite to eat. I've already tried the mission next door but it seems they're filled up and not being familiar with the surrounding area at all I really don't know...."

"Say no more," I said, stopping him short. "We've an extra bed upstairs that's hardly ever used. You're more than welcome to it, if you like."

His face lit up like a halogen lamp. Obviously he wasn't expecting me to grant his plea so readily, his hands and elbows kneading his knees and thighs in disbelief until finally, not knowing what else to do, he clasped my hands in thanks and asked, as if to pinch himself, "You're sure you won't mind?"

"Not at all," I assured him. "Stay as long as you like."

"And your wife?"

At this I had to laugh, not so much at what he said as the thought of the look on my "wife's" face when she finds out what I've done. I couldn't control myself, my laughter growing more and more maniacal with each stage of her frustration from doubt and dubitation to anger and disgust, then exhaustion once she realized there was nothing she could do; the key had been handed over and only a monster would take it back. The idea of her squirming as if covered in lice had me damn near rolling on the freshly-trimmed lawn my accomplice helped preen, himself at first laughing right along with me, then suddenly silent and stony, a look of consternation on his vagabond brow. Perhaps he thought he'd made a mistake and threatened his chance at a hot and a cot. I thought I'd set his mind at ease by throwing my arm around his gritty neck and saying, "No, Jim, I'm sure she won't mind." Then I clanked my silent partner's glass and smiled and said, "*Salud!*"

After the lemonade we collected his things and went inside. I insisted he use the bathtub (as polite as possible) and while he soaked I threw his washables in the machine and sent his woolens to the cleaner's and made sure the middle bedroom was in order. Once he had finished bathing I invited him to anything he fancied in my wardrobe (turned out we were the same build) and as he dressed I went into the kitchen and prepared a mighty meal of spaghetti and meatballs, kielbasa and cabbage, soup, sandwiches, cheese, crackers, beer, pickled herring, wine, ice cream cake and coffee and when he came out the bedroom and into the kitchen he just about wept at the sight of all before him and I just about fell to the floor on my knees, laughing. He looked every bit the raw recruit. The sight of him standing there before me in those clothes, the clothes especially handpicked for me upon *my* conscription, was almost too much to bear. All the same, I maintained and after some time of his standing in the doorway scratching himself and salivating and wondering when it would be appropriate to take a seat and eat I withdrew a chair from the table and said, "Please, be my guest."

Before the word "Thanks" reached my ears he was sitting down and diving hands-first into the spread. I sat back and grinned and wiggled my ass like a webworm.

After tea and toothpicks we retreated to the front room for cigarettes and coffee whereupon, now fed and fully relaxed, he again set in on his various adventures. His bed and board now seemingly secure, his manner of speech changed from suspicious and forced to composed and, at times, eloquent as he told about his travels down South, especially Mississippi where he'd nearly been dragged toward a tree with a rope for asking some redneck for a lift and, failing that, a smoke, then on into New Orleans which was beautiful, sure, but the stench of piss and vomit made him so dizzy and nauseous he had to take refuge inside the doorway of a whorehouse till the wind blew East and he went West toward Texas and New Mexico where he aided in the stealth entry of a poor Mexican family claiming to be descendants of Diego Rivera and who, after he'd helped them arrive safely across the Border, beat him blind and stole his clothes and left him for dead and naked with two broken legs which he dragged along the Rio Grande eating insects and honey till finally coming upon a small town with fresh water and a hospital and after recovering miraculously in just three weeks' time he again was on the road making damn sure he was walking away from the Border north toward Carlsbad and just as a tornado began its dark, ominous swirl Lizzie walked in through the living room door.

At first she just stood there, stunned, speechless in awe at the sight of this strange man sitting comfortably in her home puffing out smoke and wearing my clothes. In her hand was a bottle of liqueur which, no doubt, she intended as a gift upon completion of my daily tasks and, considering it such, I leapt up off the floor toward her and kissed her flushed cheek and before she could pull away I took the bottle and said, "Ah, Drambuie! How thoughtful! It'll go perfect with the coffee!" I then turned to show the label to Jim who responded as if on cue with an aristocratic nod. Threatening to burst aloud at this, I turned back to Lizzie and said, "Now you stay here and make yourself comfortable while I go and fix us all an ice breaker," before scurrying off toward the kitchen without so much as an introduction.

Once in the kitchen out of eyeshot I let loose one of those surd, convulsive bursts which fix to fold the stomach like a falafel pita. Figuring I hadn't much time, I quickly recovered and fumbled for a few glasses and poured us all a spot before trotting off toward the front room to sprinkle saltpeter on my tinder.

Upon returning I found Jim, like a gentlemen, had given up his seat on the futon to Lizzie who peered on in amazement as he stood in the center of the room retelling his tales and waving his arms through the smoky air with the passion and gusto of an East Coast conductor. Stifling my laughter, I set the coffee and liqueur atop the buffet and fetched a chair for our own private *Kapellmeister* who was so caught up in his stagy technique he didn't even seem to notice my presence, not even when I intruded upon the proscenium to set a small table on the floor before the futon and present both him and

Lizzie with their cups before taking my seat for the last of the *melodram*, the bulk of which was nothing more than a mere embellishment of before. All the same, it was all new to Lizzie who seemed wholly enraptured by this strange man's antics, allowing herself a smile every once in a while and sometimes even a facetious giggle which only managed to fuel Jim's engine until finally, after Cuba and Columbia and Big Sur and the Border and Carlsbad and bonesetters and pretty young nursemaids not nearly as dazzling as Lizzie's blue eyes (a nice touch, I thought) and tornadoes and sandstorms and Santa Anna and Afer he fell back in his chair with a thud and a sigh and a wide, princely smile on his dry, parched lips. I had to applaud him. He had given quite a performance on Lizzie's account and as his prize I handed him a smoke and a pony of Drambuie which he tossed down at once in a fierce swallow. I handed him the bottle.

For a while no one spoke. Not an awkward silence, mind you, for it wasn't at all awkward (at least not for me) nor was it entirely silent. Something like the rustle of leaves after a storm, a storm which threatened to tear off the roof. I looked at Lizzie; her hands held her knees as if steadying herself should a bough suddenly burst through the window behind her. Her lips were pursed in a thin, pretentious grin which wouldn't serve to deceive a schoolboy when suddenly, out of frustration at the persistent silence, she cocked her head at Jim and said, "You know, I don't even know your name."

"Oh, pardon me, ma'am," said Jim, mortified. "James' the name." He rose from his seat and, wiping his palm on the thigh of my pants, thrust out his hand. Lizzie took it as eager as she would a dead mackerel. "And I just wanna tell you," he added, "how fortunate I feel to have come across two of the most kind, most genuinely warm-hearted people in all Wisconsin. You truly are blessed, the both of you, for taking into your home so freely a strange man off the street and feeding him spaghetti and sausage and soup and offering him strong coffee and fine liqueur and cigarettes and letting him tell all his silly adventures."

"The pleasure's all ours, Jim, I assure you," said I. "Isn't that right, love?" with a salamander grin.

At first she said nothing, just smiled the kindest, most warm-hearted smile she could muster. Then: "So, Jim, you say you've been living on the street?"

"That's right, ma'am," said Jim after exhaling a blue-gray plume. "Been about, oh, six years now, I guess. 'Mazing how fast the years fly by, innit?"

"So, then," she began, ignoring his intromission, "I understand you're staying at the mission next door."

"No, ma'am." A sip of Drambuie. "Your Jeffrey has been so kind as to offer me the middle bedroom...and let me again express how honored and pleased I am to have stumbled upon in Superior of all places a bath and a bed and...."

"Excuse us, won't you, Jim?" she cut him short, pinching my knee before storming off like a cyclone through the kitchen door.

Jim shot me a look of concern as if to say, "Was it something I said?" I gave him a wink and rose easy from the futon and filled his glass and said, "Not to worry, Jim. Be back in a jiffy. Feel free to have a listen to whatever music you see," before taking leave to play pots with the wifeypoo.

She stood bent over the sink, her beautiful face erubescent with rage, her dazzling blue eyes staring straight down the drain, then hard at me as if to say, "Better start explaining, boy, and fast!" I had to use up the better part of my reserve to conceal the smirk which had already betrayed me, turning it instead into a hollow beam of ignorance while peering toward her with questioning eyes as if searching for the meaning of this sudden *tête-à-tête*. Once she realized I was taking the defense she moved her King's Pawn and sighed, "Please tell me this is all a joke."

"All *what* is a joke?" [Pawn meets Pawn head-on.]

"You know damn well what I mean!" she snapped, forcing her Queen out from behind the front line, just to feel me out. "You let a strange man into our home and feed him and bathe him and then, as if that weren't enough, then you invite him to sleep in our bed?"

"Not *our* bed," I corrected her, having no choice but to bring out my Knight. "Surely you wouldn't think I'd give over *our* bed of bliss and paradise so readily. No, I'm sure he'll be quite comfortable in the middle bedroom. However, if you think he'd prefer the other...."

"Oh, stop it! You know goddamn well what I mean," she sneered, retreating her Queen. Then: "Christ, why do you have to be so snide all the time?"

"I don't know," I shrugged. "What does *snide* mean?" [Pawn to King-Rook three.]

She shook her head while composing her next move, moaning, "Look, we don't know a thing about him."

"Sure we do. His name's Jim and he's traveled all over America and stuff and he's seen all these fantastic places and everything...."

"He's a freeloader, can't you see that?"

"He's not...not in the least. He's an honest guy. He even helped me with the yard work this afternoon."

"Oh, I see," said she, shifting her eyes while fingering her Bishop. "That explains why you were so charitable with the Drambuie, now, doesn't it? Feeling a bit guilty, were we?" [Bishop takes Pawn.]

"Not at all," I objected, ignoring her trap. "Like I said, he seems like a nice guy and I just thought we should show our appreciation is all." [Knight takes Bishop.]

"*Your* appreciation, you mean." [Pawn to Queen-Knight three.]

"Whatever. Anyway..." (sensing vulnerability) "...he's not a freeloader, as you say. Would a freeloader have been so resourceful in his adventures?...His *lone* adventures, I might add." [Bishop to King-Knight five.]

"He's a liar!" [An errant Knight move.]

"We don't know that for certain."

At this she shot a look as if to say: "Surely you can't be *that* gullible."

"Okay," I continued, trying to keep my advantage, "so what if he tends to exaggerate a little? That doesn't make him a liar, does it?" [Bishop takes Knight.]

"I don't trust him," she said simply, folding her arms. [Bishop takes Bishop.]

"He's given us no reason not to. And besides..." (sensing something amiss) "...even if he has told some crazy stories...*I* trust him. Doesn't that count for anything?" [Pawn to Queen-Knight three.]

"He's a bum!" she exclaimed. [Castles.]

"Easy," I said, wafting the air as if to smother her voice. "He can hear us, you know." [Pawn to King three.]

"I don't care if his *mother* can hear us. He's a liar and a bum and he's sick to the skin and if you can't see that then perhaps you'd be better off packing your things right alongside him and then the two of you can run off together and have your own wild, fantastic adventures." [Queen takes Knight. King in check. A bluff move.] "Speaking of your things," she went on, her voice sarcastically soft, "why the hell is he wearing your clothes...the clothes I bought especially for you?"

Her bluff no real threat, I thought I'd slip the attack with a diversion. "Because," I admitted, "his clothes are in the wash downstairs." [King to King two.]

"What?! You mean *my* washing machine?!"

I nodded.

"God, that's just like you! What are *we* supposed to use now, huh? Answer me that." Silence. Then: "Nothing, that's what...not until you scrub it good and clean with bleach and baking soda, right!" Her entire body convulsed uncontrollably as if Jack Frost himself were nibbling her lobes. "Ugh!" she quivered. "I can see his undies rolling around in there as we speak." [Pawn to Queen four.]

At this I broke. I had no choice. [Pawn takes Pawn.] I burst out laughing right in front of her beautifully agitated, erubescent face. It must have been minutes before I was able to look at her again with a level eye and when I did I noticed her arms were folded and her head was cocked and her lips locked tight in a bloodless pout.

"That's it," she said at last. "He's leaving," before tossing back her hair and turning as if to flee. [Knight to King-Bishop three.]

"He can't leave," I said, catching my breath before righting myself for a subtile move. "Not yet." She glared on, curious. I continued: "His clothes are still at the cleaner's downtown. They won't be ready for a couple days, minimum." [Knight to King-Knight one.]

She stopped dead in her step and spun around. "I thought you said they were downstairs?" she asked, bewildered and (I sensed) somewhat relieved. [King to Queen-Knight two.]

"Some are," I responded, smiling. "Some are downstairs and some are downtown." [Knight to King-Bishop three.]

She stood in the doorway with arms akimbo, no doubt wondering what the hell kind of game I was trying to play. She then peered about the room a moment as if testing the air until finally, sensing a breeze, she nodded her head and with a smile said, "Oh, is that so? Then I suppose only *some* of his bags will be hung on his back as he hikes his way to Michigan...*tonight*." [Pawn to King five. Playing the same game.]

"Nope."

"Oh really? And why is that?"

"Because his bags are being washed as well." [Soldier's wind. Pawn takes Pawn.]

At this she shook her head and frowned and looked at the ground and cried, "Why? Why are you doing this to me?" [Bishop to Queen-Bishop five.]

Pins in my skin. "Just what is it, exactly, I am doing?" [Pawn to King-Knight three.]

Her frown turned into a scowl. She must have noticed a weakness somewhere for suddenly, without warning and with both hands on the battle-axe, she curdled her neck and snarled, "He's leaving and that's final!" [Bishop takes Pawn.]

"He's got no place to go." [Pawn takes Bishop.]

"That's not my problem." [Knight takes Pawn.]

"How can you be such a bitch?" [Knight takes Knight.]

Fatality. One must never show one's true emotions in the eyes of one's enemy.

An efflorescent smile on her petal lips, she stepped from the doorway toward me and, with a dignified air, said, "This is *my* apartment and I say he's leaving, and if *you* don't like it then you can leave too...*love*," before turning on her heel and marching straight out the kitchen through the front room past Jim and the Drambuie on into the master bedroom, slamming the door behind her. [Rook takes Knight. Checkmate. End game.]

No bluff. Her threat was real. And to think I thought elsewise knowing full well before every argument she'd always have the advantage, the stronghold of every game before the first piece was moved. This indeed is her place, as she reminds me countless times, and if I have any notions contrary all I need do is look down at the board before me...the King and Queen are always inverted. They stand there like stone pillars, fixed, indifferent, evidence of the silent agreement upon entering this domain: so long as I take refuge in the warmth of her rays I must accept these terms as law lest I wind up like poor Jim who must now be sitting in the front room like a dazed Lazarus watching the boulder roll back over the light hole.

I found him on his stool, his hands between his knees looking intently up at me as if to read my thoughts. Where do I begin? I remember thinking. How to begin telling this man all I had promised upon drawing a chair at the head of the table was, in truth, nothing more than a whiff and a lick? Then again, why say anything? Surely he must have guessed something amiss the way Lizzie blew past him like a lodestar satellite. All the same, there he sat, silent and still, his eyes as two huge saucers reflecting my sorrow, a faint glow beginning to grow above his head like a halo. Honestly, he looked every bit the saint while sitting there silently, patiently awaiting the verdict to be thrown in his face. If only he'd looked more criminal, more Apache than Apostle I'd not have stood there stumbling like some guilt-stricken instigator. As it were, his silence and disarming half-smile made him seem damn near magnanimous. Hell, might as well tell Heaven I invented the H-bomb. Luckily, just as some meaningless words were about to be uttered, his magnanimity rang true and rescued me from confession.

"Look," he began, rising from his chair. "It's alright. You don't have to say a word. I heard everything. Just let me collect my things and I'll be on my way."

"No, Jim, it's not alright!" I felt like yelling. "It's nowhere near alright and, by God, I'm going to do something about it! First off, you're not going anywhere! If anyone's leaving it's me, though not before I have a few more words with the li'l missus. In the meantime you just sit tight and light another smoke and pour yourself a sipper and leave the rest to me...only remember, if I have to handcuff you to the radiator, YOU'RE NOT GOING ANYWHERE!!!"

Instead what did I do?

I looked toward the bedroom and shrugged my shoulders and shook my head and said, "Sorry, Jim, but she's not been feeling well lately." Then I led him toward the door.

Down the stairwell on the way outdoors he was silent. Not the slightest objection to the arrant turn of events, just acceptance, acceptance in silence, and it's this which cut me most. If only he'd have been the least bit vocal in expressing his disappointment he would have provided me (however unintentional) a soundboard by which to relieve the superabundant, pent-up sense of impotency which consumed me then. As it were, his silence reaffirmed the sad truth of the matter: in the presence of this woman I had indeed become impotent. What little strength and self-propensity I had at all in my frail shell had been chewed up, digested and had passed through the bowels and primrose hole of Her Majesty, the Maharani. I have traveled through the viscera of Ushas and Varuna and have come out a eunuch.

Nearing the doorway leading out into the front porch he finally mentioned some words regarding his belongings still swirling in the washer and I might have said something about having them ready first thing in the morning when I opened the door and peered out and nearly bowed down in reverence at what I saw. It seemed my prayer for relief had been answered for there before us, drowning out the outside world, was a downpour fit for a Testament scene. All I could do was smile. Jim, on the other hand, could not. In fact, my smiling must have provoked him some; for the first time since meeting him I sensed indignation – a wholly deserved indignation, of course. I smiled the brighter; it made him seem more human. All the same, I thought I'd come clean and, turning toward him, said, "Look here, Jim. Let's forget about all that was said. There's no way in hell I'm letting you leave...not with it raining slate iron sheets, right?" He smiled. I continued: "However, I can't very well bring you back upstairs. Knowing Lizzie she'd most likely call the cops and have us both removed...by force." He ceased smiling, nodded solemnly, then looked quizzically toward me. What, he wondered, was to be done?

On the porch was a couch I'd grudgingly dragged downstairs once the cats had clawed their way through the corduroy upholstery. It was torn to shreds and smelled of bad litter but at least it was dry and would stay so for the night. Any normal person would have been embarrassed as hell for attempting to pass this frazzled dust mat for a bed, let alone offering it to someone else as such, though it was all we had and after explaining to Jim that I, myself, had spent many a night on the same couch and the cushions were actually quite comfortable he agreed to the proposal with a handshake and a smile. After all, what else did he have? I crept upstairs for some sheets and a pillow and a plate of whatever was left from the spread and when I returned he had already made himself comfortable. I remember envying his complacency, given such surroundings, and wondered if I had felt it so sufficient when taking refuge on this porch amid a pouring sky of stars. Then again, our reasons for doing so varied dramatically – all except one: nowhere else to go. As I said, he looked so peaceful lying there on that clawed and tattered couch I felt damn near covetous of his lowly situation, though still not without fault for it turning out thus, and when he asked for a good book and a candle by which to while away the waking hours I leapt up unreservedly and (him being a learned man) retrieved my stolen copy of Dante's *Divine Comedy* translated by Longfellow and bade him goodnight.

Covetous, did I say? That describes to a T the way I felt when tramping up the stairs toward the bedroom and our bed sheathed in satin sheets and icecaps. While Jim would be surrounded Dante's torrential landscapes and candlelight and lightning and the rhythmic sound of rain I would be surrounded by a different kind of storm...an inner storm of icefalls and frozen skin and silence. Jim had complacency and a good book to embrace; all I had to embrace was the emptiness of shadows. All the same, I smiled. A strange satisfaction swept over me then, even when confronted with Lizzie's azurite eyes which bore right through me. I was no longer there. I was lying on the front porch, bathed in candlelight, surrounded by the sounds of a natural born storm, nibbling a piece of cheese given to me gratis and thumbing through the beautifully eerie imagery of Dante Alighieri.

The upshot of all this didn't arrive till days later. The downpour lasted seventy-two hours and while Jim, I'm sure, couldn't have been more pleased at his meteorological luck I was left to wonder when in the hell that goddamned storm would end. Upstairs the atmosphere could best be described as macroclimatic, the weather ranging from the regions of the kitchen and the morning coffee on into the evening and the icy cold bedroom enough to force an Eskimo into seclusion and sacrifice the topography to the stuff of myths and legends. And though Jim never once intruded upon his hosts by invading the boundaries of our airy hospitality, his very presence upset the balance of the polar pulls, forcing the clouds from out beyond the towering peaks of Mesopotamia on toward our own imaginary Kingdom of Micomicon. Not that the signs were wholly illusive; an electric current had occupied the air for months at just enough voltage to cause a paralysis – a peaceful, ill-provoking jolt which could scarcely stir the convictions of garden slugs. Thus, that morning upon awaking and finding broken her strict and quite clear intentions concerning the "freeloader", Lizzie made use of every opportunity to display not so much her anger (as I'd spent the previous night preparing for, mentally collecting my things in a neat, depressingly small pile) but, rather, her *disappointment* I should so readily disregard her wishes for the favor of some stranger. Defending myself against this attack was useless, for there simply was no attack, only disappointment, as I say, and to acknowledge this spectral fusillade would have meant the same as taking up the axe against an army of ghosts. Consequently, my apparent indifference to her personal suffering only infused salt upon my supposedly injurious behavior until finally, not allowing any more of my garish disrespect, she decided once and for all that under no circumstance would she allow that thieving liar and rogue of a man the use of her solely self-advantageous, yearly-leased roof. I had to laugh. I had heard this threat before. All the same, I thought it best just to be done with it and acquiesce with her wishes for one reason: just as the final tear strolled down her hot cheek and nimble chin and neck, as the last fierce gasp from her thunder-gust throat ruffled the foliage of a flowing land I looked out the window and sighed with relief. The rain had finally ceased. The storm had been weathered. I leapt down the front steps to tell Jim the good news.

I found him sitting cross-legged on the couch, his face aglow with perfect contentment. In his lap was the copy of Dante's poetry, open to what must have been an especially juicy passage for he wore an enormous grin, damn near wolfish, while his fingers stroked the pages as some young maiden's buttocks. Embarrassed, I turned away to notice his bags already packed and resting neatly in a pile by the door, ready for travel. Embarrassment turned to envy.

After what must have been a full minute he finally looked up from the book and, still grinning, said, "Oh, hello. I hope you haven't been standing there long." I shook my head. "Only," he continued as if to himself, "it's been so long since I've come across Dante, his vision and language, a man all at once of the past and future." After this, his fingers continued to float across the page as if to utter a final prayer before WHAP! he slammed shut the book and set it gently on the cushion beside him, then leapt off the couch and said, "So, this is when we shake hands and part, is it?"

Taken a bit aback by his matter-of-fact bravado, I shook his hand and watched in silence as he slung his bags across his back like a dock loader before heading for the door when finally I spoke up and shouted, "Wait!" He stopped dead in his tracks and spun around. Not knowing what I wanted to say, I said the first thing that came to mind.

"This is silly," I began. "There's no need for you to run off so soon, is there? I mean, at least let me offer you one more meal."

He stood a moment as if in thought, then shook his head and said, "I appreciate that, Jeff, but I really think I've put the both of you out enough already."

"Nonsense! It's only food. We have more than enough. Besides, you'd be doing me the favor." No reply. "If nothing else at least let me pack a few sandwiches." Still nothing. Then: "A ride. For Christ's sake, at least let me give you a ride!"

"A ride? Where to?"

"Wherever you need to go. It's the least I can do."

He thought a moment, then agreed with a nod.

"Good," I gleamed. "Wait here. I'll be right back," before dancing up the steps to get the keys to Lizzie's car.

Needless to say, the idea was shot down before the words crossed my lips. The thought of handing over even *more* to this man, a man who'd already received more than he deserved (by "deserved" she meant "earned"), was far too much to bear. Why couldn't he have just slipped out the door in the middle of the night without waiting till morning to try and weasel more? she wondered.

"Look," I began, spreading mustard on rye. "None of this has anything to do with him. The sandwiches are *my* idea." She shook her head as if to say, "I should have known." Then: "Oh," I continued, containing a grin, "there's one more thing. I told him I'd give him a ride."

Silence. A slight electric shock. I finished making the sandwiches and packed them in plastic, then turned toward her with an open palm.

"What? You mean *my* car?"

I smiled.

"You're crazy! There's no way I'd let you do something so stupid. What if he tries something?" Confused, I cocked my head. Mocking me, she did the same, then said, "What...what if he tries to hurt you and take off with the car?"

Not really knowing how to respond (that is, not exactly sure if she was concerned for me or for her car), I shook my head and closed my palm, then turned to walk away, hissing over my shoulder, "Too late. The offer's been made." I then stole toward the bedroom to find the keys atop the dresser resting next to her open tip box chock-full of fifties. "Hmm," thought I. "Perhaps a bit of gas money for the road," before slipping a bill in my back pocket and walking off toward the kitchen to bid my benefactor farewell, though when I poked my head around the doorframe I found her hunched upon a chair, her head between her knees. She looked exhausted. I thought I'd just let her be.

Downstairs Jim was standing by the door, bags in tote and rearing to go. He looked restless. He relaxed a little when I handed him the sandwiches, offering in return a shy, meager smile which thickened considerably when I dangled the keys. It was obvious he felt he'd overstayed his welcome. I wished him well-being and away we went.

On the highway headed east I began to notice something strange, a very important something which, if unchecked, could well mean nothing short of disaster. What was this? I wondered. Had I lost the money? I felt my back pocket; the bill was still there. Was it something with the car? I scanned the gauges, everything good. Lizzie came to mind, her sitting the way she was. Could this be bothering me? Perhaps, yet something else lingered, something so worrisome it compared only with dread. It engulfed me so completely I nearly pulled the car to the side of the road in a panic but before I did I thought of Jim. I looked toward him. He was gazing out the window, oblivious to my mood. This calmed me some, though nowhere near so much as to put my mind at ease. Beads of sweat formed shallow puddles on my brow; vein-like rivulets streamed down my swollen face; palms wet; tongue dry; thoughts of blood, daggers darting wildly through my overcharged mind. Again I thought of Jim. Why so silent? I wondered. Was the idyllic scenery really so enrapturing? Or was something else occupying that vagabond brain of his? Could Lizzie be right? It wouldn't be the least bit difficult, and who would be around to see it? Shit, he could be halfway to Michigan before he had to ditch the car...if that was really his destination. I found myself searching thin air for a sign, any gesture which would either confirm or deny the crazy thoughts I was thinking. "Thank God for the fifty bucks!" I said to myself. I just hoped it would be enough to buy back my life.

Were we just outside Ashland when finally he broke from his reverie, saying, "Hmm...this looks good. You can drop me off just up there, if it's all the same to you," pointing toward a truck stop a few feet up the road.

"Alright, Jeff. This is it," I warned myself. It had just reached that desolate hour of the day (midway between lunch and early supper) when the only sane people around one could rely on were either napping or tending to some menial task which sapped all their attention. I felt stranded, only myself to turn to should my worst fear come true. My only escape route (should the fifty bucks fail) would be total submission, hoping to evoke just the slightest bit of pity in my would-be assailant. Failing that, I was fucked.

The car stopped and he was the first to exit. A good sign, I thought. At least he was giving me a chance to make a run for it. Then again, I could have just sped off the instant his feet hit the dirt if for some reason I hadn't put his bags in the trunk for safekeeping. Cursing my self-mutiny, I slumped out the car like a catholic jerk about to face the stick.

His bags now out and resting at his feet, there was nothing left do but shake hands and part (I hoped) and when finally he offered his hand with obligatory grin I thought I'd just have done with it and reached into my back pocket and pulled out the fifty, slapping it coolly in his palm. For a long while he did nothing but stare, first at the fifty, then at me, his face a slab of expressionless stone. "Jesus Christ!" I thought. "If this guy doesn't give me a smile, a *genuine* smile, and soon, I might as well hand over the damn keys right now!" Still silent, the fifty clutched tight in the hand that received it, he dropped both his arms and as if in a trance, eyes glossy, teeth clenched and rigid, he stepped slowly toward me and leaned and raised his arms around my neck and shoulders and me frozen with fright expecting a sharp pain in my upper back or spine and instead feeling his rough chin on my cheek and his chest against mine and squeezing and in my ear a soft, kind voice saying, "Thank you." Then he let go and took up his bags and without another word began walking toward the stop.

I fell back in the car. I felt lower than a wormhole. I could barely see the road through the tears in my eyes...tears of pure humiliation. Whatever faith I'd left at all in my previous ability to read people's character had fallen to ash and spiraled away in a tortuous storm of self-abdication. How could I have pretended to think such a man as Jim, a man who had first-handedly seen every unpolished treasure in this unholy land (which I never did doubt) and who so intimately related into mine and Lizzie's ears the details of such travails, in doing so giving back so much more than we deserved – a man who knew exactly what it meant to give as well as to receive, who asked for nothing more than *the essential stuff of life* – how could my feeble, inane brain have believed such a man capable of violent arrogation? How could I have even invented such an idea...or did I? Did the idea come from some outside source, some outside influence? Why, yes, was it not Lizzie who first mentioned it to me? Was it not her inner eye (once dead-on in accuracy, now just dead) which pretended to see into the very soul of this man? Damn that eye! And damn my eyes! Damn the day they set sight on her Circean beauty! Damn the night she cast me in her seminary spell! Damn the way she succeeded in secluding me apart from humanity, apart from myself! Damn her eyes, those spellbinding, silver-blue eyes burning holes through my heart and skewering my soul! Damn her hypnotic locks of golden-spun sunshine! Damn her skin, her mesmerizing, phosphorescent skin and passionflower mouth and nose and ears and neck! Damn her! Damn me! Damn it all to Hell!!!

     *   *   *

 I must be completely honest with myself. Though I speak now of mine and Lizzie's relationship in purgatorial terms, the truth is nothing could satiate my goatish ego more than sitting here surrounded by her hellfire, alone, the fragrant, native warmth of her hyperborean breath crystallizing my skin and massaging my underlayer, a lunar caustic finger rub, pores spread open like a million snow hares' asses spitting out ice pellets, sunbeams and uranium, the white hot heat of her icy blue eyes like two acetylene torches melting the bones of my skeleton like wax, a tropophytic daydream, an evergreen in Egypt, a firedog's claws on a slate of glacial ice. This, truly, is peace. Even as I lay here in her porcelain tub swimming in sweat and steering through ice slates and slivers of old soap like perfumed chips of bone, a steady injection of Beethoven's mad genius blasting through my eardrums like oceanic lightning bolts of pure African ivory synchronized isomagnetically and orchestrated intersexually with the pyretic striptease of candle flames in steam clouds, a weird hypnotic nebulosity melting my skeleton and hardening my skin (a nihilistic nimbostratus), my own private aurora borealis of red-orange and yellow golden torsos dancing like snakes atop pink and purple pillars, sea blue and green cylinders of jasmine and mulberry, chamomile and melon....Even as I sit here surrounded by dichotomies, cylindrical or otherwise, I know this to be the best, the most pleasing and gentlest habitat for a mental refugee. Here I am in my element. Here I sink or swim, breathe or wheeze, live or die as I see fit. Here I juggle andiron tongs or jump through glass plates and land on upturned nails without contracting so much as a scratch. Here I produce television shows or reproduce paintings or spit in the eyes of those I love most. Nothing is forbidden...all simply *is*. Yea or nay, integral or naught – all are one and all are at my bidding. All I need do is choose...or *not*. To choose against choosing....Is that not also a choice? Apathy is just that: the mind's passionless act of choosing not to choose. I am apathy incarnate. I am and am not. I am like the snail, the passionless, spineless snail which slithers along the ocean floor in search of nothing, my white porcelain shell surrounding me at all times, protecting me from all that is not myself. I am withdrawn and I drone. I breathe and wheeze and take in the warm, fragrant, embryonic air around me...or cease breathing entirely and live forever! Why not? Why must I build boundaries before choosing my destiny? Did man need wings before choosing to fly? Like hell! All he truly needed was a *desire* to fly, a will made of steel and a concrete decision to want to fly, then the spark and the action of his unearthly will and before long he was flying, first a few feet above ground, then over puddles and ponds and wheat fields and trees and lakes and oceans and up and up and up and on into the sky and through clouds and storms and sunbeams and on toward the apex of the once-forbidden atmosphere, then further on still till he landed on the moon, then soon there was nowhere else to go again but down, down into the oceans and lakes and trees and wheat fields until finally there was nothing left for him to land upon but buildings and flag poles and people...but I don't want to fly. I don't want anything. I only want my shell, my white porcelain shell and my ocean floor of soap scum and spineless apathy. I am like the snail. I choose without choosing. I am and am not....

If my thoughts seem scrambled or altogether incoherent it's because tonight I am thinking with a contradictory brain. Though I speak of "choice" as if it were a reality I know for a fact the exact opposite is true: "choice" is no more a reality than politics or television or Lon Chaney are realities. I know this is true because Friday follows Thursday and Thursday follows Wednesday and after every sunny Monday invariably follows that day of days when my heart starts wheezing and my bones start melting and the embryonic fluid starts flowing like formaldehyde. I am thinking now of that reality of all realities: Tuesday night.

(Reality: an endless glass corridor with windows painted on.)

...And novels. Novels also occupy my mind, or, rather, *the* novel, the one true work that will finally put an end to all this silly writing business; all impotent dreams...the slaying of waking convictions...

(Novel: a crystal sarcophagus in the center of City Hall; a casket with arms and teeth and a thickly coated scrotum; a polyacrylic mass sufficient unto itself: the novel.)

...And words! And words and words and words and words and words and words. Silly, inane words like the prattle of an invalid...an *uninspired* invalid. All teeth and hair and tits and ass and cosmetics and movie stars and clothes and shoes and smells my Christ the endless smells of smells she smells a thousand million different smells like onion garlic baby powder sewage pools of cabbage stew and wet hair and underwear and chamomile and melon and good morning darling sleep all right okay I guess my back's a little sore I don't know why and you well not so bad myself so you got a sore back eh, he, he, yeah what no not now I gotta pee okay fine then what's for breakfast I don't know whatever you want what no not that I thought you knew me by now oh what the hell's the use I said no stop doing that can't you see I'm sore just go take a shower or something I'm off to see my sister and then the bank and work and mmm my favorite television shows sound just dandy all day all day all day all (damn it all to hell!) ah darling welcome back you look wonderful how's the bunion well you know it's all that walking up and down and up and down that goddamn floor all day all day and not having a proper pair of shoes and all and someday I'll have myself a surgical procedure and no not now why can't you just leave me be my back is still sore I need time to rest my feet and wash my crotch and eat and watch more movies great action scenes and polished teeth and hey what's that actor's name again you know the guy with the great ass I mean smile oh stop you know what I meant for Christ's sake why can't you just lighten up for once and stop being so defensive all the time for Christ's sake for Christ for time for time for lights out and warm covers and smoke and ice and hey why won't you touch me now all of a sudden what are you gay what'd she say what hey wake up I said wake up wake up wake up wake up wake up wake up wake up awake what huh oh is that what you want and now well all right what the hell (Hallelujah!) all hands down the panties and teeth and ears and eyes and nose and neck and nicotine lips and boozy breath and breasts and two soft velvet engulfing flames of passionflower flesh...but no nectar. Not anymore. Now all my tongue can ever taste is the alkaline solution of sweat and saliva, cigarette butts and Beaujolais....

...And words. Festering teeth marks left by a novel's noxious bite. All novelists write words, words and words and words; words drawn in monogram decoded with cellulose; words served on spinning plates with tiny plastic cutlery; words no meatier or heartier or tastier than a tree squirrel's tail bone smothered in mule dung; words brought into being solely for the purpose of instructing us how *not* to become, how *not* to be, how *not* to enjoy something, someone, anyone, anything...but nothing? No, not nothing. Especially not nothing. Especially not the novelist. All novelists seem to know about are words, words and words about purring cats and dogs barking, birds chirping, warm winds blowing, Santa Claus and candy canes falling from snow-white skies, Easter eggs, crazy kids running through green green grass holding hands walking down dirt roads harmonicas poking out of faded back pockets, baseball games, birthdays, bar mizvahs, dull candlelight glowing through incense smoke thick as opium plumes, Communion, confession, comprehension of the Trinity and the Cross and Crucifixion and Body and Blood and oh by gosh by golly by gee who's that girl I've never seen such no not her the other one with long blonde hair and deep blue eyes and bare knees bending over by *Christ Falls A Second Time* Tara, Sara, Jessica, Jennifer, Ashley, Marie, Michelle Michelle Michelle Michelle marine blue and bronze green breeze blowing foamy salty sea air swirling up and under gauzy summer Sunday's best sundress, hot, bubbly, juicy Georgia peach daydreams topped with whipped cream and barbital, wedding bells, Pachelbel, chocolate cherry cheesecake, greeting cards, supermarkets, muddy cars, consignment stores, flat tires, commercials, magazine ads illustrating mother and daughter laughing and delicately caressing one another clipping coupons for ready-bake cookies and fat-free salad dressings, opalescent soap bubbles bursting like atom bombs, anniversaries, birthdays, more birthdays, Barnes and Noble gift shop coffee house certificate receive $25 when you spend $250 membership reward cards, bottles upon bottles of green green green green green, sleepy-eyed queen bees sleeping and awaking all honeycombed waistlines and atrophied areolas, once-a-week intimacies tossed off in the key of Z and etched upon stained box spring mattresses brutal and poetic, piles upon piles of sheets and sheets soiled by spoiled brats, pets, night sweats, swollen lymph nodes, broken blood vessels, kidney bean soup and hot buttered cornmeal cakes served at backdoor bonfires burning *à la dérobée* all bright orange and red and green and Halloween yellow haystacks hiding strange and curiously shaped ponies poking, divorcees, lawyer fees, funeral marching soldiers singing happy dancing corpses donning mustached grins and gin and tonic necktie polished tooth enamel pearl-studded onionskin all Pompeii blue and pink and creamy methylene and stardust-sprinkled suntan lotion abdomen reductions under posh, expensive sport coats cut just low enough below the waist to cover up the wet spot....

The music stopped. A stifled muse.

Another disc. A new song. The birth of a new scene, or, rather, the rebirth of an old scene born one thousand times continuous, each birth a new face, each new face a manifestation of a vista I have never seen nor ever will see, a face all at once revealed and concealed, unknown, unknowable, unseen and in transit, unknowable as ether-induced intermezzos mingling moonlight and sunbeams and rabbits' feet and mole hair and copper wire; an angel stuck in limbo and dangling on strings of silver and arsenic and ether and hydrochloric acid and argon and uranium; invisible gold strands dotted with digitized images of hair and eyes and skin and sunlight seeping thin through clouds of smoke and ozone, beads of sweat and asphalt....

"Oh, there you are. I thought I heard you splashing."

Another voice. Another new vista.

"I was looking all over for you. I should have known you'd be in the bath."

Another song sung in the key of Z. All Egyptian notes and vanilla plum time bars.

"I don't know why you to listen to that crap. And when they sing....God, I hate that. It reminds me of opera, all acting and fakery." (All brutal and poetic.) "Besides, this is more relaxing, don't you think?" All bursted blood vessels, bright ocean-blue bubbles combusting, exploding in...

"Here. This is for you."

...A glass. Another bloody chalice...

"I know how much you like your Beaujolais."

...The blood of a new and everlasting lost faith, a never-ending scourge of ascending and descending lymph nodes, fallen teeth and follicles...

"Even though it's not for *me*."

...A dark horse with deep blue eyes and bronze skin and ivory smiles...

"To be honest, I can't stand the stuff. If I had my choice I'd choose Merlot..."

...And icy, poisonous breath...

"...but I'm sure you knew that already, didn't you?"

...The sacrament as commanded by Her Majesty, the Maharani of Imported Beer and Pickled Herring; a holy accord in cahoots with the Patron Saint of Swollen Pancreas and Psoriatic Assholes...all sour...all like...like...Sara. Sara, you were led on. All you were offered were novelists' tricks and time bombs ticking inaudibly underground inside...inside me...inside...inside Sara...Sara....

"What were you thinking just now?"

Silence. A sip of wine.

"Come on, I'd really like to know."

More silence. Still more wine. The tied end of a leaky intestine...

"Oh, I see. You don't think I'd understand, is that it?"

Spilling more and more and more wine and silent time bombs ticking inaudibly underground and over towns and inside empty heads like insular nuclear fallout shelters complete with rubber compressed-air-tight-cabin-pressure-seals and soundproof skin and bulletproof bone and watertight eyes and ears...

"Are you trying to ignore me?"

...And tongues and teeth and artificially-achieved gold-and-gloriously-bronzed-skinned bodies rolling on around and over one another in a clumsy, heartless display of capitulated heat...

"Fine. Ignore me, then."

...Like brave young men bending beneath the weight of...

"Ignore me while you sit there in *my* tub soaking your precious skin and drinking the Beaujolais I bought especially for you."

...A capital idea.

"Aren't you at least gonna ask me how my night went?"

Silence.

"Really. Don't tell me you're still upset about the other night."

Every night's an *other* night...a ripple in the reservoir...a slip of dystopian membranes....

"Fine. I'll tell you anyway. Like hell, that's how! First off, I forgot my apron. You know, the one with the satin edges.... Well, I had to borrow one from one of the cooks...an actual cook apron! I had to fold it four times before I could get the damn thing to fit right, and even still it looked like I had a dirty bed sheet wrapped around my waist. That set the night right off, let me tell you! Then, who do you suppose walks in the door but Caruthers himself, and not just him but his slut wife and daffy half-brother, all with those ridiculous smiles on their stupid faces...and who do you suppose Angela hands them to, huh? *Me*, that's who! And right after I told her I was hung over, too...the bitch! Anywho, I'm scrambling like hell to get everything in order with my head pounding hammers and the cooks shouting orders and nuthin's in order 'cause my apron's missing, follow? So, first off I can tell Caruthers expects me to put the napkin in his lap just 'cause I did it once before to be cute...and with his half-witted wife sitting right there, even! Well, I had to do it. Then he orders the tenderloin, okay, but he doesn't want the potato 'cause he's on the Atkins diet, right? Fine, only the boy we just hired behind the grill doesn't know how to cook a medium-well steak yet 'cause he's new and I have to bring the fucking thing back three times before he gets it right. So, my head grinding razors, I finally get a decent meal out to the guy with his wife and half-brother making snide comments under their chins and wouldn't you know it...the fucking potato's been on his plate the entire time! The asshole cook never said a word! So now I look like an idiot in front of the owner and his slut wife and retarded half-brother like I don't know what the hell the Atkins diet's all about. Well, the good thing about it all is at least Caruthers finally got to see first hand how truly fucked up and understaffed that place really is...only, I really can't stand that idiot wife of his. She didn't say a single word the entire time...just stared at me with those bumbling-twit eyeballs of hers....Hey, are you even listening to me?!"

To be sure. Bumbling-twit halfwit wives...underdone eyeballs...overstaffed Atkins diets....Now, come down here, my dear, and draw a diagram for me in the soap suds with your teeth....

She leans in. "I spoke with Irene before leaving the restaurant. She and Ian will be expecting us within the hour."

A princess...a frozen drama and her leprechaun, both on the prowl and tossing about town their desultory poetry like two meatless, motionless cannonballs exploding odorless, colorless, tasteless confetti and scrolls and scrolls of silk-and-satin-bound pages upon pages of words and words and words all waxen and atavistic, ataraxic nerve endings always severed, never mended, never meeting or competing, never seeing or conspiring, never beating or even bleeding, never creeping quiet down a dark alley broke and blinded by the moon in both eyes and bloody at the knees, never mind her bloodless heart and unclean surgical castrations like grandmothers contracting pleurisy or cancer or psoriasis, all molten bones and land mines I'll never be able to escape her lips, her lips, her lips and eyes and ears and nose and neck and lips and teeth like a billion tiny angels' toes protected by her lips, her lips like two dark-red crescent organs breathing fire into my veins and nose and Egyptian musk and dusk and dynamite and her smile like ice cold passion and her voice like cathedral bells proclaiming the Second Coming into my very soul and eyes and ears and nose and neck and skin and lips and neck and neck and neck and...

She pulls away. Standing, laughing. "And don't forget to wash your ears. They smell like dirty dishrags."

...And ears like dirty dishrags. Ah, well, even dishrags have their uses, dirty or otherwise. Even dirt possesses some level of vitality, a way of life for worm and snail; a New Jerusalem for the dredges of society like poets and lawyers and politicians and bankers and bartenders and tycoons and accountants and Caruthers and their half-wit wives and coat-tailing brothers and Atkins diets and tenderloins and television shows and portfolios and marriage counselors and white cotton underwear soiled to a dull gray and SUV's and soldiers' limbs dangled like dice from the rearview mirrors – all possessors of a secret knowledge of rotted teeth and follicles and ears like dirty dishrags, of Calvary on the ropes, of a distant, endless war waged with promissory notes and cartilage and televised victoriously, a soulless dance of heartless nothingness, of darkness and of dirt, of broken bones and ozone and tears frozen to oily skin, a vast and sandy desertion, a breach of the imagination producing nothing more than nothingness, a meaninglessness so useless, so beyond the dawn's early light that no badge, no bright coin, no mountain of gold will ever be able to shine its way through the thick, black, endless nothingness...

But I betray myself....

Book Three

The Sun vs. the Serpent

M idmorning.

Standing on the back porch slightly dizzy from a hangover smoking a cigarette watching the sun rise slowly through trees, waiting for the morning coffee to stir me to life. I'll have to wait a little longer; it's still in the maker. Normally I'd wait indoors, leaving the sunrise for those with more ambitious ideas for its rays, though for some reason I feel restless. Must just be the dizziness, in which case it makes no sense standing on a second-story porch smoking a cigarette wheezing in the warm, oxidizing air. There's a contradiction in there somewhere. Why the cigarette? Because the air is too warm, too oxidizing. Why the back porch? Because Lizzie disapproves of tobacco use before noon...

Which is a good thing. I've been trying as of late to locate the good in things, the positive. Take, for example, the sun. The sun could be a good thing...if one could ignore its brightness and warmth. The sun is a thing too easily taken for granted. I much prefer a *cool* sunny day, or, better still, a cool *sunless* day, when one must remind oneself the sun still exists. It's then when the sun truly takes on its near-mythic significance, makes one realize its true vitality. Only when it glares at you with its bright oval face do you feel like averting your eyes in disgust. No, a thing like the sun is best when it's sought out.

How's *that* for a positive?! Shit, I surprise even myself!

Speaking of which, only halfway through the cigarette and already I feel the beginnings of a serious bowl movement. Christ, these things hit like a sledgehammer in one's rectum, makes one forget all about the sun and the trees and the warm breeze and the coffee's not finished yet think I'll try one more puff...

Oof! Bad idea! Well, can't rightly waste a whole half of a decent smoke, can we?

No, siree. So...

In we go. Into the cool, sunless shade of the kitchen with a cigarette between my lips. Feels better already, by God. (Another positive.) Good enough to see how much further on the coffee...

Too far. Can't wait. It's poking out, it is.

Straight to the crapper. Crack a windowpane for two reasons, though the smoke will take care of the other. Still, I'd hate to come off *completely* careless, you know. There's a level of respect shown when one isn't *too* obvious, agreed?

Agreed.

Ahhhhhhhh....

So, sitting here humming on the porcelain receptacle listening to the drip-drip-dropping of the coffee machine just entertaining myself watching smoke curl from my fingertips and lips waiting for the inevitable to walk through...

"*What the hell do you think you're doing?!*"

Talk about the obvious. I answer with an exhalation.

"Goddammit, Jeff! You know I hate when you do that! It makes you look like a loser!"

Hard to argue with that one.

"And anyway, it stinks!"

Again, dead on. She's rolling this morning, boy. I'm about to applaud her perceptiveness but before I can put the cigarette in my mouth to free up both hands she's out the door and down the hall so instead I let out a loud fart which is just as good in any case. Before long, though, she's back and this time with a lighter and a stick of incense...patchouli, no doubt.

She places the holder on the sink just out of reach (clever girl), lights the end, inspects the flame a moment, then blows a kiss to put it out.

I was wrong. Spiced orange blossom.

"There. Now I can talk to you," she says, a weird smirk on her lips. She holds out her hand and offers me what appears to be an envelope through the swirl of smoke. "This arrived for you the other day. Tell me what you think."

An envelope, all right, addressed to me...and opened.

From Sven Stenborg, former classmate and chum. This can mean only one thing...

Yup. The son of a bitch is getting hitched...to Melissa Moore, his high school sweetheart. Hell, was there ever any doubt? One tall, tasty number, that Miss Moore. Witless as a country housecat, but tasty...and, man, did she ever adore Sven! Captain of the hockey team and prom king to boot! What chance did she have?! Besides, one had to admit they were made for each other: not one original idea between the two of them (she became an accountant, he a sporting goods store owner), but who needs ideas when you've got a slap shot like Sven and legs like Melissa. Swear to Christ, sometimes after class (economics, the only one she and I had together) I'd have to wait at least twenty-five minutes before I'd finally stop salivating from gazing all hour at those candied gams of hers. I'd have myself such an optic feast on those mile-long legs (not to mention her tits and ass and face, which weren't none too bad, neither) my blossoming libido damn near developed diverticulitis from all the blocked emissions it was forced to perform. Still, I knew it meant disaster if I so much as set a finger on those lustrous stems. Luckily, this was a risk which existed only in my imagination. As said, she wholly adored Sven, and now it seems he'll be the one who'll enjoy a long, happy life of greased internal tissue. Not only that, but he'd like me and my "other" to attend and witness the contractions, indicated politely by the RSVP insignia at the bottom of the invitation, my only thought being: How the hell did he get this address?

I look up at Lizzie. She's still standing there smirking and looking down at me as if to ask, "Well? What d'you say?" I respond by gently placing the invitation back in the already-opened envelope and tearing up the lot. Halfway through the third tear I hear: "Oh, so that's how you treat your friends, then, is it?"

"What makes you think we're friends?"

"Well, he sure as hell sounds more like a friend than those jerks at the bar."

Hmm. This needs explaining. I shoot her a look as if to say, "Alright, now, out with it. Tell me what you know."

She knows she's caught. She fumbles a bit, searching for the proper expression to bring to light – something with just enough guilt without losing any of her high stature (which isn't too hard since I'm the one on the shitter) – finds it, then churrs, "He called the other day looking for you. He wanted to mail you the invitation...formally, you know. He sounded nice, not rough or stupid like your other jack-off friends."

Silence.

"Besides," she continues, "if I'm to be a part of your life don't you think I should know all about you...everything, even about the friends you had back in high school."

More silence.

Then, stern: "Look, don't do this to me! After how I talked you up and told him what a great guy you are and how you would have got in contact with him long ago but you've been so busy with your writing....What, do you want to make me a liar?!"

Enough of this. A permanent impression is developing on my ass cheeks. Besides, there's no more drip-drip-dropping – the coffee must be finished. I raise the torn invitation, kiss it, then place it lovingly in my shirt pocket.

She smiles triumphantly, then turns and leaves the room. I soon follow.

On the way out I toss the cigarette butt in the toilet...along with the burning orange blossom.

>Telephone: Bzzzzzz...beep...beep...beep...brrrrrring...
>Operator: City, please.
>Me: Superior.
>Operator: Name?
>Me: Stenborg.
>Operator: One moment.
>Telephone: Bzzzzzzz...brrrrrring...brrrrrring...brrrrr...
>Man's voice: Hello?
>Me: Sven?
>Man's voice: One moment.
>Another man's voice: Hello?
>Me: Sven?
>Sven: Yup.
>Me: Hey, Sven. It's Jeff.
>Sven: Jeff?
>Me: Woolverton.
>Sven: Woolverton?
>Me: Wolf.

Sven: Oh! Hey! Wolf! How da hell are ya?! Me an' da boys been talkin' boutcha...wonderin' how da hell ya been holdin' yerself and all dat. Haven't heard so much as a beer fart from ya in a while, ya know.

Me: I know. I've been busy.

Sven: So's I hear. Writin' a book and all dat, are ya now?

Me: Yup.

Sven: So...what's she about?

Me: Oh, I guess she's about a couple hundred pages by now.

Sven: Huh?....Oh! Ha, ha! I get it! Writer's jokes, eh?

Me: Yup.

Sven: Yeah. Yup. Hmmm. So's anyways I suppose ya heard da good news, eh?

Me: Yeah. Congratulations, Sven.

Sven. Oh, hey, tanks, Wolf! Say, when are *you* gonna take

da plunge, eh?

Me: Don't know.

Sven: Well, best not wait too long, ya know. Dat Lizzie o' yers sounds like a hottie!

Me: Yeah.

Sven: So...ya gonna tie dat knot or what?

Me: What.

Sven: I says ya gonna tie...

Me: Sven...Look, I really don't have much time to talk. I just called to say congratulations to you and Mel and let you both know Lizzie and I will be...

Sven: Wait, Jeff...don't go yet. I'm glad ya called. See, dere's something I need ta ask ya.

Me: Me?

Sven: Yeah. See, my brudder Björn was all set ta be my best man, ya know....Well, just d'udder day he had quite de unfortunate accident at de rifle range over dere and I was wonderin'...

Me: Rifle range?

Sven: Yeah! Shot himself in de foot, de dumb duck! Can ya believe dat?! Only a week till de wedding and dey say he won't be up n' about fer a month!

Me: So what do you need from me?

Sven: What else? Ta fill in.

Me: For best man?

Sven: Nope. Usher.

Me: Usher?

Sven: Yup. Usher. See, Ski's gonna fill in fer Björn fer best man and fer Ski's spot we brought in my udder brudder Willem who, anyways, was already in since he's usherin' a-long wid my first cousin Tad only now he's not and besides Mel tinks de ushers should be equal and all dat ya know one from each side so's when Willem moved up 'er twelve-year-old second cousin Seymore moved in only just d'udder day de liddel shit got da pox so's now we're in a mess and ta hell wid Mel's idea of usher equalidy and all dat y'know one from each side besides I'd radder have you dan some twelve-year-old any day so whaddya say....Will ya do it?

Me: I don't know, Sven...

Sven: Oh! Wait! Hey! Speakin' of Mel...she's here, ya know. I betchya'd love to say a few words to 'er, eh?

Me: No, Sven, really...

Sven: Hold on dere, Wolf. I'll go gedder.

Woman's voice: Hello?

Me: Hi, Melissa.

Melissa: Hi....Who's this?

Me: Jeff.

Melissa: Jeff?

Me: Wool....Wolf.

Melissa: Oh! Wolf! Hey! How are you?

Me: Fine.

Melissa: Yeah. Say, Sven says you're gonna fill in for the wedding next week.

Me: Well...

Melissa: That's so great of you, Wolf! I knew you'd come through for us in a pinch. I always thought you were a pretty cool guy.

Me: Yeah.

Melissa: Yeah....Hey! Remember economics?!

Me: Bits and pieces.

Melissa: Yeah, me too! I remember how you'd always sit there with your eyes closed and your head down....I always wondered what it was you were thinking about.

Me: Hmmm.

Melissa: So....What were you thinking about?

Me: Nothing much.

Melissa: Yeah, right. Nothing much, huh? A smart guy like you...probably thinking about how to solve the world's problems, right?

Me: Right.

Melissa: Yeah, right. Well....Anyway, thanks again for filling in, Wolf! You're the greatest!

Me: Yup.
Melissa: Here's Sven...
Sven: Wolf?
Me: Yup.
Sven: So's I guess you'll hafta get yerself fitted fer a tux right quick seein' as de wedding's next week dere, eh, bud?
Me: Yup.
Sven: Great! See ya den, dere, Wolf! You rule!
Telephone: Click. Bzzzzzzzzzzzzzz....
Me: Fucking hell.

* * *

Showtime.

Sunshine and shoe polish. A few falling leaves. Early autumn Lake winds surging like electric currents stirring the sting of expensive perfume and cheap cologne, lotion, chewing tobacco spit, skin toners, eye liners, aloe-treated lip balm like ear wax dipped in embalming fluid, ultra low tar cigarette smoke and Winterfresh gum, open pores, inverted vertebrates, invented sexual glories, leopard-skin-printed calico panties sprayed liberally every half-hour with underestimated feminine secretions, fluoride prophylaxis, flushed pride, lost-and-found forever, future arguments over Arm-and-Hammer baking soda, ambiguously modern hair products, armpit sweat, nose-hair shavings, starched shirts stuffed to the neck with tanned and deboned and pre-seasoned man flesh plucked hairless and bending like dandelion stems beneath the weight of expectation and me in the middle of it all, smiling, somehow immune to the charge most people seem to get when attending these painfully contrived social events. Sentimental puppetry, that's all I see... but wait. One mustn't be so cynical, especially when one is wearing the same painted-on adaptation as one's own ancestry on one's back and standing in the midst of such grand histrionics, taking part in the breaking and passing and eating of fresh bread on flower-patterned banquet tables scared as hell and praying not to knock the red wine all over the bride's and groom's future nuclear family Thanksgiving Day table spread and doing just that...

But that's not till later. Right now I have other private demands acting as responsibilities, *viz.* offering my elbow to every crook and granny that saunters in through these arched entryways; a degenerate act of the staunchest purport even the pimple-faced youth who serves as my second fails to find just the smallest satisfaction from assisting these walking carcasses. We are of the same ilk, my companion and me. Somehow we've managed to build a small bond with even smaller talk in-between grandmother's and grandnieces and grand processions down and up the Scarlet Carpet Boulevard. Tad, his name is. Quite the wily thirteen-year-old, this one. Already at his young age he displays in full that single rare quality this Northern population has somehow disinherited: *wit*. And a monstrous one at that! So much so I've found myself inspecting the upper region of his forehead just above the temples for circular scars where the horns have been removed. Well, I too have my scars and they'll not allow my pride to be wounded by some nibbling pubescent prankster. Thus, a contest: who can outdo the other in severity, scope, and, of course, surreptitiousness. This last is where the wit comes into play. What good is it to pull one over on oneself? The culprit always; never the victim. This our spotted Tad understands, which makes him a worthy player. The prize? Who the hell cares?! It's enough we're still breathing in this stifling, toxic atmosphere.

So far we've barely breached the sophomoric; simple, yet skillful pranks of little inspiration and much less risk of public chastisement – a mere cracking of the knuckles before breaking into a heightened rendition of Beethoven's *Tempest*. For instance, Tad's first trick was to escort some anonymous middle-aged hag down the aisle with his tux tail wagging out his unzipped fly. Sophomoric, I say. I followed quite easily with a routine, yet daring display of arrogance disguised as ignorance: upon returning from waltzing some young pony whose perfume nearly made me faint I chose the fullest pew and, under the guise of being beckoned from the back by someone of enormous gravity, I forthwith proceeded to feign a shortcut through the trough, forcing each one of those stuffy bastards to stand as I tripped and trod and plodded at my leisure through the full length of unbent knees. Not necessarily genius, though still it must have inspired Tad some since he followed with a decidedly evil and sinister plot which impressed me as stretching far beyond his young, unimpressive years.

He assured me he must have the prime suspect for his next venture. He did not say who, though I soon believed this person existed only in one of his demonic fantasies for streams of whom I'd have considered pure fodder passed by without so much as a flinch from his fire-red eye. Finally he found her: an elderly woman barely able to walk on her own, yet there she was, alone, with no one to act as intermediary between her and the young and terrible Tad. And though spotty, his face emitted unmistakable charm which won her over instantly, enveloping her in his confidence as he led her unwittingly past the flock toward the front pews reserved specifically for the wedding party only, then left her there, alone, only her own crippling age as excuse for the inevitable confusion as he strode calm and smooth back toward the vestibule, smiling victoriously. It was clear I had the Devil on my hands...a thirteen-year-old, pimply-faced Devil. I'd better come up with something damn special.

So far I've drawn a blank. To follow Tad's abandonment of a helpless elder with anything less than unholy evil would mean defeat for both my pride *and* my scars. A thirteen-year-old boy! With acne, even! Well, there lurks in the dark shadows of every master's hall a crouching, spring-ankled, super-coiled and poisonous...

Wait! I've got it! Brilliant! And just in time, too!

I ask Tad to hand over the gum he's been chewing all

morning like a deranged billy goat. He hesitates, wants to know why. I hesitate as well, not really knowing for sure myself; the pieces are still a bit jumbled. I decide to just let out with it and arrange them as I go along.

"It's like this," I begin, solid as asbestos. "Ever hear the one about *The Wanker and the Wife*?" He nods. "You have? Where?"

"Isn't it some story by Oscar Wilde?"

Clever shit. "What the hell do you know about Oscar Wilde?" I ask, a bit too challenging.

"He's my mom's favorite," he explains. "She used to read him to me when I was a kid. Boring as hell. Put me to Z's in no time flat."

"And you remember him?"

"Yeah...well, the titles, anyway...that and he's a fag."

"Your mom told you *that*?"

"Yeah. She said if I ever play with another man's dingy the way Oscar did she'd cut mine off and send it to China."

"Right." Now it all makes sense. "Anyway, *The Wanker and the Wife* isn't some moral tale by your mom's favorite faggot. It's the ultimate prank in the perfect situation." A lie, of course, but still...steady on. "See, the gum is the key. Any gum will do, but it's best if the chewed tint is natural as possible. In other words no bright blues or pinks or purples or even yellows. Anything resembling dirty milk is best. So, then...out with it. Let's see what you got." He parts his lips and out pokes what looks like a petrified maggot. "Perfect. Now, another key element is the layout of the timber, or, in this case, the pews. Notice how the Gospel Side and the Epistle Side face the same direction. Also notice how we, as ushers, have complete control as to the comings and goings of the unsuspecting termites, or, in this case, ants. Follow?" He gives a weak nod. Must develop faster. "Okay. Now, in order for this to come off correctly one must make use of all these elements and more. First, the gum, which you've got and I need." I hold out my hand. He spits the slimy larva in my palm and grins, proving himself a budding opportunist. "Well enough." I roll the gum into a ball with my fingertips – "Now....Observe." – and stroll down the aisle with a dignified air straight toward tiny Tad's latest (or should I say *eldest*?) conquest.

She's staring straight ahead, obviously lost in reflective prayer. Pitiful. Still, this only makes the moondog eyes bob to the surface a bit more easy when I say, "Pardon, miss. I'd hate to disturb you." She startles, like an infant near a loud noise. "Only," I continue, "I'm afraid we have a problem." She remains silent, staring emptily up at me as if we speak separate languages. I smile my softest, most unsophisticated smile and conclude: "A problem with your seating."

"Oh, dear!" she sputters. "Oh, dear! Oh, dear!" All the while shifting about the pew as if she just sat on her favorite poodle. Pitiful. Pitiful.

"It's nothing to worry about," I assure her. "Believe me, madam, it's not your fault." This calms her some. "You see, the *younger* usher should have paid more respect to the fact that these seats are, in fact, reserved." Again she squirms. This is getting painful. Better hurry.

A smile. An outstretched arm. "If you'd be so kind as to take my elbow, dear lady, I'd gladly direct you toward another, more secure seat in the section behind us."

Finally, recognition. "Oh, yes! Yes! Whatever you say, young man. Whatever you say." She grabs hold of my arm and up the aisle we crawl.

Too easy. I have the sense I could lead this bag straight out the door and still she'd thank me kindly with a cherry on top and chocolate chips besides. However, I have other plans so I just drop her off a few pews up.

"God bless you, child! God bless your precious soul!"

Yeah, okay. Enjoy the show, lady.

Walking back my aim is on the aisle seat three pews up and, gum in one hand under the guise of straightening some hymnals with the other, I plant the wad flat on the back of

Apples of Arcadia 195

the empty pew. Mission accomplished. Smooth as a Hessian assassin. I smile a smile to suit my skin and saunter back to Tad to proceed on with the seminary lesson.

As to be expected he's clueless as to the motive behind the gum in the pew. To be honest, I figured it only a moment ago myself. Now that it's there, though, it's as if the rest of the plan is self-prescribed...preordained, as it were.

I see on Tad's face he's disappointed about the bag. "Not to worry," I tell him. "I still give you credit for your daring. Let's just say the intricacies of my scheme outweigh the feeble spasms of some wrinkly old prune." He chuckles. "Now, it's obvious I used the hag to plant the wad, right?"

"Right."

"And it's also obvious, given the unobviousness of its color, that the placement of the gum has some relevance as well, eh?"

"Aye."

"So...can you guess?"

He pauses a moment. Thinks. Then: "Does it have anything to do with that Oscar Wilde dude?"

"Only in the sense it does not." Hmmm. Seems I overestimated my boy. "Now, listen up...here's the whole. See, I got the idea from my desperation. The pews were filling and the service beginning and all that, right? So, I'm thinking to myself I only have a few shots left since all the shirts and skirts will soon be asleep and folded in their drawers...then it hits me."

"What?"

"*The Wanker and the Wife*, of course. The prank that practically *depends* on desperation."

"Ahhh."

"Right." Who does he think he's fooling? "Now, here's the works. You've got a room full of sheep at some gratuitous gig and every single one of them is there with someone else. Nothing works better than a wedding...or maybe a funeral, but I'd hate to meet the soulless bastard who'd try this stunt before a rotting corpse." I can tell by the cool flash in his eye I may have given the Evil One an idea. "Then again, forget it," I say quick. "Funerals are too stoic...too unceremonious. For this we need lust...a bubbly, all-around fiery heat with boobs and lace and bells on, got me?" He nods, though I still notice that flash around the rims of his retinas. Even the word *boobs* had no effect. In seconds I prepare myself to someday read about Tad the Man's adventures in the public pages, then go on: "And us being ushers makes it easy to exploit all that for our own amusement. Why settle for petty diversions? Now, your old lady bit wasn't bad, for a beginner, but what if you were to incorporate *two* old ladies or even *three* in the same trick?" Nothing. His mug now a deadpan pit. Obviously too much talking...

Tutto bene! I see them! Both strolled into the vestibule, arm-in-arm and smiling stupidly...unsuspectingly, I mean. I nudge Tad in the shoulder to wake his attention. "This is it," I tell him. "These are the lambs I'll expel from the fold." He crimps his brow and shakes his head, and he's right. Horribly dramatic, but what the hell. The moment deserved more than the sound of a rousing snore. But now a new moment. I toss on an auspicious smile and leave Tad where he stands to approach the next stage.

The woman is an attractive piece of fine Victorian furniture with mother-of-pearl fingernails and brass springs with matching earrings dangling shoulder-length in the shape of hollow shells meant to symbolize her subaqueously consummate homogeny with Neptune or Poseidon or some shit. The beau compliments her perfectly as an unassuming accessory of penny loafer shoes (no socks) and steam-pressed khaki pants cuffed twice round the ankles showing embarrassingly untanned skin in contrast with his hands and face on which he wears a distant, searching gaze beneath a mask of well-rehearsed indifference. Perfect. It's this underground gaze I'm relying on. God knows the unvirtuous thoughts bubbling beneath the surface of those seemingly obedient eyeballs of masticated maleness and subservient sexual gentility. One can almost see the smoke wafting from the pores of this man's dormant volcanic pride. Still, even more perfect than all this is the fact that over an unnerving carnation pink pinpoint Oxford shirt he's donning an impeccably tailored-to-the-hipbone navy blue wool blazer. The perfect dark backdrop for squashed dirty milk maggots.

Both smile as I approach and chime, "Hello there, folks. Lovely day for a wedding, innit?" I then offer the divan with the velvet curves my elbow while shooting the meridian stud a submissive grin (a trite, all-too-easy ploy to gain the dude's confidence) before leading them like royalty up the bloodred-carpeted aisle.

We come to the pew with the maggot-in-wait where just enough room awaits the two to snuggle in tight (I chose this pew for this reason). I bow kindly and direct the lady to her seat with a wave. She smiles and slides in. Her man soon follows (by now the submissive grin has done its work as he can hardly wait his turn to be treated like King Louie) and just as he's about to turn his eyes toward his seat I say, "Sir, you'll find both the hymnal and program in the bin directly before you...*here*." He looks where I'm pointing and plants his unsuspecting ass on target and leans back. "Thank you very much," he says, smiling. I smile back. "My pleasure," I say. "And if there's anything more I can do for you or your lovely wife, please, don't hesitate. I'm at your service." He nods. I notice a slight flinch in his brow meant to indicate to me he's about to be annoyed...and he's right. Mustn't dramatize. Time to cut this one short...for now. "Enjoy the ceremony," I conclude with a grin and a glance in both their direction, then slow and easy I pull off and begin the walk back. On the way I catch the eye of a cute young redhead. I give her a wink and walk on.

Tad can barely hold in his belly as he stands there bent over, his red face even redder with violent, silent laughter. To be honest, I'm a bit amused myself. Still, must maintain composure; there's still much to accomplish. Already I hear the organist upstairs pawing over the opening measures of a Pachelbelian march.

I give Tad a kick to the shin to get his attention. "Come on, man! Pull yourself together." He regroups, then glares up at me with spiteful eyes. It appears he thought us existing on a more kindred plane. "Look," I explain. "Take it easy is all. I may need your help."

His eyes turn from spite to skeptic bewilderment. "Help with what?" he wants to know.

"Alright," I start. "Ears up. This bit's only half over. The gum on that geek's blazer is only part of the gag...and a small part at that." His eyes now relax into lazy curiosity. I go on: "So far we've been focusing on humiliation, on the easy task of embarrassment...and we've succeeded." Tad grins, chucks his chin. I advance: "But now it's time to move on to bigger game...from jackrabbits to rhinoceros, get me?"

"How?"

"Simple. By using the knowledge of how easily these asses are embarrassed and humiliated we can then use that to turn them around and against each other, see?" Curiosity turns into confusion. "Okay...quickly....The gum on the guy's back...embarrassment, right?" He nods. "And not just him but his wife as well, and most likely anyone else who notices. See, embarrassment is like a disease...extremely contagious. No one likes to think a fellow human being could be so vulnerable...especially if that human being is one's own spouse. People tend to look upon that sort of thing with suspicion. The husband will be embarrassed for his own misfortune, the wife simply 'cause she's married to the sot. Savvy?" He seems to be getting it so I keep going. "Good. Now, relying on this theory of universal humiliation, I'll go and tell this dandy about the gum. He'll get all red-faced, maybe panicky. Who knows? Meanwhile, his wife will begin to resent his very existence for having brought so much humiliating attention upon them both....That's when I step in like a savior. I'll bear their embarrassment and lead them both toward salvation... or so it'll seem. That's where you come in." His ears suddenly prick up. "See, the husband will be led out the back by me, then directed down to the bathroom by you. I'm gonna tell him you told me about the gum so there's no smiling, you hear?! Not even a titter! It's key you look sorry as hell for the guy....Otherwise he may catch on and we're both done for, got it? Can you handle that?" He looks at me as if insulted. "Right. Moving on, you drop the guy in the crapper and come straight up. I'll tell you why in a moment. First, I'll let you know while you're tending to the gummy stooge I'll be soothing the wounded ego of his wife, Ma Superior. She'll be personally escorted by me to another section of the church while I clean the pew...a much clearer, more advantageous section, to be sure." Tad's obviously dumbfounded and this is dragging on. "Look....She'll be moved across the aisle to the Epistle side and back a few so as to have a better view of her husband who'll be clueless about his wife being moved. He'll come back from the john bewildered and, with any luck, after the music has begun. He'll have no choice but to sit in his old seat. He won't have time to look for a new pew or his missing wife who won't be so missing as he thinks. And here's the kicker...waiting for him in his wife's place will be a young, beautiful woman." Tad's eyes brighten. "That's your job. When you return from the shitter you'll hold yourself here in the vestibule waiting for a good-looking bird to come along...good enough to have this guy drooling, got me?"

"Where will you be?"

"I'll be pretending to clean the gum off the pew. See, I'll only clean a little...enough to make the wife believe there's nothing left of it, right?"

"How come?"

"So she'll get the wrong idea when her husband moves in closer to the girl. He'll only be avoiding another mess but all she'll see is a mischievous, snuggling hubby-poo." He laughs. "Of course," I continue, "he won't be so innocent. He'll *want* to snuggle up to this girl. Shit, who wouldn't? And with the wife gone and nowhere to be seen it'll be like bachelorhood all over again. He won't be able to resist."

"And he'll pay for it later, right?"

"You got it, me lad." Not bad. Thought I was wasting my breath.

But he hesitates, shakes his head and stares down as if in thought, then sighs, "Nope. It'll never work."

"Why's that?"

"Because," he says, "you'll never have enough time." He points to a clock behind me. "It's almost three. This thing's about to roll."

"You take care of your part and everything'll be fine."

"Bet you five bucks."

Christ! Opportunist? I meant Plutonic extortionist! Still, his proposition isn't *too* much of a risk. I figure I have at least ten minutes till this thing takes off, maybe more – I've attended enough weddings to know the bells and organs don't call till both the bride *and* the groom have their toes to the line. Ten is plenty of time to get the geezer downstairs and out the way. Now, Tad will be tempted to throw a wrench in the works, especially now that money is involved. I've already counted on that, though he'll not be so rash once he's face-to-face with the grunt of his own gum's hatred. Then there's the girl, which is entirely out of both mine and Tad's hands altogether. She's the bet. If I bet anything it's on whether or not she'll walk in through these hollow arches before the bells and organs belch forth their first notes. Somehow, given the way things have worked out thus far, somehow I haven't a doubt. She'll show. I sense it. I sense it the way a vulture senses the vicinity of a fresh kill.

"Let's make it ten," I tell him with a Dostoevskian grin.

He smiles and hesitates. I doubt this bratling shyster has even *half* that. What he *does* have, however, are parents, and it's this I'm sure he realizes when he says, "Alright, then. Ten."

Game afoot. We shake on it (oily, degenerate) and I'm off up the aisle on my way to meet the first phase.

On the Epistle Side I spot an opening a few pews back behind the man and his fucked-up blue wool blazer. A bit further than I'd have liked, but not bad. I mark it in mind and approach the bob and booby sitting soft and comfy as Kashmir underpants.

"Excuse me, sir." He turns, privy to my tone. "I'm awfully sorry to tell you this, sir, but the other usher just informed me of some rather unfortunate news...unfortunate for you, it seems." I give a pause to allow the screw a turn. He leans in, furls his brow. By now the wife is listening in, curious as hell to know what this is all about, no doubt secretly thanking her stars I'm not addressing her. "Before I say," I continue, "first allow me to apologize for not noticing sooner and preventing this most embarrassing situation." The seed now planted, I notice what appears to be anger in the eyes of the man, pure dread in those of his wife. Time to deliver the hammer. "That said, sir, I regret to inform you that you are now leaning back on what appeared to be from the perspective of the other usher a brightly-colored and rather freshly-chewed wad of Wrigley's spearmint gum."

Instinct gets the better of him and he jerks around, revealing a long, elastic string stretching from his back to the wooden pew.

The wife gasps in horror. "Oh my lord!" she says over and over. The man, less reverent in the House of His Holy Majesty, says, "Son of a fucking whore!" and gets a sound whap on the arm from the li'l missus. I have to turn away else I'll lose it and blow my gob in both their faces so instead I look back toward the vestibule which isn't any better since Tad's there damn near rolling on the marble floor in a fit of hysterical laughter and laughter is the one thing more contagious than embarrassment so I guess I'm screwed and there's no way around it till suddenly a flash of brilliance saves me: the old bag. I concentrate on the back of her head, on the thinning gray rag resting atop her frail, charcoal skull and I imagine that blank, pitiful stare permanently engraved in the wrinkled canvas of her face and myself in her place all withered and beaten and passionless and empty and the next thing I know I'm sad again and things can continue as planned.

By now the wife has taken control, yanking the gummed-up blazer out from the hapless grasp of her husband. Poor bastard. He needs a guiding hand so I offer him my shadow in return for Tad's ten dollars.

"Sir," I say with an air of compassion. He looks up, willing for any diversion. "Sir, if I may," I say, "I've heard cold water works best in this situation." He nods and stares at nothing... or is it the hymnals? In any case, he's hooked. He's so damn lost right now I admit it makes me numb just to stand in his presence. No need for the old bag. I wave my hand up the aisle toward the rear of the church and say, "Right this way, sir, and I'll show you to the restroom."

He turns to his wife and with his eyes politely demands the coat. She scowls, then relinquishes it with a sigh as if to say, "Fine. If you think you can do better," and we're off.

Up the aisle and approaching the vestibule I say a silent prayer Tad has managed to right himself by now.

Nothing. Nowhere to be seen.

"Tad?"

The husband and I stand beneath an archway waiting.

"Tad?"

The husband peers about, then at me wondering what the hell's happening. I wish I knew, but if that shitling thinks he's getting ten bucks for this he's mistaken.

"Tad." Yoo-hoo, asshole. Time to come out now.

A small figure peeks out from behind a large door. It's Tad, rubbing his eyes red with tears and trying his damnedest not to look us in the face.

"Tad, this is the gentleman whose coat you commented on. See to it he finds the basement restroom all right, won't you?"

He nods, careful not to look above his feet. "This way, sir," he says as if in pain.

I hand over the husband who looks at me with hollow eyes as if I just commanded he be shown the German showers. Not far off, though the gold isn't in his teeth; it's dangling from his wife's lobes in the form of foreign currency.

I find her sitting hands folded, bearing her husband's grief like a brand new black satin shawl. This is going to be easy.

"Pardon me, miss."

She looks up, recognizes me immediately, then smiles. I smile back. Seems we have a secret bond, one which excludes her unfortunate, pathetic husband, replacing him with a well-dressed, handsome, able-bodied young man.

"Pardon me," I say again, pointing toward the pew, "but I really must remedy this, your husband's horrible accident." She frowns. I lean in closer, getting a whiff of her perfume. "Believe me," I continue in a whisper, closer. "You'll be much more comfortable in the position I have in mind."

That was risky. Something in her smile, though, seemed inviting, assuring. And anyway, an older woman married several years rarely gets reminded of her sex, especially by a younger cat. When it happens the initial reaction of repulse is suspended, replaced instead with a renewed sense of worth, a tingly human wonderment made evident by her eagerness to accept my outstretch arm.

I lead her hand-in-hand to the empty pew I noticed earlier and, with a bow, lower her to her seat as one would an empress or a presidential meretrix. She smiles graciously, peering up at me with soft, moony eyes. Anxious to flee, I kiss the back of her hand (powdered rose petals) and retreat toward the glycerin disaster.

Leaning over the pew pretending to scrape the gum off the sick wood I realize I'm in view of the redhead two rows back. She's not so young as I thought, that competent gleam mingling lustily with her plush, ripe lips and chest. Lucky I'm bent over; tuxedos leave little room for private appreciation.

I can't imagine what she finds so fascinating. Why hand over all your attention to me, cutie? Then again, what else do you have to turn those hazel-green eyes toward? Nothing but a few stale words on poorly recycled paper and the mundane, over-used and unimaginative, typically decorated, more-she-than-he gaudy exhibition of gentile copulation. It's enough to make one lose faith in the act entirely. Whatever the man may say ("She deserves a glorious day!" or "What matter is it to me? She's the doll, here! She's the one and only!") the fact remains that for him this day is as close to death (a *living* death) as any caponizing event; a tragic, unavoidable accident with mindless, flesh-eating machinery. But what effects the accident? And who allows the machine to continue grinding, continue producing, continue its dehumanizing existence? Is it Man? Woman? Child? Society? The World? Maybe it's you, young attractive redhead with your hazel-green eyes and grin and glowing skin like fire underwater steaming, wine and cigarettes and sexual ingenuity. (The world reproducing itself again....A long, drawn-out mechanical orgasm.) Or maybe it's my prick, this rubbery piece of boneless meat that acts as a stake and claims my bit in the bloodless mechanism; another steel wheel with oily skin and rusted teeth that cling like mad to surging currents and passing chains of thoughts and ideas, yet remains in its place, fixed, stoic, boneless, castrated. Still, a wheel is nothing without a machine, and a prick is nothing without a cute young redhead to degrease it periodically and keep it clean and running smooth. The thoughts and ideas of fleeting worth can go right on reproducing inside the machine man has created for himself. He will not grow. He will not evolve. He will not move except around his axis. His culture and social inventions have proved themselves nothing more than the most efficient, most popular product needed to keep the machine running smooth and clean and greased....

Whoa! Almost lost it! That little train of thought nearly cost me a tenner! Must remember to try and free myself from the hypnotic power of a girl with red hair. Still, one more smile can't hurt so I toss her a slow one which she gracefully returns, then off I trot toward the vestibule to find my mass of gorgeous female apostasy...

Which won't be so difficult after all, it seems. Just halfway up the aisle and already I see what appears to be a young, pale-faced, made-up-to-order, sun-deprived girl with long, invisible legs cloaked in sarcophagus-white lace and clenched before her breast a few sad, wilted stems of sunset-yellow lilies. Lamentable...especially the fact that tradition demands such stunning stems (the legs, not the flowers) must be kept under wraps, hidden from her adoring, tradition-loving audience. One would think it'd be the opposite. You'd think tradition demand she display those glorious stems to all and sundry, anyone who cares to get an eyeful before they're shut away and locked tight forever. Ah, well, Melissa. We'll always have economics, you and I. Maybe if Sven hadn't had had such a great slap shot we might have had Phy. Ed. as well. Adieu, my dear. Dream well. Dream of ice cream cones and puppies and kittens and candle-lit baths that last ten months...

Speaking of puppies, I see Tad too, though he doesn't look as cheerful as I expect. Seeing Melissa at the ready means this thing's about to kick...and without *The Wanker* catching hell from *The Wife* where it counts. That means Tad gets his ten bucks. In light of all this, I half expect to see the cocky shit hopping with euphoria, pointing an oily finger in my direction and sticking out his tongue while thumbing his Nordic bunghole. This is not the case. Not at all. Instead he just stares, watching me approach, then turns to the right as if inspecting something, then again at me and then to the floor. Very odd. Still, a bet's a bet so I feel inside my coat for my wallet.

"Well, if it isn't the lady in white lace come to claim her black polyester man."

"Hey, Wolf."

"Hello, Melissa. You look incredible."

"Thanks, Wolf."

Christ, she looks terrified! "And you, you little devil." Tad looks up from the floor. "I suppose there's the not-so-small matter of your ten dollars to attend to, eh?"

"You don't have to rub it in, do you?"

Huh?

"I mean, what? Isn't it enough to know you're the luckiest dude alive, man?"

What the hell's he on about?

Before I can ask aloud again he turns his head to the right. Mine follows.

It's her. The doll. The one and only standing, examining a life-size pewter statue of Saint Joan posing all lionhearted and aflame even before the Brits got a hold of her; head tall, neck strong and taught, eyes intense and zealously scouring the blood-stained horizon for fleurs-de-lis and victory and her land's Dauphin and God, spears consecrated, swords sharpened and polished and pointed at the enemy, the dark heart of humanity, the swollen ego of Man, the thorn in the side of Woman, the tinny copper gleam of those eyes and limbs and armor reflecting off Lizzie's, the latter's spotless skin adopting new metallic tones and textures like stone that's been sculpted and molded by the anonymous hands of some higher being, some nameless, faceless Creator who, by chance, gave birth to the ideal, the ordained, the objectified delights of the flesh and blood and bone and all bodily fluids together in one package; i.e. the perfect weapon. A spear of pure light. The scepter of the Almighty in silver headdress and silk garters.

She hasn't seen me yet. She still looks at the statue. I've really come to enjoy these moments, moments when watching her without her being aware, oblivious to my eyes scanning her over, not maliciously or with ill intent, not in order to find some flaw in her appearance or demeanor (of which I've found most women to be horribly suspicious) but in wonder, curious as to why it works the way it does. Why do women's hands and feet join so fluidly at the wrists and ankles, like doves suspended in mid-flight and dangling from clouds on elastic strings? Or why is it, when watching from behind, the neck and back of a naked woman seem to take on properties of such a noble, gentle nature it makes a man want to at once fall prostrate and surrender himself completely to this vision, this abstraction of something he, himself, will never possess: a beauty he can never own, only reproduce with pen and ink or oil or watercolor or crayon or pastel. And even then it's not the real thing, only a reproduction, a colorful piece of nothing unable to be anything but a reminder of how poor he really is, how pitiful is his being and how great and glorious is hers. Degas saw this. As did Picasso. And De Kooning. And Gauguin. And Cézanne – all those great illustrators who recognized and acknowledged true femininity...and feared it, feared it as they might the treatment for a cancerous growth. Artists like Rubens, Bathus, Duchamp, Jean the Elder, Sickert, Spencer, Waterhouse, Warhol, even Da Vinci...but not Michelangelo. With him it was the opposite, which is doubtless why, after accomplishing what no man ever had or ever will, he renounced it all, everything, every colorful embodiment of human *male* perfection, even the statues. He knew it was false, a very potent and fragrant depiction of his depraved imagination. Art like Michelangelo's leaks poison into the bloodline of men and women alike, setting off a slow paralysis which inevitably renders the soul and spirit (for lack of better terms, an example of this paralysis) both into a state of regression, a throwback to the days when men were Men and women were curious, suspicious creatures with skin like silk and all else like the stuff of clouds, easily whisked away if left to the elements which never fail to conspire against him. She must be contained, held under restraints, kept back like a secret one must never know or understand or bring into the light. Long ago, artists like Michelangelo initiated the myth; today artists like him perpetuate the same myth, attempting to inoculate the fears of mankind until he no longer notices he is afraid, no longer feels the icy poison in his veins. Truly, he gave the world a gift. He gave the world a fiction so great and so desirous the imperfections of the real world, its beauty and mystery no longer mean anything anymore. He replaced the world of Man with a dream for the heavens, for God. He made Man forget the feel of the cold earth beneath his feet. He made Man forget he exists.

Thoughts like these seem dry and futile when peering like a criminal at the embodiment of this dream, this myth. So what? *What else?* What does man always do with his myths and legends, all the good and greatness within and beyond him? Destroy them? Exalt them? Set them proudly upon the mantelshelf atop his electric fireplace next to the family photos and Christmas cards and facsimile Mozartean sheet music? No. Not the wise man. Any wise man knows there are no such things as myths, no such things as legends. Any intelligent man understands this and does what the situation calls for, what his nature demands: he converts greatness into a commodity. He makes money.

I approach her softly, her face in perfect profile and still pointing toward the diocese's copper-plated Joan. (Just now it strikes me the oddity of this statue: a warrior, a *woman* warrior frozen in one of her violent lunges toward...what? Hypocrisy? Sure, hypocrisy, as well as its favorite offspring: the Holy Royal British Empire (R.I.P.) but what about irony? Could she not foresee that she, a woman warrior fighting in a world of men, would in the end only be granted this medallion, this stone-and-copper memoriam for her courage under the blade and strength and determinedness to conquer the enemy? Who, then, should be the one to commemorate her glory? Why, none other than the enemy itself. The ultimate insult. A worm-eaten bone thrown to Irma, the goddess of wind and fire and war and revolution and sent to us in the flesh and burned at the stake. Beautiful. Ironical.)

"Hi."

"Oh, hey. I saw you seating someone so I thought I'd just wander around a bit till you came back."

"That's fine."

"I know."

Silence. I utilize the time to remind myself of my duty.

"This is an odd thing," she says, nodding toward the statue. "I thought churches only had statues of Jesus and Mary and angels and stuff like that...not soldiers with swords and armor and angry expressions on their faces."

"That's Joan," I tell her. *"Jeanne d'Arc."*

She turns to me as if belittled. "I know who it is," she hisses. "I'm not stupid." Pause. "And another thing, you don't have to say her name in that silly French accent. You're not French and I'm not some dumb bimbo who buys into that brainy crap."

Time to turn it on. I give her a golden smile and nod my head with the courtesy and charm my custom suit allows, then I offer her my arm while leaning toward her, purring, "Of course you're not, darling. You're the woman I've been waiting for."

It works. Her mouth melts into a buttery grin, a private token thrown at my feet, aimed at my ego in appreciation for my recognizing her for who she truly is: not a woman...that is, not *just* a woman, but *the* woman. The one and only. The satin doll presiding over a land of tinsel puppets.

She takes my arm and we're off. Strolling past the bride-to-be she steadies her gait and spins her head and whispers in my ear, "So that's her, then, is it?"

Rhetorical. Ignore it. Feel her eyes shifting out and up and in and out again.

"Hmm," she says a few steps later. "So that's what all the fuss is about?" Keep eyes glazed and empty. "Well, she has a decent shape...but that dress doesn't do it justice. And her face....What's with all that make-up, I wonder? What is it about weddings that turn normally pretty women into utter hags?" She turns back slowly as if to answer herself, then forward again and says, "Or, I guess, in her case... *abnormally* pretty, hmm?"

That's my cue so I give a congratulatory chuckle to which

she warms and snuggles closer into my folded arm and torso and further up the aisle we tumble. The bride and her entire ceremony now brought to their hands and knees before her, she strides through the center of it all with such style and grace and confidence even Father Lust B. Damned hasn't a chance. All eyes are on her; she feels it. We both feel it. And it's this, this constant optic grazing by all this prodded cattle feasting on something they can't understand or won't until they end once and for all with the cud and begin slicing steaks off their loin ends and rumps – all these eyes fixed on my Lizzie like jealous ghosts roving through a world of flesh and stone and sex like white eiderdown pillows hidden under satin sheets, silver-white and sun-golden skin glowing, soaking it all from within, storing it for safe keeping, retrieving it after to savor and salivate over when I'm not around but I am, I'm here now in the flesh and blood and so soon will be the glycerin disaster from downstairs already tonguing over his peppermint cud, maybe even evolving the courage to reach for the carving block and butcher's knife and is this really worth it? Worth a measly ten bucks? Of course it is, maybe more – definitely more...but money...money's not the issue, is it? No, it's not, of course it's not, it's this, all these people praying for a good show not to be disappointed watching her walking not even noticing me by her side standing, soaking it all like golden skin breathing under satin sheets heaving, roving like me like jealous ghosts gazing, watching her all her and me all me it's me...no, it's not, it's her all her and me hiding somewhere beneath her better decide soon the empty pew is coming up only a couple steps away it's her, remember, not me, not that dandified puke bucket downstairs in the blessed holy water closet with penny loafers pinpoint Oxford shirts and artificial tans and teeth and sandbag wives sitting all alone across the way waiting, waiting...for what? For a guy like me to come along and on and in her pink carnation powdered lust and lost forever man? Never. Not for that, not for them or this or anything, not nothing, not for Mr. and Mrs. Peppermint

Apples of Arcadia

Empty and withered bags and pews of swarming maggots and jealous ghosts grazing on my Lizzie's skin like satin for a measly ten dollars, not that, not them, not for any of them, not good, not for goodbye empty pew....

A few rows past the mark there's an empty seat so I take her to it. Not optimal by any means (a woman with hair like peacocks' feathers sits directly in front of her) and I can tell by her expression she means to let me know as much. So be it. I have no reserves. This is all there is.

She motions for me with her keys to bend down.

"Don't forget to wait for me after this," she says, a hint of fear in her voice. "I don't want to stand around too long alone in front of all these strange people."

Instinctively I look up and around at all the strange people and soon my eye catches those of the cute young redhead. She's still interested for some reason. Must be the way I bend over so easily when beckoned by the sound of the female voice like...

Keys jingling.

Eyes scolding. Icy fingers plucking hairs off the back of my neck and thighs. One hand lunging forward toward my chest, keys resting cold on thin folded cotton...

"Here. Take these. I haven't any pockets."

...Then back to nothing.

Turn back toward the redhead. She too stares at nothing. The magnetic power of nothingness. The grinding sound of keys jingling cold female voices singing metal gears grazing spitting hot sparks and icicles....Well, at least that would be something....

On the way back toward the vestibule the Victorian divan is winking. My turn to turn to nothing...

...Nothing but young Tad standing with an outstretched palm. I peel a ten spot from the lining of my coat and hand it to him. He shakes his head, then walks off and takes his seat in the chair reserved for him in the rear.

The bells have all chimed and the organ upstairs starts

wheezing out the old standard. Melissa pries the caked mud off her painted hooves, waiting for her father to come and throw her over his shoulder. The groom has his feedbag on and is whipped repeatedly by the best man to remind both of the proper time and place whereby to relieve themselves. I lean up against a stained oak archway leading out and light a smoke, watching the dry autumn leaves pinwheel out of control to the ground.

Reception. Seven...something.
Standing now thoughts all sticky-fingered stealing what the other is thinking scuffling his feet pretending to dance with the pretty girls in pink sashes. There's one in particular who's drawing them in droves. A clamor of scratched soles kicking goateed lips grinning metallic blue eyes, teeth and sunned skin gleaming under stroboscopic light. It's enough to make one wish he were among them, among her, among the rich blue and red and sunny yellow smoke surrounding them, around her. Her. Two steel blue eyes smiling at them smiling back at her, her two bronze arms and legs naked all except for thin ribbons of semidiaphanous smoke and hyalescent light like the wings of exotic moths caught and torn off and ground to powder...

"Wolf?"
Thank God. An avocation.
"Hey, Wolf. I thought that was you."
It's the best man, Ski. And judging by his stagger it appears he's taken quite a fancy to all this newfound swank at the hands of Stenborg's folly, especially unlimited access to the bottom-shelf bar.

Ski leans in and slaps my back, spilling a mouthful of booze on my shoe.

"Shit, man," he sputters. "What the hell you doin' leanin' 'gainst a wall? The party's out there, dude...can't you see?" with a nod toward the dance floor. "Damn, what I wouldn't give to know the name of that buckin' filly."

"Lizzie," I tell him as if it were the answer to a game show question.

He nods as if he understands but doesn't so he inspects his skull for a germ of recognition...finds it, the flicker of thin florescent light behind the eyeballs which slowly turn in my direction. "*Yours?*"

I smile.

"Well, hell," he chortles, another nod. "That's some piece o' work you got there, Wolf. I mean...shit! That's somethin' to be proud of, man!" Again I smile. It seems it's all I'm able to do. "So," he leans in, smirking. "Tell me....How'n the hell d'you manage that one?"

I was wrong. Seems I can shrug my shoulders too.

Ski leans in closer. "Don't get me wrong, bud," he starts with a grin. "I mean, I'm not tryin' to tell you what you already know or nothin' but....Damn, dude! What the hell?! I mean, you got every fuckin' guy on the floor wantin' to be where you are right now...only you're *not*. You're *here*, you know? And they're *there*. Doesn't that concern you a bit?"

Nothing. A breeze of false liberty.

"Hey, man," he goes on. "I'm not sayin' *me*, y'hear? See now...." He holds up his left hand. "I'm taken, bro. I'm spoken for. And besides..." (with a wink) "...I'm a friend, Wolf. I'm a friend! Ha! Ha!"

Another slap. This time the other shoe.

Lizzie asudden appears before us, her hands on her hips, lips apple-red and panting and shifting her weight from left to right to left again. "God, I need a drink," she groans but my hands are dry. Ski sees this and smiles and offers his. She smiles back, accepts.

Silence dangling steel icicles on nose hairs hanging...

Ski presents a chisel. "Stephen," he says with a drop of prussic acid.

"Hi. Elizabeth," breathes she. "Well...*Liz*, actually," with a darting glance at me, my muted ox tongue.

Ski looks at me, then at our *Liz*.

They touch hands. Her hand around his and his and hers around his and his contaminated glass. Contaminated. Contemned and. Hated. Hands. Contemned and. Hands. And. Goddamn.

Hand upon my shoulder, squeezing. Sticky fingers feeling. Ski's ox tongue speaking. "It's nice to finally meet you," it says. "I've heard a lot about you from this guy here." Feeling contemned and fingers. Feeling. Hand upon my Lizzie. Squeezing. "I can see why he kept you a secret, though." Hated. "It's obvious he wants you all to himself, eh?" Hey Ted. "And who can blame him, hmm?"

"Well, *I* can blame him." Ho! Me holly yang gel speaks! "I mean, if he'd introduced us sooner I'd not had needed a drink..." (Pause.) "...I'd have had one already."

Ho! Ho! Ho!

Now Ski: "That's true. Very true." T'hee hee. "And I'd not be in need of a partner for the next dance." *Hmmm.* (It's good to have friends. All friends like fingers feeling rings on hands and spoken-for fiancées, what!)

Ski releasing me, saying, "See here, Wolf. The weddin' party's headin' over to Schultz's in an hour. You in?" I nod, more as an attempt to say no more words. "Good. Meet us in the parkin' lot...eight bells."

He turns to go. Lizzie stops him, raises his drink. "Wait. You forgot this."

"Keep it," he breathes as if in a whisper. Then, to me: "Remember, Wolf..." (again the left hand) "...A filly needs a harness." Then a parting smile as he turns toward the bar.

I look at Liz. She's watching Ski, the *rearview* of Ski walking off toward away. Now she looks at her drink, at *his* drink, and now at me. Now a sort of sad, inquisitive look not at me but inside me, inside what she thinks she sees and apprehends, what she thinks she's seen before in every man she thought she knew; a yellow-blue-green flame, a conflagration between the laminae of memory and the recollection of false hope, the imaginary promise of culling what falls from trees, from the branches of a cypress or a hickory or a sycamore, not her sycamore, not my sycamore, not even a sycamore but a rosewood or a eucalyptus or a chinaberry tree, *someone else's* chinaberry tree. Now a look of disappointment, a dejection bordering on despair, and now again the drink and now the dance floor and the people there until finally there's no memory anymore of branches or sycamores burning in the minds of men she thought she knew too well.

I tell myself to remember this look.

Then I start to walk away.

"Where the hell do you think *you're* going?"

I don't know. I honestly can't think of anything to say, which isn't so bad, so I just say, "I don't know."

She scoffs and looks at me as if I just recited her the call number for *Les Fleurs du Mal*. "You were just going to leave me here, weren't you?"

"Leave you where?"

"What the hell do you mean *where*? *Here!* By myself! Standing *here* by myself!" Pause. "Weren't you?! Tell me, goddammit! Say something!"

All these *things* to say and nothing breaching the surface. So be it. After all, an ox tongue knows no English, only *Ox*... and a little Heifer now and again, when it needs to. Do I need to? I don't know. As of late the world of *knowing* seems to be drifting fast into the world of *motherfucking shit, piss, cock, patchouli stank and cat hair cotton-mouthing off and early-morning snubs and drunken silence screaming holy bloody Christ and terror think of easy things to say then lay the neighbor's sister dreaming sitting naked at the wobbly kitchen table sipping Earl Grey and bourbon...*

"Hey! I'm talking to you, asshole!" A gush of booze. The guts of his battalion gone, beleaguering feet. "I'm waiting! Christ, can't you even think of a single thing to say?! Why is it so difficult for you, huh?! Why are you so weak?! Why am *I* always the one who has to talk?! Why?! Am I the only one who cares?! Why can't you just once act like a man and stick up for yourself and *say something*?!"

Gone. All gone. The insides of Ski's army the victim of a vicious Norwegian apoplexy.

A flash! "Can I get you another drink?" I say, eyeing the empty glass in her hand.

Something?

Wrong. All wrong. Obviously not the best way to stall a steam train. Still, even a banana peel holds some commodity somewhere as shown by the balancing act the thin reddish-brown lines of her eyebrows form when attempting to equate what was just said with the sought-after gravity of the (sadly) tepid situation. Then she surrenders and turns and walks off toward the dance floor.

I was serious about the drink. Still am. To be honest the thought of alcohol is the only thought that makes sense at this point. Not here, though – the bars at these things aren't suitable for a sophisticated waster. I feel inside my coat pocket and find Lizzie's keys and smile and head for the door.

Disarm.
Unlock.
Open.
Close.
Insert.
Turn.
Fire.
Start.
Engage.
Depress.
Divorce.

Driving down Tower Avenue now with a terrifying thirst and twenty dollars less than I should have in my pocket. So be it. We all get ours. And if there ever was a town where a man needs no money (that man being *me*) then this is it. Lots of potholes to fall into should the eyes of fortune be a gargoyle's gaze.

Pothole number one: The Dugout. Not a bad place where

a guy can get his sauce in peace with elbows resting on real mahogany while listening to tracks laid down sometime mid-Twentieth Century. There's even an old-time pinball machine propped up in the corner like Thomas Edison's tombstone that spits out gold coins if you know how to massage the slots just right...but that's not the reason most Superiorites stop here. The true draw is Samson O'Brien, the owner and head bartender of this joint ever since the word *Dugout* was tacked up atop the awning of the entryway door. Not necessarily an oddity of this town, Samson, though most certainly a separate character. Being so, Samson takes great pleasure in exercising his right as bartender to both astonish and piss off his smiling, dough-faced customers who sit at the bar like bewildered children watching him twist animals out of balloons filled with bilge water, then proceeding to beat the lot over the head with the same, the entire line of silly twats cheering for more. For some reason, though, Samson has excluded me from aim of his shit-grin remarks and taunts for personal twisted glory. No, not some reason...*cunt*. It's the least he can do is act congenial for all the juicy tail I've sent his way via late night college-types tipsy in their cups. And where's the next best joint for a stiff drink, they ask? Where else? Out the Lounge and off toward the Dugout they all trot. Ol' Samson gets his wick dipped and I get my Dugout drinks gratis. Win: win.

Pulling into the lot and straightaway I notice a jet-black Escalade with tinted windows and dual chrome exhaust spot head-on toward the concrete Dugout wall, a personalized plate reading: *BAD ASS*. A stray tourist from across the Bridge, I think as I park Lizzie's car near the entrance and flit.

Under the awning, in through the door and instantly I catch a smiling nod from Samson behind the bar. Belonging to that ilk of bartender who, due to long, exhaustive hours with nought to do but stare at sporting news highlight loops and eavesdrop on the conversations of intellectual midgets, Samson has fast discovered a far better way of wasting one's time: books, particularly the banned ones. Like most literary newbies who've before found their entertainment elsewhere (films, magazines, bottles, boobs, etc.) Samson had no idea the written word could be so potent – not until I handed him my copy of Henry Miller's *Opus Pistorum*. Since then he's shaken me for my full scatological catalogue as well as gone digging on his own, never failing to lay all he finds at my feet like fallen baby birds. This nodding smile means he's just raided a nest.

Before I even reach the bar there's a Heineken waiting for me, propped atop a copy of *Portnoy's Complaint*. Not a bad dig, I have to admit. This one I usually keep for myself, not realizing an audience still exists for Roth's juvenile rants beneath the guise of a neurotic Jew. A bit stale these days. Still, I thought his treatment of impotence sincere. I raise the Heineken and take a large pull, allowing a moment for the acidic sting to turn to pleasure, then I set down the beer and flip *Portnoy* to a random passage....

Ah, yes, it's all coming back to me. Some of the stankiest filth one can imagine comes out of this book...*some*, I say. In truth, nothing can top Herr Miller and the twisted, smutty evil and all around madcap carnival of lickerish sex he somehow pulls off in *Opus*. All else after that just seems phony, a knockoff – pornography with a purpose...

"Jeff? Is that you?"

To the right. Sadie Sunderson. The matriarch of all boys lost below a sea of tears and alcohol. "Hello, Sadie."

"Hi. I thought that was you, but I wasn't sure. You look so different with that tuxedo on. So...*regal*."

Christ, I forgot. I'm still dressed in ancestral gear. This should make for some uninteresting talk.

I look back at Sadie. She's smiling a seductive grin – eyes shining, sea blue hiding behind fallen strands of astrakhan with crow's feet in the corner; billowy, crooning cheeks red with imagination; white teeth perfectly aligned and glowing under rather thin, though perfectly capable lips – the same grin I've received from her a thousand times before though never could return because of Steve...though now there's no Steve. Perhaps he's gone. Perhaps she left him. Perhaps she finally woke up and realized he's been gone for a long time, lost beneath the icy waves searching for his son. Perhaps he's just in the john. Whatever the case, that sleepy, sideways grin of hers is worth the wait.

"So, what brings you here away from the Lounge?" I ask, nudging in closer.

"Oh, nothing," she purrs. "Just a drink," with a wink.

A clue. Nonchalance mixed with booze. What follows is rarely misunderstood.

Closer. "Just a drink, hmm?...What, are Samson's White Russians really all that smoother?" with my own clandestine twist. All smiles and stares and whispers under skirts.

"Not a chance, Jeff." (Sleepy...sidewise....) "You spoil us there, you do."

"Only you, Sadie."

T'hee.

"Oh, you...you lie."

"In suit, Miss 'Just A Drink'."

T'hee, hee.

Hmmmmmm....

She's leading me along now with her giggles and grins and I realize it doesn't matter if Steve's here or not – I can always make it well again with a handshake and a free drink, if need be. I lean in closer, so close I can set my head on her shoulder and taste the inside of her ear if I wanted. "You lie, Jeff. You lie. You're such a liar, you are." And you, Sadie, are a silly, nervous flirt with your stirring of ice cubes in glasses wet with sweat on torn napkins sopping, pearls on skin and necks twisting, tightening to the sudden acidic sting turning slowly to...

"Petcock!"

I look up from Sadie's neck to see Samson smiling down at me, a look on his face as if he just discovered the ropes. An unseasonable nuisance. Still, he returned *Portnoy* back to me safe and unstolen and as of yet hasn't asked a dime for the Heineken. I suppose a little etiquette is in order. I give Sadie back her neck (for now) and smile and say, "Petcock?"

"Yeah, petcock," he repeats through his teeth.

"What the hell is *petcock*?"

"That's what you're supposed to tell me. It's the word of the day."

"What...*petcock*?"

"Yeah...*petcock*." A troupe of middle-aged ninnies down the bar gives a titter. Samson smiles at them and says, "And no, it's not a term of endearment for your hubbies," at which the titter turns to cackles, then back at me: "Come on, man... *petcock*."

I'm on the spot. I have to admit I've never heard the word. All the same, to say this to Samson just would not do. Bar games are normally for the dull and daft-witted and I'd be neglecting my duty if I didn't greet Samson's rather inventive gesture with at least an equal try. So...

"*Petcock*," I begin, "is onomatopoeia for the sound the Australian silver rooster makes when attempting to court an auk. *Pet-pet-petCOCK*. See?"

A bit silly, I know, but not too bad. At least Sadie thinks so, complimenting my dry antics with one of her flirtatious giggles. Even if Samson's unimpressed, I've still got one in the bag. And still no Steve.

Samson points to *Portnoy*. "Thanks for that," he says, grinning. "I never knew Jews could be so...filthy. I feel liberated."

"From what?" I'd like to know.

"From myself...my views against Jews. They really do seem like a likeable bunch."

"You can say that from just one book?"

"Why not? I mean, even if this Portnoy character whines like a sissy and can't seem to get his mother out of his head, even when boning some *goy* bitch....Shit, that really got me, his obsession for *goys*....I mean, I've fucked a million of 'em and I'd gladly trade in half the lot for just one Jew cunt.... *Oops!* Pardon my Hebrew, miss." (Sadie smiles.) "Anywho, about Jews...about 'em being so likeable....I guess I never understood the way they felt about it till that book."

"About what?"

"About them...us. The *goy* thing, you know. It's really sad, isn't it? But of course it is. I don't have to tell you, being one yourself."

"What? *Goy*?"

"No...Jew. Aren't you?"

For Christ's sake! "What the hell gave you *that* idea?" I say a bit too harsh.

"It's okay. You don't have to be ashamed."

"Ashamed of *what*?! I'm not Jewish!" (Sadie starts a giggle.)

"Come on, Jeff," sighs Samson, crooking his neck. "Be honest with yourself."

"Meaning what?"

"Meaning...the whining, the whimpering, the grooming, the hair, the eyes...the nose" (Sadie's giggle turns flat into a guffaw) "the boyishness, the bookishness, the inferiority complex manifested as arrogance...the unabashed obsession with blondes...I mean, damn, man! Who else would have even *heard* of this book, let alone lend it out?"

"Philip Roth is this country's greatest living author."

"You don't believe that."

"Who else?"

He thinks some, then, with lips tilted, sneers, "*You*."

"Look," I begin, a bit taken aback by that last dig of his, "I'll say this one last time and I'll say it *slow* so you'll understand. I'M...NOT...JEWISH!"

Some thirsty ass is whining for a drink so Samson's got to go. Before he leaves he smiles and looks at me and says, "Look, it's one hell of a coincidence, is all...the Jew thing, I mean. Think of it....Perhaps you are and you just don't know it." And he's gone, sludging his way through vats of Guinness and leek soup and fields of Kelly green clovers.

Sadie's still laughing, though in a much more enticing way than Samson ever could. I decide it's time I lean in and give her a better reason to bare those alabaster gleamers of hers and as I do, staring at the bar waiting for something brilliant to pop into my bean, my eyes focus on a familiar image resting before her: *BAD ASS*. The label of a key ring.

"Yours?" I ask, nodding toward the bar.

She looks down at the ring, smiles, then purses her lips like a schoolgirl and says, "Dave's."

I have to laugh. The whole thing is painfully funny, most of all the obviousness of it which I failed to notice. A chaste woman on the loose? Ha! A saucy minx! To think this near-middle-aged mommy of two grown men traded one in for a memory and the other for an Escalade...*Dave's* Escalade! But who the hell is *Dave*?

Before I can ask a tall, bald-headed dude with buff limbs and leather and one lone silver-hoop earring dangling like a dinner bell takes the seat next to us...and says nothing, not a word. Body language says it all, however, and soon I'm met with a cold reaction from Sadie and icy-eyes from the stud.

Times like this it's best to take control.

I offer my palm to Sir Hank and say, "Oi. You must be Dave. I'm Jeff, a friend of Sadie's."

But only his eyes move. He then turns to Sadie, catching her nod and warm, motherly smile convincing him all's well below the danger zone, then at last he leans over and takes my hand and squeezes like an anaconda, then back again to his silver-clad-leather nothingness.

Sadie just shrugs and gives one final giggle, then off she goes, following his lead.

Samson reappears as if part of the script. "Here," he says, slapping a book beneath my long, non-Semitic nose. "Time to teach *you* about *my* people. We're not so bad with the pen either, you know." *A Portrait*. "Lots of accolades and awards on our end, too. 'Specially this one." Saint James of the Holy Disorder. Solicitous Joyce: Daedalus. "Not much for cot talk, him, but he's got his paws on other things, namely religion... something your lot can appreciate, eh? He, he...." A clock in turn for a cross. A cross in turn for congress. Insincerity and stupidity. "And even if it's all high-minded, puffed-up artsy psychobabble..." An Irish story on aesthetics suited for the palates of sex-starved altar boys who've contracted the pox from some poor hussy's purse. A showing forth of toxic emotion... "...You have to admit how good this guy is, don't you? I mean, *Ulysses* has been dubbed the best book ever written...beyond the Bible, that is....And by an Irishman, even!" An epiphany on paralysis. A showing forth beyond the lines on Samson's face tracing out his lineage like thin blood dripped in oil. "So, here, then, take it..." Paralyzed. Epiphanized. "...and tell me what you think."

I run my fingers lightly over the leather cover, over the raised *James Joyce* in metallic green ink, then gently push it aside and say in me best Hibernian brogue: "Pure shite."

Then I finish my beer.

"Well, hell's bells, Hemingway!" spits Samson. "Mister High N. Mighty on his throne preachin' to the masses, now, is he?! Well, then, let's just see you do better, you mouthy, Nazi pudder! Ha! Let's just see you do better!"

But I'm off. No time to respond to cunt-struck Bogtrotter jingoism.

Slipping *Portnoy* in my coat pocket I step off my stool and make for the door. About halfway down the bar I hear Samson's voice yell, "Hey, you! Hey *Jew-boy*! You still owe me for the Heineken!"

In the lot again I notice the Escalade. Inspired, I back Lizzie's car from the entrance and wedge the driver-side door T-bone-style across the *BAD ASS* plate and toss the keys in the backseat and lock the doors and bolt.

On the trot and skipping up Tower Avenue now like a man who sacked D.C. suddenly Samson's words come to mind: *Perhaps you are and you just don't know it.* I have to admit the mick puff has a point. I never thought about it much till now, most likely because of its absurdity, the total preposterousness of it, and it's this, of course, which attracts me to the idea. What if I were Jewish, not in any *practicing* way, God no, but what if there was some distant line which traces my blood back to the days of the Red Sea, back before the sand dunes of Jerusalem swarmed over the Holy Circle of Humanity and buried it there for good, the shrill, foreign screams and ill sound of splintering bone still being heard today? How would this affect me? How would I view myself in the mirror the day after this affliction? Asking myself this very question, this horror of introspection, I have to answer: *I don't know.* I know nothing about them. I know nothing about the inner space of the Jew other than that which us budding daisies were fed whilst sprouting in seclusion from the feculence outside the Holy See – which was, put simply, *horseshit.* Nothing other than stale myths and fables were brought before us during those most impressionable years (a brilliant move on the side of Tyranny – a tactic practiced by the most successful minds at the head of any oppressive state dating back to the days of Zion) that all we have to fall back upon are the perpetuated cliché-facsimiles of a dying race, a race that has been dying now for over two thousand years. *Jude*, Hebrew, Israelite, Sadducee, rabbi, the high priest, Talmudist, the Old Testament, the Koran, kike, hook-nose, hairy quim, ear wax, killers of Christ, messiah, Isaiah, Zechariah, Jeremiah, Joseph, Jonah, Ezekiel, Zephaniah, chariots of fire riding high into the sky, golden wheels spinning on wooden axles, the Exodus, exegesis, the Axe in the hands of Jesus, jewelry, fish, pickles, Pall Mall cigarettes, lamb, duck, David, Solomon, Saul Bellow, the Nobel Prize for Words, *The Solitary Life of Man*, *The Magic Barrel*, Leonard Bernstein's *Candide*, Brian Epstein's Beatles, Groucho, Harpo, Zeppo, Gummo, Chico, Spinoza's *Ethics* being lost in its own lifetime, naked pride, police state, put in ghettos,

Apples of Arcadia 225

forced to extract teeth in reverence of His Heinous, the antiholy Fritzie Heine, lice, starvation, gum disease, abscessed roots spitting puss onto parched tongues and into withered stomachs, Sons of Ahab, six-pointed stars, newfound pride (silly and premature), free-lance economics, silk fobs, silver watches, gold coins, banks, vaults, glass temples foundering with money, money, money, money, money pouring out the eyelets, Judenhut tipped sideways on ancient skulls, tradition, mysticism, salvation, illness, doom, death. These are the thoughts that immediately come to mind when I think of the Jew, a race I can no more identify with than the Aztecs or the Incas. And like the Aztecs and the Incas they are lost, slated to the elements, unrooted in time and space...the children of History, that is all. So who, then, writes history? Not the Jew, that's certain. He won't even write his own history, the story of a fated people sent blindly on an errant mission to bring salvation to a miserable, miserable world. No, he writes only about neurosis, about the *failure* of this mission. Optimism is no more in the Jew than in the fawn on the side of the road struck listless by the grill of a passing semi.

About Samson's other observations...hell, it's all I can do not to laugh. The whining? What the devil does he mean *whining*? When has he ever heard me whine...other than when he forces me to pay for one of his watered-down, all-ice-and-soap-scum aluminum rail drinks? And even then I don't whine...I sulk. An honest form of objection whereby nobody's affected but me own pathetic self, see? Anyhow, all I can say is that McPaddy rates a lot more than he's received. And the whimpering? Again, not a peep. I swear that soggy bog man's been dipping in the whiskey during work hours again like the time he nearly puréed his thick mick fingers when attempting to blend a sombrero with tequila and Tecate after midnight last Cinco de Mayo. "Hats off to the Irish!" he'd say on this hallowed day, never mind the fact that we Irish have our own ridiculous, vomitous holiday. Okay, I will say this: my boyishness and bookishness both are character traits I will not defend as I consider them flaws of the first order. Still, they are mine, as much me as my hazel-brown eyes and overdeveloped nose: they cannot be changed. So be it. My arrogance, however, I will defend and stringently, though not as some deviate, semiconscious inferiority complex gone awry (talk about artsy psychobabble!). It's no secret to anyone who's ever been accused of arrogance that, while arrogance for arrogance's sake does exist and is easily sniffed out by any semiconscious spectator due to its smell which closely resembles shit, arrogance for *one's own* sake also exists, though is not so easily sniffed out due to the fact that, instead of shit to compare it with, the semiconscious spectator now finds himself face-to-face with a bouquet of cattails. He's baffled, in the least, because he *wants* to smell shit, he sees this chap before him who couldn't care less about Venus or Mars or Neptune or Lithuania or the Olympics or cars or his kids' names or the market cost of his home or how wide is his wife's ass or how he's been having an affair with her best friend now for over a year and how they play footsie beneath the poker table every Tuesday night or Monday night football or the news or elections or the weather on the West Coast or Planet X or Pluto and he needs to have a reason why this is so. When faced with this complexity of noncompliance he needs a value by which to fix his intelligence upon, then...by God, it comes to him! Yes! Arrogance! At last he smells shit, which, no doubt, wafts from his own fuming asshole at having to clench his intestines for so long in anguish and confusion. And so, because you choose to play another game, you have this pulsating letter *A* etched into your skull like a criminal in some puritanical novel. Man's sanctity is saved! Hallelujah on high and pass the lima beans and gravy! However, what the semiconscious spectator like Samson fails to notice is this letter *A* pulsates only under his own semiconscious gaze. The arrogant chap with the scarred skull has no idea his cranium has been tampered with. All's well in Hoboken, as far as he's concerned. In fact, insofar as arrogance goes, he has no idea as to even the meaning of the word. He's immune to the symptoms of this social disease. To him it's all champagne and oysters under warm sheets and one entirely unsocial, unarrogant girl...which raises Samson's final snub about blondes. Well, shit! What else am I to diddle in a Northern port town?

I've been walking now for almost twenty minutes and my tongue needs an anodyne. All this thinking about champagne and oysters and unsociable girls and tequila have my taste buds in a stir. Still, not one friendly face by which to bum a few bucks. Scowls, that's all I see. Must just be autumn and the ice storms that follow after. People's brains must be adjusting to the bastard borne of a bitch which is Lake Superior weather. (There. A mention of the weather. An unarrogant moment.)

I'm peeking in the windows now to see if I recognize a face with a mouth that's benefited from my liberality behind the slab and I see none...though I do see something else: a fellow bard. Well, to be honest we are neither fellows nor are we bards (we enrolled in the same creative writing course at the University, that is all) though we do share one commonality: alcohol. He has some and I want some. Perhaps I can cash in on all those constructive marks we put on each other's papers all those years ago...that is, if he remembers me. It's worth a shot. The worst he can do just stare at me blanklike, then back at those Bolshevik Beatniks he's sitting with. It's settled. I step away from the window and stroll toward the tavern door.

When attempting to borrow money from someone whom one might consider an acquaintance (however loosely, in this case) it's always best to be as indirect as possible, to bring about the subject as if by accident or an *Oh, there's just one more thing* type afterthought. In other words, one must have what higher Western society calls "tact". To demand money, even if you have every right to do so, is sure to end undesirably for both the borrower and the borrowee...more so for the latter for obvious reasons, of course. With this in mind I stride past the table in question as if it doesn't exist toward the bar and order a water served in a nervous glass light on the ice with a lemon twist, the demands of which are met by the barman with a "Who the hell do you think you are, buddy?" glare which turns flat into a "You sonofabitch bastard!" scowl when I turn and walk away without leaving a dime. Fuck 'im. He is presently not my concern. I'm off to float and hover over and circle like an osprey my former pen chum...that is, an osprey in auk's plumage.

They (the Bolsheviks and Anthony, I think is his name) sit elbows-together around a small circular table in the corner under a hanging lamp whispering to one another, the whole crew looking like some dark scene out of *Brothers Karamazov* or the stark, lye-bleached embodiment of the Communist Manifesto. Either way, they seem quite serious in their army-green wool pants and Dr. Martens and turtleneck sweaters with pads sewn on the elbows. All are smoking heavily, a thick, electro-orange fog obscuring their hands and eyes and black plastic, round-rimmed glasses which each must push repeatedly up off his radical, oily nose. Serious, did I say? I meant *sarcastic*, what with the whispering and the militant, pseudo-bohemian-intellectual garb that went south of style the day Lenin sacked St. Petersburg. Still, it's the money that's important so, to infiltrate the party's objective, I steal a seat near the crowded table of wool pants and padded elbows and whispers and light up a smoke and lean in for a listen.

A beady-eyed, skin-and-bones type is speaking:

"...an invisible ship sinking in a bottomless sea. That's the whole point, the real significance behind Sartre's *Nausea*. It's got nothing to do with art for art's sake, but the *opposite* of art...the bluish film beneath the green....The pettiness behind all that anguish." (He leans back as if awaiting applause.)

At first nobody speaks, just smokes. Then, finally, a fatty with a sparse goatee exhales and says, "So, what you're saying is that anguish has no place in art?"

"No....I'm saying anguish isn't art at all...but the *opposite* of art....Which is to say, self-serving and superficial."

The fat one laughs. "But isn't that the very essence of art? Ha! Ha!"

No one laughs with him. They all just sit and smoke and every once in a while sip off their cups.

Anthony speaks:

"It's obvious you're no artist, Kent. Your views on art are childish and simplistic."

"Don't forget narcissistic," says the skinny one.

"Not only that," begins the fourth, a squirrelly-looking blond with yellow eyes, "but you're not qualified to have *any* opinion on the matter whatsoever."

"Oh? And why's that, Lars?"

"Because, Kent, you're Episcopalian, and Episcopalians make lousy artists."

"Here, here!" cries Skin-and-bones. "A toast to such marvelous revelations!"

At this the fat one – Kent – gets red in the face and leans back in silence. The others drink and smoke, also in silence, until Anthony:

"Jarvis, you began something, didn't you? About art for art's sake?"

Jarvis looks at Kent and smiles, then, at Anthony:

"That's right, Ant. Though I wasn't speaking necessarily about art, but the *absence* of it."

"Absence *where*?"

"Everywhere. Art isn't something made or created, if you will, but something the mind perceives in place of this *need* for creation, this human desire to put a name on something, on an emptiness he doesn't understand."

"Bullshit," coughs Kent.

"Look, Kent, I told you..."

"Tell you what, Lars," starts Kent. "You can go ahead and take your marvelous revelations and your Episcopalian-bashing observations and cram them up your pee hole!"

Then, to Jarvis: "Look, I may be green, but that's not to say I'm disposed to believe this country-trash theory on human nihility you're continually trying to sell us." Jarvis smirks. Kent continues: "It's art's duty, the duty of the artist to..."

"Wait," cuts Lars. "What do you mean by *art*, anyway? Let's have a definition before we let you continue."

Kent smokes a moment, then nods and says, "Art, as it is understood by a non-artist, is the manifestation of emotion."

"Man's emotion?"

"What the hell are we talking about?! *Chimpanzees?!*"

"Right. But what is emotion?"

"It's what makes man human."

"Qualify that. What do you mean by *human*?"

"What do you *mean* what do I mean, you twat?! Human! *Human* is human! *He* is human! *She* is human. *I* am human. Even *you*, you albino bastard, even *you* could be human, if you wanted to."

"You're missing the issue, Kent," starts Anthony. "What Lars means, I think, is the abstract idea behind it." A thoughtful puff, then: "*Humanness*, in relation to the artist, is really only a language for the artist's perceptions...the artist's *art*, if you will. Neither truly exists as an entity unto itself, is that right, Jarvis?"

"That's it, Ant! And if the artist doesn't exist then neither do his emotions. See, it's this emptiness, this meaninglessness of existence...or, I think, *lack* of existence, which forces man to create. He's only looking to validate his nonexistence which, in the end, accomplishes nothing. Art...art *for art's sake* accomplishes nothing. Therefore, art is the opposite of creation, see? It's all very simple."

"What, then, would you call this?" asks Kent. "What are we doing right now?"

"How do you mean?"

"This conversation...is this not something?"

"It's sound...that is all."

"And music? Is that just *sound*, as you say?"

"Yes. We only *perceive* it as music because our minds need justification for..."

"Wait....Ha! See?! A contradiction! How can a man perceive a mind that does not exist?"

"Simple. He created it."

"What?! *His mind?!*"

"Yes."

"From what?!"

"Why, from nothing, of course."

At this I nearly blow it and burst out laughing in all their pasty faces, surrendering my unsociable position. Luckily, like the substance of their mock-artsy talk, their cups have all been drained and now they're discussing whose turn it is to fetch a refill. Anthony (like a guru surrounded by his disciples) without a word accepts the burden as his own, unsettling himself and sauntering off.

That's my cue. I squash out the butt and follow him to the bar.

The bartender eyes me as we approach. I ignore him, of course, and concentrate instead on Anthony. He hasn't changed all that much since school – still wearing his clothes too small and combing his hair forward to the right – the only real difference being that he seems much more mature, more composed than before. He was always a bit obnoxious, jittery; too many cubes in the kettle, so to speak...especially with his writing. He could never concentrate on any one point more than half a paragraph before losing hold of the sealing thread and, rather than regain grasp, jump straight into a new bag where all was isolated and the only light which shone in was through the tinselly, star-shaped holes he liked to invent, though, truth be known, these curious oddities were always accidents, byproducts of confusion more than any planned attack. He confided in me as much one day over a burrito and a Pepsi in the school cafeteria. "I can't help it, Jeffrey," he'd whine, chomping into his tortilla. "All these words and images just keep rolling and rolling and I can't stop them."

A swallow, then: "If only I could think of a way to control them...to make them roll only when I need them. How easy it would be then." *Easy?! Control?! How naïve can one man be?!* Shit, in that case control would be the worst possible thing, the black metal blanket which suffocates the umbilical flow of creativity. The only thing one should wish for in such an instance is the ability to keep up, by God! Control! Ha! What this poor, supposedly tortured soul was really relating to me then was that he was scared, petrified of the inner workings of the mind, afraid of what he might find should the laurel wreath be placed gently upon *his* head because once that happens there's no turning back. It's all forward after that and to forsake it is to spit in the eye of Aphrodite. No, he wasn't looking for any advice from me then. He was looking for absolution. He was looking for a way out.

And now here he stands, a wad of stiff bills in his hand ordering drinks for the entire table, a cool, indifferent grin stretching his pale, cenobian mug. He must have found what he was looking for. All the same, it's clear he isn't looking for much else as I've been standing here nearly five minutes and he hasn't bothered looking over. He'll have his drinks soon. Must make my move.

"Anthony? That you?"

He looks up and searches the room for my voice, finds it, then smiles and says, "Jeffrey."

We shake hands. Slow. Composed.

He asks if he can buy me a drink, to which I raise my glass as if to say, "Why not?"

"What's that you're having? A martini?"

"Not exactly," I say. Then, with a smirk: "A *vodka* martini *on the rocks* with a *twist*."

He nods, calls the bartender. "A vodka martini twist... with everything else." The bartender turns to me as if in disbelief. I give him a wink as a sign of reassurance to which he just grimaces, then scuffles off.

"So, Jeffrey," starts Anthony, deftly thumbing his wad,

"tell me....What have you been up to these days?" Then, after the once-over: "Socializing?" meaning the outfit.

"Only part-time," I chuckle. He responds in kind, then turns and stares ahead, ignoring me completely.

This might be harder than I thought. However, the sight of all those bills he holds so loosely in his paw still has me optimistic. I slide in closer and think of something friendly to say but before I can he turns to me and says, "No, really, Jeffrey. What have you been doing with yourself?"

The coolness of his tone has me somewhat concerned. It seems he's setting me up to be berated, the idea of which has me forthwith puffing my skin and proclaiming, proud as can be, "I'm a bartender."

"Still? Isn't that what you were doing back in school?"

"Only part-time," is all I can think to say.

He takes over, peeling a few bills to hand over to the man who's fixing my martini, saying, "You know, Jeffrey, it's funny. I've thought about you a lot lately...probably because of my students...they remind me of you sometimes, though not in their writing...no, not in that way at all...but their passion, their near-manic passion which drives them to perfection." A pause as if in thought, then: "To think...I often thought you'd have won the National Book Award by now." He turns from the money to see my reaction. Then, receiving none, resumes his counting. "A bartender, eh? Well, if that's what it takes, I guess. My only hope is...."

Christ, he just keeps talking and talking and if he keeps talking any longer the bartender'll be back with the drinks and he'll have paid and away will go the wad. After that he might think it a chore to bring it back out again.

Fuck tact.

"Look," I say, cutting him short. "That's all great, really it is, but what I need to know is...can I hit you up for a touch?"

He just stares, his eyebrows raised, motionless. Now the drinks have arrived and the bartender gets his money and a nifty tip besides and I'm left waiting there like some bum off the street. Finally he turns to me and says, "Why should I?"

How to answer this? Do I even answer?

He relaxes, then puts a hand on my shoulder and says, "What I mean is....What's wrong?"

"Nothing's *wrong*," I tell him, a bit uneasy. "I'm just a touch low is all."

"In that case," he begins, handing me the martini, "let's drink to nothing wrong." He takes a sip off his glass and I follow, watching him the while. Then, licking booze off his upper lip: "As to the touch....It wouldn't be in good taste." Then he pockets the wad and rounds up the table's drinks and walks away, over his shoulder saying, "Enjoy the martini, Jeffrey."

I'm left standing here with my ass hanging out my pants. Behind I hear a titter. I turn to see the bartender shaking his head, laughing. "Here's to all *that*, pal," I think as I raise the martini in his face, then down it in a single gulp. He just rolls his eyes and walks off.

I light up a smoke and, trying my damnedest to contain a cough, walk away from the bar past the pigs practicing their intelligentsia accents through the door into the street.

Aaaaachhh! Passion?! What does that slow, composed, secret-society-pledging-stuffy-shirted-tight-ass know about *passion*?! To him it's just a word, an image he can't control, a *language* by which he can slowly, compositely, scientifically interpret the correct path toward perfection....*Perfection!* Shit! Who does this bastard think he is...*Norman Mailer?!* Like hell! He's just some scrawny, long-limbed, frontward-hair-combing scared little boy who wears an invisible cloak over his invisible pride he bought from some invisible institution specializing in manufacturing shields to preserve the *amour propre* behind concentrated invisibility. All said, like his hack, nihilistic theory on art, he doesn't exist. He's nothing, a nonentity, a speck of dust on a book upon a shelf assembled weak inside an invisible study. He's pissed himself and gone hiding so often he's become nothing more than a semi-translucent mist puff, a dim, slightly colored streak of blurred cowardice staining the landscape as he passes, his achromatic, toxic, piss-spouting nothingness in tow...which is all good, by the way, because if he *did* somehow muster the courage to control his bladder long enough to put a few honest, concise, *passionate* words on paper and seal them tight with a lick and a stamp and a colorless, scentless, immodest watermark in the shape of a garden hose on the flap and send them...*where?* Who's going to receive these honest, concise, passionate scribblings set on paper by a self-proclaimed nihilist and nonentity? What weight could these words possibly possess? All may as well be drawn on soiled toilet tissue with invisible ink 'cause that's all they're worth to a marketable American public. Nobody likes a nihilist, I think I heard once someplace choking down a packet of salty crackers with cold soup and warm, watered-down orange juice under harsh florescent lighting...a recurring memory ignited by chronic insomnia and bad beef and no sex for over a month....

But back to passion and its abuse in the hands of invisible fools! Ah, yes! Many more recurrences coming to the fore like drops of spittle on the tongue after licking yellow snow...."*You know, Jeffrey,*" one of them says, invisible ink pen in hand, "*you must try to curb this tendency toward... hmm...misogyny...as well this artless, disturbing penchant for violence you seem to possess. One might easily mistake it for misanthropy.*" Brilliant! A book title, that, b'Jaysus! All credits due in the Secret Sect of Word Herders eventually find their owner, do they not? A natural, magnetic force to rival the migration of birds! So, then, here's another feather for the coop: "*It's getting better, Jeffrey, really. You seem to be spending more time correcting, taming your craft than you have in the past.*" Did I detect a slaver? A slight trickle on the chops? "*Now, I don't want you to get the wrong idea about these markings. They're not a reflection of you as a writer, necessarily...only the effort you've shown me so far, understand?"* C – !!!!!!!!!!!!!!! *"Understand also, Jeffrey, I honestly was impressed by how much you've trimmed things down...so much better from all the emotional clutter of your previous pieces. Keep it up and soon the grades will follow, hmm?"* Keep what up, you rotting scion of a bootless crop? The death rattle? The sink into obscure, sand-filled, infertile lands where you reign supreme? And then, if I'm successful in what you preach, in what you're *paid* to preach, I'm sure to get as my reward.........*grades*?! What the hell good are *grades*?! I'd trade just one pageful of my own emotional, violent, misogynic, misanthropic clutter for all the grades you could possibly hand out in your entire lifetime standing behind your invisible pulpit spitting words, words, words, words, words, words, words, words, words, words, words, words, words, words, words, words, words, all words and no emotion stacked neatly into neat paragraphs, all starched and pressed and steamed and neatly packaged in pretty green and blue and gold dust jackets with silver filigree etched in the sleeves and neatly wrapped and mailed and sent off and delivered promptly to all the pretty malls and shops and bookstores in every pretty American city, every pretty American citizen cheering with perfect glee in the face of all this enterprising efficiency and industry distributing such pretty pleasantries. And while all this cheering and perfect American glee-giving is happening where is our purely venerable and positively celebratory member of modern American society? Why, back at his pulpit, of course, counting bills while instructing the next generation of lost, soulless, emotionless, non-misogynic, unmisanthropic, piss-spouting, book-minded machinists....

No road. I look up from the concrete to see a winking flame red-yellow neon sign. *Lounge*, it says. So be it. I let a sigh and step inside.

Joe's the first to greet me, a look on his face like a cocainized orangutan.

"Holy Fucking Christ!" he snorts. "What the hell's all that about?" meaning the tux. "What, did somebody die? Oh, Jeff, please tell me it was Angela," meaning his wife.

That's what I like about Joe. Always blurting improper questions and always answering them himself. What I like *best* about Joe, though, is the way he opens a bottle without any questions at all...just pure hospitality with a grin and a nod and a wink and no books to lend or earlobes to lick. Just booze – booze and various slices of ass. And maybe a filthy word or two...for seasoning.

"Couldn't stomach the proceedings, hmm?" he smirks, setting the bottle before me on the bar. "Shit," he laughs. "It's just as well. I mean, who the hell are those things for, anyway? Not me...not you, obviously....Then *who*?" He waits. I shrug my shoulders. Then: "Damn....What they oughtta do is just gather everybody at some bar someplace...some real shithole, get me?...Then, once everyone's good and pissed, hand out bucket after bucket...donations for the damned, or some shit like that. Round after round, as much as a man can pour....Then, once the newlyweds are out and snoring, box 'em up 'n ship 'em off to Korea or Taiwan or Russia or some other Third-World country...show 'em both the true meaning of *TILL DEATH DO US PART*, eh? Ah, well," he sighs. "Who am I to say anything, anyway? A bartender, is all," he says, wiggling his ring finger. "Just a bartender," before sliding down the bar to answer the call of another customer.

My eyes follow his glide, shifting perpendicular from his waist to the line of customers like dry leaves responding to an encouraging breeze. Just nods and glances of recognition as signs of respect (a respect depending solely on what one can do for the other) before a lifeless finger is lifted like a vain Jehovah enjoying His most recent creation and away it goes, gentle signs of respect now bowing before spits and curses and orders for submission. *A bartender*, says Joe. *A bartender is all*.

Back slides Joe, a small glass of something brown and icy in his hand. "This is for you...from the end of the bar."

It's Steve, smiling and laughing and patting some burly

husky on the back with his paw, letting the world know this is most likely the happiest day his sad life has ever seen. Very well could be he already knows about Sadie, most likely took that hammer to the head with a sigh of relief. And now there he sits, laughing and smiling and soaking up as much of the good stuff his hairy mug can suck sitting next to what looks like he could be his brother the way they joke and poke and cajole one another...or perhaps he went the other way. Could this be? Could Steve have found self-expression face down in a pillow? Ah, well, however it goes the guy looks so insanely keen if he is tickling dick what prick would chide him for it? Not me...not while holding a prepaid whiskey, anyway.

He looks up the bar in my direction. I hold up the glass in salutation. He does the same, then down they go.

Goddamn! One never gets used to that molten metal injection of American whiskey. I follow it immediately with the dense wetness of my beer, then struggle like a blind man in a boat sinking through all the tears and endless streams of saliva flowing through my mouth and eyes and in my ears I hear, "Hey, there he is! Hey, Jeff! Jeff! Hey, Jeff, down here! Jeff!" I wipe my eyes with my cuffs and slowly focus and look up.

It's Jesop, sitting perked and lit and beaming with high-voltage as if he just self-administered electroshock therapy, though forgot the conducting gel. He looks frazzled, to say the least, weaving and spinning about in his stool as if prodded up the asshole. An offensive image. To escape it I peer to his right and see none other than the delectable, adorable Nora sitting primed and primped like a princess on her throne, a look of composed satisfaction glittering her sylphine face and lips smiling lust toward me. I check my reserve and finally find an advantage to the monkey suit I'm wearing; by the way she's got her eyes half-open and mouth bent and melting no doubt there's more than her father's electrifying company on her mind. So noted. I smile and turn to Jesop's left and there, pouting over her bourbon, sits Julie donning gauze bandages after her latest visit to the surgeon's office. No doubt this too has much to do with Nora's royal pose. The prophecy is fulfilled. The scabby mole has been scraped off Julie's pig nose.

"Hey, Jeff," spits Jesop, spinning and slithering like a congo eel through wife and nymph. "It's Jeff, the *second* best bartender this dump has ever seen! Ha!" meaning second to Joe, his nephew, of course. "Hey, Jeff, what's with the getup? What, you get hitched or something? Ha, ha!" Nothing. Still gazing up Nora. "Hey, bartender...hey *first* best bartender, ha, ha....Hey, get our good man Jeff, there, a drink...whatever he wants. Ha, ha, ha!"

Here's Joe, apologizing with his eyes. No need. "Let's split it," I say. Joe smiles and trots off.

"Ha, ha! The *second* best bartender, yep. Whaddya say to that, there, Jeff, eh? Ha, ha, ha!"

The price of a free drink is all. Eyeing Nora, addressing Jesop, saying, "You got it dead on, man. Dead on. A master of seminiferous flesh and bone incarnation." He crimps his brow and chuckles and whispers something electric into his sliced wife's ear as Joe delivers the shots. "Kudos, Jesop," I shout, brushing off the ice chips. "Here's to you, sir. The first best father of the second best daughter this third world has ever seen." Then down it goes.

Vodka. How uncolorful.

Hmmmmmmm....

Steel clamor gunpowder bursting napalm shattered glass and bone explosions coming from somewhere near the door. A crowd, it seems, all shouting and whirling around the center of some person I can't quite...wait! Shelby's husband it is, all bare-assed and hanging shit-faced sitting sloppy forearms and legs slung noodle-like over the edge of a wobbly shopping cart, smiling....Laughing, more like, the boys of Our Fair And Goodly Elevated Wheat Harvest Seed panting, taunting all on-lookers on. Onward. Onward carts the carting. Shelby duly behind, striding.

"Make way!" they shout. "Make way, everybody! Make way for a union boy!"

So *that's* the meaning behind all this hoo-ha....One more grainer makes the select ranks of union attendee, eh? Aye. So be. So even I find time to toss a smile as does every other soused mouth outside the hole once Shelby hops behind the bar and loosens all the taps and spouts. After scraping his tips off the rail Joe grabs a beer and sulks. He's got nothing to say. Shelby out-ranks him by ten years....*Ten years!* Damn, that's one helluva lot of oyster sucking socket sauce ordered extra rich by our Doc who...is he here? Ah, ha! There he is, sunk square and anchored amidst an undercurrent of ennui and emptiness and flat ass cheeks sitting uneven between his own private version of wife and daughter...though no nymph, no siree! Nowhere near! No, Doc's got himself grounded smiling weakly up and watching Shelby's bottle-assed hubby crowned and carted like a king around the stools and booths and tables, the queen pulling taps and pouring bottles in his honor. A valuable lesson, there, Doc: a valuable lesson book *vs.* limbs of union caliber.

The atmosphere has been infected now by all the grain-inspired commotion and firewater pouring freely from bottles of all sorts and colors. Even Joe finds a smile, and it's easy to see why. It's Rebecca now...Rebecca the unconnubial cunt juiced and sitting legs open in front of him. A good reason to smile, no? In fact, the booze now lubricating all the right connections, I take the time to offer yon Nora my attentions, her response being something like the skirted girl in school always sitting in the back of the room legs parted eyes wide open and wandering always licking a cherry-red lollipop, pink lips soft, responsive, adjusting to all advances aimed toward her from all directions, all connections lubricated well and wide open and wondering...wandering....

Asleep.
Awake. The one and only fondling dreams and sheets and pillows snuggling soft between naked thighs and knees and me beside her smoking, awake.

(Asleep.)

A cigarette between my fingers and lips sucking smoke and wondering just why...or how. I already know *why*...or what, I mean. I just don't know *how*. How do things work the way the do?...Or don't?

Damn. I'm getting nowhere.

Asleep?

I pull back the covers slow, soft to get a peek of just what, or *how* things work the way they do (don't) and I see her, lying naked on her side away from me, the hump and hollow of her golden outline blushing silver in the moonlight behind me...

Nothing. No answers. It's there, all there, the glory of the female outline like a landscape one could (must) climb over and over again indefinitely till the end or the beginning of indefinite sleep and still no answers, no familiarity...*or is this it? The familiarity of the female flesh like a landscape one must paint over and over again expecting perfection?* What is it they say about practice? Makes one *prefect*? Like a president or a priest or CHRIST! it's no wonder things don't work the way they should, all these thoughts about presidents and priests and nothing running through my head...

That's just what she said....

Her: What is it? What's wrong?
Me:

Her: What? Was it something I did?
Me:
Her: Was it something I *didn't* do?
Me:
Her: Come on, tell me. You have to tell me. How can I make things better if you don't tell me what's wrong?
Me: It's nothing.
Her: What do you mean *nothing*? How am I supposed to take that?
Me: What I mean is...it's not you.
Her: Well, if it isn't me then *who*?
Me: That's not what I meant. It's just...
Her: What?
Me: I don't know.
Her: What? Are you thinking things?
Me: What things?
Her: That's what I'd like to know. What things are you thinking?
Me: Things...
Her: About me?
Me: Sometimes.
Her: Not always?
Me:
Her: What, then?
Me: I don't know. Just...things.
Her: (Sigh.) Well, this isn't working. I mean, if you can't talk to me it's not going to work, is it?
Me:
Her: Is that all you have to say?
Me:
Her: (Sigh.) Goodnight.

And that was that. Nothing going through my mind the entire time. Just her and nothing, the pillow talking nonsense and sheets sopping sweat behind her naked back and neck and arms and legs and knees and (naked?) nothing.

Now me. Now my naked flesh alongside hers and what? Separation. That's all I see. Too separate two forms so different, yet similar, hers so singular and mine so...separate...separated. Mine so straight and not hollow and hers so separated, detached, attached to something else, something not my own, not my lanky cock lying naked and languid inside my thighs, asleep, snuggling its dry nose into the hairs below, not hers, not where it should be, the stubborn, lazy prick...
    Asleep. Caressing my hand slow along the hollow of the hump leading down her naked thigh and knee and must be careful not to wake her with a tickle. Feeling now the smoothness of her skin, the warm nakedness coming up into my palm and fingers and on toward her back, just the fingertips slow over the round shoulders so perfect...even the imperfections. I feel this perfection in my palm and on my fingertips and feel John Henry stirring from a rousing breeze like sunlight blinding Arizona heat, then back down, accustomed to this breeze and this sunlight and heat, the stirrings as deceiving as a coyote's smile.
    Snoring. Breathing heavy now and sleeping under silver light and golden hair falling, smothering her round shoulders and perfect neck and back heaving under satin sheets and naked hollow hiding blushing silver pillows nestling under heads and between knees and thighs....Nonsense. Thinking nonsense now. Time to kill the cigarette and slow, quietly crawl out of bed.
    And dress.
    And easy, silently slip out the backdoor and down the alley skipping round the bend at the end of the block and off toward...
    Where? The rousing of Lizzie's nakedness along with the early winter night air have ol' Johnny Boy rubbing his eye and smacking his lips. He's hungry, he growls, and I can't blame him. Like a bear straight out from hibernation he's thin from living off his own fat for too long, ready to ravage the first piece of live meat he sees. And this being night and these his

natural surroundings he knows just where to hunt.

On Hammond Avenue past the tracks and Broadway heading south toward Belknap the obvious comes to mind: Nora. Since that blue moon wedding-day's night in alcoholic haze she and I've been treating ourselves regularly to each other's unctuous, nocturnal tissue and springs of secretory oracles; a clandestine feast suited for a wintry lad and lass who've found themselves surrounded by thousands of fat, greasy mammals but not one unlit match, only cigarette butts and expired bottles. Such a delicious creature, the nymph. Mounds upon mounds of well-tenderized skin and lips and warm iron lust-blood pumping through hearts and veins and deep red-purple flesh and not a sinew in the lot...and I should know. I've traveled over every inch and from every imaginable direction. Night after night I'd plunge my tongue and fingers and sometimes even a toe into the pure orgasmic flow...that is, up until the scare.

As said, the smiles I received from her nymphean lips were assuring, to say the least. And what man can resist the assuring lips of a nymph? Those truly are the great cosmic bait hooked on braided steel strings. No man escapes...and no man ever wants to. It's a veritable vicious circle that'll continue on through infinity till man is able to grow his own nymphean lips and sinewless flesh in his Olympian soil. In other words, never. Never and always: never the soil, always the nymph. So there I was, face to face with those lips and that smile and I said to myself – Fuck it. What's the use in fighting? Why run? I'll just end up back at the beginning again and most likely only achieve a sprained ankle or an ill-stretched tendon. No, just nod and accept your lot, I told myself...then I lit a cigarette and straight toward her I strode to smell and taste perdition.

And it smelled and tasted funny. Not funny as *unusual*, but funny as *elbow-bone-bumped-hard-on-sculpted-marble*; a mind-numbing tingle that seemed to drone well after all the juice had been drained and the skin dried. First off, her being what she was, I tried my best to prepare for what I might encounter should all things work properly – namely, the strange and unusual, which, in actuality weren't strange and unusual at all when compared with the events leading up to the revelation.

After the Lounge shut down and the cattle shooed back to the corrals all who remained were Joe, Rebecca, Nora, myself and some saucy, raunchy redhead who somehow managed to set her hooks into Joe some years back and won't let go, now belonging to that laughable category "good friend" – meaning she's got some grating bit of dirt on Joe and is using it to full advantage, which is odd since so long as I've known Joe he's never been clean. In any case, there she was, with us, swiveling in her stool and spitting out obscenities the likes of which I've only heard from drunken slags. She even bragged about it, her language, as though it were the product of years of erudition, transpired by the masters of secret institutions and unraveled only to the truly devoted scholars of serpent-tongued deformity. Such words are infectious if one hasn't been inoculated as Joe and I have, and maybe Rebecca too as a front desk manager at a prestigious Canal Park hotel... though as for Nora I couldn't be sure. I thought of Julie and her own searing brand of poisonous hisses, though possibly Nora's come to accept them as coming from a mouth she'd already defanged, so to speak. And now here's the redhead, shit-faced and shit-mouthed and aiming her scaly, defecating tongue straight at Nora...and all because the latter looks so damned enticing in tight pants and glittered skin. This was jealousy, plain and simple, and it wasn't long till I recognized a grin of recognition on Nora's deep red-purple lips. I smiled too. Without having to worry about future cuts and bruises from fish-and-milk-starved alley cats with rusted claws and bent tails all could commence creamy and smooth as Parisian mousse.

After a few drinks and a few velvet feels of Nora's thighs and wings Joe decided to leave – a party he'd promised some waster he'd attend. So be it. We each tipped our cups and piled into Joe's car and sped off across the Bridge.

In the West End, it was – a faded blue-gray, broken-down ramshackle of a house with boarded windows and stacks of beer cans piled upon the split-plank porch. I shook my head for poor Joe and his moral sense for promises. Still, I knew this wasn't to affect me long. On the ride over, Nora opting to sit on my lap with plenty of room besides, I got a good feel of what lies between the knees of butterflies, her squirming and giggling the while with delight. It would prove a short bit of time before I'd find myself sticky with sweet, prismatic dust.

We filed inside the shack and the first thing I heard were obnoxious shouts coming from somewhere near the rear, the redhead shouting back, then a volley of cuss words and curses followed by more shouts and finally ending with all downing a mouthful off a piss-yellow bottle. Evidently, the shanty was the West End abode of the redhead's stock straight off the boondocks hoping to rezone the entire neighborhood (and, judging by the look of the surrounding huts, succeeding) and I admit I was a bit nervous given the condition of the house and the uppishness of my outfit (the tux, remember). However, this was a nervousness easily kept at bay; if these truly were the redhead's friends, and if the redhead was truly a friend of Joe, then, if things suddenly turned sour, at least I'd be able to walk out the front door with all my teeth. Nora, on the other hand, would have a rougher go of it. Already she'd been tagged by the serpentine queen and it would be only a matter of alcohol before the latter came calling to collect on whatever debt her tortile brain could trump up. I decided it best to keep a close eye on all swerves and sways of this lop-sided pendulum.

It wasn't long before the metronome skipped its axis and time stood still a moment, the elemental vacuum filled with mayhem and confusion, violence and spilt booze. Of course, it wasn't Nora's fault. All she hoped to do was use the restroom, a simple request which should be refused no one under any circumstance. As it were, this wasn't just any circumstance and this wasn't just any restroom, it was the restroom in the home of the redhead's friends. Nora was not allowed. And it might have been different had she asked permission, though how often does one think of such a thing when sitting in a house full of red-nosed wasters? Leave all to their bottles of cheap beer and backwash and head for the commode, my friend, and that's what she did...and just what the redhead waited for. Once Nora shut the door she stood and went to it and waited silent, shaking her head and giving inaudible hisses to her friends at a nearby table...to get their attention, I suppose. I saw the whole thing and would have intervened right then, though, as explained, this was a volatile situation for me too. My plan was to wait for the initial attack which would send Nora flat on her back, then act surprised and rush to her aid before the redhead had a chance to jump on top... or else find Joe before the bathroom door opened. No Joe. Nowhere to be seen. So be it. I only hoped the first blow wouldn't rend those sylphic lips inoperable.

As it were, it wasn't a blow at all but a *drag*, a pulling by the hair till a knee hit the floor, then the rest, then poor Nora peering up at a throng of soused bitches spitting obscenities straight at her, the men in the house laughing and drinking, encouraging a grand performance. The redhead stood at the fore, bent-over and utilizing a dialect somewhere between inner city ghetto and sewer rat. Nora said nothing. She knew better. Besides, I think I might have seen the beginnings of a grin....And it was humorous, in a sort of contrived-reality way. Still, it wouldn't be too funny once the redhead's courage exceeded her tongue and Nora found herself stung, surrounded neck-high in a barrelful of hissing asps. The men had all gone back to their bottles, disappointed the commotion produced no action. Cue. I stood up off my chair and proceeded toward the snake pit.

Nora was all too eager to take my hand. I helped her stand and for my chivalry got her soft arms around my waist and a shove in the back from the bitch behind us, that was all. She missed her chance and she knew it. All the same, she gained a few notches in the eyes of fellow hissers. Success all around... all except Nora. At least not till later.

On the way out dodging eyes and glances from drunken, dozy house-sitters we ran into Joe. Wanted to know what's wrong with his cousin. "No bother," I assured him. "Just going out for air, is all." Then, once Nora was out of earshot: "How's about a twenty to get us across the Bridge?"

He hesitated, most likely envious of my unrelation. Still, he had Rebecca. Grinning, he peeled a bill off his wad and handed it to me. "Have fun, asshole."

Skipping out the door down dilapidated stairs I heard the sound of rustling leaves and turned to see Rebecca bent over zipping up her boot. Her blouse was unbuttoned, revealing her tits like two long, trembling drops of gelatin. I whistled a distant tune and skipped on.

Nora waited for me on the walk. She looked a bit shaken but not bad...not unfixable. Looking up the street I noticed a yellow car topped with a lighted box approaching. I grabbed hold of Nora's waist and waived it down with Joe's twenty.

In the cab she wasted no time displaying her true nature, unbuckling my belt and releasing my swollen prick from its stifling confines, massaging it deftly with her left hand, her right hand grasping onto the doorhandle for leverage. Not giving one damn for doorhandles or for leverage, I used both hands to explore the various sights and smells of this stripped-down, horned-up pixie and for my efforts got an eye-popping burst of semi-diaphanous flesh tossed lively with assorted sprinkles and handfuls of sweet peach juice, saliva now pouring down both our chins and lips and me thinking, Shit! It's a wonder the cabby doesn't pay *me* when this ride's over!

Finally we reach the destination (her friend's house just past Sixteenth Street) and buckle and zip and slip out the cab and stagger up the walk indoors straight to the bedroom. Not much of a talker, this one. Chalk another up for the nymph. Why waste time with words when all channels are greased and pulsing? There's such a thing as *silent* talk – no one knows this more than the sex-crazed idiot who'd gladly trade his lips, teeth and tongue for just one eyeful of quivering, bare nymphean skin...sans sprinkles, even.

Anyway, we reach the bedroom and straight away off come the clothes as if missing every stitch and onto the bed we fall. She's sopping now and I'm not sure if it's her I've entered or if I've found a hole in the waterbed beneath us. As it were, there was no waterbed, just her squirming like a Scylla escaping Glaucus, my *terra firma* trident to the rescue, leading her astray onto dry land hard as rock and baked clay wet with rain slick like oil paint spread thick on eight-ounce canvas all cadmium deep red hue Prussian blue and burnt sienna "I'm coming!" she said, just like that. "Oh, I'm coming! I'm gonna come!" all Grumbacher green and yellow ochre soft incarnadine tones alternating ivory black titanium white non-yellowing "I'm coming, Jeff! I'm coming all over you, Jeff!" dioxazine purple and pink and crimson deep red cadmium "I'm coming! Oh...oh, I'm coming all over your new, clean tuxedo suit!"

As said, trysts like this became regular. She'd show up at the Lounge an hour or so before close – just enough time to swallow a few lubricating cups – then off we'd trot toward her friend's house, most times barely making it through the door with all our clothes still zipped and buckled. Yessiree, for a while things sure seemed to roll on greased rails till she told me she was pregnant.

Granted, my reaction to her telling me could have been more...reactionary. As it happened I said nothing, not a peep, not even a grunt. I saw it as silly, the idea of a baby popping out of this nymph's belly under such a circumstance, and it was obvious she had more false-hearted intentions; a full month prior to the revelation she'd been calling the apartment, asking for me even when Lizzie answered the phone. It took no small deal of cunning on my part to assure my dear all's well, that the girl on the other end was only Joe's kin (true) who was only enlisting my favor to gain employment at the Lounge (also true...sort of). So, the nymph was attempting to metamorphose into a mate? Silly. And now this spiel about babies? Hmph. I shrugged it off for what it was.

And Lo! wouldn't you know just one week after the singular conception she had a miscarriage. *Miscarriage!* Act of conscience, more like. Either way, that marked the start of the end for nymphean delights. After, she rarely strayed into the Lounge save to bum a few bucks off her endearing dad or to burn holes through my errant smiles. Now, however, a good many lonely nights added to her repertoire, perhaps now she's ready to acknowledge her folly and avow what the Almighty Creator has made her.

Rounding the back walkway approaching her bedroom window I smile as I see candlelight. Good. Late night vigils always end in weakened resolve. I step slow, soft to the glass and peer in.

She's there...in bed...her long, blonde, pensive hair and milk-and-honey complexion playing sylphidine tricks with the candle flame and moon. Too easy. I tap the glass to wake her.

Nothing. Not even a stir. Another tap more stern.

Still nothing. Soft. I shouldn't draw too much attention. No, there's such a thing as *stalking*, there is...especially when perceived by the nosey old bag in the second story widow behind/above me. I offer a weak smile and wave and proceed round to the front.

Protected now safe under drowsy canopies of shadowy pine. Stepping up the stairs now soft, slow, silent, teeth-clenched-tight-in-tention-hot-hand-oozing-cold-electricity turning the doorknob...

Opening. Silent stepping soft still tight till both feet over the plane wood door shutting slow...silent...

Shut.

Whew.

Stepping a bit more easy now down the hallway toward her bedroom I toss a passing glance in the rooms along the way and see...nothing. Nobody. The house seems empty save the rhythmic tick of a clock somewhere near the kitchen. I relax some and (still easy) steady my stride approaching candle flames dancing on naked skin...

Standing in the doorway watching over her lying in her bed I realize why all is so quiet. Not one but *two* nymphs occupy this sylvan den, the second being none other than the "friend" whose house I'm in. Hmmm. If I'm lucky this could get interesting. If unlucky I could get arrested. What to do? What...to...

To hell with it. I've already broken one law by entering on the sly. Besides, this isn't social law we're talking about: this is *moral* law. What's one more misdemeanor in the already offensively long list of immoral sufferance? I place trust in Mercury and Venus and undress and smile and slowly...

Slide...

In.

Stirring. Nora lifting her head heavy silent groggy eyes blinking trying to see...

"Jeff?"

Succeeding.

"Jeff, what are you...what's going on?"

Say nothing. Smile.

"Jeff....No. What are you doing?"

React.

Reactionary. Hands pulling free putting soft feet on cold linoleum tile legs following. Dressing. Walking.

Away.

Okay. That could've gone different. And given the circumstance any wise man would leap out of bed this instant and dress and leave the house as fast as limbs can move – that is, if there weren't another slumbering nymph lying naked beside him. An imprisoning thing, curiosity.

She's lying on her stomach, her arms spread wide in a broken halo around her head faced away, one leg straight, the other bent about a hundred degrees, airing out her labia. Nora's stirrings earlier hasn't shook her any; she's hasn't moved an inch. Must be exhausted from all the cunnilingus, the thought of which, along with the liquid curves of her lower back and ass, have me grinning with approval. What more? I wonder. I lean across to give her face a look.

She moves, lifts her head and eyes. Staring. I smile and lean back where I was.

She stares at me some more, still not speaking, not even covering herself. Perhaps she thinks she's dreaming. I wonder if I should say something. What does one say in such an instance?

"Hi."

"Hi."

"I'm Jeff."

"I know."

Hmm. "Nora?"

"Of course."

Damn. "Nothing too bad, I hope," and mean it.

"Not *too*..." with a grin. Then, peering across the bed, "Where is she?"

I nod toward the door. She smiles, then stands and walks off, naked.

So be it. Nothing left to do now but pick myself up off the bed and throw on my clothes and hope like hell the cops haven't been called.

In the living room I find them, huddled together under a blanket on the couch watching TV. I sit in the lazy boy by the door and watch too awhile in silence as an act of docility. No one speaks, just the sound of electric drivel in our ears and in our eyes and minds senseless images flicker...flutter....

After about fifteen minutes I unseat myself and walk past Nora and the other out the room away from electric light and drivel down the hall through the door outside and walking...

So *that's* what the Creator made her! And her "friend" too! Ah, well, what the hell. So long as they're honest about it. So long as legs and tongues and lips entwine in *honesty*, embracing in *lust*, not as the result of misunderstanding or loneliness or social exile or any other reason often attributed to the root of the homophile treatise. Christ, if that were the case eleven-tenths of the world would be stroking odd bedfellows under gossamery sheets and nothing would get accomplished. The idea of a world populated with femininely-inclined nymphs seems both frightening and exciting: frightening from a physiological viewpoint, the regeneration of the species and all that; exciting for someone who couldn't give a shit one way or the other if mankind regenerates. Like a spectator to a striptease with only coins in his pockets he's in it for the short haul, a quick, sharp thrill before the lights pop on and he's given the bum's rush. The Earth boasts more of this type than it likes to admit. We all – each and every one of us – possess the ability to turn our backs on our neighbors and build barricades and send forth the heavy artillery to collect what we believe is ours. Isn't this the very definition of *Human Being*: a super-intelligent, highly unpopular species ahead of all others depleting resources at such a rate every man, woman and child of said species fears extinction in its own lifetime. Hence, the gold chains and diamond earrings and SUV's and luxury jets and cocaine and booze and economic, capitalist sex and acetaminophen and heroin and all other anesthetics, intravenous or otherwise. Man needs an upper...or a downer...or an equalizer...anything to help him forget how seriously fucked-up is everything on this dear, dying planet. That said, I say Hooray for all you fags and lesbians! Yee-ha! Get yours where you want it before the politicians and corporate heads and religious rights and lefts steal everything from under us and leave us high and dry and hanging from the limbs of trees stricken with heart rot, below us nothing but jagged rocks and landmines and bones to break the fall...

Ah, well, such thoughts seem futile when slithering up the Avenue like a serpent through the chill, electro-static hours of a late-November night – a serpent undulating, ingesting, digesting all that surrounds it without concern for teeth or eyelashes or fingernails or....

"Jeff?"

Pete.

"Holy shit, man! Is that you?!"

Pete Mestopolis.

"Damn, dude! Where've you been? Ha!"

Pete Mestopolis stumbling out from Mama's Bar with two armfuls of bottles and half-masted eyes and a slanted, cockeyed grin. "Fancy this," he spits. "Meetin' you on Tower Avenue this time of night...*walking*. Ha! I'da thought you'd be steerin' a Benz up the *Grand Axe* by now, you sonofabitch bastard!"

He's absolutely tanked, wobbling about on the cracked-concrete walk as if it were a conveyer belt, spitting *Damn*'s and *Dude*'s and *Don't You Give A Goddam Shit 'Bout Your Old Friends No More*'s. I say nothing, just a feeble mention of my present situation with Lizzie and the Lounge and how taxing is my time. He pays no attention to any of it, obviously trying hard not to forget what drunken obscenity he's next to spit up. Finally he has out with it and says, "Fuck all that, man. Fuck it. I mean....Hey! I got a room at the Androy now and....Hell, I got all this booze here and....I mean....Hey! You should join me for some drinks, eh? I'm buyin', ha, ha! No, really, Jeff, you should join me. I mean....I'm glad I ran into you, you know?"

I know. I've been here before. I offer to carry an armful of Pete's booze and up the Avenue we stumble.

Straight away he starts in on the wife and kids and what a burden it's all become...actually, not so much the kids as the wife. "Fuckin' whore!" he begins, just like that. "Where does she get off acting like that, like some mental ward psycho! I swear it's enough just to keep from knockin' her out at times, the way she goes about it, you know. I mean, it's not *me*, see? It's not *me* I care about. She can cuss and throw dishes and knives and whatnot at me all she wants....I couldn't care less. Mind, I'm not gonna take it like some shit-nosed mutt. I'm gonna throw back, know what I mean? She can call the cops on me all she dares...and she *does*, the no-good cunt. It's the kids, y'hear?...When she does that shit in front of the *kids* is where I draw the line." Next he goes on about the money woes and how he's been borrowing from all and sundry, everyone, even his grandfather and especially his wife's parents who "are always good for a touch now and again, sure, though all the same they don't forget to tax on ten percent interest, the merciless pricks! And they've got more mint than the Vatican, for fuck's sake! I swear, to look at 'em it's no wonder Dora turned out the way she did....She's been suckin' her mom's teats and tuggin' her pop's balls since birth! She's spoiled as summer milk, that one! And *you*, you sonofabitch!" A nudge, sloshed and pacific. "You're no better, you old duck! Runnin' off without a word hidin' yourself in some chickie's panties not even invitin' your ol' pal Pete for a drink and a look-see! Ha! Some friend you are! Ha, ha! What, you keeping it all for yourself? Ha, ha, ha!"

    I haven't a clue what Pete's on about. He knows damn well where I've been just as I know where he's been, as well as the ugly symptoms of his wife-and-kids disease. He's shown me the festering sores several times. They've never been secrets, just as Lizzie's never been a secret. In fact, he's the only one other than Joe and a few others who've seen the inside of the cellar. A strange thing, really, Pete and I. Somehow we've managed to find each other at the beginning or end of odd turns in our lives. He just appears as if to collect the facts, the color and the smell of whatever travesty I'm involved in at the time, then he gives me his and he's off, gone back to his wife and kids and never heard from again till the next time, the next travesty. Like a splinter left unattended to and eventually healed into the skin he's always there, just below the surface, always tearing and scratching, trying to make his way to the top and out and nearly succeeding, then back down he goes, a casualty of physiology and gravity. This cycle has repeated itself for over five years now, since he first dipped his knob in Pandora's box and left it there permanently, just after his twentieth birthday. At the time we were sharing an apartment to split the rent and escape our parents' basements and he swore he'd try to look at it as a good thing, as some sort of prefiguration from the gods that the bullshit of his teen years was over and here's this gift, this symbolic offering to assure him the rest of his life would be new, different...and it was new and different, no doubt, though not in the mythic, symbolically optimistic way he'd hoped. After that he moved out and I moved on and he and Pandora set their foundation on a house and a healthy stipend handed over by her father who I'm sure only wanted to keep his little girl close by and safely out from reach of the irascible Pete who, already unable to brag a penny to his name, was now irretrievably in debt to this woman and her family. Pete got fucked, good and proper, and not just by Pandora. Every sadistic, horny member of her entire family including his two sons and daughter stand in line for their turn and Pete takes it, with barbed wire. He has to. He hasn't a choice. Symbolically, physiologically he's no longer a man; he's a splinter below the surface unable to scratch and tear its way out. He's an eroded splice of bone surrounded by flesh and blood that is not its own.

We arrive under the neon red *HOTEL* of the Androy and stumble toward the door inside.

"To the top, man! The penthouse, what! Ha!" slurs Pete as we step lightly through the scarlet-carpeted lobby toward the elevator past some man with nervous, bulging eyes and a gray moustache stained with blood or pasta sauce. "And pronto, *signore*! Before my friend and I whither to dust!" The man stares down his own reflection and grunts and punches seven.

At the top through the hall now toward Pete's room and in

my nose the inauspicious smells of old wood and wet carpet and camphor balls. Mock Art Deco lamps hang like severed heads from the ceiling. Pete smiles. "Pretty fancy, huh?"

In Orcus, maybe.

Through the door into Pete's room and it's now the gag reflex sets in. Not for poor old Pete nor even for this room, although either would be appropriate: Pete with his induced, transparent grin of self-volition; this room with its gray walls crumpling down around sick lighting surrounding one sawdust desk and two chairs and a hollow, cot-like bed propped inside what appears to be a closet, though most likely advertised as a second room. Not for either of these, no, but for me, for my memories. For the nauseous, lice-infested memories of the room in Canal Park.

"Here you are, man. Sit," says Pete, handing me a chair before disappearing with the sacks around a corner to the closet a moment, returning with a bottle, opening it, pouring a glassful for me keeping the remainder for himself. "To lost time, Jeff....Lost time and newfound friends," and down goes half.

I take a whiff: American whiskey. Suicide.

He scrapes the other chair along the floor in front of me and sits down. A flush dampens his face, no doubt from the whiskey, though I can't help sensing other reasons as well. For a long while we don't speak, only sip...sip and gulp. Pete peers about the room at the walls and furniture, then the door, then at me and smiles, then the room and the cot inside, then back at me. Another smile, damp and flushed. Then: "Well, isn't this just grand, don't you think?" Don't answer. Just sip and smile. "Three kids and a wife and here I am, crashin' in the Androy drinking whiskey with my best friend. Things couldn't get any better, I tell ya, man." Another gulp. "And to think if I even set foot on the sidewalk in front of my house...*my* house! Ha! It'll never be *my* house, not while I'm alive or dead with three kids and a wife who calls the cops if I so much as raise my voice to the dumb bitch...the dumb bitch who's *cheating* on me! Ha! Can you believe that shit?! Who the hell'd want that piece of used ass three kids wide I can't fathom. I mean, I'd hate to meet that desperate prick. Thing is, I already have. Jamie his name is...*Jamie*! I thought she turned dike on me when I first heard! An old flame, he is...from high school. That tells you something right there, doesn't it? The sad bastard's got it so bad eight years, three kids and a husband won't stop him. Still, he's not bad enough where he'll take her off my hands. He knows better. He knows with her comes the three kids and a mortgage the size of California 'cause sure as shit once that bitch and her old man have through with me it's all theirs. All of it. I want none of it. Thing is, she won't divorce. I've already tried. Hell, I've even gone to the courts myself to get the papers and all and I was close, so fucking close I could've tasted it. She wants it just as bad as me, believe me. Shit, she had the pen to the line and ready to sign...then she had a moment of clarity and said, 'Well, maybe we should wait and see what my father says.' *Her father!* Fuck that! I knew I was fucked right there. No way he'd have that burden on his hands, not without my ass six feet under, anyway. Did I tell you what that sonofabitch said to me once? 'You know, Pete,' he says, all deep and gruff like he was a lumberjack instead of a frozen food salesmen. 'You know, Pete,' he says, all gruff and shit, 'you're not exactly what I would've chosen for my Pandora, there,' he says, 'but I will say this...you have given us three great grandchildren to your credit.' *To my credit?!* What the fuck is he, a real estate agent?! A fucking loan officer?! As if it were my sole purpose on this sad Earth to supply that sonofabitch with a fucking lot of cheery, happy grandchildren to hug and kiss while the sad prick whose cock spun the cheery lot gets his dick in a sling and shot! And then, straight after, the bastard had the nerve to offer me a job packin' his freezers full of pizzas and burritos and peas and Popsicles and those fucking things you push up with your thumbs. Well, I took it, anyway. I had to. I'm busted off my ass." A gulp, quick and hard. A cough. A shake of the mane like an epileptic fit, then: "Where the hell was I? Ah, yeah...the restraining order. That's right. That's what I said. If I so much as walk past my house on the fucking *sidewalk* she's callin' the cops. Can you beat that shit?! I tell ya, Jeff, when I think back on nineteen and the days we had that place on John...remember? All the parties and pussy comin' in and out of that joint...the days I'd get you stoned before breakfast....'Wake n' bake!' I'd say and you'd say, 'No, man, I got class today' but you'd do it anyway...then I'd laugh as I'd watch you stumble down the sidewalk on your way to school. Christ, I don't know how you did it...*but you did it!* You did it, man. And now here you are...a college grad on his own with a job and a girl and everything and nothing holding you back and here I am....Damn, what I wouldn't give to go back to those days...back before Pandora and her fucking dad and those three shitting brats...back when nothing mattered 'cept getting stoned and laid and beer money...back before all this bullshit, anyway." The final gulp. An empty bottle. He lets out a slow grunt and farts and stands from his chair and sighs, "Well, hell, what's the use?...Nothin' ever changes... nothin' ever gets accomplished...nothin' 'cept the bottom of a bottle, anyway...." Then he nods and shakes his head and stumbles out the room and disappears into the closet.

Poor Pete. Always there. Always like a splinter sipping (gulping) whiskey lost below the surface of skin not his own. Lost time, he says. Time....Time for what? Time for worms to lick the starched bones of meatless creatures hiding away amongst the company of overage bellhops with bloodstains on pasta sauce mustaches grunting, gulping, farting, punching seven as if it were the Hilton in New York or New Guinea or Nairobi or Jaipur or Paris one night when lights flickered green and eyes shown their white-hot inflorescence glowing sunflower-yellow-peach iris eyes staring hollow and empty, smoke rising up from fingertips dangled loose like the arms of puppets, wood or otherwise painted incarnadine and pink and rose and red-purple and what the hell is that? A spider or cockroach or secret agent climbing, spiraling up the mucus-yellow-striped wallpaper as if it were infiltrating a conversation it could never comprehend, never decipher, never decode nor communicate, never relate, never never never never never never never never...

Always.

Suddenly it occurs to me Pete has been gone for some time...longer than it takes to find another bottle. Curious, I stand from my chair and walk toward the room (closet) and peer inside.

He's there, on the cot, his arms and legs dangling off the sides like a Gulliver in the land of Shrunken Consciousness. I take a blanket off the rack above and unfold and stretch it across his body to his neck. Then I walk past the bottles and chairs and the sawdust desk away from the glass of whiskey out the door into the hall.

Past the overage bellhop punching L.

Into the Avenue like a serpent undulating, fecundating, ingesting, digesting, defecating all it sees and swallows and me like a field mouse scurrying along its ribcage trying to escape never realizing such a thing impossible. Once you're in you're in and there's no way out unless through the throat or the asshole or death, the skin like textured steel bones like iron bars surrounding undulating meat massaging you back in, back into its belly of bars and taverns blue and green neon red white-hot luminescence blinding your eyes and suffocating your ears and skin, digesting your dreams and thoughts and your strength and your courage and your only way out is through the throat or asshole or integrated into the organism for good and ever....That's it! That's the way! One must become one with whatever is digesting him! Pete realized this, this secret ability to conquer the beast. One must become one. One must become ingested and digested, then defecated, renewed back to the earth that bore him, everything, even the serpent undulating over him, massaging his eyes and ears and skin and ingesting, digesting his very essence, that which makes him Man. Bravo, Pete! Let's all follow your lead! Let's all follow you through the belly of the serpent in through the throat, integrated into the very muscle of the beast, the very sinewy meat and tendon and bones and eyes and ears and skin so then *we*, we bones of meatless stock, *we* become the ones undulating, the ones fecundating, the ones eating and digesting, defecating....

Creeping up the alley now after dawn slithering through the backdoor like a salamander with its tongue sliced off tasting the solid air, ears pricked for any sound other than its own.

Success, then straight to the maker just as listless Eight O'clock coffee beans already ground in the freezer Ziploc baggie keeps freshness in and hangovers under restraint... now straight to the shower tossing clothes off to corners in under cascading water wetness washing away the stink of all, the stench of everything, every body and out thinking to find strong coffee brewed fresh and hot and steaming and finding instead Lizzie, her hands on her hips arms bent legs acute angled feet tapping...

Say nothing.

"You're up awfully early," she says, searching.

Shrugging. Nothing.

Then: "I stopped the coffee maker. It's useless. There's no food in this place...none at all. We'll have to go out for breakfast." I can still smell it, hot and steaming poured down the drain, rats and stray dogs and cats lapping up the good stuff our good Lizzie lets them. "Get dressed....We're leaving in five minutes."

Five minutes. Time enough to grow legs and paws and turn back into a stray dog with ears pricked, tongue lapping freshly brewed coffee bagged and frozen...

Then again, breakfast....

We go to a small truckers' café up the street a few blocks

called *The Kitchen* which is strange since all I ever see in this boxy joint are men too old to drive and women without any teeth. Still, the food's not bad – just enough salt and grease to soothe the sting of a raucous night prior.

We take a seat near a window.

Steam rising spiral hot plates spinning tiny plastic cutlery cutting...smothering....

She speaks.

"You know I've asked you here for reasons other than..."

Too late.

The waitress arrives. A cagey-looking bird with silver hair and flaccid breasts and legs like an ostrich. Always here. Always merry and bright. Always order steak and eggs over-easy hash browns extra crispy wheat toast extra buttery green apple jelly. Lizzie scoffs. Despises café meat, does she. The price of ordering and delivering over-priced tenderloins to over-stuffed Caruthers and half-wit wives who'll have the chicken Parmesan no potato house salad low-fat dressing, if you please.

She orders the cheese omelet...easy on the egg, extra low-fat cheese.

The waitress leaves.

Sipping coffee no longer Eight O'clock Ziploc fresh but steaming month-old and hammered, watered-down mule shit.

Lizzie staring. Eyes glistening silver-blue beauty boring straight through me. Stare back.

Useless...useless....Too beautiful. Too...boring.

"Here it is," she begins, before the food. "I've decided to buy the duplex, the lower apartment and ours...the whole thing. It's for sale and I've known the owner, our landlord, for over five years now. He said if everything clears with the bank...which it will, of course...he'll give me the first offer. I can't pass it up. It's too good a deal...real estate, I mean. And me being so young I'll have it paid off before I'm forty and then it'll just be extra income for the rest of my life. Sounds good, huh?"

Nothing...no food. Feeling nauseous.

"There's more. Now that I'll be making payments every month...much more than we pay now...I'll expect you to help out with at least half...as well as with the repairs the place'll need like a new roof, new siding, refurbishing the bathrooms both upstairs and downstairs...waterproofing and priming and painting the basement walls and floors, the walls in the apartments, the floor in ours...the kitchen ceiling downstairs, new windows, new wallpaper, new carpeting....Everything. So....Waddya say? Pretty exciting, eh?"

Pretty eyes smiling at me staring out the greasy window wondering where the fuck our waitress wandered off. Cups of steaming hot watery shit not hot...not cups no longer but buckets of emptiness no longer hot...not coffee no longer... anything not...nothing...

"At least you could say *something*. This is a big deal for me...for *us*....An investment for *us*, for our future. You can't rely on a bartender's salary all your life....I mean, I know you want to be a famous writer one day and all that and I think that's great, really....It's more than most people think they want to be....But still, if it were to happen to you it would've happened by now, don't you think? Besides, I never see you send anything to any magazines or newspapers anymore. I never even see you write. Perhaps it's time to face it....It's not going to happen...not for you. It's time to start thinking about other things...about things that really matter. It's time to grow up."

Time to grow legs and arms and tongues and wings and teeth like a salamander I'm not eating steak and eggs overeasy and wheat toast dipped in embryos....Nauseous. Think better. Think pink bismuth thoughts pouring down throats into stomachs no longer empty...not....

"My brother wants to have a talk with you. He owns this business, you know...does really well...sells cleaning supplies or whatever....Anyway, he thinks you and I'd be great at it.

I've already looked into it and I think it'd be something we could do together...you know, I'd be the one who actually goes places and speaks with people 'cause of my looks and whatnot and you'd be the numbers guy....You were good in math, right? Anywho, my brother says after a couple years setting up reliable clients who use only our products and what-have-you we could have a steady income someday...along with the apartment, see? So....Waddya say?"

Not talking. Not worth the sweat or saliva my tongueless mouth makes attempting to produce sounds and words and images perfecting silence. Perfect teeth and eyes and nose and arms and legs and lips smiling perfectly, grinning a perfect grin in my direction. Perfectly. Pacifying.

The food arrives. I have a moment's thought of handing our waitress a searing smack on the ass, though such thoughts come a distant second to the sight and smell of seared meat and eggs over-easy side of toast green apple jelly so in I go, headfirst into the steaming hot plate.

The waitress fills our cups and flitters off to wherever she escapes.

Lizzie daintily opens her omelet to check that the cheese is melted properly and in the proper amount. Once all's well and in order she looks to me and says, "You know, Jeff, you'll never find anyone like me...not anywhere."

I know. I'll not find no one like my Lizzie, not her, not anywhere, not while here in some café sipping caramel-colored shit steaming surrounded by men too old to drive sad, toothless hags away from all this, all this nothingness, away from anywhere, from anything and everything, away from this café where we all sit sipping something, eating anything flopped in front of our starved faces so long as it's hot and steaming, greased and salted, so long as it slides past our lips and tonsils and tongueless, toothless mouths into our stomachs no longer empty, no longer aching, no longer expecting anything but nothing...

I look at Lizzie. She's wearing an adoring smile which I

mistake as for me. For a moment I do nothing, not a thing but stare – the way someone might at the sun's reflection off the surface of a rousing sea – then I sink, back into the plate of café steak and eggs and hash browns and wheat toast extra buttery....

New Year's Eve.
Evening.
Standing in the shower again rinsing off doldrums and daydreams like snakeskin chafing intestinal slough down the drain hole again swirling too slow, too circular under toes too clean for their own good, too clean, too cunning in their ability to hide dirt and snakeskin chafing like soap scum swirling down the drain hole again like blood too clear, too achromatic, too pallid and thin and pulsating through veins too weak, too collapsed, too often prodded over and over and over again like heroin or warfare or plasmapheresis or hemophilic wounds open too often, too open, too breaching the surface like soap scum or snakeskin never healing, always bleeding too thin, too achromatic, too clear, too clean, too clean for their own good...

To the right the handle turning slow, too unassuming, too silver like two steel St. Andrew's crosses too polished, too bright, too blinding, too painful for the eyes and nose and ears like dirty dishrags too clean, too unassuming, too inclined to chase electricity too bright like skylines too distant, too distant, too icy, too cold, too cold to stand, too...

To the bedroom where Lizzie has my outfit all laid out and pressed. All black. All except one cobalt blue silk shirt selected especially by her on this night and for this occasion, this dinner and dancing at the hands of her Highness dressed all in black and cobalt blue and silver jewelry hanging, dangling off wrists and ankles and round apricot columnar necks turning...

Finding her sitting before the vanity all dressed, always stunning, always shimmering like jewelry dangling off wrists and necks and eyes always sitting before the vanity waiting, waiting for me, for my clothes always pressed and waiting to be placed on skin too clean, too...

"Hey! Snap out of it!"

Two eyes too blue watching, waiting.

"Come on, get dressed! It's after eight already! We have to be at my sister's house by eight thirty and to the D.E.C.C. by nine!"

The D.E.C.C. The Dance. The Duluth Excavation and Cacophony Compost kicking off the New Year in Style and Grace and Dignity all compromised for black ties and pants and overcoats and cobalt blue eyes staring...waiting...

"Well?! *What are you waiting for?!*"

Nothing.

Dressing.

Lizzie standing, looking ravishing in silver, black and blue eyes so stunning, so ravishing. Ravish her.

"I don't suppose you remembered the money, did you?"

No. Don't. Do nothing. Just stand here. Silent.

"Look, I know it's New Year's Eve and everything but Monday's still Monday and we sure as hell won't be celebrating if you don't make the payment on time, right?"

Left arm bent. Hands on hips. Legs parted open too far for my own good standing, toes tapping kicking pavement not there anymore. Left. Left the pavement for payments made to banks lending money left...

"Well? I'm waiting. Where is it?"

Left the payment on the buffet. Business-size envelope left white on cherry-red mahogany.

"Ugh! Why do you have to play games with me now? I told you we're late as it is! God, you can be such a child at times!"

Legs parting, leaving the bedroom not waiting for me to begin dressing black pants buckling silver cobalt blue shirt buttoning over skin too cold for its own good, too cold, too distant and icy, too far off Lizzie's voice shouting...

"Hey, asshole! Found it! Right where it should be, I suppose, eh? You're lucky!"

Right where it should be arms sliding in/out of black sleeves too short where they should be too long, too far off the wrists not like I like them a little too long like false security dangling off the wrists and ankles turning heads and necks like Lizzie's, just like how Lizzie likes them up off the wrists and ankles and pressed, not wrinkled, not too much, too perfect, too prefect, too clean like cold electricity never charging, never minding, never missing payments on time to banks always lending, all money lenders always charging more money never saving, always spending money more on black suits silver cobalt blue and jewelry always shining, shimmering, always spenders never saving, never changing, never charging like electricity too cold, too distant....

Inside the sister's car wandering over the Bridge toward Duluth to be treated regally like wild monkeys who've learned to dress themselves in black and jewelry and borrow money from banks making payments on time to my left Lizzie sitting, looking ravishing laughing with the brother sitting to my right, not so ravishing but dressed in black like the rest of us, anyway...

An odd word, ravishing. Ravish: rhymes with radish, dish, fish, pish, knish, Jewish (I'm not), Irish mish mashing potatoes sour cream and cheese grated fresh from the province of Parma, karma...karm*ish*, I mean, like something that *should* be but isn't or was or not so much anymore – alien*ish* like something concerning the reformation of foreigners for their own good, wish, swish, swash...*swither*, I mean, like something a disciple of St. Andrew might do but not me, I'm not, I'm nothingishness sloshing about in waters too coldish, too distantish, not nearish enough to where it should be on cherry-red mahogany not mine, no business-size whitish envelope concealing greenish bills and black and blue and cream like cheese from Parma too far, too distantish like

Lizzie's brother laughing on my right me in the middle too Irish, not Jewish enough, too selfish, too *ish*, too *ish* for my own good....

In the dictionary *ravish* means rape; *ravishing* inspiring joy and delight. Odd, isn't it?

Approaching the Despondent Excrement and Cadaver Collection dressed in black and silver like bacilli stepping from cars automatic like dead skin falling off flesh too cold, too cold for its own good, too good, two perfect eyes in front of me watching making damn sure I'm still behind no longer waiting for electricity too cold, too cold, too distant, too cold, too...

Warm. Inside. Up stairs like salamanders tongues out and tasting, lapping the warm air for warning signs meaning life outside our own including snakeskin soap scum swirling down drain holes again intestinal slough toes too clean for their own and other salamanders especially, with or without tongues. A salamander with or without a tongue or toes too clean or even intestinal slough is still a salamander. For a salamander to exist all it needs are legs and skin like a snake.

In the ballroom now after depositing black coats like skin like snakes and what must be at least two thousand salamanders slithering around on legs and toes in black shoes too polished, to the distant left a bar with booze like an endless line of cannons aimed straight at the sky, to the right an even more endless buffet.

First things first. To the right to all the lovely delectables this Deliciously Evolving Cantankerous Cornucopia has to offer all us toothless, tongueless salamanders slithering on toes too black, too polished toward bottles and buffets (not mine) and delectables spread out on tables steaming, tasting air too alien, too foreign, too delicious to...

"Where do you think you're going?"

To the left. Lizzie.

"Our table is over there, by the bar. Come on. Let's go

claim it."

To the left toward Lizzie claiming tables not buffets with delectables not mine never will be hers, always hers, always a buffet with business-size envelopes too white, not green or black or blue enough with cream on cherry-red mahogany not mine, never will be, never remember your memories like lice, remember, your licentious memories never forget, never, remember you told her never, remember...

Sitting. Resting salamander legs like bones too soft, too degenerated, two legs withered in pants too black, not mine, not mine, not Lizzie standing, speaking...

"I'm off to the buffet. Stay here and watch my purse."

...Forgetting. Tongue like bones too soft to speak, too ravished, not ravishing like my Lizzie always walking away on legs too long, too open, too hidden under black lace like silver blue not shimmering anymore, not for me, forgetting, never remember what you said revealing yourself to her not revealing me, not me, not mine, not....

Deciding not to sit any longer. Stretching my still-bony legs to see what use this function serves other than the distribution of food and alcohol evenly, democratically to snakes and salamanders alike so long as each pays the proper fee.

(Like me.)

Like a salamander slithering past the bar and buffet out the ballroom door down stairs carpeted not blood not red but purple, purple and blue with tiny yellow specks like stars I'm standing on, slithering toward booths and more tables claimed not by Lizzie but others, other salamanders and snakes standing around and speaking as if they still had tongues and teeth to pronounce their *Sssssssssssssssssssssss sssssssssssss*'s....

First booth: a raffle for a vacuum cleaner, the top of the line. Fitting. Moving on.

Next: someone selling life insurance at an unbelievably low rate, so low your wife and two darling children won't ever have to worry about soft legs withering off ever again they'll all be able to afford prosthetic steel aluminum alloy legs a lifetime of shine one-time, low-rate, money-back guarantee tax deductible.

Moving on.

Now books...*books*? Pamphlets, more like, with starving children on the cover shooing flies off eyes of pure and utter anguish staring straight at me. So children there are hungry also. A democratic state providing for other states not so democratic but hungry which is just as good, just in time for New Year's Eve and the dancing which accompanies it to remind snakes and salamanders they were children too...but *hungry* children? Perhaps...but *hungry* children shooing *flies* off *eyes* of *pure and utter anguish*? Perhaps not.

Now one advertising diplomacy as if it were a cleaning product Lizzie's brother not so ravishing after all, after a one-time, low-rate lifetime shine on stainless steel and linoleum, anyway.

Now a new car.

Now a new house.

Now new children sitting in back seats sleeping in rooms built just for them just till they're old enough to eat soggy graham crackers and go to schools not cold not hungry but utterly with other children away from home mummy und duddy sitting close together too cold, too distant, too drunk to do it anymore he's always away too long and she's never horny, never legs-too-long anymore under fleece robes like sheered sheepskin too soft, too hungry like children too far away, too distant, too cold, too hungry for their own good...

Too bad for them.

To the next booth a new bathtub two-person porcelain claw foot and everything. Too Victorian.

To the next now a new front bay window.

Now a new front door cedar with copper inlay.

Now a new porch to match the new cedar door.

Now a new gift certificate to a convenience store free gas for a month one lucky winner.

Now fallout.

Now a new gasmask.

Now a new tube of cool, soothing ointment to rub on and over gray flaking skin like legs withering.

Now down stairs now slithering over purple and blue and yellow stars like cream too sour, too left out in the sun too long toward rooms and rooms and rooms of snakes like tongues talking, hissing something about an auction, something silent. Sounds perfect. Soundsssssssssssssssssssssssssssssssssssss....

Art (if you want to call it that...that is, if you still have teeth and a tongue to pronounce the "*rt*") hanging all wallpaper yellow, ice-blue and heroin-orange like nocturnal emissions tossed off and flung onto premium recycled acid-free paper haphazardly with precision...*permission*, I mean. I recognize the artist...a colorist (if you want to call him that) who's made himself quite a name painting imaginary images of aquatic imagery swimming freely through waters too blue...not blue enough, I mean, like ice or steel or electricity not charged fully. It appears snakes and salamanders take a liking to aquatic animals of the icy, unelectrical variety. Me too. I rather enjoy imaginary images imaginized imaginarily. All very pretty, no doubt, though I might not call it Art. *Jism*, perhaps. Or *Hot-Jelly-Fish-Egged-On-Acid-Free-Recycled-Turtle-Spunk*, maybe. All the same, reason enough to give each imaginary, heroin-orange emission nothing less than a million dollars to the decimal point in each direction....

To the ballroom.

First things first again. Straight to the buffet to see and taste and smell the delightful foreign delectables our good Degenerated Exanthematic Carnival Carnivores saw fit to offer us good, degenerated, hungry, exanthematic spectators to help celebrate this most exanthematic, carnivorous day's night...

Hmm. I meant *exocytotic*.

Seems our good seals and sacs got more than a bellyful

each of every foreign item on the menu. All that remain are rolls and cherry tomatoes and a colossal vat of lettuce with bits of cabbage and carrot mixed in. Ah, well...roughage is good for the exoskeleton. Helps maintain the shine needed to distract approaching clamshells. I load a fresh, steaming-clean plate with as much roughage as it can hold and head back to the table claimed by our good foreign, delectable-like-legs-running-naked-in-the-garden-soft-and-bittersweet, exocytotic Lizzie.

Hmmm. *Exocentric*, I meant.

Almost there. Balancing plates of roughage like lettuce with bits of cabbage and carrot and cherry tomatoes rolling about like eyeballs searching for the safe hollows of their sockets too soft, too irritated for their own...

Gone. Fallen. Rolling away on the floor without so much as a Godspeed, my good sir. In their place Lizzie's purse.

Looking up. Lizzie smirking, scowling.

"That's for not watching *that* like I asked you to. What were you thinking? What if someone walked off with it, huh? Where would we be then?"

Nothing. Nowhere, I suppose.

Gone. Back to where she was before. Not responding. Not waiting for me to respond. So be. So leave the roughage and cherry tomatoes too irritated to be rolling away on the floor for their own good and stoop and pick up Lizzie's purse and return to your seat...

And sit.

Safe.

Sitting close to my Lizzie safely absorbing hostilities like cherry red tomatoes falling off plates and rolling, collecting, counting, recounting the falling seconds till...

Too late. Midnight. All good snakes and salamanders like me, like my Lizzie slithering under falling confetti toward the center of the room under cheers like chemical explosions leaking exocentric emissions affecting tongues and teeth and lips kissing...

Gone. Left. Leaving me behind on the edge of the dance floor not the center. Not kissing. Not....

So be it. So just stand here silent and watch her leave, off toward the center of the floor with other snakes and salamanders kissing, catching confetti on lips and teeth smiling, shining carnivorous tongues tasting her and you accepting it as punishment for not watching her purse not like you should have, not like she asked you to or did or did not or not good enough, not good, not....

*   *   *

Sitting. Safe. In Superior watching all the good people of this town dance and laugh on floors slippery with fallen confetti like skin...no. Like confetti fallen, surrounding feet dancing, laughing, surrounding my Lizzie among them, her sister and her sister's husband and brother and Lester among others, all laughing, dancing, cheering, drinking....But I've no need for laughing or dancing or cheering or drinking. I've other things to tend to, other very important things such as protecting the inner contents of frail, easily stolen exoskeletons like black like leather like a purse shining, staring back at me with silver oval eyes and teeth grinning, smirking, scowling like my Lizzie looking up watching her laughing, dancing, feet stumbling all over one another like confetti, screams and howls of abandon no longer needed only as a watchdog *woof woof* every morning day and night just like that *woof woof woof* no good, must get better at my *woof*'s like the dog I am watching over black leather like belongings too easily stolen away like my Lizzie and Lester dancing what the fuck like fallen confetti too slippery, too easily swept away too easy once the night's over days begin all over again too slow, too cold, too easily forgotten under red and blue and cream like yellow like lighting too easy, too easily reflected, deflected away from her wake up it's all in your remember your mind remember your memories remember that first night like it was not like real remember, remember what you said and how she felt imaginary and you as if floating...no, *shooting* over islands and inlets like lightning like electricity remember, remember it's all there or was or isn't or wasn't it wasn't always like this or isn't or should be but couldn't try concentrating more on the could be but isn't like inverted karmish dish fish pish knish lumpish bumpish slumpish umpish turkish divertish, diverting inverted words imaginary like images not real but could be if only she'd remember wandering through gardens like thieves stealing fruits and vegetables fresh from the vine remember not real making love under trees not falling, not fallen like confetti not real but imaginary like "Hell's Bells" Hemingway or *Mister* Miller or Jimmy "Raised Green Ink" Joyce all giants of another land entirely distant entirely imaginary not here, not now, not like my Lizzie not real not Lester of all lapels makes everything seem so unreal, so imaginary but isn't but could be karmish if she wondered about the garden fruits and vegetables still fresh still not like it was or wasn't or should be but isn't and could be understand it's all very simple like musical phrases remember like memories understand I think I wonder does she wonder what does it matter look at her dancing laughing cheering smiling perfect feet stomping, stumping gray and perfect feet falling, withering Lester's lapels not mine, not me, never will be up off the wrists like false security illusive memories like lice but her, remember, remember what remember that first night her fruits and flowers blooming like giant carnivorous appetites under semidiaphanous sheets silk martinis naked feet fuck all that remember like confetti falling from skies too cold, too perfect, too dark, too distant to comprehend instead concentrate on the now and me like *woof woof* watching her purse practicing *woof woof*'s much better again *woof woof woof woo* all right that's enough a good watchdog mustn't draw attention to treasures like black leather bags like pearls any sea king would kill for and has just look around at all the blonde-haired blue-eyed murderers brandishing blades still salivating tongues still glistening under teeth still silver mouths still salivating eyes still steel-blue staring at her, at everyone sure but her especially her naked skin not glittered not naked but distant, not distant but cold still cold even when sweating dancing laughing cheering cajoling shouting look at me look at me look at her at me look look at me looking after her purse reflecting reds, blues and yellow salamanders not necessary no longer, not needed like legs dead gray and flaking like confetti not falling but fallen, trampled on by feet like Lizzie's like Lester's no longer distant but cold, still cold, still stumping, stomping in awkward beats and rhythms not audible no longer but icy, not warm but snoring, slumbering under semidiaphanous sheets still gossamer like golden apple martinis wake up good morning goodnight goodbye good sleep good riddance Godspeed good prince no longer royal blue but cobalt silk too small too high up off the wrists no longer not my own, not creased but smooth like ice cream too too cold like New York French vanilla too far, too cold, too distant not distant enough but far, too far for my own good guess I'll just sit here safe and protect imaginary images no longer mine but imaginary which is just as good just good just so long as the coldness wears away winters always follow autumns always follow summers always follow gushing oil geysers like salamanders always follow my Lizzie no longer mine too high up off the wrists like Saturday follows Friday always follows Thursday always follows Wednesday always Tuesday not Monday or Sunday, always Tuesday no more, no longer awake but sleeping under semidiaphanous sheets still silk like safe and mollycoddled back to sleep awake no longer awake but still, still not awake but wake up in gardens eat fruits and vegetables no longer fresh but vomitous like the lapels yon Lester wears like me, like what I've become just as good in any case Godspeed yon good prince goodbye good riddance for what it's worth we're all the same all sitting escaping gray feet stomping fallen confetti one billion steel-blue eyes shining, shimmering too watching too much up off the wrists at Lizzie, Liz, Elizabeth, last chance or is it? is it me or Lester dancing and laughing like what the fuck who what wake up look up toward the lights all reds, blues and yellows but no greens, no green, no green shining down like emeralds on grass not green, not green enough, not green but gray like snakeskin dying salamander legs flaking, withering, no longer legs but stumping gray and stomping, no longer dancing, no longer green but gone, not good, not awake but wake up *WAKE UP WAKE UP WAKE UP WAKE UP WAKE UP!!!*...

Awake.

In front of me Lizzie dancing, surrounded by people, Lester among them.

To my left her purse, open. Whitish business-size envelopes easy to see inside black leather exoskeletons.

Take it.

Under the envelope the silver blue green lighter, still cylindrical. Take it.

Back.

Away from the chair and Lizzie's purse taken care of no longer like a watchdog like *grrrrrrrrrr*umbling across the dance floor too many people never did like crowds too much think I'll just...

"Where do you think you're going, huh? What about my purse?!"

Taken care of.

Taking care not to trip walking through the bar door out into the street.

Outside. Too many people. Too familiar. To the left an extended line of taxicabs.

That's the best thing about New Year's Eve. Always a long, extended line of taxicabs never far, waiting, always ready to take one away. On the wings, as it were...*is*, I mean.

"Where to, pal?"

Anywhere. Away.

Taximeter ticking.

Always must first travel over the Bridge Columbia blue no longer a matter of importance. Never liked it much. Always thought it a bit gaudy given its purpose, which is to transport passengers to and from and back to again. Too easy. Too linear. Not cylindrical enough. No longer a matter to ponder.

Heading west like always...no, not always. Must remind myself never to say *always* again.

Exiting. Taximeter stopping. Cabby thanking. Wishing me a happy new year.

Entering.

Walking to the counter lit up like...no, not like. Not *like* anymore...*is*.

"Where to, pal?"

Where to? Where does one go when one wishes to get away? West? South? North? No, definitely not North.

"New York," I say.

And mean it.

"Round trip or one-way?"

East to the edge of the earth where the sun reflects off the surface of a rousing sea and back up again...

"*Round trip or one-way?!*"

...To the stars.

Book Four
Sometime Manifesto

when my heart stops
the whole world will get quicker
better
warmer
summer will follow summer
the air will be lake clear
and the meaning
too

          - Charles Bukowski
           from *to kiss the worms goodnight*

I awoke some thirty hours later with the sun shining in my face and eyes through the half-tinted glass of a Greyhound bus. It wasn't the sun but the jarring of the bus that woke me, that and the incidental elbow nudges of the man sitting next to me. Strange. I didn't remember him sitting next to me before I fell asleep.

I hadn't been sleeping the entire time, of course. My stomach and the blunt, spine-numbing bumps of commercial travel wouldn't allow it. Not that I'd wanted to. I would've missed all the scenery. All the empty fields and tree branches and rooftops and hoods of parked cars and trucks blanketed in white stillness moving into and out of the periphery of my drowsy eyes. The first few hours were quite literally a blur, a drab, gray-blue blur of the same trip I've made countless times over in my youth from up North down to the center of the Midwest to Kansas City and Abilene, the hometowns of my mother and father, respectively. Every summer we'd pack the forest green Lumina (or the burgundy Lumina... odd, I don't remember any cars other than Luminas in my youth) and after stopping at the nearest convenience store for gas and goodies and aspirin set the speedometer at a steady seventy-five headed south on I-35 going down, down, down, down – fourteen hours down through Minnesota and Iowa, mostly, though some Missouri just the corner where Kansas City can't decide where her loyalties lie and then there we were, legs cramped, nerves frazzled, half-dead and stinking like perfumed sewer rats giving nannas and papoos and first cousins hugs and kisses and eating icebox cookies washed down with strawberry soda running off away from the grownups after the routine updates underground to the basement to rummage through my mom's dad's macabre collection of WWII memorabilia. (He was an Ally, paramedic unit. Never spoke of it, I'm told.) On those trips we usually wouldn't stop till Des Moines to stall the engine and dip our toes in the same salty whirlpool every summer...Super 8, I think it was. On this trip, though, the first stop (aside from the all too often, tiresome digressions to rural Minnesota's most backwoods communities – I swear, once I even saw an Amish family board the bus, leaving both the buggy *and* the bloody horse behind) where we came to rest was none other than Scandinavia's own Minneapolis.

I'm no stranger to this town. Suburbanites from a two-hundred-mile radius surrounding this metropolis make their tarriance in the Twin Cities (the other umbilical growth being St. Paul) at least once every few months for no reason other than to remind themselves lives more interesting than their own exist and they, too, can bend the iron bars just wide enough for a three-dimensional feel, then off they trot again back to their jobs and wives and two-dimensional lives. A sad scenario, really, and as I exited the bus into this dark, bleak city asleep and snoring with the lights left on I had to smile. I was not there on a visit. I was only passing through. I lit a cigarette and stretched my legs and waited contentedly the forty-five minutes till we boarded again.

Next was Chicago. A far more memorable stop, this, for many reasons. The sun had just risen, giving the landscape an arctic glow which contrasted eerily with the tall glass buildings and violet-electric activity convulsing through the air and streets. Already at this hour the streets were filled with activity, an activity which to me then seemed strange, vibrant, chaotic, inorganic. Standing on the icy sidewalk of

South Michigan Avenue peering into the abysmal mouth of another Great Lake and the stony façade of the Art Institute I felt cold, bony, empty. Perhaps it had something to do with my stomach. I was terribly hungry (I didn't realize this till a few blocks from the station) and after searching about in a sort of dry panic I decided just to step into a small café up the street to restock my courage with strong coffee and toast and underdone eggs and hash browns extra crispy and once all was swallowed I felt better, stronger. I paid my check and stood from my seat and once again stepped out into the cold air to greet whatever.

One thing was certain: I needed new attire. The thin black fabric of cobalt-blue gentility is simply no dress to greet whatever with. All but the shoes had to go. All the same, I wasn't about to spend the bulk of my resources on a brand-new anything. Jostling my memory a bit I thought I saw a sign for second-hand clothes up the avenue a stretch. I spun on my heels and made for the vicinity when I was stopped dead by a short, stout black man in rags selling red paper roses on green pipe-cleaner stems wrapped in white tissue. On his gruff face was a beaming grin and he laughed as he greeted me, cold heat steaming out his open mouth and nostrils. He didn't ask any certain amount for the roses, just whatever I wished to pay, or *donate*, I should say. I had no need for red paper roses wrapped in tissue, though seeing him stand there, wishing all passersby a Happy New Year even when still trying to make a sale to me convinced me he was the real thing. I withdrew a twenty and handed it to him in exchange for one of the fake roses, then again made for the second-hand store. (I soon discovered the white tissue around the green pipe-cleaner stem wasn't tissue at all but pages, two pages upon which he had typed a lengthy New Year's salutation to all and sundry which I read later on the bus and which floored me completely.)

Next came Cleveland. I wouldn't have recalled Cleveland at all if it weren't for a towering, wire-thin darkie who tried to sell me hashish. Luckily, I declined. I say *luckily* for two reasons: first, soon after approaching me the dark man was escorted off the premises by two non-dark police officers with the countenance of civil disobedience and I'm sure if I'd had purchased the dude's goods I'd be going with; second, I remember seriously considering the black man's offer. When he approached me I was staring at the hazy, noonday jigsaw and frozen smoke of Cleveland's skyline and I allowed the embodiment of that sight to enter my flesh and veins and I think I might have gathered what the black man was trying to say. I felt brown, smoldered, depressed. I moved on.

After Cleveland came a long, long landscape of nothing much at all but blurred shades of brown and gray and cars and trucks and billboards and buildings with words on the sides and fronts and churches and houses mostly dirty white but some dirty blue and dirty pink and dirty green and brown and souvenir shops and gas stations and trucks on the side the initials G.O.D. (Guaranteed Overnight Delivery) and more cars, more trucks, more souvenir stations and gas houses like churches and cars and trucks and trucks and parking lots and parking lots and parking lots. I tried to keep my eyes open playing a game I remembered as a kid, recording in my mind everything I saw, placing them into various categories. The categories I'd decide beforehand, categories such as size or color or new or old or how they made me feel or didn't or just if what I saw was worth placing into a category or not. Most times not. Still, one must at least *try* to break through the gray aluminum chains of monotony if only for a state or two until sleep comes and with this in mind I devised the category "worthy" ("not worthy" would have been superfluous, no?) and I began with a sign which read "Museum of Labor and Industry" (fitting, I thought) and Rockside Road and Bedford Heights and Thistledown and on through Youngstown and all of Ohio altogether past a toll booth rotted teeth like passing through to Mexico but the sign says "Pennsylvania" and soon another saying "Pittsburgh" and another still this time atop a clothing store saying "There's No Degree of Honesty" and me thinking Christ, I'll bet to hell this joint gets knocked over twice a week at least and on to more towns and cities and everything ending in *ville* or *burg* or *ton* (like me) then just before Columbia County a sign telling us to "Keep Pennsylvania Beautiful" and me thinking Give us one good reason why! and then I see it, patches upon patches of plain land proceeding directly into rolling hills and hills and hills of trees and trees and tree tops like tips of broccoli dipped in white icing like a million of them at least one million and me thinking for the first time ever in my life America! How beautiful! which wasn't to last long since after that Mainville and again the drab grayness and ennui and inertia and on into Hibernia through the Eisenhower Estate not leaving much of an impression barely even worth remembering if it weren't for the *Eisenhower* meaning more to my mom's dad than me I guess but Laurel Avenue, now *that's* something worth remembering stirring memories of Virgil's head and Jim guiding Italy's own Dante through the Seven Circles and Verona reminding me of Sir William penning *Romeo* and Mulberry Street reminiscent of long, hot baths with soap chips scented candles burning best not think about *that* too much too far gone away too many gray streets greeting Penn Station reminding me to forget my schooling if possible toward Apostle's House not even paying attention to meaning anymore Newark...Newark...Newark being the last thing my eyes allowed my mind to categorize before the lids became two heavy, medicated slabs of aluminum flesh and off I slid into a deep, smoke-and-steel gray Mid-American sleep.

    I awoke what felt like days after heading north on I-95 through one dense metropolis after another and I felt I must be close. The series of tall buildings and streets which looked and smelled of ancient blood coagulated into gray concrete slabs laid flat and surrounded by sand and pulverized snow and ice and illuminated by endless rows of street lamps and store signs like stage lights set off an unmistakable sense of greatness, the greatness of Progress both feared and revered, of modernity and antiquity mixed together in a massive whirlpool of fire and steel and ice and lumber and sand and stage lights coagulated over two hundred years, fusing to form an enormous glacier ice floe which does not *flow*, per se, but *rotates*, revolving round its axis collecting refuse and riches and lives and dead ideas scraped relentlessly from the surrounding land and sea and spat out once the energy is digested, the lives drained and dead ideas and refuse drifting lifeless now down dirty rivulets like dead leaves in gutters.

I thought of the man sitting next to me, the one whose elbows I'd become so acquainted with, and asked how long till we reached New York. He looked at me as if I asked to sleep with his wife, then scoffed and looked straight ahead at the seat before him. Thinking this a bit odd, seeing as he was the one who woke *me*, I tightened my belt and loosened my tongue and asked, "Is that to mean you don't know?"

Again he scoffed and said, "Hey, come on, pal. You shittin' me or what?"

What? What's he on about? Is the East Coast really so suspicious?...Of its own U.S. citizens? Is my Northern accent so thick as to instill in this man a wariness of my intentions? Perhaps so. I became suspicious of myself. Was I attempting to split this man apart from his family, his prosperity – from his own American self? A mitigating tactic? Mitosis by mere questions? Ridiculous. I inquired again about New York.

"Look, pal," he said, leaning over glaring straight into my retinas. "You know as well as I do we left New York over four hours ago. We'll be skitchin' into Boston in fifteen, get me? Now...don't talk to me anymore. My ears hurt," after which he proceeded to make a cell phone call.

Boston? Boston: Beantown....A misnomer, I think. There are no more beans in Boston – they've all been replaced by half-priced calamari and linguine and lemon iced tea and green apples and peanut butter. A city in contrast, in constant construction to try and meld its cobblestone walkways weaving through crippled, salty houses leaning over one another and the testaments of grandeur with gilded domes for rooftops and marble pillars for front doors.

Boston: A city upon a hill, I think I read somewhere. I also read somewhere Boston was the first American city to publish a book. Quite a feat, that, though I think the book was a D.I.Y. on how to tune one's voice to the proper pitch so as to be heard in Heaven, whereupon after the publication of said book a woman Quaker was hanged till dead to balance the scale.

America.

Boston: A city of immigrants, of peddlers and pushers selling everything they can to match the high-pitched copper gleam intruding their eyes and ears, the stamp and seal of New England brazened on their foreheads so their exclusion, their possible impudence in the face of honest Bostonian pride may be efficiently, expeditiously sought out and dealt with forthright, the Birkenstocks retracted, computer access denied, the keys taken back and hands slapped and feet promptly shown the front door no more calamari or linguine or green apples or tea for you, now it's all lonely walks along a sunlit Charles dodging eyes from all the pretties dressed in hairy arms and legs and shoulders and lips and chins and hair slicked back sunglassed eyeballs staring you down into the baked, blood-soaked coagulated cobblestone walkways going nowhere but under towering structures too ancient and baroque and beautiful to comprehend so instead you find a park bench someplace and befriend the geese squawking songs of true beauty and antiquity further back than Man, back before the Revolution, before Boston, before foreheads brazened with the one thing you thought you needed though you're sure would leave you poisoned but you try anyway so one more attempt to teach young children all you know ends in nothing more than advice on how to roll dice and *not* lose all one's money on a single toss take the money anyway invest it in one month's rent as if that truly were an investment something that gave something back not just took and took but you're used to taking and taking it's the only thing that makes any sense anymore – that and the Charles River and the North End and the Green Line like a wire whip and that boxy bar near Berklee, I think, or the Prudential Building dedicated to that mad but lucid flame-drunk poet eating calamari and linguine half-priced at noon in Grendel's Den every Tuesday sipping coffee in some café nibbling day-old croissants watching all the pretty people scurry by in black and cobalt blue with briefcases but not you...

But I didn't know all this till much later.

I exited the bus and walked out from what I later discovered to be South Station into an early afternoon gale searing my skin and blurring my eyes which already needed help adjusting to low sunlight reflected off snow and glass. When my skin and eyes finally settled back into their original consistency I stood a moment, still as stone, allowing the scene to properly sink into my orbs. I thought I might be close to the water; even through the ice and wind and sensory inconsistency I knew I smelled salt – salt and dead fish. Could be the road, I told myself. As it were, anyone who has ever smelled the sea realizes it as unmistakable. There is an intoxicating element to the smell, in one's nose and passages, making one believe the sea as docile as a sleeping colossus, yet defiant as the sun. *Intoxicating*, I say, because this smell has caused many, many men to seek it out relentlessly, passionately, yet cautiously as though to escape the perils which usually come from too much of a good thing. Eyes slowly lose sight, legs whither, skin becomes cold and scaly, hair turns gray and brittle and eventually falls out, wives leave, libidos drain dry, cocks become just like any other useless, pesky appendage. Once the sea is in one's veins there's no escape save death, or insanity, which could be viewed as a blessing when compared with the fate above. Still, the sea is there. It makes no apologies. Like a drug or its pusher it seeks out no one; it only makes itself available when one decides to surrender. Unlike drugs or pushers, however, you needn't any money to arrange a date. In fact, the sea prefers you a poor, desolate soul. Tastes better, I suppose. In any event, one taste, one *smell* and you're hooked. Try to leave and the invisible, indestructible chain of that experience, that intoxicating trip leaves you quite literally itching for more, for another taste, just one more smell of sweet, wet salt and dead fish and the strange, vast, dark underworld which bore life eternal. The Mother of All. The Womb, so to speak. An intoxicating thought, what!

I snapped from my reverie to discover my stomach still believed in the ambrosial benefits of dry land and after giving the layout before me the once over I saw what appeared to be an eatery, though what might just as well have been an old prop from an early Mickey Rourke movie or maybe even Jimmy Dean transported paramagnetically via Sir Arthur Conan Doyle's time machine, left adrift in an unsuspecting district of brick and steel and glass buildings peering down upon the thing with reservation and indignation over cold brass windowsills and out half-shut mail slots. In a word, inharmonious. Out of place. Perfect. I made toward it with long, brisk strides.

Instead of underdone eggs and toast and hash browns extra crispy I ordered a steak and cheese sandwich with sautéed mushrooms and onions and green peppers and a side of fries (extra greasy) and a Coke. I was right about the paramagnetic bit – on the wall above the counter was a poster shrine dedicated to a select few pop hipsters of the soda jerk era, the iconic "Rebel" among them donning horn-rimmed spectacles and leaning *laissez-faire* as if contemplating direction. Strange. I never knew he wore glasses. I did, however, know about his false teeth...and his bizarre fetish of the occult. All thoughts best left for another time and setting. I finished my sandwich and fries and Coke stepped back out into the street.

Essex, the sign said. A curvature weaving away from the wind and sea. I wove with it.

A few blocks drifting to and fro like a webster led me toward another most strange and curiously laid structure as anyone hopes to see in any New England setting. I'm speaking, naturally, of the green and red and golden lion-dragon gate of Boston's own Chinatown.

What the hell was happening?! Was I still asleep on the bus, dreaming? Were the unnameable gods above pointing down and laughing as they witnessed the bizarre sights my two eyes now showed me? They must have, for even I had to let loose a dry cackle when confronted with this scene, this ancient Asian archway leading dead into a wholly ancient, Asian environment of small, almond-colored men and women carrying enormous crates of vegetables and magazines and meat and fish and Tsingtao into cramped shops and stores and restaurants and apartments. An odd introduction to Boston, agreed? Still, somehow I couldn't help but think it appropriate, all this strangeness and wholly unexpected foreign unusualness in one of America's signature cities, her one true home of the culture and architecture and individuality which comprises her character, who she truly is, what makes her. It seems sufficient to say America is not so much *American* as many would define her; that is, they who sit in houses and on couches and digest her essence through television sets and action movies and all sorts of magazines and domestically brewed beverages. No, she – *America* – is everyone, everything, a conglomerate of what makes us all, everyone, everybody in the world an individual, a character, an essence unto themselves. America provides the streets and avenues and tall buildings surrounding anomalous cafés and two Coasts outlining one half of two vast seas and one million and one bus stations – the world provides the people. Does this make any sense? A bit naïve, perhaps? Premature? In any case, it made perfect sense to me wandering through Chinatown's own thin, wiry streets of almond-colored people performing their duties with dignity and perseverance in America's own Boston. Imagine the courage of these people!

I mean, I was *born* here (as were many of them, too, no doubt) and even *I* had to cringe if I allowed my mind to wander too close toward the marrow of reality. Luckily, the chill of an East Coast wind in January provided the needed diversion. I left Chinatown, vowing to return and explore more when the weather permitted, and sank into the underground steam of the nearest subway station.

I had never used an underground before but if it's anything like a Greyhound, I guessed, there shouldn't be a problem. Purchase a token and hop on and go, with luck in the right direction, then exit upon meeting your destination. Direction, of course, is the main thing. As it were, I had no use for it. The ends of my nerves were saved by my mind's total ignorance of anything having to do with direction. Everywhere meant the same place to me. Already I was abeam just being indoors and out from the cold. I tossed the clerk behind the glass a smile and some change and received my token and got on board.

The first thing I noticed was how many people there were and how distant they all seemed – far off, away, preoccupied with something so very important as to force them all to stare at the floor, or the ceiling, or the railing, or the rails, or their shoes, or the toes inside their shoes, or their pockets, or the hands inside their pockets, or the rings sliding off and back on their fingers, or their ears, or the insides of their skulls, or their noses, or the hairs inside their noses, or nothing, anything other than the person sitting next to them, the old man falling asleep against the window, the woman with sore feet standing in the aisle waiting prayerfully for a warm seat to open soon, the child in the palm of her hand also waiting, proving to be the bravest soul here since he's the only one staring everyone in the eye, willing to greet the old man or the old woman or child or whomever with a smile and a warm, sincere Hallo! Any chance at all I had to make eye contact with anyone and acknowledge our presence with a nod and a grin was thwarted in infancy by an overbearing smaze of cold indifference. That was the first time I came face-to-face with an indifference of this magnitude, of an atmosphere where all, *everyone* save small children is disinterested in who you are or from whence you came. There are two kinds of indifference, it seems: one born of ignorance and apathy (the ugliest kind) and another born of immoderation, of possibly once caring too much, sending off too many warm Hallos and receiving none in return, soon believing it all a waste of time and energy (the saddest kind). The first is inexcusable, the second also inexcusable but understandable – Cold hearts are not born, but created. Still, it's sad to think the human heart could be so frail, so susceptible, quick to surrender its strength in spirit just because a few cold bastards couldn't give a shit one way or another if you exist or not. The heart of anger and violence thinks this way, this apathetic, indifferent way, even toward itself, smothering itself in fear and hate and cowardice – the institution of war – an *outward* war which breeds nothing but more fear, more hate, more cowardice and indifference and apathy in the frail heart of humanity. There is, however, another kind of war, an *inner* war which, once waged and fought and won, renders the violent in spirit at total peace, an *inner* peace which radiates and permeates the ones around him, around her. First, though, the violence, the anger and hate and apathy and indifference must be confronted and fought and conquered. Till then, the institution of war within humanity will always exist, always occupy men's minds as the end-all by which to protect his four spongy chambers and the blood flow which is automatic.

Anyway, after a few minutes of this indifference I quit trying to acknowledge presences and instead concentrated on the names of stations which flew by like curious birds, floating a moment in mid-flight for a brief inspection, then off again they soared in the opposite direction. Names like Symphony, Museum, Northeastern, Longwood, Brigham, Mission Park, Riverway, Back of the Hill, Heath, then back again no more birds back to Copley and exit, enter another train, another direction, another track listing other names like Kenmore, Hynes/ICA, BU East, BU Central, BU West, Pleasant, Brighton, Harvard, Mount Hood, Boston College Oops! flew too far birdless again so back once more back to Kenmore Christ! another train another track same line but different direction listing different names like Fenway, Brookline Village, Brookline Hills, Beaconsfield, Reservoir, Chestnut birds flying too far apart now making me a bit nervous wings flapping too fast too far away from the sea so back I go back in the opposite direction, back past Chestnut and Reservoir and both Brooklines past Fenway and Kenmore and Hynes/ICA deciding now to stop can't hide underground all night watching birds flying in and out so out we go, out by where we started in the first place: Copley.

It had turned dark during my time below. I'd entered the subway up the street a ways at Boylston near a cemetery, the dim lights and streets there preparing me in no way for what I was to encounter upon exiting the stairway at Copley Station into the bright, shimmery nightscape of Copley Square.

If at that moment a spaceship had crashed at my feet I might have batted an eyelash or two, maybe, then shrugged and performed a sidestep maneuver and continued on in another direction. Thus the mind works when surrounded by alien elements: hypersensitivity to detail, all senses acute to an alarming degree, brainwaves relax dramatically, slowing to a near standstill to allow the mind sufficient time for comprehension and proper judgement (which equals one nanosecond) – then action. Action is all. Impulse takes control when one is out of one's element – instinct, some might call it. As it were, standing face-to-face with this most alien of all foreign elements my two eyes had ever seen I could not move, not one limb, not one finger, toe or nostril hair for at least forty-five minutes. I was struck dumb, immobile. Only the eyeballs moved, using much more time than sufficient to comprehend all they saw, all the orange and peach and lemon-gold lights and store signs and names of restaurants and headlights reflected off the eyeballs and smiles of well-dressed people walking side-by-side on sidewalks wider than the streets surrounded by tall buildings old and new, older than the Constitution, it seemed – every one of them unique, distinct, singular, playfully counter-reacting off one another, complimenting the next in contradiction, in ancient stout baked-red clay jagged, old and rough and grinning in the face and eyes of steel and glass modernity, a smoothness sixty-stories high, impressive, towering, powerful, yet yielding to the demands of its stony predecessor, accepting its role as solely complimentary, never imposing its towering strength and steel and glass modernity selfishly, but freely, using its smoothness to reflect the rough edges of antiquity and orange and apricot and peach and lemon golden lights and smiles of well-dressed people walking together through ice and snow on sidewalks wider than the streets even.

As said, after about forty-five minutes of this my senses finally stirred and I realized I was sitting upon the icy stone steps of what might easily had been mistaken for a preserved remain of Acropolis (in fact, Boston's Public Library) staring out across a large white opening scattered with wandering souls and ending at the front steps of what I easily mistook for the final resting place of Charles the Silly (Trinity Church). I stood off the icy stone steps of Boston's own Acropolis and rubbed my ass cheeks and made for the warm, inviting lights of Boylston Street.

Walking among these lights staring into the dark glass of stores closed for the night I experienced a very strange thing. Surrounded by strange people smiling and walking together, walled in by tall buildings new and old and cold I realized I was alone, not one soul I could call or visit or contact in any way. I was alone in the truest sense of the word, which is *with no one, nobody*. Alone, yes...but not lonely. Never before had I experienced this. All my life I had been surrounded by people, so many people, *escaping* people, there were so many, so many I never wanted to be surrounded by. They were just there, around me, surviving off the energy we stole from and gave back to one another – surrounded by people, so many people all my life...and lonely. And there I was, amidst the lights and snow and ice of a strange city surrounded by more people than I had ever been before but knowing none and feeling...happy. Not lonely...not then, anyway. Everything was too new and old and frightening for me to think about such a thing as loneliness. That came later. All I could think about then was how the baked-red brick and snow and ice and smiles of strange people walking under orange and apricot lights reflected off the dark glass of clothing stores closed for the night with no one inside...then it struck me. It was nighttime. Soon I'd need a place to sleep. I stood a moment and tried to think of what to do. Like a flash I remembered a flyer I saw tacked on the wall in Copley Station, something about a hostel. *Irish* something or other. Sounded promising. I turned on my heels and headed for the subway.

I found the place by the FleetCenter on Friend Street (a good omen, I thought). So be it. I braced myself and smiled and walked inside to greet my people (like the naïve fool I was).

A pasty-faced girl with rust-colored hair behind the desk glared as I walked toward her. Somehow she could tell I didn't fall directly off the boat. Ah, well, my ancestry would save me, thought I as I smiled my best Irish smile and asked about the rooms.

"Dere aren't nut rums," she told me, her accent thick as stout. "Nut rums...just cuts."

Fine. How much for a cot?

"Dat's twenty fer a noite, loike. Sex-noite max'mum," she chirped, almost gleefully. I peered toward her questioningly. "Wee 'ave ta kipe de cuts rowtated," she explained. "Cun't allow a squatter such as yersel ta steal a cut from some udder, now, cun't wee?"

No, wee cun't. I nodded and smiled anyway and booked myself the maximum.

"Dat's round de bend ta yer lef, den."

Right.

Around the bend I found a large room like a gymnasium housing at least thirty cots arranged military style, in a corner a few dirty beds arranged one atop another. Small wonder the Irish are so crotchety, I thought. With such small lots of space left to call their own it's a wonder they don't set what's left on fire and toss themselves into the flames. I forgave my pasty-faced hostess with her "wee cun't" this and "wee cun't" that and blessed my luck for sleeping out from the cold the next six nights and flopped atop my cot and quickly passed into a deep, Irish green sleep.

*   *   *

The next four days I searched the entire city and more from daybreak till dark for lodgings, anything which matched my means. As it turned out, my means was matched only by my ability to gaze unrestrained along Boston's vicinity side streets and boroughs and landmarks and cafés and eateries (the grazing of menus all I could afford) and schools and odd architecture, the sights of each filling my imagination enough to make me forget my aching feet and eyes and legs and hunger and despair at finding nothing, returning once again to the Irish Embarrassment to ignore the sneers and scant eye-slits of my fellow embattled housemates, all of us hoping like hell to fall fast asleep and snore peacefully without having contracted our neighbor's pleuritic disposition. No such luck. The Irish have a genius for the contagious and consumptive and by eight o'clock or earlier I'd be up and sipping coffee and dodging coughs and sneezes aimed in my direction and out the door in search of my illusive savior to come and free me from the battery of blue roses, the scent of which as diseased and paralyzing as Tennessee Williams himself.

The entire city and more, I say, and nothing. My own fault, likely...or, not *mine* so much as my narrow, encompassed mind's. I went into the search with the idea such things as flophouses still existed on the East Coast, houses which let rooms (shared bath a definite negative...but still) for as little as a few hundred a month, the only amenities being a bed and perhaps a window and a dresser, if lucky, and, if *really* lucky, maybe even a personal-sized icebox, all snuggled safe behind the privacy of *one's own door*.

At first I went for gold. The Waterfront to me, naturally, seemed ideal. I imagined a place such as sailors and sea captains and their wenches might inhabit: rooms like seamen's cabins; in the lobby a bar draped in fishnet and low lights and pieces of ships recovered from wrecks; dusty bottles lined along the mirrors and doorframes, opened and emptied; dyed-red-haired women resting elbows on real mahogany; a broken-down phone booth in a corner constantly occupied by a comatose drunk; the cost for such conditions reflecting the conditions of the patrons themselves and for one brief, brief moment I thought I caught sight of that bright, salivary glimmer – a mercantile-type joint straight off the water that, as it happened, *was* for sailors and sea captains (I thought better than to inquire about wenches) though, as it also happened, was strictly in reserve *only* for these select men, a license or permit or merit patch or some other proof of aquatic tenure needed before procuring a room. I smiled anyway and thanked the bearded man behind the door for his info and turned to go, catching a hairy grin out the corner of my eye which I read to mean "you silly young fool."

The North End, surrounded by wharves, was the obvious choice where to continue my search and the moment I passed Commercial Street and set foot inside the narrowly-lined confines of cobblestone and brick and mortar and the smells and feel of another land – truly, a country within a country – I said a secret prayer to Whomever this would be it. The idea of situating myself within a typical New England town, yet just by looking out my bedroom window fully believing I was someplace else, someplace I was not – a place I could turn a corner and listen in on a conversation in a non-English tongue, then turn another and enter a traditional Italian confectioner's shop for chocolate-covered almonds or licorice or an assortment of hard candies, then another still for liqueur and espresso in a café the likes of which only Europeans can experience with honesty and authenticity – all this had my hands clasped like dovetails inside the feathery down of my secondhand jacket. Hell, if one could forgive the imposing presence of Paul Revere and pigeon shit one might easily be tempted to call the North End as close to an American ideal as America can offer and I nearly found myself living inside this ideal...well, not *nearly*, exactly. There was an old Italian man who had a room to rent above his restaurant and, like a fool, before asking to see it, I asked how much. Three times the amount in my pocket, it was. So be it. Ideals are meant to be unobtainable, I told myself, before settling wearily for a coffee and biscotti.

Day two was sunny which I mistook as a sign. Overhearing a conversation in a coffeehouse that morning about a gallery showing in the South End, I leapt without reserve. Thinking it artist friendly, hence poor, I thought it the place to look and soon found myself wandering its streets, baffled by the tenement houses which did not appear poor at all, but wealthy, quite wealthy – wealthier than Copley. Drifting down Tremont I sensed I was dreaming, tripping through a dreamscape not intended for my eyes but the eyes of a three-hundred-year-old sun-stricken Negro or a plantation lord with amnesia. New Orleans was what I saw – not the New Orleans of my time or any time, but another New Orleans, an *amnesic* New Orleans belonging not to the South nor the Creole aristocracy nor America nor any century, a place and time transcending all time, all space, all dimensions, a landscape beyond itself, belonging to a plane which exists solely in contradiction, defined by that which precisely it is not. The buildings reflected this contradiction, a contradiction much unlike the contradiction I witnessed that first night in Copley Square. This contradiction was disharmonious, conflicting, using itself and its environment as blunt tools by which to forge its place into a world where it does not belong. It resembled somewhat Paris, an *English* Paris, if one can be conceived. The disfigured offspring of two lusty European first cousins born and abandoned on swampy American soil. A sad and disheartening scenario. Pitiful, truly. However, before I reached Massachusetts Avenue (that mad bastard of a street) pity abandoned me and, remembering the coffeehouse, I thought I'd satisfy that morning's curiosity. I found a gallery and entered it. After explaining my situation to the puff atop the ambo the uppity faggot laughed in my face and said, "What do you think this is, boy, Seattle?"

That settled it. Fuck the South End. I'd sleep in the Public Garden before penning my name to that list. I headed north around Downtown Crossing to scour a cheap meal, hanging around after to browse through all the hollow buildings and cemeteries and stone-and-pewter state houses and nickel-plated jewelry stores.

Day three began much the same way as day two – ending much the same way too – the only difference being instead of a coffeehouse it was a magazine that led me astray, a "roommate finder" magazine which promised to pit me in a house with four or five other desperate souls unable or unwilling to live alone so instead they opt to huddle backs-together the long, dark night, awaking the next morning chasing crusty dreams with stale beer and TV and surfaced, meaningless talk...all for a one-time-low-no-guarantee fee of ninety-nine yams. *No thank you*, said my not-yet-that-desperate soul. Ultimately, what interested me about these magazines was not the one-time low-rate fee but the location of the various areas in which these sad bastards lived, unveiling to me those districts and burgs of Boston of such low stature as to permit the injection of what obviously was either one of two categories: 1) college kids, or 2) diseased, drunken wasters (the only difference between the two being age). Low rent follows low-rate neighbors, thought I as I drew a list of the more oft-mentioned boroughs.

The most prevalent was Jamaica Plain. Already such a name had me skeptical but what the hell. I decided it worth a look-see. If too diseased I could always hop the train, no? About halfway inland on the Orange Line I'd seen enough. All traces of city life were replaced with exact replicas of convenience stores and strip malls and modern-day suburbia as that which I headed east to escape. I was not about to trade one gangrened stump for another. At Green Street I hopped the median and saddled the iron horse branded Oak Grove rolling north.

The next was the Red Line past Harvard (of course) and out beyond Porter (a barren wasteland) before dismounting at Davis Square, which by all means appeared more promising. Airing about the streets and alleyways I began to develop a feeling this may be it. It seemed to possess a didactic, childlike ambience; a studious, relaxed jeans-and-beer-stained-tee-shirt feel which is alive and everywhere. Also everywhere were flyers advertising the need for roommates of all sorts and I smiled. Plenty of shared baths and hardwood floors for everyone, it seemed. In then end, though, all I found was a gray-haired duffer who repaired electric guitars and who lived above his shop and was in need of some assistance. We eyed each other over a moment, then shook hands and parted ways as he was twice my age and I was not a musician. Would have been cracked ice for the both of us. Ah, well, in my wanders I espied an independent theater near the square advertising a film about the life of Jackson Pollock. Only so many hours in a day, said I before purchasing my stub and settling down to rest my skin and snack and learn the esoteric tenets behind Jack's drip-drop philosophy.

Day four by chance I wandered into a café in the hub of the Financial District already dizzy from gazing up at all the tall steel-and-glass cocoons, then more so once I found myself surrounded by far too many highly exotic moths of all shapes and colors dressed like whores dressed like nuns on break between classes expounding the Holy Trinity and cut-throat business tactics. Confused and excited in a sort of weak, perverted way I thought I'd accost one of these lovely oddities to entertain my curiosity at what she might say. As it happened I roped a tall, blonde, early-thirties, black-chiffon-and-silver-winged type who smiled at my story as I told it (little boy lost in a strange city needs a home and all that, don't you know) and told me it reminded her of this guy she once met who found a place above a bar in South Boston. A bit disappointed some other collector had already pinned her subconscious, I thanked her kindly anyway and exited the chrome-plated steel aura of cocoons that never open and headed once again for the Red Line and South Boston.

If the South End is the offspring of an incestuous affair then South Boston is the bully who steals that bastard child's meal money. The Southie mentality, as observed by an outsider, is brutal – brutal in the most brute sense pure brutality has to offer. Just walking down the street (Broadway, I think it was) I had the sense I was being chased. Involuntarily, it seemed, my head turned round my back every ten seconds. Perhaps it was the landscape – a barrenness of stark houses and junk shops and bars with bloodstained linoleum floors injured by broken glass and tears like acid and disappointed soles. One of these bars I did enter, wearily heeding the advice my exotic moth offered, though after asking the barmaid (a girl no older than seventeen, I'd bet) about vacancies she just stared as if I spoke Armenian, then said all was full but I should stop back sometime next week. "Something almost always usually opens up unexpectedly." Right. Next week on the dot, lovely. Save me a stool next to the pickled eggs and pigs' feet and whisky pail filled to its wrought iron brim with broken glass and teeth and spat blood.

I wasn't about to surrender that easy, however. I'd only two nights remaining at the Irish Unconditional Happiness and Serendipity Embargo and I admit I was getting nervous. What then? I wondered. Perhaps the Public Garden wasn't such a far-off prospect after all. A chilling thought. I pressed on till I saw through the window of a used door handle repair shop a face I thought might be of some help. I entered and explained my case to the gray-haired, headbanded hippie-type behind the counter who listened patiently, then nodded solemnly and said, "Get out! Get out now! Get the hell out of Boston! You've no business here. No one does. The yuppies have taken over...turned it all, the buildings, everything into condos. You haven't a chance. It's over. What you're looking for is over. It isn't here. It's gone....So leave! Leave Boston! Leave it to its own miserable, soulless fate! Leave! Get out! Get out while you still can!" A bit put off, if not frightened, I turned to leave and just before I reached for the door I heard him say, "On second thought, try Dorchester."

I tried Dorchester. All I found was another gray-haired hippie (sans headband) who told me, "Try Quincy."

I tried Quincy. No hippies, at least. Lots of touristy restaurants and coffee shops and ice cream parlors. And water. And naval artifacts. And long docks like mummified fingers stretched out over raw iciness. I cringed. It reminded me of the Lake. I left Quincy as fast as the train would take me.

It was dark when I returned to the city. Another day in search of nothing. Feeling down, and feeling I deserved a reward for not cracking thus far, I thought I'd treat myself to a hot sandwich and a pint in one of the many pubs I'd seen about town. In a drool, I set out in search of the one thing I knew I'd find with ease.

The first was a warm, spacious, dark-wooded Irish pub christened The Black Rose. Without wait, I tripped inside and ordered a stout and a menu. The menu came straight away; the stout took a bit longer. Seemed he had to pour it twice: once three-quarters full, letting the foam like sweet milk settle, then again to the brim. I'd never before seen it done this way. Learned later it's tradition. So be it. Made sense to me. Still tasted sweet like milk tugged off the teat of the Mother of Heaven herself.

Apples of Arcadia

The menu was also traditional, I learned. Lots of potato stew and leek soup and boiled cabbage and corned beef and rashers. I thought a moment, pretending to inspect the menu in earnest till suddenly I heard the dialect of my housemates' tongues voicing back the ingredients, then quickly ordered a burger and fries, extra English (lots of ketchup and mayonnaise and salt and malt vinegar). The bartender raised an eyebrow but took my order anyway. Hell, he was probably from Jersey.

It was still early so the joint was fairly empty save a few diehards numbing the effects of the deluge the night prior as well as a collection of stale businessmen getting their buzz on before trotting home to face the wife and TV. I couldn't concern myself with any of them. The food had arrived. After that I saw no one till every salt grain and grease puddle had been stirred, sopped up and swallowed.

So, satiated, I ordered another stout to wash down the first, then found a newspaper on the bar. Lazy, I scoured the rental section to see what's new. Nothing. Ah, well, there's always the stout, thought I as the smooth, frothy blackness swirled down the hollow of my open throat.

Two or three hours later I'd forgotten all about ethereal rental properties and brutality and embargoed serendipity and happiness and instead allowed myself to melt wholly, unreservedly into the atmosphere which surrounded me. By then the bar had filled dramatically with more drunks and businessmen presumedly without wives or television sets to go home to – all smiling and patting each other's back, every so often tossing a glance at half-mast to the front of the room and the band there thumbing their way through a three-piece arsenal of traditional Gaelic psalms of sorrow, lust and drunkenness and high, unfounded gaiety. Perfect. My previous distaste for the taint of the Irish tongue was slowly turning for better as I too became affected by all the above, especially lust and drunkenness, the stout and my eyes working well together, bouncing around the room like crystallized orbs tossed atop the surface of a bubbling tar pit at all the smiling lips and teeth and eyes and harvest-colored hair and skin not pasty but ivory, bled clean by the world's sins and the baptismal mists of her island chosen by That Nameless Wonder to bear witness to war, famine, religious insurrection, lice, invasion, the Holy Purple Empire, riots, suffocated insurgencies, slaughter, civil indifference, ignorance, Easter, apathy – all the hardships mankind must encounter and suffer and defeat with much ivory lust and smiles and harvest-colored tufts and drunkenness and the psalms of a Gaelic ancestry, ancient and heroic...if not divine. The Irish green secret. Sorrow disguised as mirth. Sadness as an aphrodisiac. Inspired, I fumbled for a pad and pen and began scribbling down a few notes.

Shortly after, I was approached by one of these fair-haired Hibernians supposedly curious as to who I was and why my head was to the pad and not in my pint where it should be, by God be damned. Not sure how to answer, or if I wished to answer at all, I just shrugged my shoulders and resumed scribbling.

"Ah, yer one a dem, den, are ya?"

One of them?

"Ya know...a scribbler. A poet, loike. W.B. Yeats an all, aye?"

Yikes. This was a touchy one. If I said no, then I'd just as well stomped his foot and spat in his eye and smothered his nasal passages with an unfurled Union Jack. If yes, then I'd be shoulder-deep in a feigned discourse on poetics with a soused, patriotic Irishman. None too appealing. Luckily, the corner of my eye caught the newspaper on the bar. I lifted it by way of saying, "Nope. Just a newbie."

His face lit. "Ah knew it! Ah knew ya's nut from round 'ere, Ah did! Ah knew it! Ah knew ya weren' jus anudder punter off de boat, loike! Ha! No offense, mate. 'Ere, den. Naim's Moike." We shook hands (strange, familiar), after which he called the bartender. "Oy! Steppie! Cuppla points an roite quick, thicko!" Then, to me on the sly: "Shaim, de way dey take on any dolt in off de stones, innit?"

The pints arrived and we clanked cups and drank, soon after which he licked his lips and asked my story, which I told him in as few words as possible. He seemed truly interested, thrilled even, his eyes and thin Irish lips moving with my words as if searching behind their meaning or, at the least, learning the pronunciations. After I'd finished he jumped the conversation.

"Chroist, Jeff! Dat's one wopper uva tale ya got, dere, 'tis. Truly. De highs an lows uva true teller, dat....Pity 'bout de Embassy an all. Dose ain't true Irish, dem. Nah, dose is de squabblers come off de boat ta make loif hell fer all cunts on deir path, loike. Orangemen, de lot of 'em. 'Ere. 'Ere's ta no more Orangemen, aye?" Another clink. Another drink. Then: "Now, me? Me mum's all Republic....All green, loike....All Irish. Now, me da's all Orange but fook 'im anyhow....Pissed off when Ah's just a lad, 'aven't seen 'im since, de prick. De fookin' prick! Fook 'is Padjo arse! Ah 'ope 'is fookin' prick falls off an fooks some shank cunt an comes back all swollen an diseased an fookin' useless loike de fookin' useless prick he is, de fook!" He took a quick gulp and calmed himself, his face turning from flame red to pumpkin orange to yellow to cream to ivory white with freckles, then continued: "Anyhows, 'bout me mum....Dead now, loike. Passed on tree years back. Dey say 'twas cirrhosis but Ah tink it was de broken heart dat got 'er. Caught up ta 'er an all...chased 'er down, loike. So's now Ah live wit me grams in Southie. A fair stake, dat, Southie. Ya set yer soits on dat yet? Ah'd invoit ya ta stay wit me till ya git yer gaff settled an all but me grams pays de rent loike an Ah don't tink she'd tink it so tops. Ya know 'ow 'tis. Anyhows...'ow's 'bout anudder point fer de foir, loike? Oy! Steppie!" Suddenly he crimped his nose and pinched his cheeks as if he'd tasted something sour and turned his head back at three suits standing huddled together behind us sipping martinis. "Fookin' 'ell!" he said as if in disbelief.

"Some fookin' suit just dropped a bomb, de prick! Dat's de dose wit fookin' suits! Always droppin' bombs roite before's ya git a fresh point, de senseless bastards!" which he washed down with seven to eight ounces of stout before resuming: "Anyhows, Ah's sayin'....Ah, yea, me grams. Nah, Ah meant me mate. Sees, Ah got dis mate, roite, an he just tossed his sick twister uva betrothed straight off de turf once he stung 'er twistin' 'is best mate's nutters. So's now he's on de look out fer a replacement, loike. Wassat? Nah, not loike dat, ya sicko! Yer one sick cunt, ain't ya? Yeah, Ah can tell! Sure it's all dat Guinness in ya! Dat's what it's fer! Ta turn ya into a sicko cunt such as yersel! Nah, Ah's only slaggin' ya, loike. Yer gas craic, ya're. Anyhows, 'bout me mate...de one wit de ex-cunt out on 'er tits an all...he's got dis udder mate who's tops in some bank, loike. Always gettin' first mates in on de ball an all. Sez he's baggin' round tirty, tirty-foiv tousand a year, he is. Not bad, dat! Y'intersted? Course ya're. 'Ere, den. 'Ere's de number....Sex-One-Sefen-Foiv....Wha? De number! De number ta de fookin' bank, ya fookin'....Pay attention, will ya? A nutter lead, dis. Roite, den....Sex-One-Sefen-Foiv-One-Tree-Sex-Tree-One-Tree...extension tirty-tree. Ya got it, den? Tops, dat. A nutter lead, 'tis. So's....'Ow's 'bout anudder point ta celebrate yer fookin'....What de fook?! Fookin' 'ell! Dat fookin' suit dropped anudder fookin' bomb, de prick!"

Come midnight I had about as much Guinness and phone numbers and nutter leads and fookin' Hibernian brogue as my shrunken head would allow and I stumbled out The Black Rose into the shadows of an icy Bostonian night into streets I barely recognized back toward Friend Street and the cold comfort of my cot. Somewhere along the way I wove past what I later found out to be Boston's home for veterans. An elder black man with a peg leg stood out on the stoop. "Hey, boy," he said, his voice low and distant. "Hey, boy, where you goin'?"

I thought a moment, then smiled and laughed and said, "Orangemanland."

I think he might have frowned, then said, "Well, jus be sho's you gets dere safe, y'hear?"

"I'll try," I slurred.

"Don't try, boy!" he told me. "Jus do it!"

I did it.

The next morning I awoke with a vicious splitter which wasn't soothed any by the whispers of my housemates, their tongues like devils reminding me of every milky mouthful I'd downed, so out I went into the cold morning air for a bracer and hoping like hell just to find one cup of strong, strong hot coffee.

I followed Causeway some, then Staniford south which lead me straight into the red brick and cobble labyrinth of Beacon Hill. Not in the mood for discovery at this point, just coffee, I fought my way through the maze down the hill till Charles Street where I had my choice of posh cafés and bakeries. I chose one at random and ordered and sat down, exhausted.

Maybe it was the hangover but just then, sipping a double depth charge and nibbling a day-old croissant, I panicked. Only one night left in Orangemanland and I was out, tossed to the icy streets of a strange city with no shelter, and not one prospect to counter that fact. I thought of the past four days, of the false hope and the people and the words I received. "Get out! Get out now! Get the hell out of Boston! You've no business being here! No one does....So get out! Get the hell out of Boston! Get the hell out of Boston now!" I watched the people walking past the window of the café, their heads high, carrying a briefcase or a bagged lunch or at least a thermos, obviously going somewhere, some destination. They had established themselves somehow. They somehow found a place inside this city somewhere. Why not me? Why have I found it so difficult? Why all these dead leads and lies and icy glares and crow bird attitudes? Money? Sure, money, but what's money? This town is made of money, literally *made* with money, money draped off the awnings and state buildings and shops and park benches and houses (all but Southie) and statues and sculptures. Surely there's enough to spare. And I'm not an invalid. I could make my way and earn my coffee and croissant and maybe even lunch or dinner some honest, yet lucrative way, can't I? Some way just as good as these others in suits and skirts and trotting off somewhere, some destination with their briefcases and bags....And then I looked at them, at all those others walking past the window in the cold morning air...and I smiled. I realized I hadn't yet fallen that far. I could still sit in some posh café on Charles Street sipping strong, hot coffee nibbling a croissant, day-old or not, watching them all go wherever it was they went, toward whatever destination they were all headed in this crazy Manwomanworld. I smiled because I wasn't them. I had no destination. My existence was nonobligatory. I could use the remains of my time and money toward whatever purpose I wished. I could purchase a ticket for a movie or a plane or a dry cleaner's clothes hanger or a Greyhound bus going south or west or southwest or wherever or I could just sit here in this café and drink coffee till my eyeballs burst. That's the best thing about panic. Only after one's head is fully submerged beneath the waves of a raucous sea is he able to float within the calm nothingness and look up and gain a fresh perspective. An experience which most resembles death. Not a Socratic death, not a poetic death but a plebian death – a *human* death. Death conquered by strong coffee and a day-old croissant.

I took out the notes from the night before and added a few more.

After the coffee and stale croissant I left Beacon Hill feeling much warmer, lighter, much less submerged beneath the waves of a torrential sea I had no business creating. In fact, I fell straight back into the waves of that sea and smiled as I allowed the mad, aimless current to dictate my movement without the slightest hesitation, without the slightest refusal to turn left or right or back or not at all. And it was then, in the midst of my mindless buoyancy, I was struck by an idea. Floating about the stoops and doorsteps of Charles Street and beyond circling Boston Common, gazing at all the museum-like buildings and architecture which to me seemed to be constructed without windows or doors or fireplaces or even vents – no possible means of entry or escape – I thought on how one might gain access to such chimera, such things of such a fantastic, ephemeral nature as these lots of space and furniture and heat...then it hit me. Realty agents. They'd know. They'd hold the key (quite literally) on how to enter and escape these strange creatures which surrounded me and of which, still, I'd not seen the insides. To me, every door was locked, every window painted black. It was settled. I'd seek out the locksmiths of cold Bostonian pride.

It was now only a question of boroughs. Which berg to infiltrate first? The answer was obvious. If this idea bore fruit there was no other tree I'd rather stand under in wait than that which housed fine liqueur and espresso and thin streets like alleyways and markets selling confectioner's chocolate-covered almonds and licorice and even pigeon shit. I headed straight for the North End.

The reception I received was far from fruitful. The woman behind the desk far too large for her diminutive mood did not hand me any keys, only eyesockets when asked about simple, inexpensive rent. She'd never heard of such a thing, she confessed. Never. Not in Boston, anyhow. Cambridge, perhaps, if one were willing to accept sub-substandard conditions, forfeiting the primary amenities such as cleanliness and privacy and heat and food and a floor. Fine, I told her. Dandy. Swell. I hadn't time to haggle. She handed me the addresses of a few offices she thought might help and toward Cambridge I sped.

The addresses she gave all sprouted along Massachusetts Avenue within a six-block stretch between Harvard Yard and Central Station. Though it was after noon already I thought I'd exit the Red Line at Harvard Square for a peek at what all the hubbub was about concerning this great-great-grandfather of American elitism disguised as education. After all, even though the happy idealist in me saw those addresses as seeds delivering salvation, the staunch realist in me knew it'd take one hell of a lot more than seeds to deliver an ideal ending. In this vein, lingering somewhere between hope and despair, I decided at least I ought to take in visually as much as possible before my eyes followed my legs chasing hunger not waiting any longer for East Coast seeds to sprout illusive vegetation and fruit. So, up I went out the dark hole of a deep tunnel into the gray-white light of a wintry Ivy League sky.

The first thing I noticed was a newsstand. The next thing I noticed was how still everything seemed. Even with all the people, the streets teeming with people, pulsating with people, hundreds of people throbbing and pulsating and travelling in synchronicity as white and red and yellow and black and brown blood cells flowing automatically through the spliced hollow of a severed artery – severed, yet somehow maintaining solidarity; a dissected, extracted existence which relies not upon basic human sustenance, basic human needs such as food, warmth, shelter, sex, love, liquor, what have you, but more, needing more, more and more and more and more and more. No longer was it a question anymore of *wanting* these extractions and abstracted elements the human mind demands and perceives as happiness, as the quintessential ingredients for a life fulfilled, but *needing* them, demanding them not as pleasures but as pure necessity, as the ingredients to *maintain* existence, *maintain* life, to *maintain* the flow of red and brown and yellow and black and white blood cells all, every one of them involved in the blind pursuit of an ingredient their minds perceive as necessary. All of this flow, all this movement, all this pulsation back and forth and through the hollow artery of a severed humanity...and still. A stillness like the hummingbird whose wings flap so maniacally fast, yet whose body remains solid, fixed in space and time and traveling nowhere. This was the movement I witnessed flowing through Harvard Square, once the center of an activity which had meaning, which produced a sting like hot iron lead searing the thick tissue and membrane of human consciousness – now nothing, nothing but a stillness. A stagnant flow like a severed artery in a hummingbird called Humanity. A meaningless, maniacal flow of bodies like blood cells whose sole purpose is the transference of a key ingredient of a happiness which does not exist.

One look at the surrounding landscape and architecture, however, and immediately I understood and forgave everything. What these poor souls must endure each day upon exiting the safe hollow of their homes undoubtedly drives them toward this state of desperation and stillness. Each building, each statue, each structure and sidewalk and fence and hedge seemed out of whack, wistful, disjointed, even the newsstands appeared to have lost their vital cushioning in the world, instead tossed about the streets and ivy like die having no use in the magnetic world into which they've been thrown and left where they lie be they boxcars or snake-eyes or hard eights or craps. Either way, there they were, shaken, tossed off, forgotten, surrounded by other tarnished paraphernalia felled by the arthritic hands of our ancestors like shortsighted gamblers, their intentions stillborn as the progeny they inspire.

What poor devils, these, to have to spin inside this madhouse, this maze of contradictions having no basis in time or space or even reality, no sense at all in a system which today thrives on ecology, on earthy sensibility, on a state which now draws the individual into a corner and forces him to reconsider not just his role nor his ancestors' roles but *every* ancestor's role dating back before the Pyramids and Stonehenge and Jupiter and Mars – back before his ancestors existed, even – before a society none of us had any part in birthing but in which we all live, all of us, each of us now facing the responsibility our forefathers assumed and handed down as though it were a blessing and not a curse our feeble brains today simply cannot comprehend. Instead we hobble about between hedges and lawns and houses and buildings as strange and bizarre and archaic and confusing as ourselves, congratulating ourselves and our ancestors for having created an encompassing maze which our minds perhaps cannot comprehend fully but which, dually, does not challenge us, does not show us the pathway leading out, only in, the labyrinth structure within, further in, for what is a wandering mouse outside its maze but a lost, confused, disoriented, disjointed, arthritic, whacked-out, wistful creature – all traits a good, proper, respectable, outstanding, lost, confused, misunderstood American citizen must aspire to possess, no?

So, in the name of the Forefathers, I hobbled away from Harvard Square and its surrounding maze-like architecture down Massachusetts Avenue toward Central Square in search of locksmiths' numbers.

The further from Harvard I hobbled the saner it all appeared. It's as if I'd left a portal leading directly to the past leading directly to a street where the present would be found only a few blocks past the novelty shops and used record stores and dark Irish pubs which I walked straight past fast as possible not even looking in noticing the numbers getting larger, closer to the numbers written in blue-ink by diminutive moods swallowed by oversized desks not odd, not odd but even so off I flew across the street finding a blue-ink match and entering.

Inside the place looked and felt like a commune reserved for the more sensitive members of society such as retired middle school teachers or librarians and their bratty, longhaired sons and bootstrapped lesbian daughters. On the walls were collages and paintings which might have been produced by the members of the commune itself – there was enough gaudy color and tepid skill to suggest as much; the same nervous, excited display one might find in a suburban preschool or a French asylum – below of which bubbled and hummed a huge aquarium housing at least a hundred aquatic diseases. A long hall sketched out the entryway, toward the far end an old man and two middle-aged, overplump women bent over a table discussing something. Upon seeing me they ceased whispering and stiffened their backs, beckoning me on with stares and a chorus of obstinate silence. I smiled at all, then scraped the mud off the soles of my shoes on the paisley rug I stood upon and walked forward to greet them.

The answer was, flatly, no. No such luck. Not even close. Another realty office directly below, mentioned they. Down the stairs and round to the left. Ask for Tracy. More my age... same interests and all that, don't you know. A similar barrel to spear from, so to speak. Great. Grand. I thanked my aged passive aggressors and scraped my soles once more on the paisley rug for luck and fell down the stairs to the left to find Tracy.

No Tracy (out on a showing, it seemed) but I did find her boss, a tall, squirrelly-looking bastard with long arms and short legs and a greasy, dollar-bill smile. I didn't think it wise to waste too much time with this sort so I just asked when Tracy might return. He grumbled a time and left it at that. I bid him good day, to which he didn't respond, and back out into the blue inkwell I tumbled.

The next on the list was straight across the street, an all-windows-type office space with trendy lamps and plants and statues of cats and charts and color photographs displayed systematically along the sill – an obvious means by which the proprietor (or proprietress, as I soon learned) meant to illustrate to all upon entering she was warm, friendly, intelligent, professional, informed and, most importantly, in charge. In short, everything I was not, which resounded of disaster. The prospect of going head-to-head with such a personality on such an empty, non-friendly stomach seemed none too appealing. Still, standing on the icy sidewalk pretending to examine the various photographs of vacancies so intelligently, professionally pasted on semi-gloss poster board I was able to peer through the window to see what appeared to be a rather trendy, though yet thoroughly cozy couch alongside a short, round table upon which sat a coffeepot with cream and sugar and butter cookies besides. Perhaps in the least my story will buy me a hot cup or two, thought I. A cookie none too bad neither. In haste, I donned my best mock-friendly smile and stepped inside.

    A man in a button-down, cardinal-red silk shirt and black pants and shoes wearing a sideways grin and long, silver-gray hair pulled back in a tail sat cross-legged on the couch I saw earlier. Given his presence of confidence and cool, subdued aggressiveness (I'd momentarily forgotten all about the cat statues) I assumed him the head agent and made as if to approach when a heavy, stout, obnoxious, panting, smiling Oriental woman cut me off and said, "Hi. I'm Terri. How can I help you?"

    Given her enthusiasm, and given that the man did not move, I realized I'd made a mistake and turned all attention toward her. She was still smiling which threw me off some. Till then all I'd received were blank stares and bum lists of addresses meant to send me on my way, the thought of which instantly bringing my feet back on common ground and now the only thought which possessed my mind was the telling of a convincing enough story by which to warrant all the free coffee and cookies I desired. I began at the beginning. I told of the bus ride past New York arriving in Boston knowing no one not one soul but finding the Irish Institute for Research on Alcohol-Related Impotency and Impish Nightmare Factory and booking the six-night maximum allowing me to scour the city hastily for some other accommodations suiting my means starting with the Waterfront and the North End, then Copley, then the South End and its unaccommodating artist community, then the hopeful but ultimately fruitless journey to Jackson's own Davis Square, then Financial District moths directing me erringly to the brutality of South Boston, then the hippie-laden trail to Dorchester and the lonesome iciness of Quincy (thinking best to leave alone The Black Rose and drunken Irish lust) returning to the city knowing no one only one night left of my six-night stay and still no prospects not one goddamn it's cold out there but it's warm in here and you're so nice to listen to all this really you are Terri, is it? swell name how do you spell that? like sherry but with an *i*? swell say you don't mind if I had a small cup of coffee would you maybe a cookie or two Terri it's cold out there it'd really help really it would really? hey that's swell thanks Terri that's so nice of you yes lots of cream not much sugar *mmmmmm* perfect say yes snickerdoodles *are* my favorite how'd you know? also extra buttery double chocolate chip oatmeal raisin cinnamon Dutch apple à la mode no à la mode? that's okay Terri one of each will do thank you, thank you so very Terri was it? right like sherry but with an *i* thank you Terri thank you so very very very very very....

After, I contented myself with a second cup of hot coffee and a plateful of assorted cookies and set down on the couch alongside the mysterious cardinal-red silk-shirted man, ingesting also the office décor. Terri, it seemed – if she was the one to credit – had the desks and telephones and computers (what must have been ten each) lined along the walls of one room which must have been nearly two thousand feet square, in the center of which, flanked by stylish, yet austere chairs and a low coffee table with art and fashion magazines mixed and, of course, the aforementioned couch (which I later found out to be a rather uncomfortable metal-framed futon), stood a six-foot high tree pruned perfectly round and rather full for that time of year, the sight of which might easily put one off his guard if he hadn't hot coffee and cookies to help settle his defense. It was then I realized I had eaten all my cookies and my coffee needed a warmer so, defensively, I smiled and turned toward Terri for a nod of approval and when I did I saw her face and eyes and I froze. She appeared frightened, bewildered, petrified to move as if I'd just defecated all over her precious cat statues. I wondered if in telling my story I'd said something offensive, the thought of which sent my gaze toward the cardinal-red-shirted man who just sat on the couch smiling, smiling and nodding. I felt as though I'd overstayed my welcome and just as I was about to thank them both for the coffee and cookies and the lesson in offensive office décor and cross one more blue-ink address off the list which was dwindling Terri stood from her chair in a fit.

"Oh God!" she yelled over and over. "Oh my God! My God, can you believe this? Can you?" she asked nobody in particular...the air, as it were. "Oh my God, this is just like that movie....What is it?"

"*Midnight Cowboy*," said the cardinal-red-silk man, his voice obscured behind a self-assured grin.

"Midnight *who*?" said Terri. "Oh no, no...no, that's not it. It's like that, though....It's like *Cow*....*Cowyo*....Wait! Yes! I got it! *Coyote Ugly*! That's it! This is just like that movie *Coyote Ugly*," after which they both just nodded and smiled toward each other for what seemed like minutes till finally Terri turned to me and said, "Oh, you poor boy! Sitting there eating only cookies and coffee! You must be starving! You poor, poor boy! Here, let me heat you some soup. Hmm...is Teriyaki chicken wild rice with carrot and cucumber okay?"

What? What the hell just happened? In a flash like hot magnesium events spun wholly beyond my control which was nothing new, only the manner in which it all occurred. By then I had resigned myself to drifting alone without a sail, so to speak, though never would I have allowed my mind to trick me into believing not only would someone provide me that sail but, what's more, push me briskly aside and take over the helm.

Terri delivered the Teriyaki chicken wild rice soup with carrot and cucumber and a hummus sandwich which was the best soup and hummus sandwich I'd ever tasted and allowed me to eat, all the while hopping excitedly about the office in a flood of shouts and exclamations like the waves of a verbal tsunami, some of which I was able to float atop and ride long enough to soak their meaning. From what I gathered, she was preparing to help me, mentally sorting all her information into categories of immediate accessibility, eliminating those which excluded themselves systematically, usually by cost and unwillingness to offer efficient solutions to that very thing: Money. This raised an interesting question, thought Terri. How much, exactly, did I have on me?

This is it, then, I told myself. At least I got hot soup and a sandwich out of the deal...that and a renewed faith in hope for humanity (the taste and satisfaction of which as pleasing and passing as the sandwich and soup). I slurped the last spoonful and patted my lips with my napkin and ground my teeth and told her.

She said nothing at first, just nodded silently and stared at the floor. I thought I even saw a frown. I was frowning too. It sounded horribly little. Not nearly enough to rent salvation, not even for a month. The silence said it. I prepared to learn the last of the brief but gloriously tasty lesson in Cambridge real estate.

"There may be someone," she said finally, breaking the hellish silence. "There just may be someone who can help us."

(Strange she said *us* just then. But anyway....)

Those words were like the sound of a siren's voice who'd stolen songs from Titania's bosom. Instantly, she spun in her chair and flipped her thumbs and forefingers through a Rolodex on her desk, found what she was looking for and made a phone call, the words of which were too low for me to decipher though I did get its gist from the high tone of its closing and Terri's smile thereafter. It was settled, she said. I was to ride with her to a house not far from the office. She asked the red-silk-shirted man to watch things while she was away and he smiled and nodded some more and Terri and I rode off to what I later learned was East Cambridge.

On Cambridge Street, it was, which I immediately found incredibly odd but also glaringly obvious, like Joyce's mirror symmetry. *From Massachusetts Avenue to Cambridge Street in Cambridge, Massachusetts.* Poetic, I suppose, if one could get past the shameless adolescence of it all. *Stephen Dedalus in a Fight Against the Feckleness of Dublin Society. Portrait of the Artist as a Young, Aimless Popinjay.* Adolescent, isn't it?

The woman renting the room was Portuguese and spoke no English. I learned later Terri had spoken with the woman's son on the phone from the office, who then spoke with his mother, warning of our coming over. This is important to understand.

The woman's house had three levels. The lowest she and her husband occupied; the middle she used as storage for an obscene amount of dishes and furniture and other, more senseless artifacts I gathered were sent from the motherland in increments over the years; the upper where her son and daughter once slept and bathed, now vacant. Both are grown and out, though not far; the son moved one house up, the daughter one house down. As such, both rooms were now open and available and each had its own door and access to its own private bath and personal-sized icebox and all for an obscenely low rent and no deposit. I dared not move for fear of waking.

Terri took control. She took my money and handed it to the woman who smiled and bowed in both our direction, then handed me the keys and, not having any other reason to stay, turned and retreated to the lower level.

Terri then turned to me. "Both bedrooms are open," she said. "You have your pick. In fact, it's all yours, if you want it." Then she smiled. I could have kissed her feet.

As she turned to go she handed me a hundred and said, "Here....Forget about the finder's fee. It isn't necessary." A pause. Then: "Stop by the office sometime tomorrow...after you've rested, of course." Then she smiled again and turned toward her car.

I followed her with my eyes till she drove out of sight, then I glanced up at the sky. It was night.

Later I found the best restaurant in East Cambridge and ordered a steak dinner with fine red Portuguese wine and soft, rich cheesecake and espresso.

Then I slept for seventeen hours.

I awoke early that next afternoon. I hurriedly got out of bed and showered and found a Greek restaurant like a wooden cellar a few blocks down the street which served great, strong coffee with real goat's cream and the richest, flakiest, nuttiest baklava I'd ever tasted (which isn't saying much, I admit) and headed to the first subway station I could find (Lechmere – Green Line) and wormed my way beneath the streets to the Red Line and Harvard Square.

I followed the same path up Massachusetts Avenue past the novelty shops and record stores past posh cafés and gates and brick walls till finally I found it. Feng Shui Realty, the sign said. So be it. Made perfect sense to me.

Inside sat the same cardinal-red-silk-shirted man still cross-legged on the couch, smiling. Terri was on the phone, talking with the same spastic energy I'd witnessed earlier. A young, lanky, pale-skinned, timid-looking creature with long red hair tied back in a tail stood nervously in the center of the room, hugging a briefcase. Both he and the red-silk-shirted man watched as I entered and took a chair near the tree trimmed perfectly round and full green in the dead gray of winter, commencing to flip through an art magazine with pretty blonde actresses posing on the cover. Uninterested, I looked up and noticed the red-silk man was still watching me, smiling, nodding.

Feng Shui Realty, I repeated to myself.

Finally Terri let up with her phone talk and let out a loud shout and spun around the room to see who was watching and, addressing all, I suppose, said, "Hold tight, now. I'll be back. I'll be right back, promise. I got this guy on the ropes. He's ripe, I tell ya. So hold tight! I'll be back! I'll be right back....Bye!"

Then she was gone.

That left just myself, the red-silk-shirted man (named Richard, I soon learned) and the lanky, pasty-faced redhead still hugging his briefcase in the center of the room, all of us still and silent and trying not to stare at one another. At last the red-silk-shirted man spoke and said, "You know you're dealing with a lunatic, don't you?"

I looked up from the magazine. He sat grinning, shifting his eyes between the pasty red-tailed pony and myself, addressing us both, it seemed...but why? And about whom? The pasty red pony said nothing, just looked in my direction and let a nervous laugh. It was obvious I'd have to saddle this one myself.

"*Who* is a lunatic?" I asked the silk-shirted man.

"Who else?" he responded. Then, once instructed in due course by his own personal dramaturge, stated: "Terri."

The pasty pony and I looked toward one another, then together toward the red-silk man, then again toward each other and laughed. It sounded ridiculous. That this woman who had just the previous day performed a miracle before both mine *and* the red-silk-shirted man's eyes should now be labeled a lunatic was simply preposterous. I could put no more faith in such a premise than the spiritually diseased belief that behind van Gogh's brilliance was the influence of madness.

Even if such a blatantly mistrustful, thoroughly inhuman statement were true, what bearing would it have at all on the outcome, on the result of such a brave, brilliant and, yes, mad existence, for is it not mad not only to *want* to break oneself away from the civilized world in search of truth and beauty and nature and lust and most of all life, an honest, modest life as only a truly mad, lusty, brilliantly creative bastard such as van Gogh could realize – is it not mad not only to *desire* this type of life but to actually *realize* it, *achieve* it? To throw oneself headlong into the violent maelstrom of human existence and experience and lonesome, creative lust at the risk of losing one's own sanity?! And lo, ye nonbelievers! Behold and bear witness to the result of such madness, such selfish lust and desire and creativity! Behold the timeless majesty of Vincent Willem van Gogh's lunacy!

Such statements reek of one thing: disrepute. No matter, I told myself. The story will reveal itself in time, if I'm allowed to stick around that long. Be still, I told myself. Be patient. Best not show too much emotion and conviction at this time. Best to forget the red-silk man's accusations in favor of nervous titters emitting from pasty red-tailed ponies.

Feeling he hadn't received the response he deserved, the red-silk-shirted man said plainly, "Go ahead. Laugh. Laugh all you want. You'll see. She's psychotic. Really. You'll see. I only think it right to warn young people, young *naïve* people such as yourselves who haven't the ability to recognize pure evil when they see it."

Again the pony and I laughed. *Psychotic?! Pure evil?!* Preposterous! I decided to let the issue and the red-silk man alone entirely, and, turning to the center of the room, asked my new ally, "So, tell me....What's your story?"

He smiled and took the chair next to me and shook my hand and began relating to me the basic runaround, namely his name (also Jeff, though spelled with a *G* as in *Giraffe*), his purpose for being there (applying for an agent position, he was) and his plans for the rest of the day, namely to wait for Terri to return to discuss further instructions. Like me, thought I. Curious because he looked so young, I asked about his recent past – where he came from, what he had been doing, why real estate? why so young? Again the runaround. All I got out of the guy besides his name was that he'd been studying music and just suddenly changed his mind, no reason as to why. Ever patient, I reminded myself.

At this time Terri returned smiling, leading some young beau who hobbled behind her as if attached to her heel. The two tended to a bit of business consisting of instructions regarding garbage disposal and parking and keyed entries and once all was discussed and understood – Terri in total control the while, the young man swollen-red-faced and nodding, not daring to say a word unless she allowed it – the papers were all signed and the keys handed over and the young, crimson bunny hobbled back out into the street tripping over his cottontail.

Terri turned to the red-silk man, beaming polished teeth and lips of pure satisfaction. "Did you see that?" she asked, himself sitting, peering out the window at nothing, nodding and grinning. "Did you see that?" she asked again. "Did you see him standing square where he was...where I *told* him to stand?! I had him right where I wanted him the whole time. You should have seen it! Ha! Harvard kids! M.I.T.! Boston Medical....Ha! He hadn't a chance. That boy didn't have a chance!"

Suddenly she realized others were in the room and shook her head and convulsed her body and said, "Oh, my God! I'm so sorry! Forgive me! I completely forgot you were there!"

Jeff with a *G* jumped up off his chair as if stuck with a cattle prod and smiled rather painfully. I stayed seated and flipped absent-mindedly through the magazine some more.

"No, not you. *You.*"

I looked up and realized she meant *me*. Jeff as in *Giraffe* sat back in his chair like a pasty, red-haired poodle with its tail bent backwards. I stood off my chair and looked down at him and shrugged and smiled and walked toward Terri.

She went on to relate to me an offer: open her office each morning disarming the alarm and sorting phone messages the important ones from the "flaky" ones and any other office duties which needed fast tending such as taking out the garbage, refilling ink jet cartridges and paper, running to the post office often as needed, greeting prospective customers when she was out and away and watering her plants and keeping safe her fake porcelain cats who, she claimed, were like her children. In return she'd pay cash every couple weeks (the monthly total equaling slightly less than a month's rent in Portugal's East Cambridge) as well as unlimited computer access for personal use or job research or whatever and freedom after noon or when my duties were completed....So? What did I think?

Was this really a question? (In fact, it wasn't. She related all to me as if it were understood.) All the same, I accepted and received from her the keys to the joint and the alarm code and her home phone number should anything go awry unexpectedly and agreed to start my services beginning the next morning and that was that. She thanked me kindly, said she'd see me the morrow. I thanked her in turn, then turned toward the door, determined to find myself a filling, hot, cheap meal.

The next morning I arrived at the office at six thirty per agreement. The only people on the street at that hour were thieves and murderers with blood-soaked grins and briefcases under their arms, their coattails and legs swinging like scythes. The wind was a frigid bitch and I had a hard time freeing the alarm code Terri gave me from my pocket; my fingers seemed frozen in the warmth of their downy sheath. At last I ground my teeth and took it out and read it, then punched the numbers into the box, then turned the key and opened the door.

Then the alarm howled mad as a Bowery scamp.

At first I did nothing, nothing but stand there in wonderment if all was really happening. Then the panic set in, the panic of this noise and at this hour, signaling my vulnerable stance to all the thirsty wolves, had me seriously considering fleeing and leaving the alarm and Terri's office and all of Cambridge to their own mad, howling selves but I couldn't. The wind was far too cold to begin another flophouse search. I looked at the paper and the numbers Terri had written. Perhaps I'd punched them in error, was my first thought. Slowly, I punched the numbers just as they appeared on the paper. Nothing. Desperate, I hit every key on the pad and even tried locking and unlocking the door, thinking the damn thing would have a moment's thought of pity for my pathetic situation and disarm itself. Still nothing. The noise from the alarm was now creeping from my ears and skull down the marrow of my spine. Fuck all, I said aloud. I'd have to call Terri.

I walked in the office to use the phone but the goddamn alarm was too loud to even hear the dial tone. I spit a curse and pulled my coat over my ears, thinking ahead enough to free Terri's home phone number from my pocket before the bitch of a wind had me entertaining second thoughts.

The shops and offices in the area were all still closed so I had to use a phone booth up the block a ways which could hardly be called a booth since there were no walls or sides, just a concrete pole with a chord and number pad attached. Again I cursed, my fingers and nerves shaking in synchronized angst as I hit the numbers on the pad, all the while thinking of what to say so as not to sound like a complete ass which was useless. In the near distance the alarm was blaring loud enough to be heard in South Boston. Rise and shine, you brute Irish bastards! I said to meself, managing a weak, anxious chuckle before Terri answered the phone.

She wasn't at all angry or even surprised, it seemed. In fact, she sounded as if she were enjoying herself, laughing through the frozen earpiece with girlish delight. She said all was well, things like this happen and, still giggling, said she'd contact the appropriate people to disarm the alarm. In the meantime I was to stand in front of the office and wait. Then she giggled her last and hung up.

Soon after the appropriate people arrived and killed the alarm and chuckled and shook my hand and left.

I walked in the office and made some coffee and slumped into a chair in front of one of the computers and sighed. I felt murdered. The sound of the alarm still rung in my ears and skull though the warmth of the indoors and the smell of the coffee stirred my senses some and I couldn't help but think how strange it all seemed. Again I looked at the paper Terri had given me, the one with the alarm code written on it. The numbers were all clear and neatly written. I recalled Terri's voice, how it sounded as though I'd awoken her and how she didn't complain the least, just giggled and laughed out the frozen earpiece. Strange, I thought. This woman is either a saint or a slyly deranged succubus. I remembered Richard's words. *You know you're dealing with a lunatic, don't you?* Still sounded preposterous. A bubble in a pot that wants to boil. An entertaining diversion, is all. Pure chimera. The smell of the coffee grew strong and I poured myself a cup and set to work sifting through messages and bagging garbage and salting sidewalks and smiling and greeting passersby in the name of Terri's good business.

*   *   *

Thus things progressed the next few months through the sand and ice season. As said, Terri saw to it to pay me just slightly below one month's rent worth in Portugal's own East Cambridge (which was working out brilliantly. My landlady rarely ever reared her frail head and body out from under the second level, only once upon hearing me poke about her odd collection of Azorean artifacts of baby blue and finger-paint green porcelain knickknacks and god-awfully overproduced, gaudy image of Mary and the Holy Trinity, the guilt of which I was quick to deflect by grasping the closest drinking glass I could find and smiling, displaying the glass as if to say, "Ah-ha! Found it! Just what I was looking for. May I?" to which she responded by nodding her head in a sort of circular motion and smiling a suspicious Azorean smile, the meaning of which was lost in translation. She let me take the glass, most likely just to get me the hell out from among her things. The only other times I ever saw her was toward the end of the first week of the month to practice the only English sentence I heard her speak: "You have rent now, yes?" For other, more complex issues I dealt solely with her son who spoke English as a New Yorker and obsessed on Marilyn Monroe paraphernalia and whose wife resembled a bulimic Shelley Duvall. Through him I learned it was not okay to smoke cigarettes in the bathtub or listen to Beethoven's Fifth past midnight on his boyhood stereo. Ah, well. Such is paradise.). In order to acquire the remainder of the rent I used full advantage of the agreement made between Terri and myself upon employment, namely unlimited usage of one of her computers for job research and personal freedom once my duties were fulfilled. At first she was excited, speaking how she couldn't wait to see the day I gained an advantageous foothold in this quaint city just bank of Boston but better and she even lent a gentle hand to this end, calling on one of her girlfriends who ran a futon shop up the avenue and who had an open sales position. (Got her one helluva deal on her trendy furniture, she did.) I declined for obvious reasons. Saint or not, I didn't think it wise to entangle myself too much in this woman's web only to find my legs and arms immobile, freed only upon amputation. No, I thought it best to build my own web, both in weight and design. She took this a bit harsh on the personal level initially, though she rebounded nicely, saying perhaps it was best. I agreed and soon after again began wiggling my webworm ass cheeks.

  The center of my web was, of course, the Internet. All my research started there, the juiciest flies and insects wrapped tight and bound for future digestion. Most times, however, all I managed to snag were a few anemic moths and anorexic dung beetles – hours spent searching that imaginary vision of man's virtual (which is to say *intellectual*) Utopia spawning only loose leads and false advertisements and all-too-often out-and-out lies. To count the number of leads I scribbled hastily, excitedly down on paper dotting the whole greater Boston area including Chelsea and Somerville only to discover such leads don't now nor never did exist, then on to the next and the next and the next and the same – to connect the dots of all these leads truly would reveal a web more intricate and ephemeral than the Internet itself.

Between February and April – the early spring of my latter caterpillar days – I must have sought and chased and tasted and ultimately spit up at least a hundred such insects, many of which I still haven't gotten the bitter sting off my tongue. Some simply crumpled like dead leaves, the wings and legs and antennae as tasteless twigs. Others still, the fattest and quickest on ethereal land, promised to lead me to the colony beneath the dry earth and all the fat, juicy insects I could stomach if only I could keep up without losing faith or tripping over the keyboard. This last subdivision of the insect world is what we clumsy, hairless mammals call temp agencies.

The first thing I learned about temp agencies was how many there are and how they all promise the same thing: employment, and fast. Great! I thought. Fabulous! Fantastico! I'm your clumsy mammal! Here's my collar! Show me to my stall!

Whoa, there, two legs, said they. Not so fast. It's not that easy. First they needed a full and accurate assessment of my skills including rubber stamping paper insertion toilet tissue refill full time put in harness to the decimal point past history gold-and-standard-quote skin fresh, well-pressed appearance horny moths smiling, hiding shining prothoracic glands in lavender blouses folded cream-colored slips fluttering under gray-like-steel-wool skirts too icy, too cold, too distant to assess properly computer geek commander-in-chief gawking creating nothing including time date data graphing setting burgundy-and-chablis-chilled-with-lemon-color-coded charting for anything-other-than-visually defunct commando bull-headed arthropods to reassess fully and accurately which stall, er, station I'd feel most comfortable millstoned, er, appointed to. Fine, said I. Sounded painless. Whatever turns a buck, aye? They led me to a room with a thousand computer screens like feed bins lined along four walls and handed me a number and time limit and told me to report back when finished. Sounds painless, I repeated to myself.

The upshot of all this was that, at then, I was completely and wholly without a doubt unemployable. My skills, as they were assessed, weren't worth the ink used to print my name on the rubber-stamped referral. However, they assured me one mustn't lose hope. They offered free tutorials, they said, noon till four Tuesdays through Thursdays in the four major mazes one must master to earn his commando star and cap and free pass to any oasis in the ethereal wasteland. Bunk, I thunk. Keep your star and cap and free pass and your rubber-stamped rejection slip, I wanted to say. However, the dollar sign spoke first and it always takes priority so I said: Great. See you next Tuesday.

On the off days I ran through mazes and mousetraps on Terri's computer, staying well past noon sometimes till five or six and always on Saturdays and Sundays since she had me come in those days too, don't you know. Anyway, it allowed me more time than ample to memorize the ins and outs of monitored organizational mismanagement and my scores on those damned assessment tests went sky high. Still, though, no dough. "It's odd, I know," said the blonde moth circling the terminal screen. "However, aside from scores, there is much to be said for experience and, well, you simply have none."

"Isn't that your department?" I said rather wryly.

The pretty blonde moth just fluttered her slip and ruffled her lips and laughed and said, rather wryly as well, "We can't build a skyscraper out of papier-mâché, now, can we?"

"Why not?" I wanted to know.

"Because," she said, smiling facetiously down at me and, I sensed, a bit annoyed, "it would crumble and collapse after the first storm."

Ah, East Coast wit! Lacerating, to say the least! A deft mixture of sophistication and blood-curdling moxie. Still, I had to hand it to the girl. After this searing tongue whip she could have just snubbed me entirely, having well established her supremacy, but no. She allowed me to linger a while longer in her wingspan as she metamorphosed a list of businesses she thought might let me in on the bottom rung, comprised mostly of hackneyed print shop jobs and messenger positions paying little more than what I was already making, but what of it? It was well worth my time watching her antennae bounce rhythmically to the sound of pen and ink scribbling fluidly over blonde-moth-and-aloe-lotion-scented notepads like panels of papier-mâché buildings crumbling, collapsing, floating, settling in the palm of my dry-earth-and-hairless, unlubricated hand.

Incidentally, a strange thing happened when whooping through mazes and mousetraps after hours in Terri's Feng Shui laboratory. I noticed an agitation beginning to develop in the atmosphere as though an obstinate fly were buzzing in and out of everyone's ear incessantly. It was difficult to place at first, the buzzing, and as such I thought it best just left alone. If I weren't affected and all that, no? As it were, however, I soon came to realize that not only was I affected – it was I who was doing the affecting.

It began easily enough with Terri dropping subtle hints of displeasure at my using the computer at all hours. Made her feel as though she were being used, never mind the fact that that was the arrangement made, that all my duties were completed and well and it was understood by all the main objective for my remaining in her employ (to use this term loosely – given the demeaning tasks and the less-than-base wage offered, *bondage* seems a more appropriate word) was none other than to grant ample time to find another position which would allow a little food money (at this point I'd been maintaining a steady diet of dinner rolls and green apples and sometimes a knifeful of peanut butter spread atop either and water – maybe a bit of coffee and a cookie now and again when Terri wasn't looking). She had a curiously suspicious nature, this woman, as though she feared at any moment the roof and walls and trendy lamps and porcelain cats and her business itself would suddenly and mysteriously implode, sent spinning aimlessly throughout a negative plane, herself with it. Never have I understood this type of fear. It seems a waste of time and precious energy to worry oneself about such sudden, mysterious events involving negative planes and aimless spinning which, to be honest, sounds rather interesting...enjoyable even. Who wouldn't want to see what's on the other side, negative or not? What a gift to drift freely, aimlessly through that portion of the Universe normally accessible only upon death. What a boon! To see the world in its inverse, inverted state reserved solely for the damned in soul and spirit, yet able to return to that other, more perverse world: the world of the living. A boon, I say, which sums up my views on death. To me, death seems a thing one must earn, like rest or happiness – the product of work. It seems a cheat to take this blessed gift of the wind with greedy hands before the work is done, before the happiness and rest and wine and sex and cigarettes have been achieved by strenuous, honest toil. Seems harrowing to think of the hereafter as a lightless abyss one falls into and drowns, forever spending eternity trying to swim back to the surface. No, never fear. The hereafter is sunny and dry, though accessible only by those who've etched out a map, who've found a loophole in the Universe be it via wine or coffee or cigarettes or sex or the written word or oil-based paint or crayon or colored pencil or clay or muddy water or the piano or the viola or violoncello or by simply just walking about and soaking everything up in total peace, total acceptance (this last being the most toilsome work of all). Heaven, if we must call it that, is not given to us by birth. It is not a birthright just because we are human and because some mythical figure Christians call Christ carried a wooden cross out from the garden of Gethsemane down the *Via Dolorosa* to the topmost of Calvary where he was crucified for our sins and resurrected for our salvation. (A lovely fable, though, truly. Takes the energy out of dreaming.) Heaven, as it pertains to this life or the next, still must be earned. One cannot get there by accident, by building a strong business or taking refuge inside one when the world suddenly decides to collapse. This our good Terri had some trouble grasping, it seemed, her fearful nature manifesting itself through an errant array of suspicious glances and remarks and thoughts and ideas which grew altogether rampant once, by chance, I happened to refashion the screensaver from cutesy kittens to a champagne yellow and pearl gray and purple twilight sunset with a moonlit ocean horizon and pale strawberry and Persian blue waves I'd created using a rather elaborate and complicated program with arrows and dots and triangles and perforated trapezoids. All in all, I was somewhat impressed with my work, considering the medium, and saw no problem with it wishing to be displayed on the screen permanently for all to gaze upon in wonder. Terri, on the other hand, did not see it this way – nowhere near. Instead, she saw it as a blatant invasion of her privacy as though I harbored secret wishes to infiltrate her system (again, the sunset display being purely accidental). I laughed it off and explained its innocence, though once she seriously began entertaining the idea I be disallowed further usage of her computers I started to worry. It became clear things were far more serious than they appeared.

(Also incidentally, apropos of nothing, Jeff like a *Giraffe* landed the agent position, which allowed more time than ample to figure out what spun this guy's string. As it turned out, he was honest about being a music student – Berklee, no less – and once he'd served his time and received his plastic degree written in invisible ink he had an epiphany: all links between money and the music industry are lies, forgeries. All the money one can ever hope to squeeze from such a bitter rind has already been handed over to the acrobatic monkeys and their agents, the true musicians the ones on their hands and knees before the show doing sound checks and straightening stray wires. Not just that, but they force-fed him the most earthy and esoteric of all musical fruits: Jazz. Now he's got Miles Davis and John Coltrane and Charles Mingus on the brain while the rest of the world worships the guy who can put down a half bottle of Jack and smoke a joint and walk across the stage and sling an axe and spit obscenities into a juiced-up mic. What's a young virtuoso to do? Well, what *this* young, lanky, pasty-faced, ponytailed virtuoso did was trade his plastic invisible ink degree in for a licensed trade that actually paid. Enter Feng Shui Realty and Terri Lu who now Jeff as in *Giraffe* considered his personal savior. Soon to be married, he was, and after the first taste of such lucrative residuals as he experienced in the first week – the pay these people receive, a finder's fee, is equivalent to one month's rent which, in some cases, is as high as five thousand dollars easy – Jeff like a *Giraffe* was smiling from pasty ear to pasty ear. Seemed he'd found his true vocation after all and just in time too, what with the wedding only a few months off and all. And all he had to do was trail this obnoxious, stout Oriental woman's shadow awhile to learn the cornering "wind water" art – that and cut off his tail. A bit too slovenly, thought she, for such a prestigious position. Oh, and never wear those ridiculous Birkenstock sandals ever again. This wasn't a hippie commune after all, reminded Terri. Now that Jeff with a *G* was just as she wanted – a true member of Feng Shui Realty and all it represented – and me in her debt and Richard, who somehow managed to keep his tail, stopping in every day without fail and some quiet, meek, mustached Jew tallying numbers and figures in the corner once a week,

Terri was able to sit back and enjoy the makings of a fine male harem to be revered and adored by all who stepped in through her spotless glass doors.)

One good thing which grew from the confusion of the sunset screensaver incident was the initiative in Richard to finally break out from his silent philosophical pondering and thoughtful nodding and interact with someone other than his own intellect – namely, me. In truth, he'd been dropping seeds off this tree for weeks by then, noticing my interest in temp agencies and, consequently, computers. As it were, he had taken upon himself the leap into the game: the human race to build one's own personal *Übermensch* machine and he had done his research. Already he had found and sent for the perfect unit coupled with perfectly integrated circuits and chips and dual digital disc drives A and D rewriting capabilities megahertz upgrade card backside cache and modem information all flowing perfectly between the hard drive and RAM and motherboard and this month's latest state-of-the-art CPU and transmitted fluidly through the perfectly-flat-aperture-glare-free-clarity-true-to-life-virtually-no-distortion-edge-to-edge-viewing monitor and now, he said, all he needed to bring his creation into completion was the perfect printer whereby to bring into the world all the perfectly beautiful images he's sure to begin creating soon. ("The purpose of this whole venture," he related to anyone who asked, "is to make this damned thing do everything my retarded brain cannot." A smacking statement, that.) There was a technology convention happening in Boston by the Prudential Building, he told me. Would I care to join him? he wanted to know. I didn't think it my scene and was about to let him know as much before he cut me off and said, "Come on. You can help me out with the printer. Besides, there's something we should talk about." This last bit pinched of just enough curry to season my brain so I thought, What the hell. I could stand to lose my element for an hour or two. Anyway, it would give me a reason to ditch the office and Terri's self-conspiring nervous energy. In light of all, I agreed and off toward Haynes Convention Center we hobbled.

I say *hobbled* because after about a block or two I noticed he suffered a severe limp. "No cartilage," he said grinning, knocking his knee with his fist. Then he sang: "*If you want honey in your docket....A soft cat on your bed....*Ever hear of *Frank's Wild Years*? Tom Waits?" No answer. "*You want honey in your docket....A soft cat on your bed....A shot mare in your stable....A handkerchief instead....*So, whaddya make of Terri now, hmm?" Again no answer. "I told you she was crazy. Crazier than you or me, anyway. She only helped you that day to get a hold of you, you know? That's her style... her *machinatio*...how she works. Dates back to the day she plugged her wires into some young techie kid....Yeah, that's why she's so crazy about those computers. She hasn't the slightest idea how they work...got this kid to do it for her, a kid sorta like you...only not as skinny. Anyhow, she was doin' maid work for this lawyer guy upstate who had this son... good kid...quiet, but good, you know?...Honest....Trusting.... Didn't take long for him to fall into her trap. She's a master, Terri. Crazy...but masterful. Evil. She seduced the kid and forced the poor bastard to buy all this equipment, the whole business...had him set up the system and the website...the works. *If you'll want honey in your docket....A soft cat on your bed....You'll have to find a Hester in Tangier....*She only helped you that day 'cause she knew if she didn't then I would, you being an artist....She knows I have a soft heart for artists...the struggling ones, that is. She works that way. She wants to be the one in the center of it all...the one doing the good...the one in control, don't you know. *Tight socks at the diner...get 'er from behind her....Eczematous...cider toast....*" Suddenly he stopped dead in the center of the sidewalk and stared down a short, frail man with hollow eyes and a scraggly beard who refused to move from our path. They spat and snarled at each other, neither willing to budge till finally the frail, hollow man subsided and cursed Richard for the devil and we continued. "That's how you treat that sort," growled Richard. "Learned that in the joint, he did. Never move for no man or you'll mark yourself. What? A mark, is all. A lackey in the hole. *Black clowns or a sleezy....Billy in the hole.... Fly me to Cameroooooooon....*Hmmm. What I was gonna tell you is this...the best offense is defense. Take aikido. Wind over water." He stopped hobbling and crouched down into a defensive position, his arms crossed in front of him and swerving like snakes. "Anticipate the next move and...move," he hissed, twisting his waist as if dodging a floating bullet. "Aikido. *Best fall down sideways with a bald toupée....Not a theft or a scheme before I stole one today....*" We hobbled on. "How do you think I stayed around so long, hmm? Wind over water, that's how. Anticipate and move. I've been dropping in that place since she opened the door....Taught her how to get a trademark for Feng Shui....She's helpless, y'know. Totally. Pitiful. Can't do one thing on her own....Totally inhibited by her lack of inventiveness compensated by her evil ability to spot the weak and mind control. Learned it from her lesbian friends, she did. Sure. Remember that call she got the other day about a plane ticket?...A friend needed a deal and she was frantic on the phone trying to find one....Lesbian. She dotes on 'em 'cause they taught her all she knows....A secret pact or something. Evil. *Today's magpies....Rodriguez Solitaire....* She doesn't have my number....Thinks I don't have a phone. Doesn't even know where I live, see? Anticipate and move. Wind....Water....*For today's magpies...Rodriguez Solitaire.... You'll have to find a Hester in Tangier....*That other Jeff is a piece of work. Good kid...but twisted. Stuck in that whole evil lesbian web as well...his fiancée, I mean. That's why he and Terri get along so well. They act well with each other, is all.... That is, she acts and he *reacts*. Smart kid. He knows. He's in there for the quick cash and Terri knows it, but both win. Both feed off the other. See, so long as he's beneath her she gets a piece of the fee, did you know that? Yup. That's why she's so smiley when he's off on a showing. No matter how much he pulls in she's right there beside him licking her lips like the evil lesbian witch she is. Won't last, though. Soon she'll get jealous of his success and send him off...send him to the wolves. I told you. Pure evil. Don't say I didn't warn you. Zoobabweee....Zoobabwaa....Zoobabazweebazayow.... Aikido. Anticipate, move. Wind over water. Step aside and feel the cool breeze blow. Aikido. *Fly me to Cameroooooon.... Today's magpies....Rodriguez Solitaire....And good flight Ma Zelda tooooooooooo....*"

The next morning I thought to heed Richard's advice. I arrived early at the office and composed an elaborate letter of gratitude to Terri adorned with such absurdities as how she saved my life and how quite possibly without her enduring faith in charity and generosity in strength and spirit I'd most likely be lying face-down frozen on a park bench someplace and how forever I'd remain wholly and proudly and happily in her debt. It worked wonderfully. After the letter there was no more talk of screensavers or infiltrating computers or suspicions as to my reasons for remaining in her employ. I was welcomed back into the harem an equal member...an equally *memberless* member, that is...sans ponytail and Birkenstocks, even. Another Jeff like a *Giraffe* grazing lazily in the shadowy bounty of a perfectly round and leafy Feng Shui Realty.

*   *   *

As it turned out, the temp agency came to naught. Can't say I was surprised. The only pity was all the time spent attempting to master all those damned programs for no reason other than to further train myself in a profession for which I would not fall. Now, even more so, the making of the rent sat heavy on my chest and, since Terri no longer offered her lesbian friends as accomplices in the matter, I was forced to draw from a rather murky and malnourished well.

Plasmapheresis, it seems, rewards a person with strong, hearty veins a small fortune if he can withstand the drawing and returning and redrawing of his life fluid twice a week; enough for cigarettes and steak with cheesecake and espresso and fine, red Portuguese wine. However, this practice does have its disadvantages such as dizziness and fainting and maybe even death but certain weakness and a weakened immune system and a stomach too weak to withstand steak dinners and cheesecake and espresso and especially fine, red Portuguese wine. In the end it also came to naught. Seems there's such a thing as *moderate* malnutrition which, in my case, meant lack of protein – easily remedied if only the steak would've stayed where it was supposed to. All the same, it was enough to end even the promise of one day maintaining steak dinners and the like, as well as the all-illusive rent money. After only three weeks I was given a pamphlet illustrating the importance of a healthy diet and an escort to the door, not to return till I was seriously dedicated to retaining decent sustenance. Just as well. I hate needles, especially ones that poke veins.

Elsewhere I found little other than dull confirmations of definite maybes and misfires, the most notable being a martini lounge a few blocks up the avenue from Feng Shui which promised more money than even Terri or Jeff like a *Giraffe* had seen and all I need do was perform my well-tried, one-act pomp for every pompous asshole in Boston Metropolitan and I was close, so very close to making my way if only I could have forgotten everything I knew.

The interview went well enough. Given the décor of the joint (neon lights done up in the likeness of martini glasses with olives and neon pink swizzle sticks; padded pillars in the center of the room with matching sofas meant to send off the illusion of soft, plush comfort at the owner's expense; drinks twice the price of a golden bracelet) I had a feeling I understood what the owner was aiming for. Upon walking into this place one got the impression he was stepping into the neon folds of some young, prep yuppie's wet dream with Beatnik tendencies and all it took was a simple mention of

On The Road and I was in (the airbrushed yuppie owner's favorite novel, it so happened). I was to purchase one pair of black tuxedo pants and shoes and bow tie and one white tuxedo shirt with or without ruffles, my choice. How beatific, I thought. Nevertheless, the getup didn't strike me as very Kerouacian – no denim or police badges or nicotine-stains whatsoever. Turned out the dude was not aiming for Beatnik waster at all, but the opposite: Las Vegas swinger. All this should have seemed obvious, given the neon, and I nearly forfeited my role right then. The idea of pouring drinks to Frank and Dino all fucking night was none too appealing. All the same, the outfit was cheap and easy to find and I showed up the next night determined to master what Freud so aptly coined "amnesia of neurosis."

The bar manager was a lanky, sickly-thin, dark-haired, pale-faced Irish wench in her mid-thirties who took orders from none but the owner who never showed up evenings. She showed me the bottles and the till and I barely paid attention. The whole experience seemed to happen in the distance as though I were witnessing the production of a play I wrote, directed, acted in and reviewed and now forced to repeat because some drunken ticket taker passed out in the marquee failed to bucket the cash. Little inspiring. Money, though, of course, is the prime inspirer (so I told myself) and I set out to work over the customers as though ol' Blue Eyes himself commanded it.

After an hour or so an attractive young brunette with full lips dressed in full Vegas regalia stepped coolly behind the bar and introduced herself. Tammi, her name was. There to supervise me, said she. So be it. So long as she stayed out of my way and flashed her ivories once in a while and bent her back and neck to the beat of Frank and Dag and Pete and Joe and Sam and Al and Stan and Jack and Johnny Steinbeck's heroin-beatifying son on keyboard and our Dick's own Tom Waits on harmony and all diggin' it straight up to the top of the stratosphere, man, yeah....

Once the night caved into a slow crawl the young buxom bird Tammi swooped down off her stall and began scooping the tips off the rail with Naugahyde-red talons. "Didn't the manager tell you?" she cawed, her feathers now visibly thin. "It's customary," she explained, "for the supervisor to cut the tips the first coupla weeks. Here," she said smiling, handing me a twenty. "Here's your cut."

At first I didn't take it, thinking it some sort of initiation trick and if I set one finger on that unholy bill I'd be branded an utter dupe. Soon, though, by the steadiness of her gaze, I realized she was serious.

"It's only for a coupla weeks," she assured me. "Though, in your case, since you're obviously so well experienced, I'll see to it the manager settles for one."

Fuck you and your pale-faced, sick Irish wench manager, I wanted to say. However, money still the prime motivator, I told myself one week wasn't so long and after that all my money woes would be ghosts. I took the twenty and folded it and smiled weakly, picking the feathers off the tips of my incisors.

"Tell you what," said Tammi, obviously still not satisfied with her victory. "A group of us are going out for pizza after close....You're welcome to come too, if you like." Then she grinned and said, "I'm buying."

Bitch. All the same, free food's free food and, given the way her eyes twitched half-shut the way they did, perhaps there was something else on the menu besides pizza. It was worth a look-see. I accepted.

Once inside the pizzeria I abandoned all notions of a free lay. Appeared Tammi invited me as gesture only, evident by my place opposite hers in the long queue of lounge wasters entertaining a late-night mock-Italian mood, most of which were Las Vegas' own employees fresh off the assembly line. Even the pizza was out; seemed I'd have to pay for that as well. So, I thought, the old adage rings true: Nothing's free in Vegas.

A balding, bulging waiter standing in line in front of me must have noticed me staring down Tammi. "She's a looker, eh?" he said, catching my attention. I just shrugged. "Yeah, she's had her run. Settling down, though. A coupla kids and a husband to boot. Not bad for such short work. She must have freaked some, what with her age and all." I looked at him questioningly. He looked back, then asked, "How old do you think she is, man?" Again I shrugged, hoping to hasten the answer. "Thirty-six," he said. "And every year counts, if you catch my drift," with a filthy, hairless smirk.

Thirty-six?! Shit, she could have passed for twenty, the thought of which suggested my cut in tips and this, mixed with her age, suddenly had me questioning everything: this pizzeria standing in this queue talking to this balding relic of a profession I thought I'd escaped but nobody escapes Hell, it seems, personified by the buxom maid two kids deep and a mate and an age approaching decline. Once I allowed this cogitation to settle all the money and pizza and the one week seemed like one hell of a lopsided trade-off for a lifetime of collecting twenties and peeping at feathery birds' breasts and thighs and without a word to Tammi or the balding wait in front of me I turned and walked free from little Italy and Las Vegas mock-ingenuity, promising never to return.

The next morning at the office Terri took it upon herself to display yet more displeasure at my rash decision making. She viewed my not wishing to accept the well-paying drink-slinging position as irresponsible and I soon realized why. Since she welcomed me in the fold and sheltered me from the cold and snow and ice and cruel, non-lesbian influence she saw herself as my sponsor, the one who'd receive the credit should this daring venture of mine succeed. Now, however, it appeared as though I were purposely sabotaging it all and Terri began questioning her position at the helm, once again turning the atmosphere sour. Not in the mood to lick her folded, yellow skin to sooth prevaricated wounds, I finished my duties and with the previous night's twenty left the office in search of lunch.

I found a posh burger joint near Harvard Square which, I came to realize, was dedicated to that one literary character I could not outrun: Stephen Dedalus. (The name of the joint reflected this Hibernian antihero's mirror image with enormous steel-black wings and angular Art Deco décor, giving the Guinness and burger and fries a surreal taste, like eggs and toast and bacon baked in a Victrola and puréed and served in a monkey-brain mold.) Nevertheless, it was lunchtime and the entrées were half-priced. Being such, I bellied up to the counter to gorge seared, ground animal flesh – sans brains, if you please.

About midway through the meal a gray-haired, red-nosed Paddy two stools down inquired if I'd like his fries. This being a posh joint dedicated to masochistic Irish antiheroes, the potato servings were rather humble compared with what I'd been accustomed to. I inspected his plate for evidence of sloppy droppings and overzealous use of ketchup, but found none. Smiling, I accepted, then gorged some more.

"Ah, good ta see a foine young feller such as yersel eatin' de way y'are. 'Tis a soine o' good health, aye."

Aye, indeed. A mouthful of fries leaves little room for conversation so I just kept chewing, every so often nodding, following his words with my eyes. His face beamed with a ruddiness which was inviting and I soon found myself paying more attention to him than to my meal.

"Naim's O'Sullivan," he said, his palm stretched out to greet me. I wiped mine across my pant leg and greeted him in kind. "Pardon fer askin', son," he began with typical Paddy geniality, "but Ah's cun't help but noticin' yer rather gloomy disposition. Is sumptin' bodderin' ya, boy?" Not too sure if I thought it wise to tread that path, I hesitated. However, his beaming mug and ruddiness pulsated with a kindness and a resourcefulness – a resourcefulness born and grown only to downtrodden souls – so after all I thought I'd at least let him in on the ground floor. Perhaps he knew of a trapdoor. What harm could come of it? I told him the status of my affairs beginning with no job or money and ending with no rent or prospects. (I thought it wise to keep Terri out of the picture.) He listened politely the while, not once cutting in with trite comments or advice, then, once all was disclosed, he nodded solemnly and said, "Aye, a trublin' situation, dat, don't Ah know it. Still, boy, yer aloiv, is dat nut so?" I shrugged. "Ah, don't lose yer sense o' loif, now, son. Could be all ye gut lef, don't ye know?" I smiled and nodded. "An' so...in loite o' all an' listenin' ta all yer flowery talk an' such Ah ask ye....Are ye educated?" Educated? Educated in what? "Ah ask only fer de simple raison Ah may be able ta help ye, 'sall." Eagerly, I told of my degree. "Ah, dat's good, 'tis. A grand bit 'o paper t'ave en one's pocket, dat. Good fer ye, boy. Good. Good." And the help? "Ah'm givin' ye de number ta me brudder-en-law. A good soul, he is. Koind. Simply love's ta help udder good, koind souls such as yersel." He handed me a napkin with the number scribbled on. "Head o' de whole entoire Cambridge public school system, dat one. Ring as soon as ye possibly cun, y'ere?" I nodded. Then: "Best o' luck ta ye, son, an' remember....So long as ye still got loif en ye d'ain't nuttin' worse den de stone cold o' death." Then he smiled and staggered off.

After lunch I went straight back to the office to use the phone with Terri and Richard looking on, both impressed at my luck in turning events. *Per'aps a tooch o' green ain't sooch a bad ting!* I thought as I punched the numbers into the machine.

The Public Head of Cambridge Operations wasn't in but his secretary was and through her I learned where to apply for what positions and the papers needed. Turned out headquarters was just a couple of blocks off Cambridge Street on Thorndike. Always searching for new sentinels, said she. All I'd need was my college transcript and detailed work history and three letters of recommendation. All cake. I smiled and hung up the phone and set to work collecting credentials.

Terri was good for a letter as was Richard. For the third I conscripted the head of the Sociology department at the University. Gave me all A's the last two years in the lab so I thought there must be a bit o' gold dust in there someplace. Bastard took three weeks to respond. When he finally did, though, what he delivered was pure ochre. The papers all in order, I high-stepped my way toward Thorndike Street in confidence.

The positions available were for substitute teachers, no license required which struck me as unbelievable. Seems the size of the bucket far exceeds the well. If you have a degree and a tongue which speaks moderately fluid English – and haven't any felonies – you too can teach secondary education in Cambridge, MA. No honest experience necessary. A degree? Perfect. No rap sheet? Even better. A warm body? You're hired! Here's your schedule and steel mesh vest and ammo and green apples and blue folder of assignments as trivial and meaningless as the paper used to get you through the doorway now off you trot to dodge spit wads and curses and stray dice always tossing craps or snake eyes, never sevens or elevens or hard eights or boxcars....But that's not till later. As it happened, the interviewing process was anything but trivial. A character screening fit for a presidential hopeful. All polls and reference checks and speeches made before committees. It was nearly a month before I heard word, yea or nay.

In the meantime I occupied my unemployed brain by toying with Terri's computers, still trying to figure out this medium which has grabbed hold of the human psyche with plastic, statoelectric hands. Even an abstract landscape of an ocean sunset with oyster-pink waves and a mother-of-pearl moon on silver sand seems natural as an orange peel when canvassed through this screen of dots and zeroes and ones arranged precisely in a purely hypothetical sequence which the mind accepts as truth, reality, as the reproduction of an icon which simply must exist since the mind, the inscrutable monkey-brain-mold mind perceives it so. This is the great quandary of our generation: the defining and prescribing of truth. The mentality of the monkey was a great and dominant one when monkeys ruled mankind (some of which still dangle off trees and scratch themselves bloody, the droplets falling below like leaky faucets onto the heads of snails and salamanders) and we, the children of simian generations, must now witness the culmination of this dark period of evolution made manifest by the overgrown Mongoloid which is mass media. Man in its monkey stage still exists and still demands its self-prescribed truth, its own myopia as the ultimate, the one true *Truth* in a fallacious world. And the media perpetuates this truth, reassures the eager mind of the monkey his diseased eyes don't deceive him – it's the *world* that deceives him, that's diseased, fallible, untruthful to a destructive, alarming degree.

The message is fallacious, sure, but everywhere, on every corner of every street, in every magazine, printed on every teenager's shirt or pants or panties or shoes, on every adult's car or house or electric gadget it's difficult not to see it as Truth, as the symbol of a civilization which has evolved into the glorious age of super-comfort, a super-commercialization which allows its citizens a piece of the greater whole if only he or she can afford it...or steal it. There is no more guilt, no more fear of retribution or vigilantism. There's now only the pursuit of a justice which is subjective, fallible in the eye of a nation of monkeys whose entire organism has grown inward, myopic to the naïve degree of Adam, the outside world now processed and reasoned only through some great cataclysm which, because of media, now seems rather trite when compared with such troubling concerns as a warm house or car insurance or small tits or cocks or teeth not white enough. A simian dressed in silk and steamed khakis. A monkey chasing fairies. A cataract diagnosed as *tobacco amblyopia*.

All this comes as the result of a bizarre episode again culminating in a disorienting hangover.

One early gray spring day I determined to hole myself in Terri's office to escape the icy rain coating the outside world and, following my regimen of plastic media inspection, I tripped across an employment site advertising the search for "talent scouts" (which, of course, meant the mere corralling of young, eager monkey-minded citizens and their dollar-bill resources). The wage promised should a "scout" succeed was staggering. Myself an expert on the cardboard art as a devoted understudy of the Cutout Queen herself, the thought of obvious beauty transformed magically into dollar bills had me squirming. I showed Richard the ad to wink him my intentions. "Beware of the word *talent*," was all he said. OK. Whatever that meant, so noted. Talent, as was commonly associated with the word, would not come between me and the promise of dollar-bill beauty.

The initial meeting for prospective scouts was held that following Tuesday in Quincy which straightaway made me nervous. The way I turned tail and ran away from that sliver of the Coast came rushing back...but that was then, a distant coil which had since rusted and dissolved. Much stronger, if for no reason other than I'd learned the direction north, I hopped the Red Line and made for the meeting.

A large hall with padded walls and red and blue carpet housed twelve long tables lined cafeteria-style in pairs down the center of the room like columns in a rag mag, the caption a projector and screen and two somewhat young, somewhat attractive women dressed in black and one somewhat nervous, fidgety young stud with sideburns and gold rings and obviously a model, judging by his shoes. I was impressed by the turnout – six, sometimes seven to a table. Should be a good show. I took a seat in the rear of the room and awaited the entertainment.

The sideburnt man spoke first. Had a prime photo shoot in L.A. in six hours, he explained. I looked around the room. A few eager blondes bought it, smiling and nodding their pretty simian heads. He went on to stumble through a glossy interpretation of a model's life – the money, the attention, the smiling, the stress, the cigarettes, the sea breezes, the tofu sandwiches, the beach houses, the vomit, the tan lines done in the shape of nylon-chord nooses, the lacerated anus, the bruised tonsils, whatnot – and after he had baited the hook with juicy, squirmy ones he collected his notes and excused himself and made way amid the throng of stares and nods and disappeared out the door.

Once gone the two women assumed control, using a more tactical approach in laying down intentions. The women in the audience were obviously turned off by this, listening now only out of politeness and eagerness to get back to wherever the stud came from. The men were amused, that is all. Throughout the presentation, as the two women described in detail the purpose and duties of a hard-working scout, a feeling of sterility fell over the room like a lead blanket. No one made a move for fear of contracting some rare disease, some blinding, raw effect of the radiation which pulsated out the projector and off the screen into our eyes and skin, the faces and bodies and lips and teeth and smiles of the obviously beautiful like cancer, a life-threatening malignity one feels one should avoid for better health but cannot. One lacks the will. Like tobacco, he (and she...mostly she) is addicted not to the product itself but to the destruction of that product, the promise of pleasure when burnt to the filter and inhaled and exhaled, taken into the capillaries and retained and absorbed and thrown back out again, only the cancerous residue remaining. Such is beauty – obvious beauty – and such is the feed we all partook in through projected light and pictures and promises of more, then more and more (more *what*, exactly, was left entirely to the inhalant). After, the infusions and needles yanked rudely from our veins, it was time for business.

(I think it appropriate to mention toward the end of the presentation a number of skeptic sheep started *bah-bah*ing their opinion, namely regarding the fact that as of yet no

Apples of Arcadia

mention of any real money had been made, only profiles and promises and already we'd been sitting for over three hours and not one penny earned. Nearly half of the room decided they'd had enough and got up and left. Oddly enough, these were the most obviously beautiful of the bunch.)

The faithful sheep terrified stiff in their seats, the two women now saw fit to demystify scout success. They divided the room into five groups – four sheep to a group – and invited a challenge. Each group would be given four pictures, or profiles, then made to sort each profile in order from most beautiful to least as quick as possible. The quickest group would win a prize – a tenner for each member (the first tangible mention of true dollar-bill beauty). We drew numbers. I was pit up with three lascivious bitches with dried bloodstains on their claws. They wanted that tenner, obviously, and when the pictures were passed out I got the hell out the way and let them scratch it out, the celluloid eyes and teeth and frozen smiles flying wild with snarling tenacity and vicious accuracy and wouldn't you know....They won! Those bitches came through! Easiest tenner I ever earned.

After the challenge the presentation approached a close. Those of us remaining were congratulated for our diligence and given a mission: to approach and gain the confidence of no less than ten hopefuls for next week's meeting. We were to use the knowledge of obvious beauty learned in this free instruction and put it to use for the good of some obviously undiscovered talent and the industry and our careers (the eventuality of which was becoming less and less obvious... but what the hell. Terri had just stocked a refrigerator full of cheese-broccoli soup.). We each were given a pocketful of cards with the company's name and logo printed on and told not to return with a single one left and be confident and courageous and best of luck and out the door we all charged like Pamplonian bulls injected with testosterone and adrenaline.

It took three days for me to approach my first prospect.

All that time I spent drifting in and out of crowds, my gaze constantly inspecting each contour and dimple, each dark sliver of an eyelash or the shadow of an enticing bustline but all I saw was naught, the obviousness of a beauty which has been reproduced and super-imposed upon the lips and brows of men and women alike. Three days, I say, approaching not a single soul...not because I wasn't courageous or confident enough but because I honestly couldn't find anything worth approaching, worth the projection of my voice. This would not do. Either I'd have to figure out a plan soon or just chuck those pathetically obnoxious cards down the swirly Q, which in itself would design a plan, no? No, there's something of importance to be learned here, I realized, and with this in mind I wandered aimlessly still through the dense populace of quite possibly the most concentrated area of obvious and sophisticated extraneous appearances disguised as control disguised as confident, courageous beauty...then it hit me. What's more obvious than beauty? Why, the opposite of beauty, of course. I would approach those whom I found the most hideous, the most unwarranted to receive a card from any agency, the ones who'd attract my gaze purely out of disgust. This would be my angle by which to ditch all those cards and maybe gain a little green besides.

The weather warm and sunny, I chose the Public Garden as the center of my web, wiggling my way about the city in a spiral pattern tossing cards at those whose being radiated ugliness; blonde ugliness, black ugliness, brunette ugliness, sky-blue-eyed ugliness, pretty-girl-in-one-hand-cell-phone-open-in-the-other ugliness, smirking-staring-at-the-poor-homeless-bastard-sleeping-on-the-park-bench-ugliness, pig-nose-sniffing-cloud-stank ugliness, thin ugliness, muscular ugliness, glass-shards-dusting-bleeding-orifices ugliness, red ugliness, yellow ugliness, white ugliness, brown ugliness, no-more-hope-to-sell-anyone-anymore ugliness, ugly ugliness. The system was a success. In less than two days I sent each and every card out my pocket into the world via the hands of smiling, nodding faces who'd felt Fate had finally seen things their way. Most of my cards magnetically found their owners down Newbury and Boylston and the whole Back Bay area. Others found shelter under the gilded rooftops of Beacon Hill around Government Center, the gold ugliness thick to a suffocating degree. Some drifted through the air like leaves, following the sprightly pattern of exotic moths fluttering about the Financial District in and out of windows and doors of concrete stalks and state houses spread like eagles' wings. Others simply salivated along the jowls and snouts of pig ugliness sucking down oysters in neon pink skin-tight T's and jeans in the den of Ye Olde Union House (Friday night like ugly scout Christmas). Others just simply fell asleep and snored their way into the hands of apathetic drifters and tongue-tied partisans and billboard babies and students hanging out in Harvard Square, themselves asleep and snoring, specializing in dozy ugliness and with only a few cards left in my pocket and my stomach grumbling angrily I felt a bit loose and daring. A group of young people – much too young for college – stood huddled together chatting on the sidewalk before a trendy Italian shoe store just off the Square. Immediately my gaze was drawn toward the center of the group, a long-dark-haired filly with feathery skin and arms and legs that could sink a sailor. The others gathered round her as if she were Circe, the young men and women both transformed into slavering beasts. Hypnotic ugliness, thought I and made way toward her to brand her as such for the sake of my own private odyssey.

    The moment I handed her the card I realized I'd made a mistake. When her small hand reached out to accept the card, her eyes and lips smiling in such a way as to make the whole world pulse and undulate with an astral glow, I saw inside this young woman a being that was not ugly, not in the least, but radiant, glorious to an alarming degree. This is what caused prostration among all who surrounded her. There was no castration or sterilization, just reverence, reverence for being allowed to bask in the light of a truly beautiful being. And when I handed her that card, knowing what I knew, I felt lower than a serpent handing Eve the poisoned apple. There must have been that same smile, that same radiant glow surrounding Eve then. That must have been what the serpent set out to destroy...and did. A lustrous beauty lost forever. But here was another. A beauty far too reverent to be obscured by envious darkness. A beauteous light which must not be dimmed...at least not by my hands. I snatched back the card and tore it up and began walking away. After a few steps I heard a beautiful voice yell, "Asshole!" I nodded and walked on. Then I tossed the remaining cards in the recycler and went searching for lunch.

Next Tuesday I arrived in Quincy mostly to satisfy my curiosity at which insects my web had snared. Standing in the entryway of the alveolus smoking a cigarette I watched them all scurry in on atrophied limbs and wings like dead leaves dipped in calcimine, all the while laughing to myself under a blue-gray smoke cloud – a laugh much like the weep of a surgeon who just performed his best work on the wrong unconscious body. A shaking of the head at a wasted effort. Nearly all the insects I'd tossed cards at showed up, most rolling untangled from the Public Garden; one or two moths (not so exotic, I now noticed); a student hoping to boost her grade; a middle-aged Miss Priss I unearthed while using the shitter in the Ritz-Carlton; some skinny, acid-blond musician swaggering doped and dazed near the corner of Columbus and Massachusetts; a jewelry store clerk; a shoe salesman; a waitress who wouldn't serve me till I showed her my wallet. The only ones who didn't show were those whose boyfriends or girlfriends or spouses were there tugging their antennae, eyeing my hands and lips for any uncouth gesture which might give it all away. My only fault with these few was not giving both a card to gnaw on. Then again, too obvious. Best be selective. Allow the salt to sink into the wound a while, then wait for the winces and the screams to begin seeping out the pores. Till then, a puff off a butt and a peek at a waddling subterranean promenade.

Nearing the end of my cigarette and through with curiosity I was about to flick the butt to the curb and head back to Terri's for a piping bowl of cheese-broccoli soup and garlic hummus on wheat toast when a burly guy with a goatee lumbered out the door into the entryway. "Fucking wasters!" he spit at once, tapping a smoke and searching like a blind man through his jacket for a light. I offered him one out of habit. He nodded, took in a healthy drag and exhaled and smiled, then nodded again and continued: "Fucking sons of bitches. All my cards sent spinning through this fucking city and not one juicy set in the lot. All wasters, I tell you. Pasty-faced wasters with noses like cucumbers and elephantiasis of the fucking teeth, for fuck's sake. What the hell am I supposed to do with that, huh, I ask you? Tell me that!" I shrugged, unsure if he was addressing me or the invisible spider dangling between us. "Why the hell am I asking you, anyhow? It's useless, I tell you. Fucking useless....Wait! Who the hell are *you*? What are you doing here?" I answered in the direction of the meeting room. At once his face dropped. "You mean you're a scout?" he gasped. I nodded. "Oh, hey, you didn't hear any of that, right? What I just said, I mean....I mean.... Did you hear any of what I just said?" I looked at him as if his head was about to explode. Finally, not knowing which was the proper answer, I shrugged. "Look," he began, flicking ash off his smoke in nervous jerks, "that wasn't for you, you know? I mean, you weren't supposed to hear all that, know what I mean? I mean, what's your name, kid?" I told him. "Oh, that's you! Shit, man! You've got the best eye in lot, I say! Damn! I've got ideas for yours, lemme tell you....Jeff, did you say? How's it going, Jeff? I'm Jared....Jared Thomas." We shook hands. Dry. Nervous. Like flicking hot ash. "Say, Jeff....What are you up to right now? Any plans?" I answered in the negative – maybe a meal as an afterthought. "Oh, hey, no worries! It's on me. The least I can do for one of my top scouts. Come on. There's a seafood joint just off the harbor with all-you-can-eat crab legs that burst into your mouth. Only, I gotta ask you once more....You didn't hear that back then...about elephantiasis of the teeth and all....You didn't hear that, did you, Jeff?"

Negative.

Sucking tender white flesh out of boiled-red-apple crab daddy legs dipped in melted garlic butter washed down with fresh coleslaw and ice-cold amber ale I allowed Jared my ear, of which he was eager to take full possession. Turned out he was the head eye at the talent agency, the wizard behind the velvet curtain pulling all the levers. He'd only been operating in Boston a few weeks and already he was disgusted with the city. "Too fucking stuffy, these people, I tell you. Like statues with flesh and organs added on. Ceramic cyborgs, what! Not like back home, anyway. Michigan's the only state for me, boy." Kalamazoo, Michigan, to be exact, where he had spent his early years as a musician banging out tunes (originals, no less) and touring the States along an upside-down horseshoe from Maine to the Carolinas to Tennessee to New Orleans to Texas to New Mexico to Idaho to Colorado to Washington then skirting along the Canadian border collecting drunken memories and a minor dose of scabies. "Shit, a musician's life," mused Jared. "Nothing like it. Miss the hell out of it."

So what became of it?

"Y'know, you put out a few discs, do a few local gigs with some big acts that travel through....Played a set with the boys from Metallica once...well, before the *Black Album*, don't you know....Heard the demo for *Nevermind* when boozin' in the studio after a session...some suit nobody even knew put it in...thought it was some heroin-induced Black Francis BBC recording till someone told me who it was....What the hell did I know?...No one ever heard of Nirvana before then...all liars, those who say different....Sad story, really....Got mixed up with that dirty blonde, he did....Sold her soul to the devil, that one....Sad....Took all, everything down with her, too...all the music....Sad....Sad...." He went on to relate how after a few discs and no sales the discouragement and lack of funds was too great a force to overcome and he gave up music to chase the dollar and just in time too. "Fucking school loans," he coughed while gnawing a corn muffin cake. "Like anvils tied to my ankles. I couldn't move an inch and not feel their weight pinching my bones. I had to do something, some sort of sharp gig to saw off those damn chains." Enter the scout agency which at first he was hesitant to delve into further, though after I assured him I wouldn't be returning anywhere near his agency or even the building, and after an icy-fresh mug of amber ale to drink on it, he spilled his operation.

Seemed the Greater Boston Area was the last of a great chain of cities where he'd been setting up signs and posters and advertisements and whatnot trying to get people in, the ones who are interested in some quick cash (both the scouts *and* the talent, it turned out) and who are willing to ignore the holes in the whole works in favor of the blinding light emitting from the borrowed projector at the front of every meeting room. "How it works is like this," he explained. "We have a website, right...real *professional-looking* website my buddy and me built with his computer back home....A wise one, him...not music but *tech* school for *his* money. Anyway, on this website sit a few pics of lookers and passwords and whatnot...you know, to get the juices flowing...professional like...and the cards you and those others passed out are like invitations to a party hosted by these lookers...aphrodisiacs, get me? The prospects see this site and think it's legit...which it is, more or less...and they come to the next week's meeting to find out more....That's where your job ends and mine begins. It's my job to get all those ugly buggers believing they've got a shot at their face in lights, see? They pay the thousand dollars....Yeah, no shit! One thousand! You'd be surprised! Anyway, they pay the thousand bucks to get their profile posted on this site my buddy and me created we tell 'em a ton of top agencies regularly check for fresh, new talent and don't be discouraged if you don't see anything right off it's all part of the business be patient and all this other horseshit. They feel great about themselves a while and we get our money and after a few weeks it's off to the next town before the cops catch up. Nah, it's all legal....Just that once the cops start snooping around a good many future thousands start drifting, know what I mean? Shit, in Orlando we had the cops bust in right in the middle of a meeting, over three dozen wide-eyed watermelons ready to burst. Fucked everything right up. After the cops bust in on you there's not much you can do. No amount of explaining can fix anyone's mind after that display, believe me. Anyway....Where was I? Oh, yeah...the thousand bucks. That's where you caught me, the cursing and all....A natural recoil given all the puss-faced, leprous mugs those no-talent pricks brought me. I mean, shit...even J.C. Himself couldn't perform the miracle needed to make those buggers believe they've got it! Christ, once this Egyptian bitch brought me nothing but toddlers.... *Toddlers!* What the hell am I supposed to do with toddlers?! This ain't no kiddie-porn site, after all. I mean, shit....I do have my morals....What? What are you laughing at? What? Do you need anything? More Beer? Crab? Coleslaw? What? How's about some pie? Some hot apple pie à la mode? I hear this place has great apple pie. Like down South, they say. Steaming hot with cinnamon and everything. How's about a slice, huh? Waddya say, there, bud? Waddya say, there, pal, huh?"

After the apple pie and beer and coleslaw and espresso at my request it seemed he still wasn't sure of my oath of secrecy and – to show his allegiance, I suppose – we drove to his friend's house in Wollaston (a mansion, really...whether or not this was his techie friend's mansion he wouldn't say) and we pissed the night away tossing empty beer bottles off the attic balcony onto passing cars all Jaguars and Mercedes and BMW's and I think I even saw an Aston Martin.

The next morning I arrived at Feng Shui an hour before

noon hungover and reeking of imported booze. This raised everyone's eyebrow – Richard, Jeff like a *Giraffe*, the Jew and especially Terri who had her gaze glued to my soggy steps the while. But what matter? I was there in the flesh, was I not? And before noon, even. I completed all my duties and poured my first coffee, after which I fell like a wet noodle into a chair in the back of the room.

After about fifteen minutes Terri approached me, shoulders slumped, an unnatural look of displeasure in her eyes. "Jeff," she began, her head hung as in mourning. "Jeff," she began again, "I'm sorry. This isn't working out."

"What isn't working out?" I asked.

"This," she said. "You....*Us*....I don't believe you're serious anymore."

"Serious about what?" I asked, already sick to my stomach with talk.

"Look, Jeff, I'm not about to argue with you. I just don't think you're ready for the responsibilities I gave you is all." Then she held out her hand, that malcontented look still glazing her eyes. "My keys, please," she said finally.

Like a fool, I looked across the room for an ally. All had their heads down over their desks like school children, afraid to show their eyes for fear of attracting this woman's wrath. Even the Jew who showed only once every couple weeks was struck prostrate. Jeff like a *Giraffe* had his pasty neck bent in some papers under the pretense of finding work. Richard punched some meaningless commands into his computer, now complete and anchored squarely in the corner.

I peered back up at Terri whose eyes had become stern. "My keys, *please*, Jeff."

I handed her her keys.

"Joseph will cut a check for the work you've done," she said. Then she hung her head some more and rolled toward her desk.

I stumbled to the Jew. He handed me a check (pittance... barely enough for a bus ticket) and a look which I took as meaning, "Sorry, man. Wish it were more." I smiled and nodded and made for the door, not sure which direction I should turn – toward the bank or back toward my bed. One thing was certain: there'd be no more cheese-broccoli soup.

"If any person thinks the examination of the rest of the animal kingdom an unworthy task," said Aristotle, "he must hold in like scorn the study of man. For none can look at the elements of the human frame – blood, flesh, bones, vessels, and the like – without much repugnance."

Mulling over this tasty morsel sitting on a plastic stool wet with rain on the veranda of a Harvard Square café too poor to order (Myself, I'd devised a rather repugnant practice: watch and wait for a customer to unseat, leaving behind the recycled waxed-paper container, then assume a refill as if it were my own. A bit crude, I admit, but every cent counts.) watching all the bloody human frames scurrying by like so many hairless, joyless creatures from some distant animal world in some distant, joyless universe where ambivalence is the natural law I suddenly understood what Aristotle was poking at. Even if these words are out of context (he was merely introducing his comprehensive study of the animal in our Universe – the *only* universe, according to Aristotle), they ring with a majestic tone. What he meant, I surmised, was the extracted parts, the singular elements of every animal in our Universe, man especially, are repugnant, off-putting, difficult to visually digest without that sting and leveling feeling of nausea grasping one's throat and solar plexus. Only when visualized as parts of a whole do the singular abstractions take on substance, a meaning indefinable and profound as a thing which is indispensable – an animal tripping joylessly through his own kingdom not because he's unhappy in the philosophical sense, but because he *chooses* to be unhappy. He *chooses* to be joyless. He *chooses* ambivalence over mirth, sadness over joy, tears over laughter, coffee over tea, wheat over white, the axe over the cleaver, his friend's wife over his own, his own house over the world, cream over sugar, ham over rye extra mayo provolone cheese side of chips baked not fried extra ketchup over all. He chooses all these things and he's unhappy with his choices, perhaps even sad with the fact that he has to choose in the first place...but he doesn't. After all, to *not* choose is also a choice, is it not? So, then, you hairless, scurrying elements of man's only Universe....Choose nothing and smile for once, you sad, repugnant bastards!

Thus spake Aristotle.

Of course, it's easy to conclude thus when there are no more choices to be made, when all is neither cold nor hot like untainted coffee or tea or the warmth of wet ass cheeks sitting frigid on some plastic stool on the veranda of some Harvard Square café. Why Harvard Square? Stumbling through the vicinage searching for anything and nothing alike I found a flyer tacked to a pole just outside black iron gates and brick walls advertising the Harvard College Library's need for an assistant. I shivered through the cold, wet, gray columns of Widener to apply and was promptly shown the door, directed back outside the confines toward an obnoxiously bright office on Holyoke Street next door to an expensive café made to resemble a Paris Metro entrance Art Deco style. This café had no veranda. I stumbled up the alley instead.

About this time – about the time I'd procured my first empty container – none other than Richard came tripping up the street, himself stumbling rather awkwardly. His eyes beamed when he saw me. It appeared he had something important to say.

He took the seat beside me, then smiled some more and nodded and said, "Well, you've done it. You've secured your Cantabrigian throne." At first I thought he meant the cold, wet plastic stool. I was about to scoff him then and there before it occurred to me there was something else, something more deserving this one favorite term of his (he had used *Cantabrigian* before – several times, in fact, each to describe

Cambridge elements stemming from the mossy, stony soil of England and sent over via frock coats and sodden, wooden vessels, himself included). After he'd successfully landed his *Cantabrigian*, that gleeful beam failed to dim from his eyes. It was obvious there was more.

After the customary pause he continued: "The director of Cambridge Public Schools called the office yesterday. Asked Terri some questions about your worth. No, no...nothing to worry about. She was so glossy speaking to the guy all she managed were a few weak squeaks and sputters till he asked if you could be trusted around young kids." Another dramatic pause. Then: "*Oh yes. Yes, of course, of course*, she said as if it weren't a question. Then again, she couldn't say anything elsewise....I was watching her the while." Then he chucked my shoulder and said, "You're in....You're in...Cantabrigian, kid...*Cantabrigian*....*Go do some world shakin'...some world shakin'....*" Then he smiled, nodded and stared at the street in silence a while before finally snapping out of it and, grunting to his feet like a wounded veteran, said, "I have the director's number written down at Terri's office. Stop by sometime after she leaves...around six. Got the place to myself then. Stop by. Besides, there's something else I want to talk with you about." Then he smiled down at me and said *Cantabrigian* once more and sang as he stumbled off....*I wish I had a news machine... I can feel it in my jeans....*

The next day I did as Richard suggested. I arrived at Terri's office just before dark in case Terri was ordered a new assignment hunting down low hotel fares in San Francisco or the Netherlands or some other groveling lesbian errand. I walked slow past the office windows on the opposite side of the street to sneak a look. No Terri. I skipped across the street and hopped in through the door.

Richard was there like he said, though not alone. A frail, scraggly-looking man with half a beard and no top hair stood beside him bent over with hands clasped behind his back, both peering like peeping Toms into Richard's monitor. The moment they heard me they jumped out from their trance and flicked off the screen and turned nervously toward me. The scraggly one turned away immediately, not even bothering to straighten his back.

Richard grinned his silk-snake grin. "Ho, he shows! The Cantabrigian king! Here, here!" with a chuckle and a nod to his hunchbacked twin (I later learned this dwarf's name was also Richard...or just Rich, to thwart confusion). Then, still to the shrunken Quasimodo, "This is the prince our Terri saw fit to toss headfirst out the glass castle gates."

The hunchback tossed up a glance, then back to the floor. "That bitch," he scoffed. Then, after a shake of the mane: "That bitch...that bitch is crazy-*eee*...than me...crazier than I am. Crazy-*eee*...like a lesbian Komodo dragon with a urinary tract infection...shun. Crazy." Then he laughed...or coughed, more like.

I looked at Richard. He was grinning and nodding in approval toward the dwarf, then toward me, at my sideways glance. He must and understood.

"Rich lives up the avenue at the Y.M.C.A., doncha, Rich?" Rich nodded, still looking down. Richard went on: "He could come live with me but he prefers it at the Y, ain't that right, Rich?"

Again Rich nodded. "It's cozy-*eee*. Nobody there messes with my records and CD's...*eeeez*....Not like at the other place," he explained.

"This man's a music encyclopedia," elaborated Richard. "Knows everything from Beethoven to Barber to...who's that conductor you admire so much?"

"Koussevitzky!" spat Rich, promptly gnawing his thumbnail after.

"Koussevitzky," nodded Richard.

Silence. Then: "Sergei Aleksandrovich Koussevitzky," began Rich. "Born 1874, July, in Vishny-Volochok, Russia, to a poor family...lee...left home at 14 to study music in Moscow... scow...double b*aa*...b*aaa*ss...r*eee*...remarkable...r*eee*...recordings...ings...married into money and moved to Berlin to r*eee*... to conduct his first orchestra...stra...phen...phenom...nul... then to Russia to conduct his *own* orchestra...his own *Russian* orchestra...stra...also phenom...phenom...nul...pair...then to Paris to escape the Revolution...shun...best r*eee*...best pair... best orchestra in all Paris...is*sss*...pair...phen...then America and Boston in 1924 to rival Bernstein and champion Harris and Hanson, Copeland, Schuman, Stravinsky....*Stravinsky!... Symphony of Psalms!...The Firebird Suite!...Phenomenal!... Like balls of rainbow smoke blown in heaven dipped on angel-tip strings and swung from God's own toe....*" At this Richard gave a loud grumble I took as meaning to bring Rich back and rolling on the proper rails. "Koussevitzky," resumed Rich. "Greatest conductor in all of Boston...stun... all...in all...*the world...all the world...all*..." (another grumble) "*Stravin*...self-taught...the Berkshire...Tanglew*oooo*...wood... steam ships floating up and down the Volga...ga...lee...slow... miracles of color and new precision...pre...shun...fine...finely new and...lee...new...nuance...stra...skee...died June 4, 1951, in Boston...stun...Koussevitzky."

"Koussevitzky," repeated Richard.

Another silence. Then, apropos of before: "Here's the number I promised you...the school director," said Richard, handing me a torn piece of paper. "I think it best to call after lunch...allow the tuna fish to settle some, got me?" with a grin and a nod. I nodded as well. That number was like roast beef and gravy seeping in through my skin.

At this I was prepared to turn the computer king and his court jester over to whatever game they were engaged in and leave off to celebrate the digestion of new hope. Before I could break free, however, Richard called me over to his desk and pulled out a stack of pages he'd obviously taken off the Net. "Come on," he said, nodding toward himself. "Come sit down. I want to show you something."

I sat beside Richard and peered at the pages. The hunchback stumbled nervously behind me darting electrokinetic glances over my shoulder. It was then I noticed the smell of week-old sweat and moldy cheese. My appetite and desire to celebrate waned. Sober and in a hurry to flee, I gave Richard my full attention.

Turned out what he'd discovered that was so important was a sleep study conducted in one-month's time at a local research hospital near the Cancer Institute. Something about the cardiovascular effects of intermittent bright light. He smiled triumphantly as he reeled off the criteria and purpose and procedures of the study, all with obvious intent to declare that I – my age and sanity and good health (I hadn't told him about the recent pink slip from plasmapheresis), lack of funds and total lack of anything resembling hindering responsibilities – I would indeed prove the ideal participant, both intermittently and cardiovascular alike. Needless to say, I was skeptical. Giving the pages the once-over I noticed too soon the bit about IV's and rectal thermometers, neither too appealing. "They'd compensate handsomely for that," assured Richard, still hoping for a sale – for what reason I couldn't tell. Could he still be trying to maintain this self-proclaimed notion of starving-artist-inspired philanthropy? And after his silent oath proclaiming the opposite that day in Terri's office? Whatever the reason, the money was the bait. Two thousand dollars it was, and all for only nine days' work. Appetizing, no? So much so, in fact, the stench of stale sweat and moldy cheese wafting off the encyclopedic monkey hanging over my shoulder couldn't swage my newfound salivation at refreshed hope and hunger. I smiled wide and thanked Richard for the free flea, then tucked the pages under my arm for light afternoon reading and made as if to leave. Before out the door, however, Terri's first-day hospitality came to mind and I strode toward the back room and cooler and made myself a smoked ham sandwich on marble rye smothered with chipotle mustard and horseradish mayonnaise and onion and fresh romaine and capers.

The next morning I dialed the number Richard gave me.

A feathery hen obviously at least twice my age picked up and directed my next move, namely to make myself manifest in the confines of her coop for a thorough inspection of crow and coxcomb, then a quick walkthrough noting any previous damage and a prick of any fingertip and my name signed on royal-blue-lined yellow legal pad paper for the sake of America's misguided progeny...well, misguided *Cambridge* progeny, anyway. Could I report first thing tomorrow for an interview? my feathery hen cooed, to which I replied a hearty *Cockadoodledoo!*

The rest of the day I tripped lazily through the Common and Public Garden tossing stale dinner roll crumbs at ducks and hissing geese.

The next morning I awoke early to seek and munch a breakfast worthy of an unfledged soldier filing blindly into battle. Not possessing the resources for previous such ventures, I soon found East Cambridge boasts the absolute when it comes to industrialized *ante meridiem* hasheries – all empty cubbyholes etched in brick walls and tasteless cafés built from chrome. All other less *American*, more unique and tasty eateries didn't open till noon. I found only one sit-down joint which served an authentic, earthy English breakfast and used up quite a troubling sum sucking runny eggs on burnt wheat toast and dry bacon and tough steaks sliced too thin. Even the coffee failed to inspire rage, barely able to leave even a stain. In far too disparate a mood to see ill portent in all this, I slurped my coffee and eggs and dabbed my lip and left a generous tip besides and sauntered out into a sunny New England spring landscape.

Up Thorndike Street near the Center for Multicultural Convictions I ferreted out the number corresponding with soft cooings made by middle-aged feathery hens in baby blue dresses and silk tanned-skin-toned hosiery and stepped inside, soon to realize I wasn't the only cock invited beyond the wire that day. In fact, there were three others, all pale-skinned and timidly clutching portfolios in their thighs and laps and instantly I thought of Jeff like a *Giraffe* still crooking his neck in Terri's office and I smiled, seriously at risk of losing it altogether. Luckily, pity consumed me and instead I took my seat and folded my hands in my lap and tried my damnedest to come off most dour...er, serious.

After about an hour of twiddling my wingtips I was cawed into a cagey office with no windows or fake plants or reproductions of Impressionist paintings but there was a large desk placed square in the center, a solitary chair facing its front. A bantam fountain gurgled conspicuously in a far corner.

The pruned bird behind the desk asked that I be seated while she crooned over my credentials. She seemed especially interested in my transcripts, specifically my degree in Sociology. It was her field as well, I soon learned...or, actually, not Sociology, necessarily, but *social work*, the statement of which made me cringe. (The confusion between the two – one a very serious study of humanity locked at the horns and struggling like crazed mountain sheep to break free; the other a perpetual meddling in the affairs of these sheep's offspring – is a constant metal thorn in the sides of all who subject themselves to the insanity which is called human science. Even if it all be just impartial theory anyhow – the behavior both of sheep and their offspring – impartial theorists these disillusioned caseworkers most certainly are not. As it happens, they are interested only in practice, in the locating and untangling of a web which needs untangling, sure, but by whom? Who may presume to know another human being so well to prescribe an anecdote for all his ills? Who presumes not only the diagnosis of a disease but the method by which the healing process will take place and when and under whose guidance and supervision? The social worker presumes, of course, and the younglings and ewes are the ones who must suffer, who must stand by and watch as their lives turn into statistics and their strengths and powers as individuals are stolen and sold over to the State and categorized as publicly unfit, unsound, a travesty, a martyr for someone else's need to sleep well at night. And after still the sheep remain horn-locked, the younglings and ewes still confused and scared and possibly even more heartbroken than before. In the end only the symptom has been cured, its acidic guise and social detriment. In the end the social worker proves nothing more than a parasite using heartbreak as a commodity to buy back the respect of the four-year institution which bore him.) All the same, it was an inward cringe I made and outwardly I managed to maintain a juicy smile to match the prosperity the situation promised, the social bird opposite me never more the wiser. After only fifteen minutes my credentials and smile got a rubber stamp and my hand a feathery shake meant to welcome me into the ranks....And just in time, too. By then the gurgling of the miniature fountain in the corner had full control over the inner gurgling of my bladder. I released the social bird's feathery wing and fled the wiry cage in search of the nearest toilet, barely finding one in time. And as I stood groaning over the piss pot pouring bucketsful into the porcelain reservoir I remembered the other cocks clutching tight their portfolios and their tails taped to their inner thigh and suddenly I found myself smiling and whistling and in a deep, gurgling voice singing...*If you want honey in your docket...A soft cat on your bed...A shot mare in your stable... A handerchief instead....*

The very next morning I received my first assignment via a five a.m. phone call (for this reason alone I'd purchased a used telephone from a secondhand store, the owner of which assuring me all was well – the chord was fully intact inside and all the buttons pushed down and popped back up again and so on, etc. It was the connection fee which killed me, damn near a month's worth of dinner rolls and green apples. I asked that it be tagged onto the first month's bill, of course never intending to pay a penny. There was only a month left in the school year. After that the damn machine would be tossed straight into the Charles.), a voice on the other end sounding like Ma Baker's lymphatic second cousin told me if I wanted the gig I was to report to the registrar's office of Cambridge Rindge and Latin before seven or I could forget the complimentary wake-up call tomorrow or the next day or the next until All Presidents' Day for all she cared, thank you very much. I thanked her kindly in turn and flipped my ass out of bed straight toward the frigid commode for a quick shit and a spritz bath, then off I skipped toward cheery ol' Clamor Bridge o'er Lachlan.

Finding it finally after roping some quivering homebody out for a pre-dawn stroll down Broadway near Kendall telling me with jittery teeth it's just up the avenue before the library take a right down Dana or up Ellery or well around there anyway, then away he speed-walked straight toward the bakery and me stumbling, sweating in through Rindge and Latin arches marching straight toward...what? Some office somewhere, but where? Not certain of anything at this point, not even the time, I wandered wide-eyed down the hallway peeking like a felon through glass-encased wire till on the second floor I found a wooden sign with a rather suggestive arrow attached. "Main Office" it encouraged. To its left a clock. "Six fifty-two" it sang with a smile. I smiled back, then followed the bald phallus.

Around the corner a buzz like the hum of a nuclear reactor. Some twenty-odd teachers clogged the entryway, each toting fat blue folders with multicolored papers bulging out the sides like confetti lettuce in a huge blue hoagie no teeth could ever handle.

After a full minute my presence was finally noticed. A stout-breasted squab in a paisley skirt and sandals asked the reason for my standing there stiff as a Grecian woodpecker's poker. I shrugged and offered a nervous grin.

"Okay, then....Your name?" inquired the squab.

I told her. The sound of my own name bounced off and around between so many pillars of pure explosive energy was a most sobering experience and after that I perked up quite dramatically, so much so I too found myself infected with the common disease, the symptoms manifested as fear-fueled megalomania coupled by apoplexy of the jaw, wrists and finger joints resulting in the compulsive clutching of inedibly fat iceberg-blue folders and coffee-and/or-tea-and-nicotine-stained teeth.

The squab smiled and handed me my blue folder. "You'll be covering for Evelyn this week," she told me, then pointed toward a wall upon which hung cabinets like the comb of a hive. "That's her cubby there," she said. "Each morning check the cubby to retrieve the student list or any new assignments Miss Evelyn sends in. Got it?" I nodded. "Good." Then she turned toward a computer screen and punched some keys and stared some, then again at me saying, "She'll be here all morning...Room 142. She asked that you stand in with her so the students can see you by her side...smooth transitioning and all that, see?" Again I nodded. "Fine." Then she turned and stared at the screen again, this time for good.

Room 142, I repeated to myself.

Strolling in through the coop swing door floating wired after downing a raw concoction mixed one part adrenaline two parts diluted apathy I fled the drowsy stares of fluffy, uncouth chicks and sought instead the head hen, finding her pecking seeds off the blackboard ledge. I coughed to get her attention.

She turned and smiled, then with a wave invited me behind her desk. Once there in a whisper she asked my name. I told her, also in a whisper.

After, Miss Evelyn Hen Turned Mute Swan spun round toward the class and said, "Everyone, listen up. Listen up, everyone....This is Mr. Woolverton. He'll be taking over class this afternoon. Please show him the same respect you all show me, right?" A snicker from somewhere near the back. Miss Evelyn paid no attention. "Now, listen...if I hear otherwise from Mr. Woolverton...well, I won't be pleased, understand?

Do you all understand me?" Another snicker. Miss Mute Swan Turned Tired Ostrich then looked to me and smiled as if to say, "There. See how easy it is?" I smiled back as if to say, "You poor, plucked bird." Then I sat by her desk and waited for lunch.

After lunch I returned to Mother Hen Evelyn's classroom and assumed the padded seat behind the desk. The entire setup seemed to swallow me whole with wooden teeth as I watched the children returning from their meal laughing, taunting, spitting, cursing, roughhousing, playing with the sort of joyous abandon resulting in either victory or injury or both, the adults hovering over the sidelines shouting warnings and commands, shadowing the playing field with their unladen fears and laws and world that cannot stomach chaos, which is suspicious of primitive ceremonies of pure enjoyment, which witnesses the antics of youth and cringes with visions of splintered bone and torn skin and hospital bills, brain damage, lost teeth, bad credit, misused opportunities resulting in misfortune, missed planes, trains and ocean liners crashing into cliffs and sinking to the bottom of the sea, the golden treasure trapped and locked inside the hull, lost forever. This is the crux of the matter. The innate mind of the child doesn't think a second of crashing planes or trains or sinking ocean liners and certainly won't shed a tear over lost gold or oil or silver bracelets. If a child thinks this way it is only because his mind has been tainted by adult greed and jealousy and shameless fear of loss and mystery. Without a doubt, the adult feels a sort of violent compulsion to teach and protect, to control not just a certain situation or a series of situations but bodies and minds as well – and not just those of the young or the elderly or the invalid but the bodies and minds of his neighbors and co-workers and evangelic devotees and club members and financial advisers and pets and friends and enemies. Everyone around him raises his suspicions and these suspicions turn to fear which turns to impotence which turns to anger which either causes death or turns to action, to violence. A very natural, human impulse, violence, no? Very natural. Very *of* nature, of the most primitive impulses borne as instinct in the psyche of man and beast alike. The beast, though, uses violence either to eat or to show its invaders the size of its teeth, not to plunder gold coins or oil or silver bracelets or Antwerp blue diamonds or treasures lost deep below the surface of the sea. To the beast gold coins mean indigestion, that is all. And to the child the glint of gold and silver and diamonds all mean only a moment's sorrow handed down to them in trade for forgiveness for the violent acts of an adult mind.

Thoughts like these kept whirling through my bean as I watched the wild fury of excited youth scurry round the room over desks and chairs and hands and feet and walls and window sills and the water-stained tiles of the suspended ceiling, finally settling like feathers to their seats with no prompting from me, just by habit. And as they sat there in silence watching me watching them all wondering what the hell, the violence and sorrow in my head seeping out my eyes and mouth through a smile, I heard a voice from the back ask, "Well? What are we supposed to do now, man?"

For what seemed like minutes I did nothing, nothing but rest my elbows under my chin and smile. Then I shrugged and said, "Do whatever you like."

Nobody moved. They obviously thought it a trap, a juicy slab of taffy dangled loose before their mouths only to be snatched back and their fingers slapped once they lifted their hands. Soon, though, a few brave souls from the back stood up and, letting loose a bawdy laugh, strutted to a far corner and squatted and began rolling dice.

The others just watched them, then me, at my reaction. Seeing only a smile they too unsettled themselves and began roaming the room. Some stayed seated, making sketches in their notebooks. Others flirted awkwardly with the boys and girls sitting next to them.

I wandered toward the back of the room to try my luck and

lost a tenner.

    The following week kept fairly close the same scenario. Each new day meant more bills lost to young snot-nosed shysters whose pettifoggery consisted solely of acute vulgarities tossed as loaded die down sticky sleeves toward a wall – a winner every time. It was all I could do to keep a few bucks inside my pocket before lunch, at which time I often found myself wandering aimlessly off campus toward nowhere in particular, just down a street or avenue toward a building or tree bent just strange enough to catch my eye, my legs entranced by its osteoporotic curves and leaves and pink and blue petals new on the bud, my mind working frantically to justify either returning to or fleeing Miss Evelyn's Juvenile Lounge/Casino, in the end always returning, not because of any sense of duty or responsibility but because I hoped to win back my damn money. A funny thing, pride. Always seems to empty one's pockets faster than a sure thing or a strange man on the street selling promises of redemption. At the end of the week those snotty bastards took me for every penny, the consolation being a fat check arriving in the mail the following week for all my hours spent guarding and nurturing the minds and bodies of tomorrow's brave new leaders...or criminally-minded raconteurs. In any case, since all were still breathing I'd proven my worth in the eyes of the System and was promptly offered another gig, then another, then another and another, each tossed sporadically across Cambridge's webbed landscape, each rarely lasting more than a few days and all meaning one thing: one more fat check secured.

    My financial albatross now seemingly on the wing (if hovering somewhat near), I could resume my wanderings without the usual setbacks of frustration and hunger, the entire city of Boston again alive and writhing under my toes and fingertips. Eager to escape Cambridge the first chance I could, directly after the day's last bell I'd hop the Harvard Square train headed east beneath the Charles through the underbelly of the giant, eventually darting like a tapeworm out its lifeless throat onto the streets and buildings and tenement houses of Fenway's baroque architecture, specifically the dichotomous façade of the Museum of Fine Arts.

Stepping through the Ionic phizog of the Huntington entrance one gets the sense he's about to be greeted with feathers and fresh grapes only to find a maze of glass-encased artifacts and bones and mummified bodies and King Henry's bloody chessboard before him. Days I spent tripping like a somnambulist through this tomb's dark rooms and alcoves, a specter trapped inside the history of man's greatest ambitions which always seemed to fall just short of the mark, as proof a fierce, stony palace erected atop a catacomb where only ghosts and spirits are allowed to shadow its walls. In this frigid, air-conditioned atmosphere the passion of past glories always comes off placid, embalmed, glass-encased, impractical – mere decoration for plaster walls and hallways. Artists not just of this country's history but of all mankind's spilt blood and wine and sweat and toiled to the bone for this, for the inspiration of a grand hallway where spectators come to pay their fare and step into and through, then out the other end like digested fruit, inspired to stay and linger maybe a moment, though ultimately moved along by forces beyond their control. Even the Impressionists, those brilliant re-inventors of color and light, even they seem stale and achromatic when strung in this atmosphere: Cézanne a fearful anarchist; Gauguin a miserly imperialist; van Gogh a textured postcard sent to creditors and estranged loyalists. The whole of the great fractured eye of Impressionism, when tacked on a wall like butterfly wings, resounds with joy and sadness: joy in life – that a life once existed and created with this eye; sadness in its death and rebirth as a novelty. Nowhere does one come in contact with this tragedy more than in the museum. Perhaps that illusory *Imaginary View of the Grande Galerie in Ruins* (however unconsciously) hits this sentiment dead on: the hallways and rooms of the great

Louvre in ruins; clear blue sky with flush trees and birds seen through a fallen *plafond*; pillars crumbled like cake atop the surrounding rubble; a solitary figure in the middle of it all, painting. *Creation out of nothing*, the frequenters of concerts and museums would sermonize. Fortunately, I'm neither...or *wasn't* until those wasted spring afternoons. Soon I found myself wandering beyond the stony columnar façade of Fine Arts toward more obscure, less obnoxious museums in hopes of refuting what I'd found previously...namely, *nothing out of creation*.

Throughout Boston and Cambridge I searched, plodding my shuffled feet through cold monasteries and esoteric tombs and shanties, all like their predecessors – dead, embalmed – till finally I came upon the most disconsonant, most blatantly misrepresented, out-and-out incongruous venue of them all: the Fogg. Like a wild beast caged in an architectural zoo, this building devours in one fierce swipe, tasting nothing but the sinew left stuck in its teeth. And maybe, if one's quiet enough (or *frightened* enough, I should say), one can hear the sucking sounds emitting from the walls and archways encompassing a mock Italian courtyard where transients of cultural entrails can be seen sipping coffee and/or tea, perhaps nibbling some biscotti, all whispering to one another and smiling and every so often bobbing their heads and shifting their eyes to take in and absorb the surrounding roughage, however predigested. It was inside the Fogg I came face-to-face with Monet – not the Monet of sparkling Parisian glory but the Monet of the mirage, of the years when his eyes became his worst enemies. Fortunately for us, these years were his most vivid. During these last crippling days Monet was in full possession of the secret which he sought after so stringently in his youth and which, because of his fierce ambition, eluded him. At his last, when he had nothing left to either gain or lose, he sat himself down and in vibrant, brilliant hues and mad, wild, precise strokes he finally painted what he saw – not with his eyes, as it were, but with his heart. He proved to us all the power in beauty, the true nobility of the artist, the truly *innate* nobility which can only reveal itself fully when loss or gain or even the five senses become powerless against it. Monet realized this. The power and light and beauty of his *self* simply could not be contained as made evident on that canvas before me and – I suppose because of its vividness amidst the darkness of mendacity – I raised my arm and reached out and caressed Monet's brushstrokes as I would his wounded eyes.

A red light flashed on. Instinctively, I turned around and, noticing cameras in the corners and above me, I panicked and made for the exit, passing a security guard on the way out. The guard went in and I left, sweating steel pellets as if I'd attempted to bludgeon the Pope.

Outside again surrounded by neo-Georgian pretensions I wandered up the street a ways to cool my brow when I noticed a familiar figure working its way up the opposite side of the street. It was Richard, hobbling as usual and whistling himself some far-off tune, an aloof expression spanning his eyes and forehead. I had a moment's thought of turning a corner and avoiding him, his aloofness none too inviting. Instead, I stuck my course. If his aloofness were true he wouldn't notice me. If false, perhaps there was some way I might benefit. A meal, in the very least. Mustn't look too eager, however. Just a pinch of the ol' pallor often associated with mind-damaging hunger. Like Hamsun's nameless scavenger...minus the crippling pride. I hunched my shoulders and donned a wan expression to match my would-be benefactor's brow and crossed the street and made toward him.

As luck had had it he was on his way toward a Thai joint just off the square. Would I care to join him? he wondered. Was this really a question? I wondered back, pretending to think it over some, careful not to drool down the front of my used Brooks Brothers pinpoint oxford shirt, bulletproof and borrowed from East Cambridge's own academic arsenal.

The Thai joint was really an open-walled hovel in the hollow of an elitist mall. At least they paid attention to detail, made evident by the yellow slants tossing salads and pouring hot soup and cracking fresh pepper before the salivating eyes of whites, ourselves included. Richard spotted a table on the second level and nabbed it. Within minutes we were served. Richard ordered iced tea with lemon. I ordered a beer, my first in almost a month. I allowed the sting to linger like stars bursting in the back of my throat, then I sighed and smiled and attacked my sprouts and noodles.

After what must have been a full five minutes I looked up to notice Richard wasn't eating. In fact, he'd barely touched his food, only stirring the cubes of his iced tea. I slowed my pace as a polite gesture, seeing as he clearly intended to foot the check. My stomach somewhat full and bubbling anyhow, I dropped my sticks and sipped my beer, waiting for whatever the price free sprouts and noodles would cost me.

After a few more minutes he finally spoke up. "You know why I didn't say anything that day in the office, don't you?"

I thought things might turn thus. True, I'd questioned his silence regarding that day, given all he had said before about assisting naïve, starving artists via his soft heart, but to be honest I'd have expected nothing different. The way I explained Richard's silence – much like the others' silence, I suppose – was in the fact that Richard didn't know me from Adam. Why stick his or his *Übermensch* machine's neck out for the sake of some bum, some transient, a complete nobody obviously passing through one door and out the other? Only a fool would be so reckless, so daring. And Richard was no fool, this I'd calculated rather quickly. In fact, by then I was beginning to think him quite cunning – as cunning as his namesake, the deformed monarch-in-seed sick with having to await his turn at the throne, frightened mad it may never come. It was his nonchalance which betrayed him. Only a calculating mind acts so unperturbed – only a false portrait reveals itself so focused, so undistorted. All this I'd sorted out straight after that last day in Terri's office and I'd not thought about it since. Obviously, though, Richard had, and since he was now so willing to make amends via spicy Thai cuisine and beer – served gratis – I suddenly found myself more than willing to let drop all I'd untangled.

"What day is it you mean?" I asked, resuming hold of my sticks.

He crimped his brow and tossed me a rampant grin as if to say, "You know damn well what day I mean, asshole."

I smiled. I had to. Obviously, such games of transparent origin would have to cease; we knew each other too well...or, rather, *of* each other, the other's scheming intellect. I poked the sprouts and noodles and stabbed a slab of soupy beef with my sticks and, still smiling, munched contentedly.

Then I waited.

"It's all very simple," he began, his confidence surging. "You were being cut off, see? Severed from Feng Shui royalty...severed from all the resources Feng Shui had to offer. You needed an anchor, a darning needle...someone to stay behind and keep the line alive. If we both were out where would you be then, hmmm? Drifting through the city alone, that's where...a nomad...a puddle hopper...a dog on a leash but no master, hmm?" Grinning, he skewered a thin strip of chicken, then dipped it into a bowl of steamed jasmine rice and bit down and chomped emphatically. Seemed he'd just proven something. I waited silent to find out what. Finally he swallowed and sipped his lemon iced tea and continued: "My one regret is I didn't have a chance to tell you sooner. I did warn you, though, didn't I? Didn't I warn you she'd turn on you...kick you out with no real reason, hmm? Didn't I?" with a self-acknowledged grin. Then, a shrug: "Ah, well, you should consider yourself lucky. You've taken all you could from her, anyway. What else could you have gotten from her, hmm? *Food?* Nonsense! What use have you for food? Food for you will only be a diversion...a pesky nuisance dealt with only when the pangs become too unbearable. Besides, you're Cantabrigian now, understand? *Cantabrigian!* A member! A true bloodline member of an American elite! You'll never have to worry about food again! For you, food will always be there, always just around the corner....All you'll have to do is hold out your hand and down it will fall into your palm like manna...like food from the gods, the heavens....Ambrosia fit for a Cantabrigian king!..."

So much for scheming intellects. This guy's plotting was so thin I saw it floating just below the surface of the murky broth in my bowl, suffocating. Ah, well, he was right about the food. In fact, he seemed to hit it dead on. The main thing, aside from severing this Cantabrigian bloodline he was so obsessed with, is food. Just keep eating, I told myself, and as often as possible. The rest will fall into place...or not. In any case, if the food will be there then so will I – with knife and fork in hand, salivating.

After the meal Richard invited me to go walk with him. I thought I'd decline. I was feeling somewhat fatigued, what with the teaching gig and the museums and near misses from the hands of Monet security. As it were, I couldn't decline. In my mind I still owed him for the meal, even if Richard himself never implied as much. Besides, to turn down any such request might mean fewer offers of free Thai in the future. In light of all, I accepted with a smile.

We headed for the T. Seemed there were a few mouse holes and niches he wished to show me. Said no trip through Boston would be complete without them, the sound of which had me immediately suspicious. By his tone you'd think he'd already written me off, already blown the whistle and had my papers signed and slated for the first train headed straight for the Northeastern border...minus the tearful salutations. Still, as always, merry and bright. I trod along with him, my eye on the constant lookout for hammer claws and blood-red bandages.

We jumped the T at Park Street. (The sun was at the hour when good, decent people of cities large and small leave the streets and avenues and alleyways for the marauding sort – the sort with missing fingers and peg legs and acid on the breath; the sort the night streets were meant for, a refuge from the hours marked by screaming cars and bikers and pets shitting on park lawns and alabaster faces shooting empty, polished smiles.) From Park Street we skirted south along the Common on Tremont, turning left at Boylston toward a red and green, Halloween-orange centriole: Chinatown.

I didn't tell Richard my first impression of Chinatown. Didn't think it prevalent. Some things simply don't transfer well into words. Still, Richard was quick to point out all *his* impressions as though Chinatown just simply appeared from his own willful imagination. "See over there?" he said, nodding toward two slants unloading a fish truck. "Still working, toiling through the dark hours. The assiduous seed of the foreign man sprouting roots under concrete slabs and stares and buildings toppling over him. The roughened hands of the underclass, hmm? Weary travelers, yes? The great hub of American activity seen from the hollow crack of a street filled with spit and blood and bone and bits of rotten vegetable." He pointed through the window of a restaurant. "See them? See the mothers and daughters and fathers and sons eating, talking. See them laughing?...Crying?...Consoling? Another world, isn't it? Distant, yet close...so very close...alarmingly close....Like Koussevitzky leaving his native Russia to conduct an orchestra, get me? A leap...a bounding, continental leap of courage and conviction...the conviction of a restless spirit...." Suddenly he stopped and turned and looked behind us as if being followed. "Feel that?" he asked. "Feel the energy? The electricity pulsating under your feet?...Under your being?" He looked forward again and grinned. "Feels like the earth is planning on destroying something."

We walked on, leaving Chinatown through its gates of green dragon heads and lions' claws up Washington through Downtown Crossing and Quincy and State, finally taking rest on a bench just outside Faneuil Hall (by this point the man's hobble had turned to a severe limp), at which time Richard suddenly became nostalgic, recounting bits about his family, his father specifically. "The creative one," he began. "Always creating something...always turning over ideas and thoughts in his head...creating. Those stones," he said, pointing toward a narrow strip of cobblestone alongside a wide strip of black pavement outside an expensive restaurant. "When they tore up this street to make way for concrete my father made sure he was on the job, to steal away as many of those stones as possible...as many as could possibly fit in our Volkswagen. I never found out why till fifteen years later." He stared hopelessly at the stones – lost, I guess – till: "Turned out he stole those stones to build a garden for my mother in the backyard. Said he couldn't stand the idea of those stones, stones that had been in a street he'd walked over so many times before... couldn't stand the thought they should no longer be there... stolen....So he stole them first to build a garden....For my mother. He died soon after." He snapped out of his reverie and looked at me, then he smiled and stood from the bench and said, "That garden...that stone garden stolen from the emptiness of this black, empty street....It's still standing. After thirty years that goddamn cobblestone garden is still standing." Then he stood and laughed and shook his head and smiled some more – the kind of smile used to fight tears – then I stood with him.

Together we limped on past expensive restaurants and night-clubs and Boston's Ye Oldest Oyster Hole through a damp tunnel like a sewer leading us under the city's most expensive concrete project to date (recently leaking), emerging through an opening like a gateway to the underworld of Boston's own North End before a sharp left and the apricot-golden glow of Northern Italy's own Hanover Street.

We walked slowly through a throng of smiling people standing, walking, entering and leaving smoke houses and taverns and pastry shops and pizzerias and restaurants, the waiters standing, smiling, carrying plates of green and purple salads and red or white meats and pastas covered in red or white sauces and cheese and peppers and bottles of red or white wine, the waiters opening either, each with a *Thhhh... Pop!*, the faces and mouths of the people laughing, acting surprised, tasting, cheering, drinking, thinking nothing about anything having to do with something other than standing, smoking, buying things, eating, cheering, drinking, laughing, seeing the eyes and mouths of the faces next to them turning into smiles, free of anything having to do with fear or hate or ugliness, just silence, happiness, Richard and I walking through them, watching, all of us smiling, laughing, looking, seeing, floating....

We entered the door of a fancy café made-up to resemble European marble-chrome nobility and sat and ordered two espressos and two snifters of Drambuie. Richard insisted on paying. I didn't argue.

We sat there for some time, sipping our espressos and snifters, soaking in the aura, the astral glow of electric light reflected off marble floors and tables and countertops like stars, the constellations of gentility seeping in through our souls and hearts and stomachs warm and gentle and soothing as the coffee and Drambuie. Some time, I say, till Richard again thought he'd break the religious silence.

"Do you know the Golden Ratio?" he asked. I confessed I did not. "The Golden Ratio," he continued. "The Golden Cut. Da Vinci's divine method of genius...of *madness*...the mad brilliance of his art....The Divine Proportion created...no, not created...*discovered*...uncovered throughout Nature in everything...everything...even that outside of Nature, which is to say, Man." He took a sip off his espresso and eyed the snifter, leaving it be. Then he lifted his head and stared out the window to the street – the same stare I'd seen that day in Terri's office – then said, "The Divine Proportion...da Vinci's divine method....The map, the blueprint....Nature's blueprint for the Universe." Again he turned toward me. "The divine proportion of balance between two extremes...two endpoints: Life and art. Excess and abstinence. The beautiful and the good. The necessary blending...a *rationalizing* of chaos, of the world's brilliant chaos into something divine, coherent, understood, understandable...*bearable*," with a sly, devilish grin. Da Vincian. "The Universe not made, not born or created, but *existent*...coherent....*Coerced*, get me? *Forced* into being by *law*...by *Man's* law of beauty, *his* method and proportion...*his* chaos...*his* mad, chaotic beauty made divine, proportionate, aesthetic...*numeric*. The world not seen through the eyes of Nature but the eyes of mathematics... the eyes of Humanity. The proportion, the distance...the *balance* between the beautiful and the good, between excess and abstinence, life and art...this balance exists only in the imagination...as a *number*, understand? The beauty and soul and spirit of the Universe bottled and contained and labeled *Golden*, only to be used for Man's personal aesthetic eye, his own personal soul and spirit and divinity...his own life and art...his own Acropolis, his own Great Pyramids, his own canvases and cathedrals...his own nautilus shell...."

We drank down the rest of our espressos and snifters in silence – a contemplative silence, one could say – then left the café back out into Hanover Street toward the Waterfront and the endless row of wharves like great concrete tentacles reaching, trying to pull the great purple-gray body behind them out of the water onto dry land into the surrounding buildings.

Past the Waterfront approaching Atlantic Avenue I noticed Richard's limping had reached such a state as to cause pain, his face wincing with every step. I asked that we stop, that we hop the next train in the nearest station and call it a night. I myself was exhausted, weary with the thought of the next morning's five o'clock call. Richard refused. Grinning through his winces, he assured me there was one more thing he wished to show me – in fact, the very reason he asked me on this walk. Thinking black coffee thoughts (the Drambuie had a rather backsliding effect on the espresso), I agreed. We walked on.

Turning right down Kneeland, then again on Utica, at

last Richard stopped and pointed up at the topmost level of a warehouse building, a strip of electric activity lit against the black of night. "There," he said, still pointing up and looking at the lights. "There is where I see you...where you'll one day work, uncover, create using digits and commands...monitors and images...light and electricity...technology instead of clay, get me?" He looked away from the building toward me. "A modern man...a man of the present and future...of the here and now and beyond. Not a creator...not an artist so much as a *coercionist*...a seer. A man reliable on himself, dependent not on the past, not even so much the present, but the future, which is to say, modern. A modern man not creating, but seeing...."

He stopped and stared toward me, a glazed look in his eye – a stare which seemed to bore right through till I realized he wasn't staring at *me*, but *behind* me. I turned and saw nothing, nothing but an enormous black hole in the brick wall of an abandoned building.

I looked back at Richard. He just stood, staring, lost in something I could not see. His lips moved some, inaudibly, as his eyes began circling, perusing the sunken darkness of the empty hole in the wall till suddenly his arms raised and his legs moved, dragging him closer toward the hole. "I see roses," he said finally as if entranced. "Roses...white, pink, yellow petals falling to the surface....A man...broken...lying naked in the far corner...the light visible only on his feet, on the ankles and soles...his toes black with bruises, the joints misplaced, bent backward....A woman in the corner nearest us...kneeling, weeping...trying to catch the petals before they hit the floor...each petal falling faster...fast like stones...so fast she can't move fast enough to catch them all, only a few which she holds in her dress pinned up against her breast... but with each petal she tries to catch another falls free, falls to the surface like a stone...falls through...lost...so she weeps some more....Music...music...." He lifted his head and eyes toward the night sky as if attempting to hear the moon. "Such music...the music of falling rose petals...of Wagner and Liszt and Barber...of love and doom and nakedness and toes bent backward, unable to take another step...of lying naked in far corners, unable to move just one step or even rouse one eyelid to ease the misery of a woman kneeling, weeping, trying to catch just one more pink or white or yellow rose petal falling to the surface of the earth like stone...."

*   *   *

The next two weeks were marked by constant five a.m. phone calls, each directing me toward new and different schools and classrooms stretched out about the vastly flat and over-centralized Cantabrigian cosmorama. I found myself in every setting from spinning well-fed bratlings in circles chasing tails and half-dead-deflated beach balls across filthy paved-over enclosures to tossing algebraic quizzes in the direction of half-closed, fully glazed eyeballs deftly studying the insides of lids and/or the inner thighs of thoughtless missies to everything between...especially lunch. Invariably during this hour of freedom I'd see just how far and fast I could escape the chains of giants, the farthest usually just around the corner to an organic café or else the library to scan the shelves for early editions of masterpieces to steal. (A favorite pastime of mine, one which has yielded some rather interesting add-ons to my home collection, including Kierkegaard's complete "poetic" works as well as the aforementioned Dante according to Longfellow to Spengler's *Decline* to Whitman's complete works of prose, purely his own and purely free of poetic refrain. Still on the lookout, though, for the infamous *Ulysses*...before Woolsey got a hold of it, I mean. What a curious piece of poorly mishandled and oddly damaged Victorian furniture it would make!) After a quick, tasteless bite or a quick thumb-flick through some dusty, under-financed vault I'd invariably return, shoulders slumped, miserable with the thought of having to sit myself at the front of some dark room the next four hours dodging empty stares from the pupils of malnourished eyes, the next morning invariably promising the same till, as luck had had it, with just one week left of makeshift academics I again received a call from Rindge and Latin asking if I'd finish the year in their athletics department. Seemed one of the knee-benders decided to take an early leave. So be it. I double laced my Stacy Adams and ran over my one-two-three's and crossovers and after straining every body part from nostril-hair to nipple I grabbed my roll and apple and hopped the train to meet my pay.

As to be expected, the "athletics" in *athletics department* was a canard. Turned out all one must know to keep proper order in these environs is CPR and the location of the First Aid box, each invaluable in a gymnasium swarming with hypercalcemic skeletons and asthmatics. If both CPR and First Aid fail, one's next option is the ambulance, which never happened on my watch – which is most likely why the head "athletics" instructor once approached me to inform me a full-time position would soon be open...as early as the next school year. I looked up from my group of flying hands and feet to see if he was serious and, seeing he was, at once froze in fear, the thought of joining these ranks as a career acting as a sort of paralysis. Fortunately, I was able to pass off my fear as consideration, stating after I'd rather think it over. "Understandable," he said. "I'd expect nothing different for so serious a decision." After which he walked off, smiling. *Victoire double.* He saved face and I saved my salary.

Next issue.

About this time, now with a steady teaching gig soon terminated, I began thinking seriously on other options pending my release from the chains of Cantabrigian giants. Immediately coming to mind was the sleep study Richard downloaded one month prior from the hub of our world's illusive web, the idea of which, formulated by my very own, very fresh experiences, was one of little enthusiasm. Still, I hadn't many options to choose from; my chances for suitable income were scarce – short of becoming a pimp, the thought of which led me straight down dark alleyways seeded with firearms and syringes. Besides, the only cunt I could think to call on was Terri's moldy quim, and no John in his sane mind would pay one farthing for that juiceless slit. I'd starve for sure. In light of all – or nothing – I decided the sleep study was the thing.

Strange enough, the entrance procedures were actually quite assuring. After a brief physical examination (including a none too brief or soothing but assuring rectal probing) to everyone's satisfaction the only question then was the status of my mind: whether or not I would suddenly crack halfway through the study and fling pudding and/or poo at the walls and faces of Boston's most noted medical technicians. And so, I was given a rather extensive questionnaire demanding to know everything from my favorite color to my desire to ever murder anyone (to which I most soberly replied: None as of yet, thank you) to three different reviews with three different shrinks all demanding to know one thing: my ability to act calm and rational on a consistent basis under rather pressing circumstances such as loss of a loved one and/or hair, limb, medication, employment, eyesight and/or virginity, freedom, life, faith in God and/or Satan, any skill whatsoever resulting in my ability to gain an income resulting in a feeling of inadequacy and impotency in the face of a bastard society, all resulting in the answering of just one question: Are you now, and will you remain for the next four to six weeks, sane? (To which I most calmly and rationally replied: I think so.) Quite assuring, indeed.

After the psychological screening and, more importantly, my rubber stamping, I was sent on to the next stage where I was told in detail the exact instances of the study and the peculiarities expected of me as a willful participant, *viz.* abstinence from alcohol, caffeine, nicotine, red meat, narcotics (over-the-counter and/or otherwise), hot baths, massages, chocolate, cigars, orgasms (self-induced and/or otherwise), pleasurable bowel movements, trips to theaters for reasons other than educational, letter-writing to persons other than grandparents or anonyms, fish, pasteurized milk, foreign influence (including but not exclusive to cuisine and/or art culture), tap water, physical exertion (including but not exclusive to hanging naked from unstrung chandeliers), loud music, arousing images and above all a steady bedtime of eleven p.m. each night for three weeks straight, each morning rousing at seven a.m. sharp. Should I choose to ignore these prescriptions I could kiss the sleep study and all monies owed me goodbye. If, however, there wasn't a relapse I could consider myself a rich man...rich by my own hand-to-mouth standards, that is. In any case, two thousand dollars richer than I was. All I had to do was sign my name on the dotted line and accept the consequences as such. I did so without reserve.

Also about this time Richard began calling on me more often than necessary to tempt me away from my obligations to the sleep study and back into the gutter without so much as an apology. Even if he were a self-admitted teetotalist and non-smoker he was nonetheless a caffeine addict and (as a result, I suppose) an out-and-out insomniac. More than once I literally had to force myself out of his company before my eleven p.m. curfew lest I forfeited all that cash. (The method by which the technicians kept eye on this condition was an electronic device worn round the wrist which monitored my movement and/or pulse: they never said which for fear I proved the manipulating sort.) What's more, the migraines from cold-turkey abstinence were such as to cause nausea, Richard's constant coffee-sippings a needle to the eye of a masochistic junky. The only reason I ever accepted the guy's offerings was because food was always involved and at that time – my last check from Rindge and Latin going straight to rent and two weeks till the study and my apples and rolls all stale and rotted – food was one hell of a motivator. Each time he'd call (my phone kept on the mantle and out of the

Charles for this reason alone) I'd don my checkered napkin and snatch my fork and spoon and butter knife and skip down the stairs out the door, careful not splinter my diminished, malnourished bones...each time, that is, till the gray squirrel incident.

As it happened, Richard had just purchased a vehicle, a metallic-maroon Topaz which he said needed breaking-in but the streets and avenues of Boston Metropolitan were too angular and narrow to allow anything other than uneven tire tread. His solution: a road trip to New Hampshire. Would I care to join him?

Would I rather stay indoors and starve?

Upon seeing him in this machine – this man who every bit resembled the stock face of America's Forefathers from distinguished gray to ponytail to rot teeth and poor hygiene right down to a debilitating arthritic limp – upon first view of this relic sitting behind the wheel of combusted oil and steel I nearly went into hysterics and lost my chance at a full, churning stomach. What happened instead, however, was I went numb. I felt nothing, no sense of irony or private glee. The sight of him behind the wheel of an automobile at once made perfect sense to me. Dispassionate, I opened the car door and slid into the passenger seat.

Approaching the White Mountains Richard decided he'd start hypothesizing. "Hmm....Imagine yourself wandering a-lone through this wilderness," he began, staring out the car window into fog-obscured treetops. "What a wilderness!...A refuge....Man's last refuge...the last place on this earth he can disappear and fall into...into the solitude and darkness of rocks and trees and leaves and bogs and rivers...everything entirely beyond his control...into the quiet and solitude of Nature...and even then he's not alone. Man will never be alone....Never...not on this earth. I'm not talking about the animals or bugs or trees or rocks or seas or any of that....I'm talking about himself...about Mankind *himself*." He paused a moment to check his speed and gauges, then continued:

"Man will never be alone...not on this earth. He'll always have his own self, his own conscience to contend with...his own failures...his own lost dreams...his own love and his own hate...his own hate of...."

Just then a loud thump sounded from somewhere near the undercarriage. Richard stopped the car and we both got out to investigate. Finding nothing wrong with the tires or anything else we peered down the road behind us. A large lump of gray fur laid motionless on the road. We limped toward it.

The mangled remains of what appeared to have been a gray squirrel was ground into the pavement, staining the surface with its flesh and blood. For about a minute we stared at the carnage, the crushed mass of intestine and bone and brain and separated limbs and skin till the ugliness of it all went away, transformed into just another bloody mass of animal seen everyday in grocery stores and television sets and newspaper magazines. And I grinned. Again I thought of the Topaz, of the absurdity in imagery, the intensity in irony I'd noticed before but forgot just as quick. That imagery and irony coupled with the image of the mashed squirrel was too much to bear and again I was on the verge of hysterics, ready to erupt and explode on the road passing through the midst of whitewashed treetops and rocks and rivers and birds and animals like the gray squirrel pummeled inside-out before us but before I did I looked at Richard, at his face and I was silenced. He looked ill, nauseous, fixing down at the carcass with disconsolate sadness and, I imagined, mad disdain for his role in it all, or, in the very least, his *Topaz's* role, the thought of which again nearly sent me on my knees. As it were, I maintained and together we walked back toward the car and drove off.

Richard didn't say a word the rest of the trip, barely even answering if asked a question or advice, just a nod or a low, weak *Hmmm*. I remember wondering if it was me, if it was something I said or did to cause his silence. It seemed silly to think it could have solely been the smeared gray squirrel which set off such a reaction. Even if seen as symbolic there still was the irony of it all as relief...*comic* relief, I think it's called. *For all your ills I give you laughter*, said Rabelais, creator of the five most sadly comic books known to Man.

Back in Cambridge and still no meal I thought I'd hang on by Richard to try and console him. As it were, he proved inconsolable. Without a word he drove straight to Terri's office and promptly sat himself before his computer, lost in ethereal oblivion. I fixed myself a sandwich and reheated some soup (vegetable-salmon couscous) and ate contentedly and waited.

Nothing. Not a word. Lost. Gone. Obliterated.

I noticed the typewriter, the same one used to type Terri's apology letter. I sat before it and typed the first thing that came to mind, then the next, and the next, and the next....

When I stopped typing I was alone. The key to the office had been placed alongside the typewriter, Richard nowhere to be seen.

I looked at the clock. Eleven fifteen.

Late.

I remembered the futon and unfolded it, setting an alarm for seven a.m. sharp.

I exited the doors of Brigham and Women's Clinical Research Center into a bright, sunny day which made my eyes burn like two hot coals dipped in lighter fluid. I felt weak, sleep-deprived, insane. I remember only bits and slices of the last few days: questions, tests, turkey sandwiches, tomato juice; mindless, ceaseless chatter meant to keep my eyes and mind open; more questions, more tests; bedpans brought in and out of the room like dead pets; pretty blonde and brunette and redhead technicians sitting bedside, all having to set ammonia cakes by their feet to muddle the stench; endless games of trivia and rummy and hangman; more questions, more tests, more dry turkey sandwiches and warm tomato juice swallowed every ten minutes whether I wanted to or would or could or not; EKG's, EMG's, EOG's, EEG's; having to lie stretched on a stiff bed in one position for what felt like days (which, in fact, *was* days...fifty-seven hours, to be exact) without being allowed to move so much as an eyelash, shit, shower, turn to one side or the other or hide my sleep-deprived erection for pretty blonde and brunette and redhead technicians till at last the plug was pulled and the tests completed and questions answered and turkey sandwiches and warm tomato juice ceased and I was allowed to fall asleep. I was awoken some hours later and fed a breakfast of pancakes with maple syrup, toast, sausage links and orange juice, after which I was told to shower and clothe myself and collect my things. The study had concluded. I could leave as I pleased.

Accompanying me to the door was the head technician, a rather tall and energetic bloke with short, curly hair and a wide, toothy smile and obnoxious taste in ties. After showing me the various buttons and levers behind the velvet curtain with proud vivacity he then lead me toward an elevator and rode me to the bottom, cheerful the while. Needless to say, I found his sunniness rather blistering. I was in no mood for geniality. The only thing on my mind then – aside from my bed, of course – was the not-so-small matter of my two thousand dollars.

"Oh, that," said the bloke. "Didn't they tell you about that during the screening?"

Unable to speak, I shook my head and listened.

"You don't get that straight away, of course," he told me. "Once the results are sent and analyzed...that's to say, once we've proven the study actually happened...only then are we compensated, the funds for the completed study handed to us...two thousand dollars of which, as you know, is yours and then, *only* then can you receive in full." He paused to gauge my reaction. Then, noticing nothing, he continued: "It's out of my hands, see? I've no control over any of that....I mean, I can't very well give you money I don't have, can I? Hmm? Ha, ha, ha...."

Ha, ha, ha, indeed.

I could have slit his throat if only my arms would have risen above the belt. As it were, I could do nothing but stare at the elevator's stainless steel doors in silence, numb, my tongue a lifeless slab of swollen meat in my mouth.

At last the elevator opened and we stepped out into the enfoldment of a blinding white lobby. It was then I first noticed how bright was the sun and I said a silent curse.

Passing the reception desk I noticed a newspaper folded atop an elderly woman's lap. The woman was nodding and smiling at passersby, an absent stare in her eyes. Her bony, decrepit fingers gently caressed the cover of the paper, an overblown photo of an unfurled flag waving, above it the words in block letters: TODAY THE NATION CELEBRATES HER GLORIOUS INDEPENDENCE! This time I cursed aloud, catching the technician's attention. Seemed he was genuinely concerned for me, my situation. Asked if there was anything he could do. I told him there was, after which he smiled, nodded, reached into his back pocket, into his wallet and pulled out a twenty. Then he thanked me. I thanked him in turn, then walked out the door.

The sun baked down upon my head through my skull and eyes and I quickly realized I'd need shelter or I'd faint. As it happened, the T stations along this stretch were above ground with no shelter. Waiting for a train along this line meant disaster for sure. For a brief moment, walking down Huntington past the universities and hospitals and museums, I envisioned the reactions of the cheery people around me should I suddenly keel over and die in front of them... and on this most cherished and hallowed day! Seeing the eyes of pure glee and sunshine turn into the eyes of confused terror and fear and, finally, neglect at so tangible a reminder of their mortality – *human* mortality, be they black or red or brown or yellow or white or orange or Czech or Grecian or Abyssinian or Icelandic or Sudanese or Muscovite or Swiss or Bulgarian; the myriad-tinted faces of all who walked this street just as fast or slow or poorly or freely on this day as any other – the look on all their faces should the life of my frail limbs suddenly decide to sink back into the earth before their eyes...this look struck me as so perfect a true sentiment as this day demands and I said a secret prayer to the Maker of All Emblems that, if the life of my limbs should suddenly return to this green earth, the spirit of my eyes could stick around just long enough to record this look to play over into eternity. A reasonable last request, no? One hell of a lot simpler than revolution or world peace or a final piece of ass, is it not? Besides, revolutions only beget more revolutions, rendering the quest for world peace useless...or, in the very least, *intangible*. In this light, the piece of ass seems more sensible, though still a bit airy...*ethereal*, as it were. No, I'd choose one last vivid frame of pure human thought over a mindless, empty fuck any dying day. Just seems more honest, lasting. Tangible.

All the same, stumbling along Huntington Avenue with no sign of death's release – just a weakened spirit – I looked around for shade and shelter and, remembering the twenty clutched in my palm, noticed an unlit neon sign advertising the promise of greasy food and ice cold beverages. I sighed and stammered toward it.

Tripping through the door I nearly fell to my knees as the stench of alcohol and cigarette smoke wafted through the air directly into my nose and skin. Just the same, I thought I'd stay. At least there was no sun. And anyway, this was my element, was it not? Only a minute or two and I'd recuperate, I told myself. I held my breath and drifted through the laughs and hisses of the other patrons and found an open stool at the bar and sat down.

After a few minutes the barman approached and asked my order. A burger with fries and a beer, I told him. He turned without smiling or nodding to place the order, returning shortly after with the beer. Then he disappeared.

I stared at the beer. A feeling of nausea bubbled up into my throat. I thought to ask for a water instead but the barman was nowhere to be seen. Desperate for relief, I turned my head toward the table behind me.

Three men sat smoking and drinking, drunk, discussing the state of the nation's affairs. The smoke about their heads and faces was so thick only the indentations of their features were noticeable, barely recognizable as human. They sat pyramid-fashion, their arms and hands stretched out across the table like a three-pointed star. In their fingers were cigars.

The one nearest me was speaking.

"...See? It's not so much a matter of security, this restless, solicitous pursuit of intelligence and degeneration...degeneration of democracy. No, not so much *security* as the blind and fruitless passion of *insecurity*...our nation's main artery open and exposed to all its enemies for the severing.

Paranoia, once this country's greatest strength...the one emotion used to unite us all for a common cause, a common good...this paranoia has now become our greatest weakness... the thorn in the paw of the jungle's most ferocious beast." He paused and peered inward, introspectively awhile, then he ashed his cigar and continued: "The world is laughing, boys. The lion's jaws are howling and all the world's hyenas are licking their chops." Feeling he'd made his point, he leaned back in his chair and puffed his smoke.

"Well, as to that," began the man on his left, scowling, "I have to say your pointing out this country's weaknesses lead us nowhere but down...nowhere but below the level of thorns and lion's paws and hyenas and paranoia and...what was it you said again? About democracy?"

"Degeneration," chimed the third man in a Southern accent, his face aflush with pride.

"Right," said the second, chuckling. "*Degeneration.* As if such a thing were possible. Hell, I wonder how you can even *think* such thoughts after witnessing the great wide wings of democracy stretched out across the Desert....*The Desert*, for Christ's sake! The land of sand and death! Where just a few years ago men were dragged into the street and shot for the thoughts inside their head wraps or the mats they knelt on and prayed to Allah or whoever....And now look! A new world where fear and paranoia and death itself are chased after and killed! And about this country being weak, below itself....*Shit!* Never has this country been stronger! Never! And we've the nation's leaders to thank for that, by God!" He paused as if awaiting a response from the other who just sat staring at nothing – at the wall, it seemed – stroking his chin and puffing his cigar. Sensing discomfort, the third man was about to speak but was quickly cut off by the second, shouting, "Never before! And you! You, with your poisoned tongue and blasphemous talk of our sad state!..." His face reddened considerably. "You and everyone like you spread the disease...the contagious filth that seeps into the minds and hearts of our young men and destroys them...destroys the sense of duty and obligation which comes with being born on this land, this great soil!"

"I's born in Tennessee," said the third man to the second, smiling. "Yessiree...Memphis, Tennessee...skies as bright an' blue as heaven itself, Momma said."

"Well?" said the second man to the first, ignoring the third. "Say something! Anything! *Defend yourself!*"

The first man at last looked in from the wall and gently ashed his cigar and smiled and said, "Look, there's no need for me to defend myself against you...against your views on democracy or the strength of this great country or whatever, what have you. I never wanted a fight. I suppose it was the heat, the color of the day...the excitement and all, you know, which made me say those things." He extended his palm and smiled again and said, "Come....Let's have a truce, whaddya say?"

The two men sat and stared at each other – the first man smiling; the second scowling, searching – neither moving for fear of showing weakness. After a full minute the third man shifted rather awkwardly and said, "Yessir. *Clear blue skies an' Momma's apple pies*, Daddy always told me. The only two things a Tennessee man needs to make him happy, an' he's right. Whenever I feel sad er cold er far from home er whatnot I just look up at the sky if it's blue er gray er white er whatever an' imagine I'm there sittin' on the front porch swing er out back in the fields er else I send a letter back home to good ol' Memphis askin' Momma to send me one of her homemade apple pies overnight delivery an' all." A brief pause. Reflective. Forgetful. Then: "How's 'bout you's? What sets you straight?"

The second man still stared at the first man's hand extended before him, then he chuckled and said, "Ha! You'd like that, wouldn't you? You'd like it all to disappear under the table with a simple handshake, ain't that so? Well, it ain't that easy! It simply won't disappear just 'cause you don't possess the gall to look it in the eye for what it is...for what it's become!"

The first man withdrew his hand and again leaned back in his chair and stared at nothing, puffing his cigar, a look of mock-contentment on his brow. Undeterred, the second man went on: "Because it's become something too hideous for you, hasn't it? It's become something so frightening it makes you sick...makes you wake up in the night and paralyzes you with fear. That's the true reason behind your words. It's got nothing to do with heat or color or what day it is....It's fear! You said it yourself, only the dread you feel in the face of it all makes you turn and run, hide...makes you deflect yourself in its eyes...makes you talk instead of lion's paws and hyenas and paranoia and the degeneration of democracy...makes you invent new enemies..."

"Yessiree. Momma said blue skies clear as heaven the day I's born," said the third man to the second, smiling, nodding. "Yessiree. And Momma never lies...not never....Never in all her life..."

"...And if you think it'll disappear just 'cause you don't believe in it then you're no better than our enemies....'Cause now it's *you...you* become the one allowing the poison to seep into the minds and hearts of our young men, destroying their strength and ability...their duty to defend us...this...our great nation..."

"...'Cept this once I's just a tike, legs kickin' lazy on the front porch swing. Momma said Daddy done went huntin' wit one o' the dogs an' shot its head clean off cuz o' some freak accident. Found out later Daddy done shot that dog on purpose fer not doin' what it's supposed to...fer disobeyin' Daddy..."

"...And when that happens...what then? What will you say to console your cowardice then, I wonder? Where will you run and hide yourself when the enemy has surrounded your own home?! Who will save you then, hmm? Tell me! Who will come and save you then?!..."

"...'Course I know why she done it...why she lied to me, I mean. It's 'cause she's scared I might fear Daddy after that day...after that day with the dog..."

"...Well *I* won't run! *I* won't hide! I'll fight! 'Cause I believe in this country! Right or wrong I believe in this country and right or wrong...whatever the reason...right or wrong I'll fight for it...fight right along with it! I'll fight right alongside any man or woman or child who believes in this country and loves it the way I do..."

"...But I didn't. I didn't fear Daddy after that day with the dog...not too bad. I just knew not never to cross Daddy, is all...."

"...And if you don't love it...any man, woman or child who don't love this country the way I do...anyone who runs and hides, who won't stand up and fight in the face of this nation's enemies...any man such as that ain't worth the spit in my mouth!"

The burger and fries arrived. After one bite I fell nauseous. I tried to wash the taste out my mouth with the beer but that made it worse. Woozy, I stood up off the stool and hurried toward the bathroom and puked it up.

The atmosphere now too much to stand, I paid for the food and beer and left the bar. Battling the sun and heat, I hopped the Green Line, thankful at least I didn't have to switch trains.

I exited at Lechmere and stumbled up Cambridge Street toward the Portuguese woman's home, then up the stairs toward my room and bed and collapsed, oblivious.

I was awoken some hours later by a knock on the bedroom door. It was the Portuguese woman. Seemed there was something pressing, a matter of eager importance as evident by her persistent knocking and the smile she forced once I finally managed to move my body out of bed and open the door.

For a full minute we stood facing each other, silent, her

forced smile met head-on by my glazed stare.

Finally, she spoke.

"You have rent now, yes?"

I shook my head.

"Good....You go then, okay?"

I nodded. (After, I remember thinking she said that rather well; no stuttering or hesitation. She never even stopped smiling.)

She didn't budge, her feet planted square in the frame of the open door, her smile growing more and more forced. It was obvious by *then* she meant *now*. I nodded once more, then dressed and collected my things, consisting of Terri's office key, the pages I'd typed on her machine and the New Year's salutation from the homeless man in Chicago. Slipping the key into my back pocket, I tucked the pages under my arm and made down the stairs toward the door. Just as I placed my hand on the knob I heard the Portuguese woman's voice and turned around. She was scurrying down the stairs toward me, waving a large white envelope. "*Para voce,*" she was shouting. "*Para voce, senhor jovem....Na sua ausência.*" She handed me the envelope, then turned and walked away. I tucked the envelope under my arm with the pages and opened the door and walked into the street.

Down Cambridge I hopped the T for Harvard. I waited three trains before I could transfer lines at Copley. Finally, I got my train and boarded and sat back, exhausted.

Drifting underground amid a wave of feet and shoulders and backs of heads and necks I followed the current till the wave grew too tall and crashed asunder. Most went west or east, searching for bright lights or a good show or at least a decent meal. I went south down Massachusetts Avenue to return a key.

Standing in front of Feng Shui on the opposite side of the street I peered through the windows to see if Richard was inside but I saw nothing, nobody. I walked further down the avenue to the corner store and asked the man behind the counter for an envelope and a stamp. I placed Terri's key inside the envelope and mailed it anonymously. I then started back toward Harvard, though after a block I turned and headed for Central instead.

Exiting South Station I noticed the sun had begun its slow decline behind skyscrapers and banks and suddenly I grew hungry. I thought of the Philly, of my first Bostonian meal, and made way toward it. Just outside the door, however, I changed my mind and started for Chinatown.

After my meal I roamed the streets. I watched the men and women and children eating, drinking, talking, laughing. I watched them all and I remember thinking how on these streets and in these buildings it was just another day and I felt calm, at ease. I saw an old man on the opposite side of the street sitting, asking for money. I crossed the street and walked past him, handing him the rest of the twenty.

No longer able to afford the train, I wandered the city. The sky was darkening rapidly and I thought it best to stay under the lights of streets and restaurants and clubs where luck could find me more easy. Following these lights and long streams of clubs and eateries inevitably led me toward the Common and Public Garden where well-dressed and beautiful people laid themselves down on the grass like the dead, their faces toward the sky as if awaiting the Resurrection. I strolled through them as calm as possible and left the soft grass for firm concrete.

On Charles Street through Beacon Hill vendors rambled down sidewalks and in the streets selling electric wands and beer and candied necklaces. Soon the streets were overrun with neon blue and red plastic strands dancing, writhing in mid-air. The pavement was sopping with spilt beverages, the reflections of naked legs and arms and faces off the puddles like limbs of maimed soldiers left aground after a battle. Uneasy, I hurried through the street as fast as I could and ran up a flight of stairs leading high above the street onto the platform of a bridge.

Over the water calm as glass I relaxed some and walked across the bridge. The sky was purple.

Toward the center of the bridge the crowd thickened and thickened till soon I could move no further. A suffocating feeling came over me and I pushed way toward the ledge for relief and looked out over the water. In the air was music – a march of some sort.

Overhead were stars. Golden yellow, fire-red and blue stars.

I thought of the envelope under my arm and opened it. It was from Widener, a response to my application.

I stared at it a moment, then watched it float below into the water.

CHESS MOVES for BOOK TWO

[Her Majesty: Odd; **Her Eunuch: Even**]

1. King's Pawn to King four
2. **Pawn meets Pawn head-on**
3. Queen out (King-Rook five)
4. **Knight to Queen-Bishop three**
5. Queen retreats (King-Bishop three)
6. **Pawn to King-Rook three**
7. Bishop takes Pawn
8. **Knight takes Bishop**
9. Pawn to Queen-Knight three
10. **Bishop to King-Knight five**
11. Knight to Queen-Rook three
12. **Bishop takes Knight**
13. Bishop takes Bishop
14. **Pawn to Queen-Knight three**
15. Castles
16. **Pawn to King three**
17. Queen takes Knight (check)
18. **King to King two**
19. Pawn to Queen four
20. **Pawn takes Pawn**
21. Knight to King-Bishop three
22. **Knight to King-Knight one**
23. King to Queen-Knight two
24. **Knight to King-Bishop three**
25. Pawn to King five
26. **Pawn takes Pawn**
27. Bishop to Queen-Bishop five
28. **Pawn to King-Knight three**
29. Bishop takes Pawn (Queen four)
30. **Pawn takes Bishop**
31. Knight takes Pawn
32. **Knight takes Knight**
33. Rook takes Knight (checkmate)

End Game

* note: a eunuch is a queen who fate granted be born a king